DEADLY SKIES

Every warning light on Hawk Hunter's cockpit panel came on at once.

One moment he was flying undetected high above the fog bank, in the next his Harrier jumpjet was being "painted" by at least three blazing threat-warning radars. Within three to five seconds, the air around him would be filled with so many missiles and AA shells that even the best of pilots would not survive.

But Hawk Hunter was better than the best.

Within a micro-second of the first warning, Hunter had gone on the offensive. In the snap of a switch he had armed his twin Aden cannon pods. With the flick of a button he activated his pair of wingtip-mounted Matra 155 twin rocket launchers as well as the single Harpoon antiship missile he carried under his right wing.

Then he yanked back on the jumpjet's vertical thrusters, literally bringing the Harrier to a screeching halt. Four heartbeats later, the air was filled with hundreds of deadly AA shells and four screaming SA-2 missiles. All of them missed. Hunter watched as the high-tech flak passed through the airspace where he would have been if he hadn't slammed on the brakes.

"OK," he whispered, jamming the thruster controls back into the full forward flight position. "Now it's my turn. . . ."

WINGMAN

SKYFIRE
MACK MALONEY

ZEBRA BOOKS
KENSINGTON PUBLISHING CORP.

ZEBRA BOOKS

are published by

Kensington Publishing Corp.
475 Park Avenue South
New York, NY 10016

First printing: September, 1990

Printed in the United States of America

Part One

Chapter One

From the narrow window of the tower, the woman could see for miles across the soaring, snow-covered peaks of the Canadian Rockies.

The sun was just beginning to set, and its warm, reddish hue seemed to give everything—the trees, the snowcaps, the mountains themselves—a sparkling, jeweled quality.

But the spectacular vista did nothing to bolster the woman's spirits. In fact, having all of that vast space and freedom just beyond her reach only heightened her despair.

Bravely fighting back a tear, she turned away from the window.

In stark contrast to the glimmering mountaintops and the lush forests at their feet, the woman's cell was barren. Except for a dirty, ripped mattress and a small wooden bench that held a cracked pitcher of murky water, the tiny room was empty. On the opposite wall from the small window was a heavy wooden door, held from the outside by a thick steel bar. This little piece of hell had been her prison for what seemed like an eternity.

She slumped to the floor and finally released the tears she'd been holding back.

How long can this go on? she wondered sadly.

Just then the cell door burst open and a tall woman dressed in army fatigues walked in.

The size seven, well-tailored combat jumpsuit did little to disguise the ripe curves of this woman's body. Bleached blonde, and looking better than a whiskey bottle at midnight, the female guard's well-cultivated Amazon look was working—all the way down to the two heavy ammunition belts that crisscrossed her full breasts. Her faddishy worn-down cap was made of the same leather as her meticulously polished boots. The buttons were cast of the same silver as her three bracelets and the ring in her right ear. Everything matched.

The overall fashion statement was topped off by an AK-47 automatic rifle rakishly slung over her shoulder.

She was carrying a bowl filled with a brownish, watery substance masquerading as soup, which she immediately banged down onto the bench. Then she walked over to the tormented woman on the cell floor.

"Not hungry?" the guard asked sarcastically, placing the barrel of the AK-47 directly onto the woman's right breast. "I can't imagine why . . ."

The guard then laughed, and quickly left the cell, the door closing with a loud thump behind her.

The lovely prisoner slowly lifted her head and leaned back against the stone wall. Even streaked with dirt and tears, her face was stunning: glistening dark eyes, perfectly shaped nose, full, rich lips, a younger reflection of the 1950's French film siren Brigitte Bardot.

Add the luxurious (and natural) blond hair, the creamy skin, the sensually subtle figure and made-for-black-nylons legs and the sum equaled an astonishing Gallic beauty.

Her name was Dominique.

The already-teetering world had turned completely upside down in the days following World War III. America alone had seen almost nonstop military action, including two major wars. Yet by some accounts, this was relatively calm compared to what was happening in nearly every other part of the globe.

It was in the midst of the battles that were fought for

control of the American continent that soldiers on both sides first came to know Dominique.

It all started when a crazed, superterrorist named Viktor Robotov (alias Lucifer) kidnapped her prior to the outbreak of the first campaign for control of the American continent, a titanic struggle that came to be called the first Circle War. By distributing hypnotic, quasi-X-rated photos of Dominique, he did nothing less than entice an entire army to do his bidding.

Such was her allure and beauty.

Even in the three and a half years since this catastrophic civil war, her photos were treasured by those lucky enough to have them. Squirreled away and fought over, it was as if they were made of pure gold.

So it was no exaggeration to say that millions of men loved her. Dreamed of her. *Prayed* to her.

But there was only one man in her thoughts, prayers, and dreams: Major Hawk Hunter, the man the world knew as the Wingman.

Often, to escape for a least a few moments from the crushing reality of her damp confinement, she would let her mind wander back to those times . . . those few precious, incredibly exciting times that she had spent with Hunter.

It seemed like an eternity had passed since they had first met in that abandoned farmhouse on the French coast in those turbulent days following the Big War in Europe. The attraction between them had been immediate, intense, and by all means, predestined.

But in the years since, fate had been cruel, allowing them only a few, isolated liaisons, then tearing them apart again.

Dominique wiped the stream of tears from her face and took a long, deep breath. She was in love with him and she was sure he loved her. She also knew that there was more to it than fate. That was the problem. Hunter could not escape his destiny because it was intertwined with the destiny of his country. More than any man alive, it was

Hunter who had been responsible for rekindling the spirit and the courage of the once-proud United States, and this was no light cross to bear.

In fact, it had been a monumental task, one that seemed to battle against the entire cosmos itself.

Freedom had been very unlucky in the past five and a half years. America and her NATO allies had been on the brink of winning the savage, conventionally fought World War III when at the very last minute, a fanatical anti-*glasnost* clique within the Soviet Union, aided by the traitorous U.S. vice president, unleashed a sneak nuclear attack that devastated the center of the American continent. With much of the country in shambles, a repressive regime known as the New Order took over and chopped the United States into dozens of strife-torn independently run yet virtually lawless states, countries, and "free" territories.

It took two years, but out of the resulting chaos emerged the New Democratic freedom fighters, led by Hunter and his allies. Determined to regain control of and reunite the American continent, these democratic forces assembled small but well-equipped armies and took on the New Order. After a series of hard-fought and bloody wars, democracy prevailed. America finally was reunited.

Yet no sooner had this been done when another threat arose.

Taking advantage of the instability that still gripped the Western Hemisphere as well as the rest of the world, a group of neo-Nazis appropriately known as the Twisted Cross seized control of the Panama Canal. Another bloody confrontation followed in which the Americans invaded Panama for at least the second time in history. It was a hard-fought battle: but eventually the newly united Americans emerged triumphant.

With the Twisted Cross defeated, the Americans turned their attention toward rebuilding their shattered continent, not just physically, but spiritually as well. The first act was played out when the traitorous vice president was brought back to America to stand trial for his crimes. He was eventually convicted of high treason and, after surviving a bizarre assassination attempt, was imprisoned for life.

In the meantime, the major cities on both American coasts began working together to resurrect the war-ravaged east and midsections of the country. By year five, life was actually beginning to take on a semblance of pre-World War III normalcy.

Then another threat arose to challenge to the United American cause.

A huge army of outlaws, mercenaries, and Nazi Twisted Cross survivors banded together under the guiding hand of a racist white supremacist drug addict named Duke Devillian and attempted to establish control over the devastated southwest heartland of the nation. Hunter and his allies met this challenge, too—unexpectedly, as it turned out—while driving a twelve-locomotive, heavily armed, miles-long rolling fortress called the Freedom Express through the disputed section of the country via the last remaining rail from the old AMTRAK days.

Though heavily outgunned and facing odds of more than a hundred to one, the United Americans used cunning and even a dose of mysticism to crush Devillian's forces in a climactic battle in the Grand Canyon. Though Devillian himself escaped, the Freedom Express rolled triumphantly into Los Angeles, a dramatic symbol of the reunification of the nation.

But vital as they were, these victories over the enemies of his country had taken a tremendous personal toll on Hunter. Not in his flying skills—which were still unequaled—nor in his ability to use his incredibly advanced personalized form of ESP. No—the toll had been one of the heart and soul. Fighting the battles of his country had kept him from Dominique, by his own admission, the only woman he had ever truly loved.

But the long years of war for him were ones of waiting and wondering and worrying for her. Finally, they had taken their toll on her, too—as a human being and as a woman.

The last time they'd seen each other was on a fog-shrouded airfield somewhere near the border of Free Canada and the Free Territory of New York. It was in the midst of the second Circle War, and the meeting was painfully and uncomfortably brief. Although she ached to hold him again, to tell him that she was willing to continue her vigil while he continued the swashbuckling struggle to restore the freedom and dignity of his country, the words never came out. She turned away from him instead, her pride blinding her, her broken heart making her mute.

After leaving him standing alone at that gloomy airfield, her life had become a blur. Unbeknownst to her, someone started spiking her food with a very low-impact but highly addictive drug called Percodex. At some point—she really couldn't remember exactly when, due to the insidious drugging scheme—she had been spirited away again, this time by an organization secretly led by the beautiful but evil Elizabeth Sandlake, the same person who tried to kill the traitorous ex-vice president.

And now for the last several weeks—or was it actually the last several *months?*—she had been locked up in this bleak tower somewhere in the wilderness of western Canada, held for no single logical reason, just a million and a half illogical ones.

Dominique's eyes were now wet with dirty tears. She was convinced she would die in this place, guilty of the twin sins of pride and stubbornness. Oddly enough she found herself strangely resigned to it.

But . . . if only she could see Hunter again, just for a few minutes, to finally say the words that she had failed to say on that foggy airfield.

She knew she would never have that chance, though. For her captors were so conniving, and their hideout so isolated that she had come to believe that even Hunter couldn't find her now.

She stumbled back to the window for a final glimpse of the mountains and the blue sky beyond before the sun set.

In the dull red and darkening sky she saw the contrails of an airplane cut across the distant horizon. It wasn't unusual to see airplanes flying over the desolate part of Free Canada, lonely contrails of cross-country long-range cargo craft, flying way up at forty-five thousand feet and higher, some of them going directly right over her head.

So this, the new plane and the trail of ice particles its engine was leaving behind, held her interest only briefly. She started to turn away from the window . . .

But then *something* made her glance up a final time.

Suddenly she saw the airplane turn sharply into a zigzag pattern. Then it began sculpting a sky-writing pattern with ice crystals from its tail.

Puzzled, she watched as slowly but steadily, the white-and red-tinged streaks left by the jet formed a giant "W" in the sky.

Chapter Two

Like a column of ghosts, the small band of soldiers moved silently through the deepening gloom of the forest.

Although the men were weighted down with assault weapons and heavy backpacks, their footsteps made no sounds on the soft yet crusty snow-covered forest floor. Steadily, purposefully, they advanced through the growing darkness.

They reached the edge of a small clearing and the group's leader held up his hand. The men behind him froze in place. Looming in front of them, in the center of the frozen glade, lay the huge, battered fuselage of a C-141 Starlifter.

"I'll be damned," the group's leader, a Free Canadian Air Force major named Frost said. "It *does* exist . . ."

His second in command was up and beside him in a second.

"That definitely looks like our C-141, Major," the lieutenant said, pulling a small notebook from his uniform pocket. "Serial two-three-four-double zero-five?"

Frost confirmed the same numbers were painted on the twisted, ice-encrusted tail section of the wrecked cargo plane.

"The big question is," he went on, "how in hell did it get here?"

It was a question right out of a bad sci-fi movie script: Gigantic Air Force cargo plane found sitting in the middle of a small field that was bordered on four sides by tall pine trees that, judging from their height, had sprouted about the time of Columbus.

Frost pulled out a small, infrared camera and quickly snapped off a dozen shots.

"There's one thing for *damn* sure," he whispered loudly to the lieutenant. "This bird didn't *land* here . . ."

"Not unless it came straight down," the younger officer agreed.

Frost refilled the camera with a fresh roll of film and began shooting again.

"Well, someone knows how it was done," he said, clicking the camera's shutter as fast as he could. "Someone up there . . ."

He nodded toward the mountain on the far side of the clearing. Several hundred feet above the timberline, barely visible in the rapidly fleeing twilight, was a Gothiclike structure perched on the side of the mountain. It was large enough by far to qualify as a castle, but its position looked so unnatural that it appeared as if it had been carelessly tossed there by a giant hand and just happened to stick.

As such, the fortress managed to look both precarious and impenetrable at the same time.

Frost turned back to the C-141 resting in the clearing, then called up his squad leaders.

"This is it, guys," he said, pointing to the haunting, abandoned aircraft. "Not a peep from now on in."

The word was passed down the line and, then, with Frost and his lieutenant leading the way, the unit silently crossed the darkened field and climbed into the C-141's bent fuselage.

Though cramped and gloomily enveloped in ice, the insides of the odd aircraft were reasonably clear of any sharp debris. Frost knew this was a good sign.

Each of the eighty-five heavily armed Free Canadian Rangers found a reasonably smooth place to sit. Then, with not a word among them, they began the anxious wait for the night to pass.

* * *

A few miles to the east, another group of soldiers was advancing stealthily toward the same mountain.

There were one hundred and twenty of them in all, the majority of whom carried high-powered assault rifles, ammunition belts, grenades, and a full assortment of mountain-climbing gear.

This contingent—known as Blue Force—was led by a tall black man named Major Lamont "Catfish" Johnson. Formerly second-in-command of the famed U.S Marine 7th Cavalry, Johnson now was one of the United Americans' most highly decorated officers. His most recent assignment had been as commander of the troops aboard the Freedom Express, the train that had blazed a path through the southwest Badlands. Before that, he had played a major role in the successful invasion of Nazi-controlled Panama.

About half the men with Johnson were also veterans of the old 7th Cavalry, a misnamed unit that was now part of the crack 1st United American Airborne Division. The other half of the column were members of the Football City Special Forces Rangers, the ultra-elite fighting force whose support had helped the United Americans achieve many of their key victories in the recent past.

Combined, they made up a group of professional soldiers that had no rivals on the American continent, and quite possibly in the entire world.

As darkness fell, Johnson led his men to a particularly secluded spot in the midst of a thick grove of towering pines and then checked his map.

"We're here," he said simply to his second officer.

Rapidly and silently the news passed among the men.

"Find a dry place," the second officer called back down the line. "Cover up, check your equipment, and then chow pack number two."

Within a few minutes, all of the men had settled in for the evening, thankful to be at the end of the tortuous fifty-mile trek into the barren territory, yet anxious for

16

morning to come so they could get on with the mission.

Johnson and his second officer crawled under the over-hanging branches of a particularly large northern pine, and with a half dozen other troopers, shared a cold meal. The evening was growing chilly, but a campfire was out of the question. This mission had to be secret, silent, and, at least until tomorrow morning, invisible.

"Hard to say just how well protected this place is," the second officer said, scanning the castle with his infrared NightScope binoculars between bites of cold Spam. "I see AA gun lights, and LED's from some SAM's, but they've got a lot of places to hide things up there."

He passed the NightScope glasses to Johnson. "Recon is tough in the mountains," he said with the comfortable tone of experience. "But according to St. Louie's spook's estimates, there shouldn't be more than about five hundred troops up there right now."

The St. Louie Johnson referred to was Louie St. Louie, the flamboyant leader of Football City (formerly St. Louis) who, besides running the largest gambling empire in the Western Hemisphere, also operated its the largest intelligence network.

At the request of General David Jones, commander of the United American Provisional Government, St. Louie had assigned some of his top agents to track down Duke Devillian, leader of the Knights of the Burning Cross, the racist terrorist organization that had tried to halt the cross-country mission of the Freedom Express. Following the United Americans' victory in the pivotal Grand Canyon battle, Devillian had been shot down over Death Valley — by Hawk Hunter himself no less — but somehow escaped what seemed to be certain death.

St. Louie's operatives also had been searching for another threat to the newly emerging American republic — the woman named Elizabeth Sandlake. Incredibly bright as well as beautiful, Sandlake's mind had been forever twisted during the last days of her brutal captivity at the hands of the vicious Canal Nazis of the Twisted Cross.

Hunter had rescued her, and eventually defeated the neo-Nazi thugs who had used her in their plot to seize control of a world in turmoil. But Elizabeth Sandlake was never the same. She had spent too many months immersed in evil to ever return to normal. The lust for power was contagious and she had caught it. Soon afterward she had set out on her own bizarre quest to overthrow the government of America and turn the country into an all-woman aristocracy, with herself as nothing less than its queen.

She convinced herself that the first step in this strange plan was the assassination of the traitorous ex-vice president. She came very close to completing this act, firing six bullets into the man minutes after he'd been convicted of high treason against the American people.

Captured, tried, and convicted herself, Sandlake was considered so dangerous and such a threat to escape that she was sentenced to serve her life sentence aboard a series of flying prisons.

Somehow she managed to commandeer one of them and escape. It was that plane that now sat mysteriously in the middle of a field on the other side of the mountain.

When all the leads were put together, it was particularly ironic that St. Louie's intelligence operatives traced both Devillian and Sandlake to the same spot: this fortress lodged on the side of the mountain here in the wilds of western Canada.

But as far as irony went, this was only the beginning.

As a personal favor, Hawk Hunter had asked St. Louie to also find a trail that would lead him back to Dominique, and St. Louie obliged. But even the top intelligence experts at Football City were spooked when the twisted trail in search of Hunter's paramour eventually wound up at this same, desolate mountain outpost.

As the first orange-and-yellow streaks of dawn began to edge the blackness away from the eastern horizon, the hundred and twenty men of Catfish Johnson's Blue Force expertly linked up with the eighty-five Free Canadians of Frost's Red Force and together they resumed their silent advance toward the base of the mountain.

Meanwhile, seventy miles to the east, on a flat Alberta prairie, the early-morning calm was shattered by the roar of a dozen jet fighters, their engines shrieking like banshees, screaming for takeoff.

It was a diverse collection of aircraft: two F-104 Starfighters, two F-4 Phantom fighters, four F-106 Delta Darts, four F-105X Super Thunderchiefs. Not one of the airplanes was newer than thirty-five years, and two of the Thunderchiefs were closing in on the half-century mark.

Still, age notwithstanding, the dozen jet fighters represented a formidable force, a fact that said as much about the pilots as the quality (or lack of it) of jet aircraft in postwar America.

There were also two OH-1 support helicopters—codenamed Seasprays—taking off nearby. One runway over, a KC-135 in-flight refueling ship lifted off in a roar of dirty exhaust.

There was one other aircraft, sitting by itself on the far side of the makeshift airfield. At a bare-ass eleven years old, the plane was just a pup compared to the geezers warming up a half an airfield away. But that was the least of the differences between this solitary aircraft and the rest of the patchwork squadron. For this plane could not only fly conventionally, it could also fly straight up and straight down. It could stop in midair, go backward and land in about twenty feet of clear space.

This airplane was a souped-up AV-8BE Harrier jumpjet. The pilot standing next to it was Major Hawk Hunter.

The AV-8BE was a two-seat version of the famous British VTOL attack jet that was later built in the USA for the Marines. Hunter had extensively modified the extra large flight compartment, and normally the rear part of the cockpit was jam-packed with his personally designed advanced flight and weapons systems avionics.

But now all of this clutter had been cleared away to make room for a passenger. It was Hunter's plan to be alone in that cockpit when he joined the assault on the mountainside castle.

But he didn't plan to leave alone.

Confident but anxious, Hunter ran his hands through his longish blond hair. There always was a certain amount of nerves before any military operation, but he couldn't remember ever being this jumpy. Sleep had been impossible the night before and the night before that. Instead, he passed the hours by going over the plan of attack from beginning to end, following it through, hundreds of times in his mind.

The key was timing. The air strike had to take place just as the combined American and Canadian assault force was beginning their ascent of the mountain. For the first several critical minutes, the assault force would be exposed as they climbed toward the fortress; their survival would depend entirely on the effectiveness of their air cover.

As he watched, the two Seaspray helicopters lifted off and turned westward. The two copters were piloted by his friends, the highly renowned Cobra brothers. Not really brothers, pilots Jesse Tyler and Bobby Crockett and their gunners Max Baxter and John-Boy Hobbs had gained both their fame and their nickname by flying deadly UH-I Cobra gunships.

For today's mission, Tyler and Company were leaving their familiar Cobras behind in favor of the Seasprays, and there was one very important reason for this: the Seasprays were almost totally silent.

Using these remarkable birds to their fullest advantage, the Cobra brothers hoped to get within a few hundred yards of the castle before they were noticed, thus maintaining the element of surprise until the last possible minute.

If their luck held, the Cobras would fly close in to the castle and launch the cannisters that were piled in the rear of each Seaspray. Those cannisters were filled with a powdery compound that when mixed with an accelerant became a unique crowd-control gas known as SX-551. In layman's terms it would probably be called "knockout gas."

According to St. Louie's spies, many of the soldiers holding the mountainside fortress were women. Enemies or not, the United American and Canadian commanders didn't relish the idea of killing a castle full of females. So they decided to try the knockout gas, which also increased their chances of capturing Devillian and Sandlake alive, as well as the many other notorious criminals known to be hiding in the castle.

But the strike force knew they wouldn't be able just to put everyone to sleep and waltz into the fortress unchallenged. St. Louie's spies also uncovered evidence that a sizeable group of incorporated mercenaries—known as the Guardians, Inc.—had joined the castle forces. The Guardians called themselves soldiers for hire but really were just killers for hire. Their ranks were of full cutthroats, murderers and Busted Wings, grounded air pirates who just couldn't get wanton killing-for-money out of their systems.

So in addition to the nonlethal knockout gas, the United American aircraft were packing plenty of deadly firepower as well. Both Seasprays were bristling with machine guns, and all of the fighters in the raiding party were equipped with air-to-surface missiles and nose cannons.

For their part, the ground troops were heavily armed with high-powered assault rifles of various designs, HE grenades, and even a few small rocket launchers.

Each soldier was also carrying a gas mask.

The two Seasprays vanished over the horizon and then ten tense, uneventful minutes passed. Finally, at exactly 0615, the Starfighters gunned their engines and rolled into position for takeoff. Piloting them were J.T. Twomey and Ben Wa, two of Hunter's closest friends. They had flown with him in the Thunderbirds before the Big War, and had served at his side throughout the United Americans' struggle to reclaim their continent. After Hunter, they were probably the most skilled fighter pilots in America.

Following the Starfighters into the sky were the two F-4's, also carrying some of Hunter's friends: the fighter team known as the Ace Wrecking Company, commanded by the bold and colorful Captain "Crunch" O'Malley and his partner, the somewhat enigmatic pilot known as Elvis Q. The rest of the pilots were volunteers from the UA's various air squadrons.

Within the preplanned time frame of exactly ninety-two seconds, all of the fighters were airborne. Hunter watched as the last Thunderchief disappeared in the western sky. Slowly, he climbed into the Harrier. He still had several minutes to kill and he knew they would pass slowly. For this unusual plan called for the raid on the castle to be underway before he arrived.

Chapter Three

At the base of the mountain, still hidden in the edge of the forest, the soldiers of the combined assault force anxiously scanned the skies to the east for the first sign of the Seasprays. It was 0645.

Suddenly, the two helicopters appeared, not out on the horizon but directly overhead.

"Damn, they *are* quiet," Frost whispered to Johnson. "I didn't hear a thing."

"Let's hope our friends up there in the castle don't, either," Johnson replied grimly.

Tyler and Crockett maneuvered the two choppers closer to the mountain fortress, going into a near hover just a couple of hundred feet away from the castle's front gates.

Suddenly the silence of the early morning was shattered by a burst of gunfire.

A dozen soldiers had instantly materialized along the front ramparts of the castle, their weapons blazing. In a second, both Tyler and Crockett could tell that these soldiers definitely were men. And worse, many of them were wearing gas masks.

The Cobra brothers immediately opened fire with their belly-mounted two-inch rocket launchers and then swerved sharply to the right and away from the enemy gunfire.

The fight was on.

By now the wave of attacking jet aircraft, having just refueled in air, arrived on the scene. Realizing that the Seasprays' initial approach had been repulsed, Ben Wa and Twomey, leading the air strike in their creaking F-104's, dove straight for the castle's front wall. The heavy cannon fire of the Starfighters sent the blocking squad of Guardians scurrying for cover.

As JT and Ben Wa circled around for another pass, the F-4's of the Ace Wrecking Company roared in and sent two more barrages of cannon fire slicing into the castle. At least a hundred Guardians soldiers, about half of them wearing gas masks, had now appeared on the battlements of the fortress and were filling the sky with AA fire in a desperate attempt to hold off the attackers.

The rest of the United Americans' aerial attack force roared into view. But suddenly the skies were filled with streaking AA fire as well as a rain of small but deadly shoulder-launched SAM's. Then a wave of Hind helicopters emerged from hidden shelters on the far side of the mountain. While they were no match for the heavily armed jet fighters, the Hinds were able to dart in and out of the AA fire and send harassment fire up at the air strike, gaining precious moments until help could arrive.

And that help came, in the form of a dozen Phantom jets being piloted by air pirates in the employ of the Guardians. The Americans saw them coming and, as planned, half turned in their direction, missiles ready.

The battle now fully joined, the troops at the base of the mountain started their dangerous ascent. They edged their way up to the castle—slowly, painfully, but thankfully free of any resistance. Already the first part of the assault plan was working: The hired guardians of the fortress were far too occupied with the attacking jets to concern themselves with a ground attack, too.

Meanwhile, Tyler and Crockett ducked under the dogfights raging above them and brought the Seasprays streaking right over the castle, just a few feet above the walls. With considerable aplomb, they began firing cannisters of knockout gas inside the towering walls of the mountain fortress.

Not everybody down there can be wearing a mask, Tyler

thought as he watched one cannister smash into one of the castle's turrets and begin to spill its powerful gas.

And he was right. Inside the castle, dozens of soldiers—both men and woman—began to stumble and fall to the ground, unconscious, as the SX-555 gas started to spread.

The forces led by Frost and Johnson had reached the gates of the castle by now. Immediately a sharp firefight erupted between the invaders and the hired guns guarding the fortress. Several hundred feet above, the Cobras were now free to tangle with the Hind gunships. A thousand feet above them, the United American jets were battling it out with the Guardian Phantoms. Within the course of only a few minutes, the mountain sky, which had been bathed in the gentle pink of early morning, had turned red with the flames of war.

And out of that bloodred sky, a lone airplane appeared, and headed straight for the heart of the holocaust.

Hawk Hunter was about to join the battle.

Chapter Four

Hunter counted fifteen enemy Phantoms taking part in the swirling dogfight above the castle.

"Nine against fifteen?" he whispered as he watched the nine true fighters in the United Americans air contingent tangle with the F-4's. "Can they hold them?"

The United Americans had expected air opposition—it was known that the Guardians had hired out free-lance air pirates based at a heavily fortified air strip nearby. But to strike the base before attacking the castle would have tipped the Americans' hand. So the hard decision had been made to deal with the enemy air force after it arrived on the scene.

Normally, Hunter would have armed everything on board and hurtled himself into the high-speed jet shootout twisting barely a mile above the castle. Actually it took a lot of willpower to prevent his instincts from doing just that. Instead, he was flashing in toward the castle at treetop height, far below the spectacular dogfight.

The truth was, mixing it up in a furball was not part of his mission. Nor was providing ground support, SAM supression, or weapons targeting. No, he had only one mission this day, dictated in writing by the United American Commander in Chief himself, General Dave Jones.

That mission was to rescue Dominique.

When word first arrived—via St. Louie's spies—that Dominique was being held prisoner in the same location that Duke Devillian, Elizabeth Sandlake, and God-knows-how-many other wanted criminals and terrorists were using as refuge, Jones knew that the plan to invade the castle and arrest the notorious characters had just taken a very bizarre and complicated twist. As a student of history and as a commander of an entire nation's armed forces, he knew that military planners frequently had to put sentimentality aside when making tough decisions. Few important military victories came cheap, in resources or in lives. When the truth was uncovered about the castle, the stark-cold reality of it was this: the possibility of catching so many dangerous criminals in one place at one time was too great for both the Americans and the Free Canadians to pass up just because Hunter's celebrity girlfriend was locked inside.

So, from a military point of view, the castle *had* to be attacked.

Yet such an operation—especially one that counted on air power as such a crucial component—would be much more complicated and costly without Hunter's expertise in planning a prestrike execution. No one doubted that the attempt to capture the fortress would be intense and bloody. But Jones could not order Hunter to take part in a military action that could prove so violent it might quite possibly kill Dominique.

So Jones slyly did the right thing. Declaring that Dominique would be "a valuable asset" in any treason trial against Devillian and Elizabeth Sandlake (because, Jones explained, she could place the criminals at the scene of the crime, so to speak), the general made it Hunter's special mission to rescue this valuable witness—at all costs.

With complete determination—and a grim wink of the eye—Hunter had accepted the mission.

Now hoping that JT, Ben, Crunch, and the others could keep the situation in the air under control, Hunter put the Harrier into a shallow dive, heading straight for the castle.

On the ground, the elite troops led by Johnson and Frost had broken through the front gate and were locked in close combat with the hired guards of the fortress. The knockout gas had eliminated some of the resistance, but hundreds of gas-mask-equipped soldiers remained, determined—by gold or insanity or both—to defend every inch of the fortress with their lives.

The Harrier hovered just above the castle, dodging a wide assortment of AA fire, as Hunter searched for a landing place. Because the Harrier was so versatile, any reasonably flat surface would do. Yet, in the midst of the gunfire, the explosions, and smoke, finding such a place wouldn't be easy.

Still, Hunter was nothing if not lucky, and within seconds he spotted a semiprotected ledge jutting from the side of the mountain, about a hundred yards from the castle's front gate.

It would take a landing of pinpoint accuracy, since the ledge was only twenty-five feet wide. Any slight miscalculation would send the Harrier hurtling down the side of the cliff and into the forest several hundred feet below.

Gingerly, Hunter eased the Harrier into position. Once he was as close as he was ever going to get, he took a deep gulp of oxygen and activated the jumpjet's direct vertical thrusters. A few seconds later, he set the aircraft down exactly in the center of the tiny ledge.

It took him only a couple of seconds to secure the jumpjet, leap out, and start for the castle gate. On the way, he donned a gas mask. He was carrying his trusty M-16—filled as usual with tracer rounds—as well as several grenades and a small cannister of the SX-555 knockout gas.

Reaching the battered, burning gate, he found nothing less than a full-scale battle in progress. Gas-masked soldiers on both sides were firing at each other from point-blank range. Some of them had resorted to brutal bayonet engagements, others had tossed their guns aside completely and were struggling in hand-to-hand combat with their foes. All the while, the sky was aflame with streaks of AA fire and air-to-ground rocket launches and the roar of the dueling jet fighters high above.

It looked all the world like a scene from a B movie about a war between alien armies on a far-off planet.

Darting quickly through the gate and into a huge courtyard, Hunter moved along the edge of the fighting, stopping every few feet to add his tracer-laden machine-gunfire when and where it was needed. Within a half minute, he was able to ease his way toward an opening on the far side of the courtyard that seemed to lead into the castle itself.

Once he'd battled his way to this opening and turned the corner, however, he found two Guardians in his path, their rifles raised. Before they could get off a shot, Hunter dropped them both with the butt of his M-16. The first man was out cold, his jaw shattered and mangled from the sudden blow. The second man, suffering from a busted nose and choking on a mouth full of broken teeth, struggled to his knees and shakily lifted his weapon. But once again, Hunter was too quick. He expertly batted the rifle out of the man's grasp and slammed him back onto the stone floor of the courtyard.

Leaning over the fallen soldier, Hunter instantly jerked off the man's gas mask. Then, jabbing the muzzle of his rifle against the man's forehead, he barked through his own gas mask: "The woman prisoner—*where is she?*"

The soldier's eyes were wide with fear, but he said nothing, shaking his head as he spit out more teeth. But Hunter had no time to dally. The hand-to-hand fighting was getting worse, as was the automatic gunfire from both sides. The dogfight between the Hinds and the Seasprays was also intensifying, as was the battle between the UA jets and the enemy Phantoms.

So Hunter quickly lowered the M-16, pressed it against the man's groin, and screamed: *"Talk!"*

The fear on the man's face turned to sheer horror. Although he was a professional, well-paid, killer-for-hire, there were some things more precious to him than gold.

"Up there," he blurted out through bleeding lips, pointing toward a tower rising from the far corner of the courtyard. "She's up there . . ."

"That's better," snarled Hunter. A sharp punch to the man's jaw combined with the fog of SX-555 gas to knock him unconscious.

Hunter continued through the smaller courtyard until he reached the small door leading into the main building of the fortress. Bursting inside, he raked the main hallway of the castle's entrance with his M-16 tracers, causing the defending Guardians to take cover. This respite proved long enough for the American and Free Canadian troops to smash their way in through the main doors of the castle, carrying the sharp firefight into the corridors of the fortress itself.

The fighting now became particularly vicious in this main hallway. No sooner had the allied forces burst in when the opposing troops were hurling flash grenades and smoke bombs at them with wild abandon while their companions filled the air with a storm of ricocheting bullets.

Hunter added his tracer stream to this hail of lead as he slowly zigzagged his way across the main hallway and toward a long ornate set of marble stairs. Scrambling up this staircase, he reached the first landing and found it split off into two adjoining passageways—one leading up, the other leading down.

Crouched behind a thick marble post off to one side of this landing, firing away with a huge Browning automatic rifle, was his good friend, Catfish Johnson, along with a dozen of his men.

"Glad to see you made it, Hawk," Johnson told him, managing to shake his hand and yell above the racket of the ancient yet still-powerful BAR. "Where you heading?"

Hunter nodded toward the passageway that led up to the castle's tower. "I'm pretty sure Dominique is up there."

At that point, a squad of Free Canadian troopers came running up the other passageway, Major Frost in the lead.

"That way leads down to the dungeon," Frost told them after quickly greeting Hunter. "We broke in through the subbasement, blew down a wall, and trapped a bunch of these Guardians down there. At least temporarily . . ."

Despite the nonstop gunfire, the constant blinding light of flash grenades going off, and the generally ear-splitting racket of warfare, Hunter turned to his friends and said: "Things seem to be under control here . . . I've got to get going . . . got things to do."

He started to move past them and toward the hallway that would bring him up to the tower when Frost reached out and grabbed him by the shoulder.

"There's something you should know, Hawk," he yelled. "We spotted an airplane way down in that dungeon. A bunch of these goons were pushing it out of the back and toward that road on the other side of the mountain."

Hunter shrugged anxiously. "So?"

Frost took a quick deep breath. "It was *your* airplane, Hawk," he said deliberately. "Your F-16 . . ."

Hunter immediately became frozen to the spot.

"My airplane?" he asked, dumbfounded. *"Here?"*

The F-16XL. It seemed like an eternity since Hunter had climbed into that familiar cockpit, savored the reassuring touch of those customized controls, felt the surge of excitement as his skill and energy blended with the raw power and unmatched aerodynamic technology of the remarkable aircraft. They said that in his hands, the XL was the greatest jet fighter in the history of aerial combat.

And in a flash, he remembered the sickening feeling, like a vicious kick in the gut, that struck him when he first learned the XL had been stolen. It was before his trek with the Freedom Express—a mission that required the capability of the Harrier to land on a flatcar—that he had stored the one-of-a-kind F-16 at Andrews Air Force Base. Yet, despite the heavy guard, the airplane vanished, spirited away by a faceless enemy.

He had vowed to search to the far ends of the earth, if necessary, to find that legendary airplane and reclaim it. And now, it was here, within his grasp once again.

"Now listen to me, Hawk," Frost told him grimly,

knowing full well the implications of what he was about to tell his friend. "Say the word and you, me, and ten of my guys will go and get it. It's not in the plan and it will take time. But we'd have to do it *right* now."

In the infinitesimal time frame of a nano-second, Hunter realized the horrible irony of the moment. Down one hallway he would find his treasured airplane; up another, the only woman he had ever really loved. If he went after one, the other would surely be lost again—most likely forever.

And there was no way to rescue both.

Oddly, the gist of an old saying came into his head. "I found two roads . . . and it was the road not taken that made all the difference."

But as it turned out, Hunter didn't hesitate more than a a heartbeat.

"We've got to stick to the plan" he told Frost.

Then without another moment's loss, he jumped up and ran into the passageway that would lead him to Dominique.

Chapter Five

With the sounds of gunfire and flash explosions echo-
ing off the thick marble walls, Hunter raced down the
dark passageway until he came to a door that he hoped
led into the base of the fortress tower.

The smell of SX-555 was so thick inside this part of the
passageway, Hunter quickly lowered his gas mask again.
Then, shoving a fresh clip of ammo into his M-16, he
opened the door. There was a set of narrow stone steps on
the other side that spiraled upward. Moving quickly but
quietly, Hunter started taking the stairs two at a time. As
he climbed, a hauntingly familiar feeling seized him. It
had happened a number of times in the past few years—
that powerful sense of destiny . . . as if he were being propelled by unseen forces along a preordained path. But
where was that path ultimately leading? What about the
road not taken?

Despite his almost mystical powers of intuition, that answer remained tantalizingly beyond Hunter's grasp.

And now, fate had intervened again. All the twisted
threads of his life over the past few months suddenly had
come together on this desolate mountainside in the midst
of the Canadian wilderness . . . his missing F-16, the de-
mented Duke Devillian, the gorgeous but deadly Elizabeth
Sandlake . . . and his beloved Dominique. All here, witnesses to—or victims of—a thoroughly *un*divine day of
judgment.

After the first few dozen steps, the twisted stairway
grew even narrower, until it was barely wide enough for

two people to pass each other. Like a bad dream, the gloom of the tower deepened into total darkness, and Hunter was forced to start feeling his way by running his hands over the rough stone walls on either side.

He had climbed about two hundred steps when suddenly he halted. His famous built-in "radar system" — actually his keenly developed ESP powers — warned him that something was waiting around the next bend in the stairway. Slowly, he eased his way forward in the darkness, and sensed rather than saw the person standing in front of him. He lunged, and the two bodies collided and began tumbling down the steps, locked in a deadly struggle.

Despite the near-total darkness, Hunter managed to reach up and jerk off his opponent's gas mask. Then, holding the struggling soldier in a viselike grip, he waited for the SX-555 knockout gas that was blowing through the tower stairway to take effect. It took thirty long seconds, but eventually the thrashing subsided, and the body went limp. Pulling out his penlight, Hunter shined its narrow beam into his opponent's face and realized for the first time that he had been wrestling with a woman.

Stepping over his fallen foe, the Wingman resumed his climb. He judged that he was at least halfway up the tower by now.

Halfway to his Dominique.

She had watched, first with fear and then with growing hope, as the battle swirled above and around the castle.

From the narrow window at the top of the tower, she couldn't identify the attacking forces, although she caught a glimpse of a couple of airplanes that somehow looked familiar. She almost let herself believe that the invaders were coming to rescue her, that the W she had seen in the sky really *was* proof of Hunter's presence and not just a trick of her tormented mind.

But then, just as her hopes were rising higher than ever before, her cell door crashed open, and a gang of six fashionably dressed female guards burst in, rifles raised.

One of the women, her voice sounding both drugged and desperate, hissed at Dominique: "Don't think your friends will save you, my lovely little thing. They're not going to get here in time."

Another of the Amazonlike women then stepped forward and grabbed Dominique by the hair.

"In fact," she told her harshly, "we're here to waste you. But not before we get a little of this . . ."

The guard suddenly ripped the front of Dominique's gown down to her waist and began crudely squeezing her lovely, heaving breasts. Exhausted and depleted beyond words, Dominique nevertheless attempted to fight back. But two more of the women grabbed her and then two more. It was hopeless. On the verge of unconsciousness, she collapsed, unable to prevent the gang of women from savagely fondling her private parts.

In the meantime, a strange odor began to leak into the tiny room. Despite her condition, Dominique sniffed it and felt her panic rise up yet another dizzying notch. Was this poisonous gas? But in another instant she knew it made little difference. She might as well die now, she thought, rather than endure the rape and then get shot.

But her assailants smelled the gas, too. They immediately stopped ravaging her body and quickly covered their noses and mouth with kerchiefs, hoping the cloth would keep out the mysterious gas.

"Enough of this stuff," one of the women shouted through her improvised mask. "We've got to finish this and get out of here . . ."

Her companions quickly agreed. The leader then picked up her AK-47 assault rifle, cocked it, and pointed it straight at Dominique's heart.

Dominique braced herself for the bullet, in the instant between life and death regretting that she never would see Hunter again. Not in this life anyway.

But the shot never came.

Instead there was a loud commotion near the cell's entrance and a sudden burst of white smoke. Instantly everything went fuzzy in front of Dominique's eyes, but she was vaguely aware of the woman with the gun suddenly slumping to the cell floor, the rifle making a loud rattle as it struck the hard surface. Behind her, the other guards also fell like dominoes, their limp bodies forming a twisted line back to the massive cell doors.

Standing in that doorway was a tall, broad-shouldered figure surrounded by the fog of white gas and with a head that looked like it belonged to a grotesque, giant insect.

Immediately Dominique thought she was hallucinating. She struggled to remain conscious, struggled to remain sane—but it was no use. She was fading fast, and had no strength to resist when the creature walked over, bent down, and picked her up.

The last thing she remembered was how gentle this monster seemed to be.

Ten minutes passed before Dominique opened her eyes again.

She gradually came to realize that she was being carried to some unknown destination, the change in light telling her that she was outside the castle.

She could also still hear the fighting in the background and armed creatures—all them with the same kind of grostesque head as the one carrying her—seemed to be everywhere. She was also vaguely aware of what looked like hundreds of airships streaking overhead, filling the sky with cannon fire and missiles.

Finally, the giant insect man lifted her into a small cabin of some kind . . . No, it was the cockpit of an airplane. Her head was starting to clear now. She blinked back the dirt and tears and gas, and begged her eyes to focus properly. When they did, she suddenly realized that the grotesque head on the person who had carried out of the castle and put her into the airplane really was just a gas mask. And now the man was removing it.

36

With a sudden rush of unbearable joy an instant later, Dominique found herself staring into the face of Hawk Hunter.

"Hi, honey." he said to her, almost sheepishly. "Are you OK?"

Chapter Six

Washington, DC

Hunter poured a glass of beer for himself and one for the man across the table from him, General Dave Jones, Commander in Chief of the United American Armed Forces.

The two old friends were sitting in a bar located in the Washington, DC, suburb of Georgetown, not too far from Jones's headquarters. It was three days after the titanic battle at the Alberta fortress.

The general spoke first.

"Well, Hawk, what's on your mind?"

Hunter took a swallow of beer and then passed a hefty-sized document to Jones. "First of all, sir, these are the follow-up battle assessments from the operation . . ."

Jones lit a cigar, and took a swig of beer between the opening puffs. He perused the first few pages of the document and said: "I suppose I'll have to read all this eventually. But can you give me the bottom line?"

Hunter refilled both their beer glasses. He could have recited the seventy seven-page battle assessment report word for word if Jones had wanted him to. It was all in there: the sound defeat of the castle security forces at the hands of the United Americans and their Free Canadian allies; the capture of hundreds of various criminals and terrorists including the unbalanced Nazi leader, Duke Devillian.

Also included were Devillian's subsequent confessions,

38

as well as the locations of the last of his fascist organization weapons caches—undefended supply dumps and storage facilities that were being hit by United American fighter bombers at that very moment. The report ended by detailing the astonishingly low casualty figures for the friendly forces.

"Officially, the operation was a success," Hunter said.

"And unofficially?"

Hunter frowned slightly and took another sip of beer.

"Unofficially, I'd have to rate it about sixty to sixty-five percent successful . . ." he replied.

Jones relit his cigar, and waved his way through the resulting cloud of smoke.

"But why?" the senior officer asked. "We wiped out most of the forces holding that castle. We captured Devillian and we've been launching air strikes on the last of his empire ever since . . ."

Jones paused for a puff on his stogie and a swig of beer.

"And you got Dominique back," he said, his voice lower in volume a notch. "And that certainly was a critical thing."

"So what's the bad news?"

Hunter took several seconds before replying.

"Well, as you know, Elizabeth Sandlake got away," he said. "And Fitz's intelligence boys think Juanita Juarez did, too."

Jones shrugged; he knew all about both women. Elizabeth Sandlake, the brilliant but unbalanced woman, was the mastermind behind the castle's operations. And Juanita Juarez, the incredibly beautiful but murderous ally of Duke Devillian, had somehow become Sandlake's second in command.

"There's no doubt that both escaped?" he asked.

"None whatsoever," Hunter said. "Fitz and his guys checked and double-checked all the prisoners and all the enemy KIA's. No one fits their descriptions."

"Damn . . ." Jones whispered. "Those are two ladies I'd

rather not have running around loose."

Hunter nodded grimly. "And then, there's my airplane . . ."

Jones searched his friend's eyes and thought he detected the slightest hint of their moistening. He knew that next to Dominique, Hunter's F-16XL was the most valuable thing in the world to him.

"Do we have any idea how or where they took it?" Jones asked, knowing the question was pointless.

Hunter shook his head no and leaned back in his seat. He quickly drained his glass of beer and poured another.

"Don't worry," Jones told him. "We'll get it back. It may take a while—but we'll do it."

Hunter just shrugged and unconsciously sank lower in his seat. Once again, Jones watched his friend's face carefully for several moments as they drank in silence. Finally, he spoke again.

"But I must say, I'm a little puzzled by your reaction, Hawk," the senior officer said. "Frankly, I thought you'd go storming out of here, hot on the trail of both Miss Sandlake *and* your airplane . . ."

Hunter smiled wanly and stared across the barroom for a long time before responding.

Finally he said: "I guess that's what most people would expect. And believe me, there's a part of me that wants to do exactly that."

"But?"

"But not this time," Hunter said, turning back to the general.

The Wingman took a deep breath and washed it down with a long swig of beer.

"General, we've been through a lot together in these past few years." he continued. "You know me as well as any man alive. You know how I feel about this country. You know I'd never stand by and let anyone trample on what it stands for."

Jones nodded, sensing what was to come.

"We've fought and won a lot of battles," the pilot went

on. "And I know that the country isn't entirely safe yet. But the way things are right now . . . well, speaking frankly, sir, I just don't think you need me anymore."

For the briefest of moments, Jones was stunned.

"Hawk, your country will *always* need you," Jones told him, immediately realizing that this was one battle he was not going to win.

"And I will always need it," Hunter replied. "But you already have plenty of good men out there: Fitz. St. Louie. Ben and JT. Crunch and Elvis. The Cobras. All of them. Plus the Free Canadians. They're more than capable of carrying the ball . . ."

Hunter took a long swallow of beer to fortify himself. He'd been practicing this speech for days.

"Plus, things have finally settled down," he continued. "For the first time since the Big War, there's no major threat out on the horizon. Our borders are secure. The air pirates are practically extinct. We don't have to worry about Devillian and his kind anymore."

"That's all true, Hawk," Jones replied. "But, speaking not so much as a friend but as an objective observer, you know that with your skills and savvy, you're about as close to irreplaceable as anyone can get."

"No man is irreplaceable, General," Hunter said quickly. "Someone will just have to step in and take over my duties."

"Because?"

"Because I've decided it's time for me to retire," Hunter just about blurted out. This wasn't going as smoothly as he would have liked. Still, he pressed on. "And this time I mean it. I have to keep my promise to Dominique and to myself. I'm just not going to risk losing her again."

Jones had seen it coming. Over the years, he had often listened to Hunter talk about that day in the future when America would be free again, when he would be able to leave the battles and the bloodshed behind and begin a more peaceful life with Dominique.

Now that time had come.

Hunter ordered another pitcher of cheap beer and the two men continued to drink quietly for another few minutes. Then Jones finally broke the silence.

"What the hell," the officer muttered in resignation. "I could try and talk you out of this, Hawk, but I know it would be useless. And the truth is, I can't really say that my heart would be in it."

Hunter managed a brief smile, though not without some difficulty.

"Thanks for understanding, General," he said.

They made a spontaneous toast, a quick meeting of their beer glasses as if to seal the end of an era.

"Where will you be going?" Jones asked him after draining his glass.

"Back to Cape Cod," Hunter said, fully smiling for the first time. "Got a place all picked out. It will be perfect for us."

Jones reached across the table and grasped his friend's hand. "There are a lot of things I could say right now," the senior officer told him. "But I'm not going to embarrass both of us. Just promise me one thing."

"Name it, General . . ."

"Wherever you go, stay in touch," Jones said. "For a couple of reasons. First, because myself and a lot of other guys don't want to lose track of you."

"And the second reason?"

Jones bit his lip. "Because," he said, "if the time comes—and I pray it doesn't—that this country is in *real* danger again . . ."

Hunter held up his hand and cut the general off.

"Don't worry, sir," he said. "If that happens, you'll know where to find me."

Part Two

Chapter Seven

Oslo, Norway

Gors Svenson uncapped the bottle of expensive whiskey and nervously poured a quarter of its contents into a pure white porcelain beer mug.

"If this bottle doesn't do it, maybe another will," he thought, closing his eyes. He drained the mug in five painful gulps.

The whiskey burned its way down his gullet and tore right into his bloodstream, seemingly bypassing his stomach and liver. Still, its inebriating properties did nothing to dull the ache deep inside him.

"Why did I do it?" he mumbled. *"Why?"*

He had only to open his teary eyes to get his answer. Sitting before him on his large oak office desk were thirty large burlap bags, all of them filled with gold.

He swiveled his chair away from the booty and turned to stare out the large picture window behind his desk. The vast workyard that stretched nearly a mile before him was deserted now. No cranes rolled, no welding machines blazed, no steel was being set in place. Instead, a cold, damp rain was coating the place in a thin and treacherous skin of ice.

"Hell is freezing cold," Svenson heard his drunken lips say. "Lucifer is never warm enough . . ."

He coughed out a pathetic laugh and took a deep gulp of whiskey—this time directly from the bottle.

For the briefest of moments he forgot exactly when he

had dismissed his army of workers. As part of the deal, seven thousand men and women—skilled laborers not easily found in anarchic, post-World War III Europe—had simply been told to leave. Fired. Let go.

Was it a day ago that he had so cruelly surprised them? Or a week? Or even longer?

He couldn't remember, and that actually made him feel a little better. Maybe drinking away his troubles—his all-encompassing guilt—*was* the answer.

But it only took another hundred-and-eighty-degree turn in his chair and a closer look at the bags of gold to remind him exactly the time and reason of his bizarre action. It had been two weeks ago, and the seven thousand people had marched out of the workyard, stunned that they no longer had a job, frightened that they were being cast out into the uncertainty of the lawless, chaotic, six-month-long Scandinavian night.

Just who had he betrayed? Svenson wondered drunkenly as he deeply chugged from the whiskey bottle again. His country? Not really—the old, well-defined democratic Norway had ceased to exist with the first exchanges of the Big War. Now this part of Norway was little more than a name—a cold dark place where highwaymen, terrorists, and bandits ruled the countryside's long night and where a man without a job meant a man without money to buy food and clothes and fuel for his lights. Where a man without a job could not afford a gun and ammunition to protect himself and his loved ones.

So then, had he betrayed his own family? Again, not really. The thirty large bags of gold—probably more money than in all of the rest of southern Norway combined—was more than enough for him, his wife, and their four children to live in opulent comfort for the rest of their lives. That is, if the guilt didn't get them first.

No, the object of his betrayal was no one other than himself. What he had sold—the secret designs exchanged for all this gold—had been the fruit of his labor for the past ten years. His plans, his innovations, his sacrifices.

Sold away not for the good of his fellow man but simply to the highest bidder, someone who would most definitely not use the knowledge for the betterment of the human condition.

Quite the opposite, in fact.

It was that piece of knowledge, the nagging kernal of undisputed truth that his secret innovative designs would ultimately lead to more death and destruction in a world that needed not one more iota of either, that now led him to push aside the nearly empty whiskey bottle and retrieve a smaller one, this one containing fifty sleeping pills.

Thirty bags of gold, thirty pieces of silver, he thought. What was the difference?

Euthanasia was practically a tradition in Scandinavia — suicide only slightly less so. And in the end, Svenson had turned out to be a traditionalist.

Now, as he began gulping down handfuls of sleeping tablets, one last thought crossed his mind.

"From one gloomy place to another," he whispered, his lips already turning blue and numb, "I now, like a coward, go . . ."

Chapter Eight

Cape Cod
Eight months later

Hawk Hunter gathered his shoulder-length hair up under his hat and once again faced the strong easterly wind.

It was up to about twenty miles per hour now, he figured, gusting to 25 or even 30 mph on occasion. That was just fine with him — the brisk ocean breeze was a pleasant relief to the eighty-five-plus temperatures of the late June day.

He gulped down a cup of ice water and returned to the matter at hand, the large field of long grass before him. Reaching down, he plucked up a single blade of the long bright green grass and gently laid its bottom end against his tongue. With a wide smile of satisfaction, he noted its sweet taste.

Not too long now, he thought.

He studied the dimensions of the field. It would take another two days at the most, he figured. Then, if the weather stayed dry, he would cut it down — all twenty acres of it — bundle it, and sell it.

"Probably get five small bags of gold," he said aloud with no small amount of pride. "Maybe six, if it dries real quick . . ."

The strong wind once again blew off his baseball cap, and this time, a kind of reverse gust nearly carried it right over the edge of the cliff. Retrieving the cap just inches from the precipice, he gazed down at the wave-battered rocky shore some hundred and fifty feet below. Then, irresistibly, he stared out at the vast Atlantic Ocean beyond. He had already lost two of his favorite hats in that fashion—blown by a gust out to sea where they might or might not float into someone else's hands. Now he was down to his last hat, and it would be a big problem should he lose it.

Once again gathering up his long hair and placing the cap—it was a fading Boston Red Sox *chapeau*—more securely on his head, he breathed in deep of the ocean air and let the afternoon sun bake his face.

This is the life, he thought again. *This is what I've been waiting for.*

His hay farm was on the edge of Nauset Heights, a place located just above the crook in the elbow of Cape Cod. The twenty-acre, roughly rectangular plot sat on a long, high cliff that stretched for five miles on either side. This put him smack dab in the middle of an extraordinary piece of the famous cape's topography. Few places on the mostly flat, sand- and windswept cape were tall enough to merit the name "heights." Nauset was one of them.

But the location of Hunter's small farm was unique in many other ways. To the east was an awesome view of the deep-blue Atlantic; to the north, the family of inland islands of Eastham. To the south was the long, thin green-and-beige finger of Nauset Beach, doing its best to hold back the sea from overflowing into Pleasant Bay and the Chathams beyond.

But to Hunter's mind, it was the view to the west that made this place so special.

Few places on America's continental East Coast offered the unique vista of the sun rising out of the sea in the morning *and* setting over the water, Pacific-style, at the end of the day. Because of its elevation and location east of Cape Cod Bay, the view from Hunter's farm featured both.

No wonder the previous owner had named the place, "SkyFire."

49

He gulped the last of his ice water, checked the dryness of his soil once again, and satisfied that all was right with his crop—and therefore with his entire world—walked back toward the farmhouse.

It was small, just small enough. Six rooms, a pleasantly dilapidated porch on three sides, big root cellar, and an attic large enough to hold his two telescopes. Next to the house was a pair of barns. One, the biggest, held his modest arsenal of farm equipment: a rake, a bundler, a cutter and twine caddy, all pulled at various times by his cranky tractor. The hay was stored in the loft, where it coexisted both with a small family of bats and a larger brood of cats. He was also able to squeeze his trusty Chevy farm truck into the barn, as well as the rare 1969 Harley-Davidson 1000SP motorcycle that he was forever working on.

In the small garage attached to the barn he kept his Corvette.

It was a 1983 model, white with chrome reverse all round, black leather interior, and the somewhat-standard 454 cubic-inch engine. Although it would not have been his first choice for year and model (a black '66 ragtop would have done nicely), Hunter had grown to love the '83 Vette. He had bought it two months before, from a barely honest marketeer in Boston, a man recommended to him by the agent who had sold him the farm. Surprisingly, other than the to-be-expected clutch problems, the car had run very well.

The second smaller barn was about a hundred feet from the first, it being the most isolated structure on the farm. Unlike the breezy farmhouse and the larger barn, this building was locked up tight—sealed against water *and* the salt air—and was ringed with a half dozen nearly invisible security systems.

Hunter rarely visited this barn—his psyche had tabbed it the black sheep in the otherwise happy conglomoration of buildings that made up his place. It contained no farm tools or hay or bats or cats. Rather, its walls held in memories—they being in the form of one, extremely souped-up but now never-used AV-8BE Harrier jumpjet.

Hunter hadn't flown in nearly six months, and to his surprise, he didn't miss it. Life on the farm had provided him with a myriad of pleasant distractions: Would the hay get too much rain or not enough? Should he cut one cord or two of wood to fuel the wood stoves that kept the farmhouse warm during the winter? How many cans of homegrown tomatoes were enough for a year? What would the price of kerosene be in the fall?

His days were now filled with the calculations of the earth—good and bad acres, the number of earthworms per square foot, the acidity of his soil—so many, in fact, that he had been able to sweep aside the numerics of flying a fighter jet. Weapons load, fuel available, and time-to-target were numbers now buried as deeply in him as the turnip roots in the farmhouse's cellar. And the way things were going, those numbers and the memories they ultimately represented—war, misery, death—would stay buried, possibly never to see the light of day again.

Two hours passed.

Hunter was in the barn, shooing away a squad of kittens from his disassembled motorbike when he heard the back door of the farmhouse squeak and open.

He turned and saw her and immediately felt a pleasant chill run through him.

She was carrying two cups of tea on a tray and a small jar that he knew contained cognac—their ritual drink for watching the sun dip down over the bay. She was barefoot. A long white, almost see-through linen dress clung to her slim yet well-curved figure. Her shoulder-length blond hair was gathered into two hastily arranged ponytails.

Good God she's beautiful, he thought.

Even now, after all this time, the sight of Dominique could take his breath away.

"You're a little early, aren't you?" he kidded her as they

51

met just outside the barn door. "The sun doesn't begin to go down for at least another hour."

"Now you are complaining?" she asked in her slyly pouting French-dipped English.

He didn't answer—instead, he kissed her, causing a minor spill of hot water from the teacups onto her delicate fingers.

"Too-il-a-belle?" he asked, casually wiping the tepid tea from her hands.

She shook her head. "You have burned me with the tea," she said. "You have insulted me, and now you are trying to compliment me—with bad *français?*"

"OK, you win," he said, taking her arm and gently leading her to their west field, a place where she grew strawberries. "In fact, you *always* win . . ."

Once they reached the small unplowed field, they sat on the splintered wooden bench and she poured a splash of cognac into their half-full teacups. Time passed and the day cooled off. They held hands and drank the slightly spiked tea, and Hunter tried to get Dominique to laugh at just one of his jokes with no success.

Eventually the orange ball on the sun passed over them and sank down into the now-greenish waters of Cape Cod Bay.

"It's beautiful," she whispered, the glow making her features even more radiant. "Beautiful as always . . ."

"Sure is," he agreed softly, taking a deep breath and then asking her: "How do you say 'This is the life' in French?"

Chapter Nine

Nova Scotia

Lieutenant Commander Stan Yastrewski—"Yaz" to his friends—finally eased the tracked vehicle out of the woods and onto the deserted highway, triumphantly shifting into second gear for the first time in hours.

"Never thought I'd be so damn glad to see asphalt," he whispered to himself as he brought the ancient two-ton halftrack up to thirty-five miles per hour on the otherwise empty two-lane turnpike.

He checked the time—it was just 11 PM. With luck he'd be back in the coastal town of Yarmouth within the hour. But that would be about fifty-nine minutes too long a trip for him—he was cold, unwashed, unshaven, and his stomach was growling like a polar bear. The muscles in the lower part of his back were in open revolt, spasmatically stinging him as punishment for the seven hours of bumping and jostling he'd just put them through.

Yaz had been plowing through the dense Nova Scotia wilderness since four that afternoon. The word "grueling" didn't even come close to describing the trip. "Pure torture" would have been closer to the mark. Yet, beneath his grumbling and discomfort, Yaz knew it had all been necessary. The location of the place he had visited was one of the most closely guarded secrets in the world. Being built seven hours from the nearest road was essential in keeping it that way.

Its official name was Kejimkujik Station. It was little more than two small structures built into the side of a mountain in such a way as to be invisible from the air. The mountain itself was on the edge of the Tobeatic Game Sanctuary, a place as far away from anything as one could get on Nova Scotia.

Kejimkujik was not a military installation per se. Rather it was a prison—one which held only one man. Yet this prisoner was so notorious that the isolated jail had been built just for him. It was a place where he would serve out a life sentence for the most damaging crime of all, that of betraying his country.

It may have struck some as ironic that the ex-vice president of the United States would be imprisoned in a foreign country. But to the leaders of the United American government, the arrangements made perfect sense. After his conviction on numerous counts of treason—the most damaging being his aiding and abetting the anti-*glasnost* Soviet clique known as Red Star in their nuclear sneak attack that had obliterated the center of the United States at the end of World War III—the ex-VP was sentenced to life in solitary confinement. Although the government quietly announced that the "most likely site" of the prisoner's incarceration would be a military prison in Point Barrow, Alaska, the real plans called for him to be shipped to the Kejimkujik facility, which had been built by the Free Canadians for just such a purpose.

The assassination attempt on the ex-VP by the deranged Elizabeth Sandlake only postponed the prisoner's eventual transfer to Kejimkujik; once he had recovered from his wounds in a Canadian hospital, the quisling was transported via half-track to the secret jail in the middle of the Nova Scotia wilderness.

Within minutes of his arrival, he was locked inside a bare, windowless room that held a large American flag as its only wall decoration.

It was here that the man would contemplate his crimes until he died.

Because operating the secret jail was a joint effort between the Free Canadian and United American governments, providing for its security was also a shared affair, and this was the reason for Yaz's trip. As part of the inner circle of General Dave Jones and the United American Armed Forces Command Yaz had been asked by Jones to make the required monthly trip to the Kejimkujik to meet with the prison's Free Canadian security officer.

During the two-day visit, Yaz had been briefed on several new security procedures instituted at the jail. He also spoke with the contingent of Football City Special Forces Rangers who served as half the guard force, and was now carrying back a sack of mail for them to be first screened and then delivered to their families.

All in all it had been a routine trip—it was the manner of transport to the place that proved to be unbearable, yet painfully necessary. He just wished someone had told him that shock absorbers were not standard equipment on Free Canadian Army half-tracks.

As part of the joint agreement, the Kejimkujik Station could not be approached by air. This rule was instituted because should someone want to free the prisoner it would be a relatively easy operation to track a flight in and out of the deep forest and thereby determine the jail's top-secret location.

Thus all access to the prison had to be made by land vehicle, and the noisy, uncomfortable, spine-wrecking half-tracks were the best means available for following the twisting, always changing, barely marked passage into the deep woods that surrounded Kejimkujik. Many times during the trip, Yaz mused that perhaps a more deserving punishment for the famous traitor would be to force *him* to make the torturous journey several times a week.

A warm, dry, if bare, cell seemed like paradise in comparison.

Yaz spotted the smoke about fifteen minutes after pulling out onto the paved highway.

It was a tall column of black and gray directly to his south, a mushrooming plume that seemed frozen in the cool Nova Scotia summer night. His first reaction was to dismiss it—the smoke was probably nothing more than a small woods fire, burning somewhere near his destination of Yarmouth. There had been a lightning storm a couple of hours back, and it wasn't unusual for a stray bolt to set a small patch of the dry forest aflame.

But the closer he got to Yarmouth, the more he knew something *was* wrong. As he came within fifteen miles of the town, he saw that the smoke plume rising over the tops of the trees in the distance was actually being fed by several fires, possibly as many as a half dozen, and that the columns of sparks and ash shooting into the air were blue and green in color, indicating that more than wood was burning.

Instinctively, he gunned the old halftrack up to its top speed of 40 mph. Still, it took him more than fifteen minutes to drive to the top of the hill that lay on the outskirts of the town where he would have an unobstructed view of Yarmouth.

When he got there he was horrified to discover that the entire town was in flames.

Twenty heart-wrenching minutes later, Yaz was barreling the half-track through the burning streets of the seaport city, feeling like he was driving through a bad dream.

The destruction was beyond description. It appeared as if every structure in the postcard seaport—from the small brick buildings in the center of town to the hundreds of fishing shacks and houses down near the water—was either burned to the ground or still on fire. What was more, the town was still being rocked by a series of explosions, telling Yaz that the small fuel storage depot next to the town's docks was going up.

And everywhere, he saw bodies.

Even for a combat veteran like himself, it took a while before Yaz could determine just what had happened. A novice might have assumed that the fuel depot—it contained a good amount of highly volatile jet fuel—had exploded and set fire to the rest of the town. But Yaz knew better. He recognized the telltale signs of many fires individually set: Rows of houses were in varying degrees of burning, as if someone had run along the street torching them in a methodical fashion. Plus, most of the bodies were in the street, indicating that the victims had some kind of warning—albeit a short one—before disaster struck. Even worse, not all of the corpses were smoldering black skeletal wrecks. Judging from the number of bashed-in skulls, some had apparently been clubbed to death.

But the most dastardly clue was the smell. On top of the sweet odor of wood smoke and the stink of jet fuel burning, the unmistakable scent of napalm—jellied gasoline used in aerial bombs—was thick in the air.

Washington, DC

Thirty minutes later the secure telex located in the Pentagon office of General Jones started buzzing.

The night-duty officer attached to Jones's command retrieved the short message, read it once, then immediately called over to Jones's residence.

"Sorry to bother you, sir," the night officer explained to the still-yawning Commander in Chief. "But we've just received an urgent communiqué from Commander Yastrewski, via the Free Canadian Naval base at Halifax."

"Read it to me . . ." Jones replied.

The night officer took a deep breath and then read the message through dry lips: " 'Port of Yarmouth attacked by unknown force before 1100 hours last. City completely devastated by fire. No survivors.' "

Chapter Ten

Off the coast of New Hampshire

His name was Rook, and this morning, like every other morning for the past two years, he arose and poured himself half a glass of whiskey.

The weather was already getting warm, and as the harsh liquor made its way into his distended belly, he knew that another day of heavy lifting awaited him.

The small island off the coast of the old city of Portsmouth, New Hampshire, had been his home since the end of the second Circle War. A South African mercenary, Rook had fought on the losing side and was present at the resounding defeat of the Circle Army at the hands of the United American forces in the pivotal battle of Washington, DC.

He deserted the field just minutes before his unit was wiped out by a United American air strike, and had spent the next few weeks making his way up through New England until he found the small deserted island and set up refuge. The ensuing two and a half years had passed in relative calm—all except, that is, for the day that the Soviet ICBM came crashing down onto his beach.

It had happened almost a year before. Rook had been asleep as usual when a monstrous crashing noise just about threw him from his bed. Dashing from his log cabin hideout, he had been amazed to see the smoky remains of a huge Soviet SS-19 missile sticking up in the sand just above the high tide water mark on the east side of the island.

His first reaction was to flee. He had been trained in the South African Army as an airborne explosives expert, and as such he knew an intercontinental ballistic missile when he saw one — especially one carrying a nuclear warhead.

Yet, at the same time, he knew that whoever launched the missile had done so incorrectly. The object he had discovered that morning was very nearly an entire missile — launch stages, warhead, everything. The missile had not separated in the upper reaches of the earth's atmosphere as it was supposed to. Instead, it had landed on his beach virtually intact.

Knowing that the warhead could explode at anytime, Rook had hastily packed his things and took to his small boat almost immediately after the missile crashed. Making his way to shore, he hid in a cave for the next twelve hours, knowing that if the warhead did explode, it would be a waste of time trying to get out of the blast area.

But when the nuclear device did *not* explode, he summoned up enough gumption to leave the cave and move into Portsmouth. He spent the next few months living in a partially abandoned section of the city.

It was during this time that he realized that the missile sticking out of the sand back on his island was worth a fortune.

One of the most profitable enterprises in postwar America was the black market, especially the segment dealing in weapons. Through a few whispered conversations, Rook was able to ascertain that the going rate for a nuclear device in repairable condition was a whopping five thousand bags of gold. With that kind of money, Rook knew he could make it to one of the Carribbean islands — hell, he could *buy* one of them! — invest in a couple of pounds of cocaine, purchase a bevy of female love slaves, and live the rest of his life in contented decadence.

Just a few things stood in the way of his dream.

One of them was that the warhead had to be detached from the missile in order to be sold, and that promised to be a hazardous operation — at least, at first. Just the radioactivity alone was enough to kill someone not handling the device correctly, and Rook had nothing in the way of protective clothing or instruments.

So, with typical deviousness, he solved the problem at the expense of others. Hiring three men in a bar in Portsmouth, he offered them a small fortune to remove the warhead from the launcher. They foolishly agreed after he assured them that there was no danger present. Carting them to the island, he directed them from afar via walkietalkie as they gingerly unscrewed the nosecone from the battered, rusting Soviet ICBM and retrieved the nuclear device.

The entire operation had taken more than twelve hours. Then, once the trio had placed the warhead into a heavily leaded canister, they walked back to Rook's cabin to demand payment. Keeping them at a distance, Rook explained to them with a cold rationality that he had lied to them and that they had been irreversibly irradiated.

Then he simply shot all three of them to death.

All this had happened a week before.

Now, on this morning, with his glass of whiskey swilling in his belly, he began to steel himself for the next crucial part in his plan; hauling the heavy lead-lined canister onto a raft he'd made and eventually sailing it back to Portsmouth.

Rook took another swig of the bad whiskey and, thus bolstered, pulled on his trousers and boots and walked out of the cabin, whistling as he turned toward the beach.

He never saw the axe, nor the man wielding it. All he felt was a cold yet sharp sensation on the back of his neck, which was replaced almost immediately by a gush of sticky warmth. He was dead an instant later, his collarbone, shoulder blade, and upper cervical vertebrae all neatly severed by one well-placed blow.

Chapter Eleven

Cape Cod

The morning dawned bright and sunny over Nauset
Heights.

Hunter was awakened by the first rays of the morning
as they streamed into the farmhouse's bedroom. Instantly
the warm light pried his eyelids open, reminding him of
the big day that lay ahead. Moving with characteristic
agility, he gingerly disentangled himself from the beautiful, naked form of Dominique and quietly slipped out of
the large brass bed.

Silently moving down the creaky stairs, he reached the
kitchen just as the automatic coffee maker was clicking
on. A bowl of oat bran disappeared quickly enough, as
did two cups of coffee. A trip to the head included a long,
hot shower and a shave and, finally, he was ready to face
the day.

Walking out to his fields, he couldn't remember the last
time he'd been so enthusiastic. Today he would cut his hay
crop, and all the indicators were looking good for the operation. The sky was clear, no rain was in the forecast,
and the wind was at a minimum.

But still, he needed to conduct one last test. Pulling up
a single strand of grass, he tasted it and found it was
sweeter than ever.

That was all he needed.

He ran back to the house and made a quick radio call
to a phone located in the firehouse of the small seaport

village of Nauset, just a mile away. Several days before, three of the local militiamen stationed there had offered to help Hunter pull in the harvest, and now he was taking them up on their neighborly offer. Once his help was on the way, he started up his tractor, got the cutter working, and headed out to the east high field.

Minutes later he was happily cutting his first acre of pasture.

The noise of the tractor had awakened Dominique.

Now, through sleepy eyes and a cup of coffee, she watched from the side porch as Hunter steered the clanking beast through the field, slicing down swaths of hay in his wake.

She had never seen him so happy—so vibrant in the little things of life. He was dwelling in the inconsequentials, reveling in the little pleasures. She knew that producing the hay crop had nothing to do with money or survival. Hunter had plenty of gold on hand, leftover payments from his days in the United American Armed Forces. In fact, harvesting the hay wasn't necessary at all—but that was the beauty of it. For the first time since she'd known him, Hunter was actually doing something he didn't *have* to do.

And that made all the difference.

She smiled and waved to the three militiamen who arrived in their Chevy pickup a few minutes later. They graciously accepted a thermos of coffee from her, each man trying his best to avoid staring down the front of her plunging nightgown. With a tip of their militia caps they walked out into the field, had a brief conversation with Hunter, and soon enough were wielding large wooden rakes and spreading the hay out so it could dry properly.

If the weather stayed good and all the hay was cut and spread on this day, then it could be bundled and stored and sold anytime after that.

The job was done by four that afternoon.

The work had gone surprisingly smoothly—all three of Hunter's fields were cut and raked and bundled with daylight to spare. The only glitch developed when Hunter tried to pay the three militiamen at the end of the workday. All three adamantly refused any money. Still a novice concerning the customs of his neighbors, Hunter quickly realized that the trio was almost insulted when he tried to push a bag of silver on them.

It was Dominique who saved the day, suggesting that as a return gesture for their help they all gather down on the west beach and steam some clams. This they heartily agreed to do. A quick call down to the village brought the militiamen's girlfriends and two cases of ice-cold, newly bottled locally brewed beer.

By the time the sun began to set over Cape Cod Bay, an old-fashioned New England clambake was in full swing.

They all ate and drank and ate some more. When the sun finally dropped down into the bay, its fading light reflected off the warm water to give the illusion that the sky near the horizon was aflame.

Hunter sat on the beach with Dominique and watched the unusual natural display.

" 'Sky on Fire,' " he whispered, almost to himself. "If I died tomorrow, at least I'd go knowing that I was happy just living in this place . . ."

She looked deep in his eyes and smiled.

"Me, too," she said.

Chapter Twelve

Washington, DC

"I guess we were kidding ourselves," General Jones was saying as he uncapped his third beer of the evening. "I guess what we thought was peace was actually the calm before the storm."

Jones was sitting in the back room of a musty bar located near the edge of Georgetown. At the table with him was millionaire Soldier-of-Fortune Mike Fitzgerald, Captain Crunch O'Malley, and Yaz. In front of them were a gaggle of beer bottles, some empty, some half filled, some still waiting to be opened.

"Are we sure that this isn't just an isolated incident?" Crunch asked. "I mean, just because a bunch of bandits rough up a tiny village way the hell up in Nova Scotia doesn't mean the end of the world is coming."

"I'm convinced there's more to it," Yaz replied quickly. "I saw that village and it wasn't just 'roughed up.' It was leveled. I mean, absolutely destroyed. There wasn't anything over three feet tall left standing. I've been in combat. I've seen the results of war. But I've never seen anything as completely devastated as that place."

"Plus there's the added problem that they — whoever *they* are — hit so close to the Kejimkujik prison," Fitzgerald added.

Jones wiped away the overflow of foam from his beer glass and then took a long swig.

"Well, believe it or not, that might have been a coincidence," he said, grimacing at the taste of the sour beer. "As it turns out, just before I left to come here, I got a report that said while the main attack on Yarmouth was going on, a bunch of odd-looking characters were spotted about fifteen miles to the east, at a place named Barren Lake."

"Barren Lake?" Yaz asked. "I went fishing there once. What was going on up in that area?"

Jones shrugged. "Who knows?" he said. "I just got a flash from Frost that said some people in the area saw a gang of about twenty guys in uniforms pulling something out of the lake at just about the same time the attack on Yarmouth was happening. The local constable became suspicious, so he followed them back down from the lake. But he lost track of them as soon as he saw the village had been snuffed out."

"You mean the attack on Yarmouth could have been just a diversion?" Yaz asked.

Again, Jones shrugged. "That's hard to tell," he replied. "But we have to assume that if the same people who leveled the village also sent an advance party up to drag God-knows-what from a lake, then they probably could have made an all-out assault on the prison if they had wanted to. My gut tells me they didn't realize they were so close to Kejimkujik."

Crunch took a swig of his beer and lit up a cigar.

"Sure is strange though," he said through a cloud of smoke, "especially when you consider that these bandits — or whatever you want to call them — really pulled off quite a disappearing act."

A sudden silence enveloped the table. Each man knew that Crunch was referring to the most puzzling aspect of the Yarmouth massacre: that despite the several military investigative teams that had combed through the destroyed town and the surrounding area, not one solid piece of evidence had been found as to how the mystery troops had arrived in the village or how they had left.

In fact, the only clue left behind by the marauders were the hundreds of footsteps found on the beach at Yarmouth. Strange as it seemed, they indicated that the raiders had literally walked out of the sea the night of the raid and withdrew the same way.

Yet no one had seen a single ship in the area.

"It *couldn't* have been a standard amphibious landing," Jones said, verbalizing what was on everyone's minds. "They would have needed three to four hundred troops to carry out that raid. But that bay is just chock-full with fishing boats, as is the entire coastline. The people in that area *live* out on the sea, for God's sake. Any ship large enough to carry four hundred assault troops would have been spotted from a hundred miles away."

"Plus no one saw or heard any choppers," Yaz added. "No seaplanes, hovercrafts, nothing. Just a bunch a footprints walking into the sea."

Fitzgerald took a swig of beer and let out a long, gloomy whistle.

"The attack on the village, these guys at the lake, then disappearing—it's all very weird," he said. "And I mean in a dangerous kind of way."

"Exactly," Jones replied, reaching for another beer. "That's why I have the feeling that it's going to get worse—and *weirder*, if that's possible."

Chapter Thirteen

Jones's prophecy came true the next day.

It arrived in the form of a videotape. Grainy, shaky, and out of focus, the footage contained on the tape had nevertheless captured a bizarre event that had occurred off the northern coast of the old state of Massachusetts, near a resort area known as Plum Island.

Quite simply, the videotape appeared to show a sea monster.

The tape—the crucial part being only three seconds long—had been sent to Jones by the head of the local militia of the nearest city to Plum Island, a place called Newburyport. The footage had been shot by two of his men who had been routinely patroling the ten miles of beach on Plum Island several days before.

The day in question had been windy, cold, and rainy, typical for the north shore of Massachusetts under the spell of a summer nor'easter. The men had just stopped for a smoke break when they spotted something about a half mile off the beach. At first it appeared as a blurry black form to them, its color barely distinguishable from the cold, dark gray sea. But after having been apprised about the massacre in Nova Scotia several hundred miles to the north, and asked to keep an extra eye for anything unusual off the coast, the soldiers immediately turned on the video camera they carried as standard equipment in their beach jeep. Adjusting the camera's zoom lens, they zeroed in on the object, hoping to get a better look.

What they saw astonished them.

Now, Jones sat with Yaz in his Pentagon office, replaying the segment of tape over and over on his VCR.

"I just can't believe this . . ." Yaz repeated just about as many times as Jones played the three seconds of tape. "What could it be?"

Jones was as baffled as he. The tape was of poor quality—the camera the militiamen had used was old and prone to static, plus the weather and the late-afternoon hour combined to make the image look out of focus. Yet, what could be seen looked like the head of some enormous sea creature ever so briefly rising up out of the rough seas before stiffly splashing back down into them.

"The goddamn thing looks like every artist's conception I've ever seen of the Loch Ness monster," Jones grumbled, "I just never believed for a minute that the damn thing *actually* existed."

"In the old days, we could have had this videotape analyzed a thousand times over," Yaz said. "You know, to make sure that it's not an optical illusion or whatever."

Jones paused a moment to light his pipe, then he replayed the three seconds of tape.

"That's no illusion," he said, freezing a crucial frame which best showed the object's horselike head, flared nostrils, and scaly mane. "Monster or not, there's something definitely out there."

Jones finally switched off the tape and turned on the office lights.

Yaz was still shaking his head. "God, first the massacre up in Nova Scotia, and now this!" he said.

At that moment, Fitzgerald walked in. He had had an earlier showing of the strange video, so his worried expression had nothing to do with sea monsters. Rather, it had to do with the telex he was holding.

"Just got this off the scramble wire," he told Jones, referring to the single sheet of yellow paper. "It's from the Nova Scotia Provincial Army commander. They've recovered three hundred and eleven bodies from the massacre."

Jones shook his head in disgust. "We've still got a long

way to go before civilizing this continent."

"I agree," Fitz said through his thick Irish brogue. "But there's something else. That village had more than five hundred people in it—there's almost two hundred people unaccounted for . . ."

Both Jones and Yaz felt a chill run through them.

"Christ, were there that many bodies burned into dust?" Yaz exclaimed.

Fitz slowly shook his head. "Undoubtably some were," he said. "But not such a high number. But there's more: According to the Army commander, apparently all of the people missing are women."

"Women?" Jones asked.

Fitz shrugged. "That's right: all the males—of all ages—in the village were killed," he said, referring once again to the telex. "And there were some women killed, too. But at least one hundred and eighty-seven people—all of them women between the ages of fourteen and thirty-six—are missing. Gone. Vanished."

"Good God," Jones whispered bitterly. "What the hell happened up there?"

Fitz could only shake his head. "Either the raiders grouped all these women together and killed them somewhere else and their bodies just haven't been found. Or . . ."

"Or what?" Yaz wanted to know.

"Or . . ." Jones answered the question soberly. "The bastards took them all with them."

Chapter Fourteen

Nauset Heights,
Three days later

"More chowder, Yaz?"

Yaz leaned back in his chair and briefly squeezed his expanding waistline.

"Maybe just a little," he replied, caving in without much of a fight. "It's so damn good, it's hard to resist . . ."

Dominique ladled out two heaping spoonfuls of the fish stew, then handed the pot to Hunter who doled out a third helping of his own.

Yaz reached for a hot roll and slapped a pat of butter on it. "God, I haven't eaten this good in years," he said.

"Neither have I," Hunter mumbled through a mouthful of the fish chowder. "That's scrod you're eating by the way. Caught a bunch of them this morning out in the bay."

They were sitting in the comfortably rustic kitchen of the farmhouse Hunter and Dominique called home. Yaz had arrived earlier that afternoon, flown in by a United American Armed Forces helicopter that had met his airplane at the airport up in Boston. It seemed as if he and Hunter had been eating and drinking ever since.

Yaz's mission per Jones's orders was to brief his friend on the strange goings-on in Nova Scotia, as well as the piece of videotape from Plum Island. It had been a tough decision for the Commander in Chief to make.

70

More than eight months had passed since Hunter left active duty, and Jones had gone to great lengths to honor Hunter's desire for privacy.

Yet Hunter had greeted Yaz warmly on his arrival— they were friends, and it had been almost a year since they'd seen each other. However, at Hunter's insistence, Yaz had put off discussing the bad news until after dinner.

"Unless you're here to tell me about an impending nuclear attack, it can wait," Hunter had said to him shortly after Yaz stepped off the chopper.

So instead, Yaz had gotten a tour of the farm and the fields, plus a ride along the beach in Hunter's laughably rickety pickup truck.

But now, as the three of them finished their dinner meal, Yaz knew it was time to get on with his assignment.

Hunter caught the look in his eye, and reluctantly nodded.

"OK," he said, filling Yaz's glass with an after-dinner shot of brandy. "Let's have it . . ."

Yaz threw back the liquor to steel himself, then took the next fifteen minutes to detail what was known about the Yarmouth massacre. Through it all, Hunter listened without speaking, taking it all in between refills of brandy. Only Dominique, who pretended to busy herself by putting the finishing touches on a dessert of homemade apple pie, showed any reaction to the startling news, gasping at several points in the story.

By the time he got to the part about the "sea monster," Yaz had downed three glasses of brandy and was working on his second piece of pie.

Finally, Hunter spoke.

"Well, I knew it must have been something heavy duty for you to come all the way out here," he said. "What do Jonesie and the others make of all this?"

Yaz shook his head. "No one has come up with anything near a rational explantion," he said, finally pushing

71

the pie plate away from him. "I mean, it was bad enough that whoever was responsible just utterly wiped out that village. But for them to disappear like that—walk back into the ocean?—and apparently take a hundred and eighty-seven women with them? It's just too bizarre . . ."

"And the women who were taken were just between certain ages?" Dominique asked.

Yaz nodded grimly. "Between fourteen and thirty-six," he said. "And we all know there are white slavers running around the world. But I've never heard of any of them abducting more than five or six people at a time."

"Neither have I," Hunter said. "Usually, they're just hit-and-run scumbags who can't count past ten."

They retired to the back porch, where a pot of brandy-laced coffee was passed around. The fading light of the setting sun provided the customary spectacular sunset, with a slightly cool ocean breeze heralding the approach of another night.

"All this gloom from Nova Scotia almost makes your monster story seem funny by comparison," Hunter told Yaz. "Jones and Fitz must be going nuts."

"They've worn out the VCR watching the videotape," Yaz said. "And I don't blame them. I've seen it probably three dozen times, and each time, it looks like a frigging monster. A real one—solid, skin and all. His head just bobs up and down once and then *boom!* it disappears."

"Perhaps the famous monster finally escaped from Loch Ness?" Dominique said, brushing back her beautiful blond hair as she sipped her coffee.

"That's what Jonesie said," Yaz replied with a laugh.

"Well, that monster he better stay the hell away from Nova Scotia," Hunter replied. "Sounds like whoever is on the loose up there would cut him up and eat him for breakfast."

Yaz took a hefty gulp of his own spiked coffee.

"Jones was back and forth on whether I should even come out here and tell you all this," he said to Hunter. "I mean, I'm the last one in the world who'd want to screw up your . . . well, your vacation. But . . ."

Hunter held up his hand. "It's okay," he told Yaz.

Yaz nodded, but he could sense the disappointment in Hunter's voice. He felt like the guy who'd just crashed a birthday party, or more accurately, a honeymoon.

"Well, Jones figured you'd want to know," he went on. "He wrote it all up in a report that I have in my pack. Forty-two pages of it."

Hunter poured out three more cups of coffee.

"And?" he asked.

"And," Yaz replied somewhat sheepishly, "he thought that maybe you could read it over, help us figure it all out . . ."

Hunter immediately looked over at Dominique, who was staring right back at him. With just one glance, he read volumes in her eyes.

"Well, the problem is that we're trying to make this more than just a 'vacation,' Yaz," Hunter told him. "It's more like a retirement."

"I know," Yaz replied. "And Jones knows that, too. I realize you're out of the business, and I don't blame you. But there's just so many strange things going on . . ."

Hunter barely suppressed a laugh. "So what else is new?" he asked.

They sat in silence for several moments. Then Hunter took a deep breath and let it out slowly.

"Okay, I'll make a deal with you," he said finally. "I'll read the report, roll it all over for a few days, and then let you know what comes out. How's that?"

Yaz could only shrug. "Well, that's great," he replied. "I mean I'm sure Jones didn't expect you to lead the charge, exactly."

"Well then, it's settled," Hunter said with a smile. "I'll be like an adviser. A big-shot consultant. And of course, you'll have to stick around here for a while, you know, to help me sort it out."

Yaz looked up at him and scratched his head.

"Jesuzz, I don't know, Hawk," he said worriedly.

"Jones thought I'd shoot out here and then go right back—either with or without you. He's expecting me back tomorrow."

Hunter cheerfully waved away Yaz's protests.

"When's the last time you took a few days off?" he asked his friend.

Yaz shook his head. "I can't remember back that far."

At that point, Hunter grinned and poured him another cup of coffee, thereby signaling that the debate was over.

Dominique reached over and placed her hand on Yaz's shoulder.

"Like it or not, Yaz," she said sweetly, "it looks like *you're* the one who's going to take a vacation . . ."

Chapter Fifteen

Near Boston
Two days later

His name was Jack Stallion, and as he gazed out from his office atop the fifty-foot-high tower, he was reminded once again that he was a man with a lot of responsibilities.

Stretched before him, looking like a field of enormous tuna fish cans, were twelve huge fuel storage tanks, each one painted in a distinctive pearl white. Contained in the tanks was more than one hundred-thousand gallons of a highly volatile kerosene product known as JP-8 to the experts, jet fuel to the layman.

As such, the dozen tanks of JP-8 represented the largest concentration of jet engine fuel in the northeast part of America.

Like many things in the first few years after the Big War, jet fuel had been at a premium. But as the country gradually recovered, reserves of the precious JP-8 grew, as did its use. The increase in jet flights from the East Coast to the West and vice versa—the massive air convoys now contained as many as seventy or eighty airplanes—demanded continuous production of the JP-8 at a half dozen refineries on the eastern seaboard. This one, located on the shore just north of Boston in a small city called Revere, was one of the largest because of its proximity to the Hub's huge airport.

And to a certain degree, Jack Stallion was the keeper of all this gas.

A man of ruddy Irish complexion and a shock of gray-white hair that went well with his last name, Stallion was in charge of the small army that guarded the fuel-tank storage area of the refinery. More than a hundred men were under his command, and their weaponry — ranging from NightScope-equipped M-16's to TOW antitank rockets, and even some small surface-to-air missiles — was judged to be more than enough to discourage any troublemakers from nosing around the sprawling hundred-fifty-acre waterfront facility.

Now, on this night, as Stallion looked out of the tower at the full moon rising above his little protectorate, he knew it was time to begin his quarter-hourly security check.

"Station One?" he routinely called into the microphone of his elaborate radio setup. "Report . . ."

"Station One, OK . . ." came the reply.

"Station Two?"

"Deuce is OK . . ."

"Station Three?"

"Trips is OK . . ."

On and on it went, each of the three-man outposts around the perimeter of the facility calling in that everything was quiet.

But still, Stallion felt uneasy. He couldn't quite put his finger on it, but something in his craw was telling him everything wasn't as it should be.

Acting purely on instinct, Stallion quickly completed the security check and then sent out a general order for his troops to go up to a Yellow Alert, the middle stage of readiness.

His troopers — mostly veterans of the Big War as well as the more recent civil wars — knew better than to question their commander's order. Instead, reacting like a well-oiled machine, each outpost went to Yellow. All weapons were checked for ammunition load and all safeties were turned off. Each NightScope operator widened his range of field, and the reserve force of troopers back in the barracks quickly suited up and reenforced their assigned stations.

As it turned out, Stallion's action would be responsible for saving the lives of many of his soldiers.

The first sign of trouble appeared ten minutes later.

The NightScope operator at Station Twenty-two was scanning a section of oily beach about an eighth of a mile from his position when he got a reading of two figures walking up from the water's edge. He immediately alerted the two other troopers in his pillbox, and one of them in turn radioed a quick report back to Stallion's tower command post.

As luck would have it, Station Twenty-two was the most isolated position on the facility's perimeter. Stuck out on the far eastern edge of the storage area, it looked out on a little-used shipping channel that at one time handled sizable oil tankers arriving from overseas. Now the channel was collared with tall bullrushes that somehow managed to live along the heavily polluted shoreline. It was in these weeds that the NightScope operator first saw the intruders.

No sooner had the warning call gone out to Stallion and the rest of the security force when the number of mysterious figures on NightScope increased to six, then eight, then twelve, then twenty. Stallion immediately bumped the whole facility up to Red Alert. Already a small force of twenty reserve troops were quietly making their way to the area, but Station Twenty-two's isolated location being what it was, they would not arrive for several minutes.

By that time, it would be too late.

The voice of the radio operator in Twenty-two took on an ever-increasing anxious tone as he radioed the situation back to Stallion.

"We have a reading on as many as thirty-six individuals approaching our position," Stallion heard the man say in a controlled but undeniably nervous whisper. "They are definitely armed."

Stallion had turned his own NightScope on the area by this time and he, too, could see the faint images of a crowd of figures walking up from the water's edge. Because of the volatility of their surroundings, the rules of engagement around the storage facility were stridently low-key and by the book. No one wanted any panic firing when just one or two bullets could light up one hundred-thousand gallons of explosive aviation fuel.

Still, Stallion knew that nothing less than a small army was approaching his facility, and according to the rules, no prior warning had to be given to anyone acting in an aggressive manner around the area.

"We count more than fifty now . . ." the radio operator reported, his voice shaky and apprehensive. "Closest is just thirty-five yards from our position."

Stallion knew he had no time to mull it over.

"Engage with secondary weapons at twenty yards," he called back to Station Twenty-two. Then he dashed across his small office and pushed a series of buttons, at the same time yelling out the message back to his open microphone that he was "flooding the tanks." Immediately, the small moats around each storage tank began filling up with thousands of gallons of Purple K, a fire-retardant foam. But it was a symbolic act if anything—should even one tank ignite, a *million* gallons of foam would do little to prevent a conflagration.

"Intruders at twenty-five yards . . ." came the staticky report from Station Twenty-two. "Twenty-three . . . twenty-one."

Suddenly it seemed as if the whole eastern edge of the facility was lit up bright as day. Even though he knew that the men in Station Twenty-two had just shot a dozen flash grenades—the so-called "secondary weapons"—at the approaching force, Stallion was startled nevertheless by the sudden flare.

"Station Twenty-two, report!" Stallion yelled into his microphone.

"They're still coming," came the almost-immediate reply.

That was it, Stallion knew. The flash grenades, little more than glorified fireworks, were intended to scare off any potential intruders and the tactic hadn't worked.

Now he had no choice but to order the use of "real" firepower.

"Engage with primary weapons!" Stallion yelled into his radio mike.

No sooner were the words out of his mouth when the first fuel tank went up.

It was Storage Tank Red-Four, a small, half-filled vessel

close to Station Twenty-two. Only later would Stallion find out that it had been hit with a somewhat rare British-made Swingfire antitank weapon, fired by the mysterious intruders. The resulting explosion instantly incinerated the men inside Station Twenty-two, as well as more than a few of the intruders. A small mushroom cloud climbed up into the night sky, lighting up the landscape for miles around and giving even a veteran like Stallion a moment of terrifying pause.

"All units engage!" he yelled, grabbing his own rifle and exiting the tower to join the battle.

He was halfway down the tower ladder when Storage Tank Green-Six exploded. Although it was more than a quarter mile away from his position, the force of the sudden blast very nearly blew Stallion off the ladder. His ears ringing, his eyes nearly blinded by the light of the explosion, Stallion scrambled down the remaining twenty-five feet to the ground in less than three seconds.

By the time he reached the bottom of the ladder, new sounds were filling the weird day-for-night scene. The unmistakable chattering of many M-16's firing at once was interspersed with the whooshing noise of rockets flying back and forth. Running full speed toward the action, Stallion saw that several of his squads were already in a sharp firefight with the vanguard of the enemy force, and more were converging on the area. Yet he could also see that a stream of more than a hundred of the enemy was swarming through the breech blown in the perimeter line near the vaporized Station Twenty-two. With no small amount of amazement, he watched as the enemy troops — dressed all in black and wearing strangely shaped silver helmets — dashed from fuel tank to fuel tank, planting what looked to be explosive satchels.

Christ, they're not here to steal the gas, Stallion instantly realized. *They're here to blow it all up!*

What was even worse, the light of the flames revealed that another hundred or more intruders were mulling around near the water's edge, observing the battle in a bizarrely serene fashion.

"Where the hell are these guys coming from?" he wondered aloud.

Once again, Stallion had to make the right decision quickly. As well drilled and professional as his security force was, it was not equipped to throw back a small invasion. Nor was it expected to. The commander also knew that even if most of the enemy sappers were stopped, all it would take was for two or three more fuel tanks to go up and the whole area would look like a suburb of hell itself.

In a split second, Stallion knew that what was important now was the lives of his men.

Skidding to a stop next to one of the fuel farm's many fire klaxons, he broke through the protective glass with the butt of his rifle and manually punched the warning button three long times.

That was all it took. The eighty-odd men left alive in his command instantly recognized the order to evacuate the area.

Just as quickly as they had run to join the fight, now the security troops withdrew from it. Stallion stationed himself at the far gate of the storage area, waiting until the last survivor hurried through. Then he, like the others, moved across the highway and into a marshy area that eventually led to the nearby beach. Already, United American helicopter gunships were racing overhead, sent from Boston's airport to investigate the explosions. But they quickly fell back, too, instantly recognizing that a disaster was in the making, one that no amount of manpower could stop.

By the time Stallion and his men reached the relative safety of the ocean waves, the mysterious intruders had also withdrawn to positions of reasonable safety and were systematically destroying the storage tanks by detonating their planted satchel charges, one by one.

The resulting explosions looked like many little atom bombs going off.

There's going to be a lot of airplanes sitting on the ground because of this, Stallion thought.

Chapter Sixteen

Cape Cod

"Get ready to take it away!"

Yaz lifted the last bale of hay up onto Hunter's dilapidated pickup truck, and with a whistle of relief, he wiped the sweat from his brow and yelled: "OK, that's it. We're loaded . . ."

Thankful that the long hot day's work was done, Yaz all but ignored the cloud of exhaust that shot out of the truck's tail pipe as Hunter shifted gears into forward. Instead, he climbed up onto the classic shitbox's rotting fender and held on for the bumpy ride back down to Hunter's barn.

He had never worked so hard in his life. Not during his teen years, not during his stint as an executive officer aboard a US Navy nuclear submarine, not in his role as a multi-faceted soldier in the days since the war. They had gathered more than twenty truckloads of baled hay today, just he and Hunter, and between the heat, the bugs and the absolute lack of ocean breeze, it had been a wearying, sticky, humid affair.

But now, the job was nearly done and Yaz had to admit that he actually felt good as a result of the day of honest work. Once the pickup was unloaded, all of the hay would be safely under the roof in Hunter's barn, protected from any rain that would have ruined the whole shebang had the dried-out cut grass been soaked while still on the ground. And then he planned to claim at least half of the dozen bottles of beer he knew were icing in Hunter's fridge.

As they pulled off the last thirty bales from the truck, Hunter explained that tomorrow they would drive up to the farmer's market in North Eastham and sell the whole lot for about twenty-five bags of silver. It didn't take Yaz more than a few seconds to calculate that the amount was equivalent to less money than Hunter used to make in a half day back in his old flying days.

But in the same instant, he realized it didn't matter. Hunter's retirement to the hay farm wasn't about money or profits. It was about living a simple life—and he was beginning to fall in love with it.

Yaz had been at the farm now for three days, and with each one he had grown more envious of Hunter's situation. To see his friend working his way through acres of hot and buggy hay, whistling happily and even bursting into periods of unself-conscious singing was a sight to behold. Here was a guy who could fly a jet fighter blindfolded through a hoop at Mach 2, good-naturedly swearing and punching his steering wheel as the battered pickup fought him for control over the rough furrows of his hay fields. Here was a guy who could instantaneously formulate military strategies that would make Patton, MacArthur, and Alexander the Great drool in envy, planning nothing more than how he would distribute his crop the next time. Here was a guy who carried the flag against dozens of enemies of America—and defeated every last one of them and yet was now losing a months-long struggle against the family of woodchucks who dined on Dominique's tomato garden anytime his back was turned.

Observing all this, Yaz was quickly coming to one of the eternal truths: Simple *was* better. In life. In love. In the pursuit of happiness.

Ten minutes later, Yaz was guzzling the first of his

dream beers.

"This damn stuff never tasted so good," he told Hunter as they finally retired to the shade of the farmhouse's front porch.

"Brewed nearby," Hunter said, plunging his smudged and sweaty face into a handful of ice. "Some weeks it's better than others."

Dominique had been sitting on the porch for most of the hot afternoon, drinking ice water and reading one of her many books on psychic phenomena. Already somewhat of an expert of paranormal subjects before moving to the farm, she now spent much of her time wading through vast volumes detailing serious studies of things ranging from precognition, synchronicity, psychokinesis, up to even odder themes such as spontaneous human combustion and radiohalos.

But neither the bizarre subject matter nor the ninety-degree temperatures could ruffle her appearance—she still looked beautiful, cool, and collected despite the blazing heat. Try as he might, Yaz just couldn't keep his eyes off her. She was dressed in simple cutoff jeans and a T-shirt, but everything fit her so damn well, the outfit appeared to have been designed just for her. Being only twenty-five years old, Yaz just barely knew of the 1950s actress, Brigitte Bardot—he had seen photos of her maybe once or twice. But like everyone who had ever met Dominique, he had to agree that she was an exact duplicate of the French sex kitten/actress. Only younger. And more luscious. And more . . .

Suddenly Yaz found himself guzzling the last of his beer, a defense mechanism to prevent his imagination from running away with him.

Goddamn, he thought, as he watched Dominique casually rub Hunter's tired shoulders. *No wonder he wants to stay down on the farm.*

Yaz opened another beer and quickly began draining it.

"Are you leaving room for dinner, Yaz?" Dominique

asked him sweetly.

He nodded and smiled. "Don't worry about that," he replied, once again falling into the habit of patting his stomach. "Though I bet I've gained about ten pounds since I've been here."

Hunter put his cold beer bottle up to his forehead. "You worked off a few of them today," he said. "By the way, there's a big clambake down on East Line beach tonight. It's an every Friday night thing. Whole town gets together. Plenty of food and booze. Fireworks, too. *Loads* of babes . . ."

Dominique gave Hunter a mild slap as punishment for the sexist remark.

"He meant to say that you probably could meet a nice woman," she told Yaz, in a sweet voice that dripped French as thick as salad dressing. "I'll introduce you . . ."

"I'm in," Yaz replied enthusiastically.

Hunter and Dominique looked at each other and laughed.

"He's learning," Hunter said with a wink.

Less than two hours later, both men were cleaned up and ready to climb into Hunter's pickup for the ride down to East Line Beach.

Loaded into the back of the truck was a bushel of corn, a basket of tomatoes and onions, plus a dozen crabs Hunter had pulled from his traps just an hour before.

Now, as he and Yaz waited for Dominique to finish getting ready, Hunter produced a small brandy flask. Shaking its contents briefly, he uncapped it, took a swig, and handed it to Yaz.

"Thanks for the help the past few days," he said.

"I'm the one who should be thanking you," Yaz replied. "I can't remember the last time I've felt so relaxed. Even though I've worked my butt off."

Hunter took a deep breath of the cool evening air. "This place does that to you," he said finally.

Yaz took a longer gulp of brandy and handed the flask back to Hunter.

"The only problem is, I've got to get back to Washington sometime," he said, his voice showing a commensurate amount of disappointment. "Although it's about the last fucking thing I want to do."

"You're preaching to the choir, pal," Hunter replied, capping the flask and throwing it onto the front seat of the truck. "It would take something pretty big to drag me away from . . ."

He didn't finish the sentence. Instead he stood up straight and cocked his head toward the north.

"Hmm, that's strange," he said somewhat mysteriously. "We're about to have some company . . ."

Yaz had to think a moment to figure out what Hunter was talking about. But then it came to him just as the faintest sounds of the approaching helicopter reached his ears.

"*Damn!*" Yaz cried out. "They're coming to get me, the bastards . . ."

He knew he couldn't last forever. Although he'd been "hiding out" at the farm for the three days, he had called Jones on the shortwave radio down in the village every morning, somehow convincing his commanding officer that Hunter and he were studying the report on the Nova Scotia incident. In reality, they had discussed it only two times and on both occasions, only briefly.

The helicopter was hovering above their heads just a minute later, its rotors kicking up dust, sand, and leftover stray pieces of hay. With a blast of engine smoke and noise, the chopper—the same deep-blue UH-60 Blackhawk that had dropped Yaz off—landed with a thump right in front of the farmhouse.

A soldier in full flight gear emerged and ran in a crouch toward Hunter and Yaz.

The usual round of salutes was quickly dispensed

with, after which the man identified himself as an intelligence officer attached to the Boston-based 2nd Airborne Division of the United American Army.

"Sorry to bother you," the officer, a Captain Quill, told them. "But I've got some bad news."

The man then detailed the devastating attack on the fuel-storage facility near Boston. Hunter and Yaz listened with their jaws practically drooping.

"It's *got* to be the same guys who destroyed that village up in Nova Scotia," Yaz said.

Captain Quill nodded grimly. "A lot of things match up," he agreed. "What's even worse is we've also got some reports of smaller actions along the coast between Portsmouth and Boston. Raiding parties of ten to twenty men, coming ashore, attacking a target, and then just disappearing. Always at night, always quick, always ruthless."

"What kinds of targets are they hitting?" Hunter asked.

"That's another constant," Quill replied. "Just like in Boston and Nova Scotia, they seem to be hitting fuel dumps, specifically ones containing jet fuel. And they're taking young women with them any chance they get."

That piece of news sent an electrifying jolt down Hunter's spine.

"This *is* serious," he whispered, almost to himself.

"Headquarters agrees," Quill told him. "That's why they asked me to brief you on all this."

Hunter pulled his chin in thought for a moment. "Has anyone ever got more than a passing glimpse of these guys?" he asked. "Or any clues to how they can appear and disappear like that?"

Quill slowly shook his head. "No, sir," he replied. "We've got foot patrols out all along the coastline and several P-3 ocean recon craft flying between New Hampshire and Rhode Island. But so far, no one has seen a thing."

There was a brief but somber silence among the trio,

broken only by the thin whine of the Blackhawk's heated engines and the sound of the surf crashing on the beach below the heights.

"What about me?" Yaz finally asked the officer, not really wanting to hear the answers. "Do you have my orders?"

"Yes, sir," Quill nodded. "We're to transport you back up to Boston where you are to catch a flight back to DC immediately."

Yaz's shoulders slumped appreciably.

"Well, it was good while it lasted," he said to Hunter. "I'd better get my things together."

"Wait . . ." Hunter said, turning to Quill. "What exactly do the boys in DC expect *me* to do about all this?"

Quill shifted around somewhat nervously. "Officially, I'm not sure, sir," he replied with a shrug. "*Un*officially, I'm supposed to tell you that there's a seat for you in the chopper for the ride back to Boston, and another one on the flight to DC . . ." At that moment, Hunter looked up toward the farmhouse and saw Dominique standing on the porch. Picnic basket in hand, she was wearing a white beach dress with her hair tied up under Hunter's baseball cap. But the look on her face was devastating. She knew that the appearance of the helicopter and Quill could mean only one thing.

But Hunter refused to let it be.

"I won't be going back with you, Captain," he told Quill politely but firmly. "And, as a favor, I'm going to ask you to wait a day before lifting Commander Yastrewski out of here. Can you come on back down here this time tomorrow?"

Quill screwed up his face for a moment and then shrugged again. "What should I tell Washington, sir?"

"Just tell them that I'm studying the report you've given me and that I'm writing an option list for them," Hunter replied. "And that I need Commander Yastrewski's assistance in doing this."

Eventually a slight grin spread across Quill's features. "I understand, sir," he said with a salute. "We'll be back at 1800 hours tomorrow."

With that, he ran back to the Blackhawk, and with another salute and a friendly wave, took off in a blast of sand and dust.

Less than a minute later, the copter had disappeared over the horizon.

Twenty more minutes passed while Hunter and Dominique had a personal conversation on the front porch.

Grateful for his twenty-four hour reprieve and knowing his two friends wanted privacy, Yaz stretched out in the back of the pickup and worked on perfecting the art of pouring beer into his mouth while horizontal.

He was considering a second bottle of beer when the hot evening breeze and the long day of work gently conspired to ease him down into a pleasant doze. One second he was looking up at the orange-tinged sunset sky and the next he was dreaming.

In the dream, he was sitting in a roomful of women—beautiful women—and for some reason, the room was rocking. The women didn't seem to mind, though; instead, they were fascinated with him, the only male in their midst. He was wearing a uniform, but they were not his standard United American fatigues. Some of the women were wearing uniforms, too, but others—they being the most beautiful ones of all—were wearing mini-skirt-style white tunics with plunging necklines. He was about to ask one of the women where he was when he felt a hand on his shoulder. He turned and found that the tunic-clad woman who had touched him was none other than Dominique . . .

That's when he heard the explosion.

It took him a few seconds to realize that the dreadfully loud noise was not part of his dream. Groggily, he sat up in the back of the pickup and forced his eyes to focus. Like a sword through his heart he saw a huge ball of fire and smoke rising like a mushroom over the small town about a mile north of Nauset Heights.

He turned to call out to Hunter, but his friend was a already reacting.

Then Yaz heard another explosion, this one smaller, more muffled. Jumping down off the pickup he realized that this rumble had come from Hunter starting up his Corvette's mighty engine. Running toward the car, Yaz could see and hear Hunter gunning the engines up to their full peak RPM. But at the same time, off in the distance, he heard yet another powerful explosion. Finally reaching the driver's-side door, Yaz started to climb in when he saw Hunter hold up his hand.

"No . . ." Hunter called to him, yelling to be heard over the engine noise. "Please, Yaz, stay here with Dominique."

"But . . . you might need me down there," Yaz stuttered, pointing toward the second cloud of smoke and flame that was rising into the night sky over the small town of Nauset.

Hunter quickly shifted the Corvette from neutral to first gear.

"Stay here, as a favor, Yaz . . ." he yelled again. "I'll be back as soon as I can . . ."

With that, Hunter popped the clutch and roared off, leaving Yaz behind in a cloud of sand and exhaust.

Chapter Seventeen

In his worst nightmare, Hunter couldn't have imagined the extent of damage in the village of Nauset.

His trip down to the small seaport town had been a fast and furious affair, the Corvette screeching and squealing all the way down the steep dirt road that led to the narrow marsh-lined turnpike, which in turn ran into the normally placid village.

But no sooner had he reached the paved roadway when he saw a terrible sight in the distance: Not only was half the village engulfed in flames, but so was the surface of the water in the harbor itself. The four small fuel storage tanks that held diesel and gasoline for the village fishing boats had somehow exploded, igniting many of the village's buildings as well as setting the harbor water itself aflame.

Now, as he roared around a corner and came within a quarter mile of the town, he saw that small secondary explosions continued to shudder through the dock area where the fuel tanks were located, spreading more fire and destruction with every blast.

Screeching to a stop right at the edge of the town, Hunter jumped out of the car, grabbing his M-16 as he did so. Several groups of people were walking quickly toward him. Some of them were burned severely, all of them more than a little dazed.

"What happened?" Hunter asked a middle-aged man who was helping an elderly lady whose dress was still smoldering.

The man could only shake his head. Tears were streaming down his face.

"They're everywhere," he said as he hurried by. "Just *everywhere* . . ."

Three middle-aged women limped by, each one burned to some degree. "It's the end of the world," one of them cried.

"They're stabbing, shooting everyone . . ." another gasped.

An elderly man was right behind the women, walking along so calmly Hunter knew he was in a state of shock.

"They blew up the gas tanks," this man told Hunter in a voice of frightening serenity. "They're ransacking the town. Raping. Killing . . ."

With that, the man staggered on.

Hunter was visibly shaking with anger by this time. Up to this point he had hoped the conflagration had been the result of an accident. Now he knew that the same nightmare that had devastated the fishing village in Nova Scotia had just arrived on Cape Cod.

He instantly took off toward the village, checking that he had a full clip in his M-16 as he ran. He could hear more explosions were going off on the far side of the town, as well as the unmistakable chattering of automatic rifle fire. Mixed in to the cacophony there was also a strange background noise, like that of a dozen of trumpets being blown at once.

He sprinted across a small hayfield and up onto the village drawbridge. There he met a woman and more than two dozen crying children.

"Don't go in there . . ." the woman yelled at Hunter, trying her best to be heard over the wails of the youngsters. "They'll kill you . . ."

"Keep going," Hunter told her, "Get as far away as you can . . ."

The woman began to say something, but couldn't. She let out a gasp and collapsed in his arms.

Upon seeing this, the children—there were twenty-six of them in all, most with badly burned arms and legs—became hysterical. The majority of them started running down the bridge and into the hayfields beyond. Yet several of them turned and began running back toward the flaming village.

Acting quickly, Hunter laid the unconscious woman down as gently as possible, and then took off after the kids.

He caught them at the foot of the bridge, and corraling all five of them, he led them back out of the flaming town. Several mild slaps to the face revived the woman, and within a half minute, she was able to follow the children over the bridge and away from the danger.

Now, once again, Hunter began to run back toward the village.

But then several strange things happened.

First of all, he suddenly became aware of a large force of armed men moving up the side of a hilly dune about a half mile from him. There were at least twenty of them, and oddly, each man seemed to be trying to race the others to be the first to the top of the mound. What's more, several of them were blowing loud and flat-toned bugles as they rushed up the dune.

But even stranger, there was something flying right above them. It appeared very small at first—just a black speck in the sky, performing a tight turn not a hundred feet over the bluff.

"What the hell is that?" Hunter wondered aloud.

Then, as he was staring at the action on the hill, he heard an unbelievable, ungodly shriek. Spinning on his heels, he turned toward the sound; it was coming from the east, from out over the ocean, and it was getting louder by the second.

Hunter squinted into the dusky sky; the very air itself seemed to be aflame, lit up by the flames from the burning village.

Then he saw it.

It was too small to be a rocket or a missile, but it was traveling at least as fast. It was silver and almost gleaming in the reflection of the flames. Within a second of spotting it, it slammed right into the gang of armed men that had been scrambling up the hill.

The resulting explosion was so intense, it knocked Hunter off his feet. He could feel the very earth itself rumbling as a result of the projectile's impact. The ground beneath him was shaking like an earthquake. A shock wave passed over that was so strong, he thought his eardrums would burst.

And then, everything was suddenly quiet.

Hunter lifted his head and saw that not only had the force of enemy soldiers disappeared in the smoke and flame of the projectile's impact, but the large hill, as well as the small forest of beach scrub trees that had surrounded it, was gone, too, obliterated in the blast.

All that was left was an enormous crater of frightening proportions.

Hunter got to his feet just as three militiamen ran out of the village and up onto the bridge. One of them recognized him.

At that moment, they all heard an odd, buzzing sound. Looking back toward the crater, Hunter saw that the aerial speck he had spotted before was now heading right for them.

"What the hell is that thing?" one of the militiamen yelled, raising his weapon.

In an instant, Hunter realized that the strange flying object was actually an RPV—a remotely piloted vehicle—a small unmanned aircraft usually equipped with a TV camera and used to scout out enemy positions.

Before they could say another word, the RPV flashed over their heads, turned sharply to the east, and headed out to sea.

Within a few seconds, it was gone.

Hunter and the three militiamen made their way back down the bridge and into a ditch next to a small tidal stream. The combination of night and the thick black smoke made it almost impossible to see clearly into the village by this time. Plus, all sounds of weapons firing had ceased.

"What the hell happened?" Hunter asked the soldiers.

"They just hit us out of the blue," one of the men, a sergeant, told him. "They came from nowhere. I was on duty down by the beach. One moment everything was clear. The next I look up and here's about three dozen guys running up into the town.

"I sounded the alarm, but it couldn't have been more than a few seconds later when the fuel tanks went up. They went right for them. Fired an antitank missile into each one of them. That's when all hell broke loose . . ."

The only good news was that most of the townspeople weren't even home when the attack came. The vast majority of the residents were over on East Line Beach about ten miles away for the usual Friday night clambake.

"Our commander took about half our unit over to East Line," the militia sergeant went on. "All we could do was hold them off as long as possible. We shot at a bunch of them down near the docks, but then, with the fire and smoke and all, we had to get the hell out . . ."

"Did you actually get a close look at any of them?" Hunter asked.

The men all shrugged. "It was hard to," one of them said. "They were dressed all in black and they moved real quick, like they had done this sort of thing before. But they were wearing funny-looking helmets. And those bugles! Jeesuz, it was like every other guy was blowing his lungs out on one of those things."

"Well, it's damn quiet in there now," Hunter said, first eyeing the town and then the huge, smoldering crater. "I say we go back in and take a look."

The four of them rechecked their weapons and then cautiously moved back into the village.

Chapter Eighteen

It didn't take them long to reconnoiter the devastated seaport.

There wasn't much left to see. The raiders were long gone and just about every building had been burned to the ground. Anything of any consequential value—cars, trucks, fishing boats, even the village's ice-making machine—had been destroyed. Fortunately, the body count was low. Hunter and the troopers came across only a half dozen corpses during the grim search, all of them civilians.

After thirty minutes or so, Hunter's small group arrived at the town's beach. Several more militia units were already there, as were about a dozen injured civilians. A militia unit officer was also on hand, directing his troopers to go out on the outskirts of the village and find any civilians who might be hiding in the fields and dunes.

This officer recognized Hunter immediately, and after a brief discussion, showed him the only piece of evidence that could be found as to how the raiders had arrived and departed so quickly. Bringing him to a section of the beach that was bracketed by two breakwater jetties, he pointed to the dozens of bootprints that led in and out of the crashing surf. It was the exact copy of what the investigators up in Nova Scotia had reported.

"Yet no landing ships were sighted?" Hunter asked the militia commander.

"Not a one" was the reply. "Even now, if they had

been landed and picked up by troopship, we'd be able to see them."

Hunter scanned the quickly darkening ocean and saw nothing. No lights, no silhouettes on the horizon. Nothing.

He quickly told the officer about the RPV and the projectile that had decimated the force of men he'd seen running up the sand dune.

"We saw it, too," the officer replied, adding that a squad of soldiers dispatched to the scene came back to report that nothing—not even a bone or a piece of clothing—was left of the attackers.

"Whoever fired that shot did us a favor, whether they had intended to or not," the officer concluded. "It killed one of their parties and scattered the rest of them, I'd say. The problem is, there are probably dozens of these raiders still running around out in the woods beyond town."

Once again, Hunter gazed out to sea. The projectile, whatever it was, must have been fired from a ship out beyond the horizon, its aim obviously guided by the RPV. Yet there weren't many guns afloat that could fire such a shell with such devastating accuracy at such a long distance.

And the question remained: Was it fired by a friend or foe?

Just then, a militia corporal ran up and reported that a medi-vac helicopter was on its way down from the United American Army fort at Plymouth. The officer told the man to round up as many troopers as he could to help get the wounded civilians ready for evacuation.

Hunter and the officer then pitched in loading the more seriously wounded civilians onto stretchers. Within ten minutes, the medi-vac chopper—actually a large, CH-47 Chinook—had set down on the beach. The loading of the wounded began immediately.

A UA Army officer emerged from the chopper and

quickly sought out the militia commander. Hunter had just finished helping load a burn victim onto the Chinook when he joined the two men.

"This is not an isolated attack," the officer was telling the militia commander. "You've got to get your men organized and set up a perimeter around the village, or what's left of it."

Hunter quickly introduced himself. "Are you saying there was another attack like this somewhere?" he asked the man.

The UA officer removed his helmet and wiped his forehead of grime and perspiration.

"There's been as many as twenty-five attacks," he said grimly. "All along this edge of the Cape. Provincetown. Truro. Wellfleet. North Eastham. All hit, some of them worse than this, if you can believe it. We've also got calls that Chatham and Harwich to the south got it, too. It's a full-scale assault. They're pulling hit-and-runs on the bigger towns. But there are a lot of reports of these people—whoever the hell they are—roaming the countryside, killing, raping, looting. And they seem to be moving to the south. That's why you've got to get a defense organized here."

But Hunter did not hear the man's last sentence.

He was too busy running. Through the smoldering village, past the bodies, up and over the bridge, and to his Corvette.

All the while his insides were turning inside out. He had made a terrible assumption—that the attack on Nauset Harbor had been a single, isolated action. Now that he knew it hadn't been, visions of his worst fears were flashing before his eyes.

Within seconds of reaching his car, he was screaming back down the turnpike, roaring at full speed back toward his farm on Nauset Heights.

* * *

Randy Montserrat was dying.

Blood was flowing so freely from the cuts on his wrists and ankles that it had soaked the pile of leaves and pine needles below his feet.

It took much effort for him to raise his head and look over at his wife, Tanya, who was tied to a pine tree about ten feet away from him. The small pool of blood around her feet was also growing. Tears welled up in his eyes as he saw that she was no longer moving.

He let out a muffled scream and once again tried in vain to snap the ropes that were holding him to his tree. But it was no use: the armed men who had so barbarically beat and slashed him and Tanya had lashed them to the trees with binds too strong to break. Now Randy, robust for his age of sixty-two, felt the last of his strength leaving him.

He was sure his spirit and soul would soon follow.

Death would bring one respite: He would not have to endure the memory of the nightmare he and Tanya had suffered in the past two hours. The men had come to their isolated beach cottage just as the sun was setting. Without warning they burst in on him, beat both of them, and then proceeded to ransack the house.

After finding little of value—both Randy and Tanya were artists and thus had very little in the way of material goods—the men dragged them out of the house and torched it. Then they marched them up into these woods and tied them to the trees, slashing their wrists and ankles as their final dastardly act.

The men left soon afterward, laughing and growling, almost like they'd become intoxicated by their acts. Through it all, only one of the men spoke. He was a huge bear of a man who was wearing a long black cape in addition to his black uniform.

He had barked to Randy and Tanya in a thick un-American accent that, instead of being killed right away, they were being left to bleed to death in the woods. The reason was the men wanted to "leave a gift" for the animals. Randy had gotten the implication right away. There were a half dozen types of animals in the Cape woods—foxes, badgers, even a few wild dogs—that would be attracted to the area by the smell of blood. Undoubtedly, soon after that, the animals would devour them.

Randy let out another howl, this one in hope that both he and his beloved wife would die soon, before the animals came.

He knew only a miracle could save them now.

It was a loud, rumbling noise that brought Randy out of unconsciousness.

Through bleary, blood-soaked eyes, he saw an angel.

"Can you speak?" the man asked him.

Randy looked down at his bleeding hands and realized for the first time that they were no longer bound. Nor were his feet. Instead, he was leaning against the tree, the crumbling bark and pine sap sticking to his blood-soaked body.

"We were . . . we were attacked," he managed to mumble, before falling to his knees in exhaustion.

The loss of blood was obviously making him hallucinate, he thought. Either that or he was already dead. Just a minute before, he felt that he was seconds from death in the deserted woods. Now, just a few feet away from him, there was a white sports car, its headlights shining, its engine rumbling, and this man who had cut the ropes from the tree.

"Who are you?" Randy asked the man, who was now kneeling over him.

"That's not important" was the reply.

"My wife . . . ?"

"She's still alive," the man said.

Randy looked to his left and saw Tanya, lying close

by, dirty and bruised but obviously breathing.

The man moved quickly to bandage Randy's wounds, all the time working by the light of the sports car's headlamps.

"You're going to be OK," the man told him. "You both lost some blood, but the cuts weren't deep. Whoever did this to you wanted you to bleed slowly."

"But how could you possibly have found us?" Randy asked, consciously feeling some of his strength return. "You certainly didn't hear me screaming, did you?"

"That's not important, either," Hunter replied.

He had no ready answer. He had been tearing along the turnpike when his extraordinary intuition began flashing with great intensity. He had learned long before never to question this powerful sixth sense of his, no matter how critical the situation might be. So, even at the moment when his one and only thought was to get back to Nauset Heights as quickly as possible, he nevertheless followed the impulse that was telling him to go slow along the deserted roadway, to look for something wrong. Driving from side to side in order to shine his powerful headlights into the woods, he found the couple just a minute later, about fifty feet off the edge of the road.

Now bandaged and revived, he loaded the two into his car and screeched out of the woods. He turned south, back to the town, but as luck would have it, a militia troop truck was making its way toward him.

A quick flick of his lights stopped the driver, and soon Randy and Tanya were turned over to the militiamen for transport back to the town.

Before being loaded into the truck, Randy grasped Hunter's hand, and with a firm grip and deathly sincerity said: "Someday, I'll will pay you back for saving our lives."

Hunter did not reply. He simply got back into his car and roared away.

* * *

They were gone.

He searched the farmhouse three times, the barn and other buildings twice. He even ran through the fields, and up to the cliff, and down to the west beach. But he found nothing. Dominique and Yaz were gone.

There were no outward signs of a struggle, but Yaz's rifle had been left behind. There was no blood anywhere, nor did the footprints in the sandy clay of his front yard look too unusual. Yet the raiders had been there; they had left a calling card. A black steel, three-foot axe had been embedded into the house's front door.

It was two hours before Hunter stopped searching and half collapsed onto the steps of his front porch. He held his head in his hands and came as close to tears as he had in a long time.

His precious, beautiful Dominique was gone . . .

Had he chosen not to go to the village, would he have prevented this? Had he chosen not to help the children or stay with the militiamen, or help load the wounded onto the Chinook, would he have arrived back to the farm in time?

If he hadn't had listened to his accursed sixth sense and found the couple in the woods, would he have saved Dominique and Yaz?

It was the last question that burned inside him — burned a torrid flame that ignited something deep within his soul, something that he thought had been finally laid to rest.

The world had not changed just because he had "retired" to the farm. If anything, it had become more insane. How many times had he fooled himself into thinking that with time, things would evolve and civilization would return? If anything, things were deteriorating — and fast.

He had simply chosen to hide away from the evils of

the world. But now the demons had found him. They had tracked him down and had invaded his homestead—the last island of sanity left on earth. They had taken away the only woman he had ever loved, to meet God-knows-what fate.

And all because his damned sixth sense had prevented him from returning in time.

One hour later, as the full moon reached its zenith, the ground around Nauset Heights began to shake.

The small field animals that lived under the barn and the cats who lived in its hayloft all scampered for safety, so great was the rumbling.

Within seconds, the entire top of the cliff was enveloped in a cloud of hot-burning smoke. The convulsions of the earth intensified as an ear-splitting scream shot out from the cliff and traveled down the hill and into the salt marshes below.

In a second, the scream turned into a high-pitched roar, so loud that many of the windows in the farmhouse shattered from the vibration. Then there was flame, and more smoke, and the roar got louder and louder until finally it could get no more terrifying.

At that instant, the small, rotting wooden structure in the middle of the hayfield burst apart in fury as the gleaming, powerful shape of the AV-8B Harrier jumpjet exploded upward.

It rose about a hundred feet above the farm, lingered in a hover for several moments, and then, in a great burst of angry jet flame and exhaust, rocketed away to the south.

Chapter Nineteen

Two days later

The commander of the Long Island Self-Defense Forces lowered his NightScope binoculars and checked his watch.

It was 2345 hours—fifteen minutes to midnight, and then six long hours to dawn. What would happen between now and sunrise was anybody's guess. But as the commander looked down the line of his troops—most of them were working furiously to reinforce the tree-and-rubble barricade that stretched for nearly a half mile along the beach—he couldn't help but wonder how many of them would be alive to see the sun come up.

And then he wondered, too, if this was to be his last day.

They were coming—everyone had convinced themselves of that one single fact. The mysterious coastal raiders, fresh from ravaging the New England coastline, were now likely to carry their campaign southward and hit Long Island. And it was here, at Montauk Point, the very northeastern tip of the island, that they would probably come ashore first.

Not since the beginnings of the Circle War several years back had the commander seen so much apprehension—some would call it panic—affecting the population of the American East Coast as had the news of the coastal raiders. He would have thought that after more than five years of postwar instability, the American citi-

103

zen would be able to handle any new threat. But if the events over the past forty-eight hours were any proof, it appeared that just the reverse was true.

He knew it was a case of knowledge *not* conquering fear, and for the most part the burgeoning born-again media of the country was to blame.

If anything, the citizens of the East Coast were better informed now than at any time since the Big War. Many local television stations were back to broadcasting regularly, and dozens of AM and FM radio stations had gone back on the air just in the past year alone. There were even a few dozen newspapers circulating in the Northeast, with many more farther south and out west.

All of this should have served the public good: Knowledge was power, they used to say. An informed public was a courageous one.

However, this latest threat brought with it a reputation for unmatched brutality, and the media had been playing that gruesome angle nonstop ever since Cape Cod was attacked. Certainly there were some indisputable facts: the raiders raped and killed almost indiscriminately, they could somehow mysteriously appear and then disappear apparently at will and they sometimes took young women between the ages of eighteen and thirty-six.

But from these kernels of truth, the wildest, most panic-stricken rumors had sprung up. Tales of impossible butchery, grossly inflated death counts, and outright cannibalism (sometimes while the victim was alive) abounded, fanned to flame by the various customer-hungry media machines.

The result was that rumors were being reported as facts and facts as rumors. What was worse, it seemed as if every news broadcaster was striving to one-up the next by applying a new, more frightening twist to the story: The raiders were actually Special Forces troops being directed by the fanatical Soviet-based Red Star clique; the raiders were bloodthirsty leftovers from the recent United American campaign against the fascist white supremacist armies of the American Southwest; the raiders were radioactive mutants from the North Pole; the raiders were UFO aliens.

Just how alarming these stories were had been proved earlier this day when a crowd of five hundred or more Long Islanders, fleeing the inevitable arrival of the raiders, attempted to cross a drawbridge down near Islip. For some reason, the drawbridge operator chose to raise his span and stop the flow. Seventy-eight people died in the ensuing stampede. The bridge operator shot himself through the head soon afterward.

Reports of similar tragedies had been coming in ever since. Hundreds of thousands of people from New England down to the Carolinas were fleeing inland, to the mountains, to the cities, to the forests—anywhere, just as long as it was away from the coast.

As this day—day four of the threat—grew longer, the news, as well as the rumors, only got worse. Since noontime, there had been a number of reports that oil refineries and fuel storage dumps were being blown up all across the country. Now again, a new twist was being added: the raiders weren't just moving down the East Coast, they were *everywhere*.

The problem was, these reports were true.

More than twenty oil refineries and fuel dumps east of the Mississippi had been attacked during the day. The vast majority of these attacks, most of which involved long-range remotely operated high explosive missiles, were successful, so much so that even the most battle-hardened veterans had to admit concern.

The coordination alone of such an enemy campaign was frightening. But so were the insidious reasons behind it. As soon as news of the fuel attacks spread, authorities immediately restricted the use of gasoline and aviation fuel for all but emergency reasons. This action in turn created more panic, as people tried to horde whatever gas supplies were left. By 6 PM eastern time, the country was caught in the grip of a major fuel crisis.

The lack of fuel also restricted the timeliness of the response to the raiders from the central government in Washington. Knowing it was wise to conserve whatever fuel supplies they had—just in case the country *was* filled with fifth columnists—the United American Army was forced to march many of its troops to the coast. This would take time and careful planning as to just where these soldiers should take up positions.

The same was true for air support. Although a dozen squadrons of UA fighter jets had been moved to bases on the East Coast, the threat to the fuel supply dictated that only the minimum of patrol craft be sent out to look for the elusive enemy.

In the meantime, the United American army brass were urging the local militias to mount their own defenses, and this is what the Long Island Self-Defense Force was doing on the beach at Montauk on this warm night.

They were three hundred and fifty strong, by far the best-organized, best-armed force to meet the raiders so far. But still an atmosphere of nervousness was thick in the air. Most of the LISDF militiamen were volunteers, well trained, but more used to chasing local robber gangs and highwaymen than dealing with a barbaric, sea going army that apparently could appear and vanish on a whim.

Plus, many of them had never killed anyone before.

The militia commander checked his watch again, and then called his first lieutenant up.

"Have the men check their ammunition and then count off," he told the young officer. "It'll give them something to do and keep their minds on the job."

The lieutenant saluted smartly and then half ran

through the beach sand back down to the beginning of the now-completed barricade. Within a minute, the commander could hear the count start up: "One . . . two . . . three . . ."

Then, steeling himself against the darkness and the gloomy crash of the waves, the officer raised his infrared binoculars to his eyes and once again peered out to sea.

The attack came twenty minutes later.

It was the Commander who saw them first and—*damn it!*—it *did* appear as if they had just materialized on the beach.

"They're here," the Commander shouted out, immediately knowing it was not the proper warning to give. He screamed: "Check ammunition loads!" as partial remedy, adding: "Fire on my command and not before!" Then he turned his attention back to the small but growing force of men approaching the barricade from the left.

The invaders, at least two hundred of them now, were clearly walking right out of the surf. Yet impossibly, there were no landing craft in sight of the beach, nor any larger mother ships farther out to sea.

But to his credit, the Commander knew that it was not up to him to figure out the raiders' disappearing act. Nor did he intend to make a courageous and therefore suicidal last stand on the beach at Montauk. His orders were simple: inflict as much damage as possible on the invaders while minimizing casualties to the militia. The commander felt the first part of the order was straightforward enough; the rest however was left open for interpretation.

In reality, the commander intended on getting two or three volleys from his men and then, if the enemy kept coming in overwhelming numbers, he planned to withdraw to secondary positions about a quarter mile away.

Another two or three volleys and then another with-drawal. He would fall back like this all night if he had to—all the way to Southhampton if necessary.

It was a viable, intelligent strategy. There were no civilians anywhere nearby, and with the Montauk region being a sparsely populated resort area, there was little in the way worth pillaging. Besides, the Commander *did* have one advantage over his enemy: Time. Because he knew, as his troops did, that so far, the raiders had always "disappeared" long before the sun came up.

Quickly adjusting his infrared spyglasses, he estimated that more than three hundred raiders were now already ashore, with many more appearing by the second. He called to his radioman to get a message off to the LISDF headquarters at Hampton Bays, some thirty-five miles away, telling them of the situation. Then he made sure his own M-16 was loaded.

Several more tense seconds passed and then the commander yelled: "Get ready!" An advance group of more than fifty raiders had reached a point about a hundred yards from the northern tip of the militia's barricade and they had obviously spotted the defense works. At this point, the commander knew he had no other choice but to engage.

"Aim!" he yelled, knowing that the longer he waited, the more effective the first volley would be. "Fire only on my order . . ."

But suddenly his first lieutenant was tugging violently at his shoulder.

"Sir!" the man said in a terrifying whisper. "Look . . . to the south!"

The Commander spun to his right and adjusted his NightScope.

"Oh, damn—no . . ." he whispered.

Approaching from their right flank was an even larger force of the enemy.

"And they're behind us, too . . ." the young officer

said shakily, pointing to still more shadows heading toward them from the dunes to their west.

"We're surrounded, sir . . ." the lieutenant blurted out.

A second later, they heard the bugles.

Until this day, Lee Goldstein had never killed a person before. He was a musician by trade, devoted to bringing people entertainment, not pain.

But now, as the sergeant in charge of the southernmost flank of the LISDF barricade, Goldstein was suddenly killing people by the dozens, firing furiously at the hundreds of raiders that had attacked the weak side of the LISDF line.

It was a slow-motion nightmare come to life. The screams of his men, the nonstop firing of the guns on both sides, the frightening drone of the enemy's bugles. The air itself was drenched in panic. Men were being ripped by bullets all around him. Death and pandemonium were everywhere.

And there was no end to the invaders—they just kept coming, running up from the beach in a bizarre helter-skelter fashion, screaming as they charged the barricades, some firing their weapons, others wildly waving huge battle axes.

Through it all Goldstein kept shooting—it was as if his hands were fastened to the M-16, the heat of the constant firing welding them in place as a death grip.

But no matter how fast he fired or how many of the enemy he killed, Goldstein knew that his end was near. The invaders had breached the northern end of the barricade and were wielding their axes like a farmer wields a sickle. Goldstein instantly learned that there was no horror equal to the sound of a man being hacked to death. The invaders were pouring into the LISDF positions from the rear, too, with many of their bullets flying over the militia's surrounded barricades and absurdly cutting down their own men who were attacking from the south.

Despite the wall of lead, the line of screaming invaders was still coming fast. They were just fifteen feet from his end of the barricade now, and for the first time, Goldstein could see them up close. Their features were craggy, their faces lined and windblown. Each one wore a beard of some kind, and none that he saw had a face devoid of scars. How ironic, Goldstein thought, that he would see these things just before his death: the lines in the enemy's face, the grime on his hands, the look of absolute evil in the eyes.

The first invader to reach the barricade directly in front of Goldstein was swinging a huge battle-axe with one hand and firing a 9mm machine pistol with the other. Goldstein shot him in the throat. The next enemy soldier in line was carrying a red-hot BAR automatic rifle. He stepped right up onto the back of his fallen comrade and glared at the militiamen as he raked the barricade with gunfire. Goldstein fired three bullets directly into his heart. Behind him were two invaders carrying a length of pipe which was smoking heavily at one end. Goldstein recognized the instrument as a bangalore torpedo. He quickly sprayed both men with his M-16, the bullets snapping off a series of sickening cracks as they punctured the enemy soldiers' skulls at close range.

Blown backward the barrage, the dying men dropped the torpedo. Goldstein barely had enough time to yell *"Down!"* to his men before the explosive inside the metal tube went off. The force of the blast caused a large piece of the barricade—an eight-by-eight piece of backyard fence—to fall on top of him and pin him to the damp beach sand. Goldstein now could not move his arms or legs. What was worse, the invaders were using the battered wooden section as a ramp to gain access to the line behind the barricade.

Scared beyond words that he was now going to be

crushed to death, Goldstein nevertheless managed to pull his M-16 up and point it through a crack in the wood beams. He began firing wildly, killing as many as four of the raiders with nasty shots to their private parts before running out of ammo. Trapped but still hidden by the heavy section of wood, he somehow was able to jam another clip into his M-16 and continue firing.

The raiders were all over the barricades by now, and brutal hand-to-hand fighting was going on everywhere. All the while the racket of the bugles and gunfire was rising to a crescendo. Yet in the background, Goldstein's finely tuned musician's ear heard another sound — a dull, mechanical roar that seemed to be coming from out to sea.

Perhaps it was the sound of some Angel of Death, he thought, coming to get them all.

Just then a great hand grabbed the end of his rifle muzzle and attempted to yank it up through the hole in the fence pickets. Goldstein squeezed the trigger and killed the man, but his hand was replaced by another. Goldstein fired again. And again. But as each victim fell away, another would grab his rifle and yank it.

Then he ran out of ammunition for good.

A second later, one of the invaders was successful in ripping the spent rifle from his hands. Then he realized that three of the enemy were grabbing onto the edges of the fence section itself and lifting it. For one terrifying moment, all he could see was the gleam of the enemy's axe heads.

With a fair amount of effort, the men managed to pull the piece of wood off him, and for a frightening half-second, all three of them peered down at him, cruel grins on their faces. The mechanical roar out to sea was even louder now, providing strange accompaniment for what should have been the last few seconds of Goldstein's life. The invaders raised their axes and screamed in unison, generating the psychic energy needed to chop

Goldstein into pieces. He closed his eyes and waited for the first blow.

But it never came.

Instead, all three of the invaders were suddenly blown away in a great stream of wind and gunfire. Goldstein barely saw them through the slits in his eyelids as their bodies were swept away by a long tongue of tracer fire.

Two more invaders appeared right above him, but they, too, were dispatched by a burst of fire. All the while the mechanical noise was screeching in his eardrums. What the hell was it? The noise, which now drowned out all the screams and sounds of gunfire, seemed familiar, but Goldstein's reasoning process was skewed as he was close to going into a state of shock.

For the next two minutes all he heard was the earsplitting mechanical noise and the roar of what sounded like one, solitary cannon that was sweeping fire up and down the beach. And then, after a while, this gunfire stopped, too.

With great effort, Goldstein lifted himself out from the rubble and tangled bodies and was astonished at what he saw.

There wasn't a enemy soldier left standing. The shoreline was covered with their bodies, cut down like so many blades of grass, some of them rolling in the heavy surf. Parts of the barricade were smoking, and several fires were raging at the north end. Many of the LISDF militiamen around him were dead.

It seemed to him the only thing left was the terrifying blackness of the night and this strange roar. It took a few confused moments, but by looking straight up, Goldstein finally discovered the source of the sound: Hovering right over his position was a Harrier jumpjet.

Chapter Twenty

When the Commander of the LISDF militia awakened, it was morning.

He was flat on his back and it seemed as if every bone in his body was aching. The sky overhead was cloudless and clear except for a single jet-black raven that was circling high above. The first sound the officer heard was the gentle crashing of the waves. He felt a warm breeze on his face. Then he realized that tears were running out of his eyes.

He couldn't believe it—he was still alive.

"How are you feeling, sir?"

The Commander blinked once and saw he was staring into the face of Sergeant Goldstein.

"What . . . what happened?"

Goldstein managed a grin even though his face and shoulder were covered with bloody bandages. "You got hit on the head, sir . . ."

"And the enemy?" the Commander asked, gingerly rubbing the large gash on his forehead.

"They were stopped, sir," Goldstein said, his voice choking back the emotion. "Finally . . ."

With Goldstein's help, the commander managed to raise himself up on his right elbow. Then, for the first time, he saw the devastation on Montauk Beach.

The barricade was gone for the most part, burned or blown away. Hundreds of sand-caked weapons—guns to mortars to axes and swords—were strewn all around him. The smell of gunpowder was as thick as that of the sea. And everywhere were bodies, stretching for at least a mile along the shore, some lying in the wet sand, others perversely tossed about by the incoming tide. Off to his left, his men were calmly separating the corpses; one pile for the invaders, another for the militia's KIA's.

"How many?" he asked Goldstein, wiping a stream of blood from his lips.

"Seventy-eight of our guys confirmed," Goldstein told him. "At least three hundred of them . . ."

The Commander shook his head and found it painful. "But how?" he asked. "All I can remember is that they were coming at us from all sides . . ."

Goldstein pointed down to the southern end of the beach. "Over there, sir," he said. "That's the reason we're still alive."

The Commander looked south and saw a man dressed in a flight suit and a white helmet, sitting on the top of a sand dune a hundred feet away.

"He saved us," Goldstein said. "Him and his jumpjet. Got here just in time. Caught the enemy right on the tideline, and rolled them up to our barricades. I still don't know how he did it, but he was able to shoot them without hitting any one of us . . ."

The commander tried to get to his feet but fell back almost immediately.

"I . . . must talk to him," he said, trying again to get up.

"Hang on, sir," Goldstein replied. "There's something else you should know."

This time he pointed out to sea. At first all the commander could make out was a long black plume of smoke, rising straight up into the sky. But as he was able to focus his teary eyes, he saw that there was actually a ship of some kind, burning about a half mile off shore.

"That pilot also solved the big mystery for us, sir," Goldstein told the senior officer. "He found out how the raiders were able to attack so quickly . . ."

The commander somehow found his binoculars, and with help from Goldstein was able to focus them on the burning wreck.

"My God," the senior officer exclaimed after examining the burning ship for a few moments. "Is that a submarine?"

Chapter Twenty-one

Not only had Sergeant Goldstein never been aboard a submarine before, he had never even seen one up close.

But now, as he steered the motorboat at full speed toward the smoking hulk of the raiders' vessel, he realized all of that was about to change.

His "Monster Johnson" speedster was in the vanguard of a fleet made up of two dozen yachts, fishing boats, powerboats, and motorized catamarans that had been hastily appropriated from the Montauk Point Yacht Club. More than a hundred and fifty militiamen were crowded onto the vessels, many hanging on for dear life as the makeshift flotilla raced through the choppy waters off Montauk. A quarter mile ahead was their prize—the raiders' submarine. Their intention was to board it, overcome anyone still left alive on board, and then inspect the vessel for clues as to the origin of the raiders.

But now, as Goldstein drew closer to the vessel, it was becoming very clear that this particular submarine was many times larger than he ever imagined it would be.

"It's *enormous*," the militia commander said, focusing his spyglasses on the vessel. "Much bigger than any old US Navy boat, wouldn't you think, Major Hunter?"

Standing on the rail next to the commander, Hunter had to agree that this was no typical submarine they were approaching.

"I've only seen drawings of subs like this," he told the commander, borrowing the man's spyglasses. "Years ago, before they built the Alaskan pipeline, someone proposed constructing a bunch of huge subs—submerged supertankers really—to carry the oil drilled up in Prudhoe Bay down to the refineries in the lower states. They claimed it would have been much safer, cheaper, and better for the environment than pumping the stuff through pipes down the middle of the state.

"I don't think any of them were actually built, but this boat looks to be designed along the same general idea—in size anyway."

As he spoke, Hunter calculated the length of the huge sub to be at least nine hundred feet, almost twice as long as the US Navy's gigantic Ohio-class Trident sub. It was also much wider, probably a good eighty feet across the beam, with a stout yet bulbous conning tower to match. And it was not entirely tubular like prewar subs—rather its overall shape was flattened-out and squat.

By further adjusting the binoculars, Hunter could also clearly see the spot on the ass end of the sub where he had delivered a thousand pound bomb during the height of the battle the night before. A tangled mass of burnt and twisted metal was all that was left of the two huge propellers that once propelled the ship. The impact of the GPU bomb—he had eyeballed it in from a height of fifty feet—had caused the aft end of the vessel to stick up about fifteen feet in the air. Correspondingly, the bow of the sub was submerged by approximately the same amount.

"It's quite a unique design," Hunter concluded, handing the binoculars back to the commander. "And if I had to guess, I'd say it was built overseas some-

117

where *after* the Big War, not before."

"God damn," the commander exclaimed, immediately realizing the implications of Hunter's statement. "Do you really think that it's possible?"

Hunter could only shake his head. When he considered what he knew about the panic sweeping the continent, added in the destruction of nearly half of the country's gasoline and jet fuel reserves and the totally bizarre battle the night before, the appearance of a gigantic submarine almost seemed like a piece of comic relief to him.

In fact, the last two days had been so strange, he was at a point where he'd believe just about *anything* was possible.

Before happening upon the battle at Montauk, he had spent most of the previous forty-eight hours sweeping up and down the waters of southern New England and Long Island Sound, looking for any signs of the raiders who had snatched Dominique and Yaz. The search had not only been unsuccessful, it had been incredibly frustrating to boot. Not only did he face the task of searching over hundreds of square miles of ocean, he also had to deal with the extra hassle of trying to get JP-8 fuel for the Harrier.

He had spent eight hours of precious time trying to convince the commanders of a reserve naval air station in old Rhode Island that he was, in fact, Major Hawk Hunter of the United American Armed Forces and that he needed as much of their jet fuel as they could spare. Trouble was, no one paid much attention to him—they were too worried about being overrun by the ghostly horde of axe-wielding cannibalistic rapists. Hunter tried everything, including offering a bribe to the fueling crew, but still, no one would budge.

Finally it took a direct order via telex from Commander in Chief General Dave Jones himself to convince the naval officers to fill the Harrier's tanks.

It was dark by the time he finally took off from the naval station, and he immediately resumed his search of the coastal waters around Block Island Sound. Then, around midnight, his extraordinary sixth sense had begun flashing. Although nothing had registered on his various cockpit instruments, somehow he just "knew" that the raiders were close by. It was only a few minutes later that he spotted the first shots of the battle between the militiamen and the raiders on Montauk Point. After that, all it took was one sweep of the shoreline to distinguish friend from foe.

Ten minutes was all that was needed for him to empty both his Aden cannons into the scores of invaders along the beach. Then he turned out to sea just as the submarine—little more than a glint of light in the pitch-black dark and a mass of interference on his cockpit's look-down radar—was submerging.

Although he could have destroyed it outright, he chose to deliver just the one well-aimed thousand-pound GPU bomb to the boat's rear end. Hitting the props dead-on, he disabled the vessel immediately. There were several reasons behind this somewhat measured response: in strictly military terms, he knew that capturing the vessel intact would provide many clues as to who the raiders were.

However, he also had an overriding personal reason for not sinking the boat on the spot: this was the possibility that Dominique and Yaz might be aboard.

And although his gut was telling him that Dominique and his friend were not anywhere nearby—and never yet had his sixth sense of his been wrong—there was still the chance that other kidnapped Americans were being held on the boat.

"Well, whenever the hell it was built, it's ours now," the Commander suddenly boasted, breaking into

119

Hunter's thoughts. "It took these bastards to come to Long Island to finally get their asses whipped."

Hunter began to say something, but thought better of it. He knew the militia officer was assuming that this boat was the one and only vessel belonging to the raiders. Hunter doubted this, though. With the number of attacks reported in New England three days before, the numbers just didn't add up.

The Commander quickly radioed the other boats in his small fleet to stop and prepare for boarding.

"Just like we planned it," he said over and over into his radio microphone. "We don't need any screw-ups at this point."

Hunter checked the ammunition in his M-16 and adjusted his crash helmet. There was a good chance that someone was still alive aboard the sub, and if they chose to fight, they would prove to be a troublesome adversary. For although more than three hundred raiders had died at Montauk Point, not all of them had been killed by the militiamen or by Hunter's cannons. Rather, more than one hundred of them had died by their own hand, killing themselves after realizing that, despite their ferocity and just plain dumb courage, their battle had been lost.

The very thought of that had been giving Hunter the creeps all morning. Only fanatics choose suicide over defeat, and from painful experience he knew the worst kind of enemy was a fanatical one.

After five minutes of shaky maneuvering, the small militia flotilla had finally surrounded the big sub. At that point, the Commander gave the word to board the vessel.

Hunter, Goldstein, and the Commander himself were among the first to climb up onto the boat's deck. Then a fishing boat pulled alongside and deposited twenty-five distinctive, green-uniformed soldiers on to the sub. These men, all of them veterans of World War III as well as the various postwar continental campaigns, composed the militia's shock troop unit. They had volunteered to go into the sub first.

Once he saw that the rest of his troops were standing close by, the Commander left Goldstein in charge of the top side and then gave the signal for the special forces to enter the sub.

With Hunter and the Commander in the lead, the small force squeezed down through the conning tower hatchway and into a long pitch-black corridor below.

Right away it was apparent to all that this was no ordinary submarine—outside *or* inside.

By the light of a powerful flashlight attached to Hunter's M-16, they could all see that the walls of the corridor were adorned with hundreds of bizarre symbols. Birds, dragons, schools of fish, seals, trees, snowflakes, grapevines, all mixed in with strange lettering—a kind of hieroglyphics, Hunter supposed.

Moving down the passageway, the symbols on the wall changed from letters and pictures to murals of battle scenes featuring black-uniformed, axe-wielding, bugle-blowing soldiers in combat against undefinable, almost generic-type enemies. There were doors all along this dark hallway, but each one had been welded shut. Removing his glove and feeling the area around one weld, Hunter nearly burned his finger, evidence that the sealing operation had taken place just recently. That also accounted for the acrid smell in the air of the passage.

They worked their way down the corridor and into the control room. Again, all the indications were that the boat was hardly like anything ever built before. The vast steering deck was also covered with hundreds of the strange symbols, but there were surprisingly few actual controls. The steering mechanisms were especially rudimentary, as were the levers for the ballasting action. The few computers in sight looked to be about vintage 1958, and try as he might, Hunter could not even find a periscope. Nor were there any controls which might be tied into any kind of weapons systems.

"It's so big," the Commander said, "yet so, well . . . *primitive.*"

"My thoughts exactly," Hunter replied.

Leaving six of the shock troops in the control room, Hunter and the others pressed on into the midsection of the boat. They found more welded doors and even more extravagant murals on the walls and ceiling. The acrid smell gave way to another odor, this one, however, of definite human origin.

"God, it stinks worse than a locker room down here" is how one of the shock troops so aptly put it.

The stench got worse as they approached a set of double hatches. Seeing they were not welded, Hunter and the troops carefully unlocked them and pulled them open. A massive wave of body odor was waiting for them on the other side.

"Jeesuzz," Hunter said, quickly wrapping his red cowboy style kerchief around his nose and mouth. "These guys ever hear of soap?"

The room they'd entered was a large barracks type affair, with stacked beds reaching five and six bunks high. The place was a human pigsty. The floor was covered with all kinds of trash, from greasy rags and ripped, discarded clothing to empty cans of oil and piles of fish bones. One corner of the room was apparently used as an open latrine. And instead of mattresses and blankets, the bunks were covered with little more than collections of filthy animal skins and tacky furs.

"We're dealing with some *very* strange people here," Hunter said with classic understatement.

On Hunter's suggestion, the militia commander assigned four unlucky soldiers to count the number of bunks inside the dark and dirty chamber. Holding their noses and working quickly, the men reported a total of 173.

"That's bad news," the Commander said. "Because if we don't find another barracks like this, that means—"

". . . that there was more than one sub off your position last night," Hunter finished the sentence for him. "And that means they have at least two of these things and most likely many more."

With the militia commander's ego deflated slightly, they moved through the smelly compartment and into the powerplant of the boat. This was where they got their biggest surprise.

"Coal?" the Commander exclaimed when he first spotted the large pile of bituminous material inside the power chamber. "This is too unbelievable . . ."

At first glance, Hunter had to agree. A submarine powered by coal? But on closer inspection he discovered that whoever built the vessel might have cut corners on the aesthetics, but they had come up with an ingenious way of fueling its propulsion units.

"They don't burn coal in the usual way," Hunter explained, pointing to the igloolike structure in the middle of the power compartment. "This thing is a coal gasification unit. It breaks down the coal and converts it into a gas."

He walked past the igloo to the bank of turbines at the far end of the large compartment.

"They burn the gas in these turbines," he said, inspecting the four compact but powerful, jet-enginelike machines. "And they turn the propellers and provide electricity to the boat's systems. The beauty of it is they don't have to use very much coal to get the gas they need."

"Amazing," the militia commander whispered.

"It gets better," Hunter replied, walking over to two larger turbines which were situated right up against the bulkhead wall. "It looks like they've built in a recycling aspect, too. These are steam-driven turbines. My guess is that they can recover some of the heat from the gas turbines' operation, use it to boil water, then make steam and drive these babies for even more power."

The Commander was astonished at the propulsion system's makeup. "Do you mean that despite its size and lack of sophistication, this boat has power to spare?" he asked.

"This one does, yes," Hunter replied. "And it also means they can stay at sea for extended periods of time without refueling."

At that moment, one of the shock troopers left behind in the control room came running into the power chamber.

"Excuse me, sir," he called out to the commander. "But you'd better come up to the control room. We just found some people . . ."

Five minutes later, Hunter, the Commander, and a squad of militiaman were staring at a very curious sight.

They were in a room just aft of the control center, one that had been welded shut before some industrious LISDF troopers decided to break in. Once through, they had discovered twenty-two individuals, calmly sitting cross-legged in the middle of the otherwise bare room chattering away in some foreign language, practically oblivious to the fact that they had just been captured. It did appear as if these men — all of them bearded, dirty, and obscenely smelly—were discussing their situation. Yet they were so serene about it, they looked like nothing more than a bunch of Boy Scouts sitting around talking about slipknots and such.

"Can this all get any stranger?" the Commander whispered to Hunter.

"Don't ask," Hunter replied.

The senior officer cocked his good ear toward the circle of smelly men. "What language are they speaking?" he asked. "It's not German, is it?"

Hunter gave a long listen, but the prisoners were talking so rapidly, it was hard to pick up many key words.

Still, Hunter had a theory.

"If I had to guess, I'd say it's at least part Scandinavian," he told the Commander.

"Well," the senior officer huffed, "if they think that just by ignoring us, we'll go away, they're very wrong."

With that he pulled out his .45 Colt pistol and fired two shots into the compartment's ceiling.

This act immediately got the prisoners' attention.

"Who *are* you people?" the senior officer yelled at the group, now staring at him with expressions of anger and disbelief. "Why have you attacked us?"

The men looked at each other and shrugged.

Two more bullets into the ceiling brought only more stares and shrugs. "Where is your captain?" the Commander yelled. "Why are you here?"

Despite the bombastic effort, it was quickly obvious to Hunter that the Commander's tactics weren't working.

"Can I give it a try, sir?" he asked the officer.

With a nod from the Commander, Hunter walked into the middle of the circle of strange men. Picking out the one he judged to be the biggest, he strategically aimed his M-16 at the floor between the man's

125

legs.

"This always works," Hunter muttered over his shoulder to the militia commander.

Then he pulled the trigger.

The victim, a bear of an individual with an especially slimy beard, literally jumped four feet into the air. When he came back down, Hunter instantly had his boot on the man's throat and his hot gun muzzle on his nose.

"Who?" Hunter asked simply, pointing to the man.

"Theut" was the terrified reply.

"This?" Hunter asked, sweeping his free hand around to indicate the boat itself.

"Knorr 'Kristsuden . . . " the man answered, his nose beginning to run due to the heat on snout of the M-16. *"Krig Bat Seks . . ."*

"Where are you from?"

"Godthaab . . ."

Holding his own nose, Hunter quickly searched the man. All he found was a kind of religious card, sealed in plastic. It depicted a crude picture of the earth, with a huge snake wrapped around it.

Hunter then reached inside his flight-suit pocket and pulled out the photograph of Dominique that he always kept there.

He shoved the photo right between the man's eyes.

"Seen her?" he asked, just barely controlling his anger.

The man was absolutely petrified, as if he knew exactly why Hunter was asking the question.

"Na . . . *na!*" he babbled shaking his head. *"Knorr Kristsuden na for skraelings."*

Hunter suppressed the urge to kick the man in the head. Instead, he went back over to the Commander.

"Did you understand any of that?" the militia officer asked him.

"Not really," Hunter answered. "He's definitely speaking some kind of northern European dialect though, maybe even a new one. Either that, or possibly a combination of several languages."

"He seemed to be telling you that this boat didn't carry prisoners . . ." the Commander said.

"That's what I thought, too," Hunter said, studying the plastic card he'd taken from the man. Just then, a thought popped into his head. "Unless . . ."

"Unless what?"

"Unless this picture is of Midgardsomr," Hunter answered somewhat mysteriously. "And if it is . . ."

Suddenly he turned and ran out the door. Moving down the long corridor in a flash, he quickly climbed up the conning-tower ladder and then out onto the deck itself.

Most of the militiamen were milling around in small groups onto the deck, inspecting the length of the strange vessel. Hunter, however, headed right for the bow.

Curiously, several ravens had landed on this far end deck of the sub. They flapped away with a squawk as he approached. Still, he could only get within fifteen feet or so of the nose of the sub, as it was submerged due to the damage to the aft end of the boat. Yet there was something down there that he had to see. He was formulating a very way-out theory in his mind, one that he had to confirm, and he knew a very important clue might be attached to the snout of the boat.

After laying his M-16 down on the deck, he quickly removed his flight suit and helmet. Then, using a battered but still-attached hand railing, he slowly made his way down the bow of the boat toward the sunken tip.

The militia commander had arrived on the scene by

127

this time, and, joined by a curious gang of militia-man, he watched and wondered just what the hell Hunter was up to.

Hunter eased himself down into the water until it was up to his neck. Then, taking several large gulps of air, he went under, still holding onto the railing.

The saltwater stung his eyes briefly, but it was a small price to pay for what he saw. Attached to the nose of the submarine was a frighteningly realistic wood-and-plastic mockup of a sea monster's head.

I don't believe this, Hunter thought.

Not only was this head fashioned to exact propor-tions, its green skin and brown stringy mane were made of some pliable material which allowed it to move and sway and nod just like a living creature. The workmanship was so good that Hunter took a couple of extra seconds to admire it before easing himself back up to the boat's deck.

The Commander was there to help him up the last few steps, and now, completely soaked, Hunter shook himself to get rid of some of the excess water. Then he explained to the Commander what he had just seen.

"It's unbelievable," he said, still shaking his head in astonishment.

"But what does it mean, Major?" the militia officer asked.

Hunter retrieved the picture card the prisoner had given him.

"This is a picture of *Midgardsomr,*" he said, spitting out some seawater that had crept into his mouth. "It's the most enduring of all the ancient Teutonic symbols. A thousand years ago, people of northern Europe be-lieved that this serpent protected them from evil spir-its. They believed it so much, they used to carve them everywhere, including on the bows of their ships.

128

"Now some militiamen up in Massachusetts took a video of what looked a hell of a lot like a sea monster off their coast a few days ago. All they saw, though, was the head, and then only for a few seconds. But the thing looked damn real. Well, I just saw what they saw, and its on the bow of this sub and probably on the bow of as many subs as these guys have."

The Commander was shaking his head furiously by this time.

"Well, the subs explain how these people were able to get so close in to our shores without being seen," the man said. "But this lifelike monster head. What does *it* mean? Are you saying that we are being invaded by an army of . . . what? Ancient Teutonics?"

"No, sir," Hunter replied. "What I'm saying is that we're being invaded by an army of Vikings . . ."

Chapter Twenty-two

Ninety miles off the coast of Long Island

The only illumination in the small cabin came from a single waning candle.

In this flickering light, six men and one woman sat around a small fold-down table, speaking in hushed tones.

"This was likely to happen sooner or later," one man said. "We couldn't expect them to continue to make landings without meeting some well-armed opposition eventually."

"True," another man said. "But this was not a regular military unit. We know they were not United American troops, but rather a local militia. It was the airplane that turned the tide."

"Airplane?" the woman asked harshly. "This is the first I've heard of an airplane being involved."

The six men eyed each other worriedly. No one wanted to speak. The woman was as well known for her violent temper.

"There *was* an airplane, my lady," one man finally murmured. "It was this airplane that saved the defending *skraeling* troops."

"And was it this airplane that also destroyed the troopship?" the woman demanded, pulling the dark hood she always wore closer to her face, giving her the appearance of a female Grim Reaper.

"Yes, my lady," several men answered at once.

"Apparently the *Krig Bat* took a direct hit on its propellers before it could submerge," another explained.

A frightening silence descended upon the room.

"So not only did this attack fail," the woman said finally. "Now the enemy knows many of our secrets as well."

"Those men from the troopship met their deaths bravely, my lady," said one man boldly. "And they believed that if they die with honor, then they do not die for no reason."

"That's nonsense!" the woman said in a voice so chilling that all six men involuntarily flinched. "If you die without achieving your objective, then your death is meaningless."

"No . . ." another of the men half shouted. "It is the honor of death in battle that is important."

The woman raised her hand as indication that the men should be still.

"I will not argue philosophy with you now," she said, her voice becoming strangely calm. "What we must talk about is how this action will affect our plans."

"It shouldn't affect them at all, my lady," the boldest of the six men told her. "We'll make sure your orders are transmitted to the appropriate people and that the troops continue their actions just as you prescribed. The American *skraelings* will not be prepared for them every time they strike. In the meantime, we will pursue our own agenda."

"But now they know how we—and the troopships—all travel," the woman told him angrily.

"This is regrettably true, my lady," the man pressed on. "But tracking and finding us or the troopships will still be very difficult for them. Even before the Big War, submarines proved very elusive. The superpowers spent much time and money trying to discover better ways to track submerged warships, and—"

"Do you pretend to lecture me on military history?" the woman interrupted.

"No . . . not at all, my lady," the man quickly answered. "I was just reviewing the facts of the past . . ."

"Forget the past," she told him harshly. "We must plan for the future. We must keep our schedule or risk the consequences."

"We are dedicated to just that, my lady," one of the men concluded nervously.

Chapter Twenty-three

The small, German-built CL-191 "Mini-Drone" RPV skimmed over the tops of the waves forty-four miles off the coast of Cape Cod, its remotely controlled flight systems performing flawlessly despite the turbulent air directly above the rough seas.

The RPV had been in the air almost three hours now and was quickly reaching the end of its fuel reserves. Sensing this, the drone's minicomputer flight control system began transmitting a series of short electromagnetic bursts. Thirty seconds later, these homing signals acquired their mark. Instantly processing the return signal, the RPV deftly dropped its left wing and turned to a more northeasterly course. Within another minute, it had locked on to its "home base."

Ten miles away, a seemingly innocuous fishing boat was undergoing a startling transformation. With speed and agility that comes only from many hours of practice, three members of its four-man crew hauled a section of fishing net up to a point twenty feet above the deck. Attaching one side to the fully extended deck crane and the other to a special set of clasps along the boat's main boom, the crew had, in effect, quickly constructed what was known in RPV lingo as a "vertical retrieval barrier."

Overseeing the operation from the bridge was the boat's captain. Once the net was up and secured, he turned the seventy-five foot boat into the wind and then settled down in front of fourteen-inch CRT display. After flipping three switches, he waited as the ghostly video image of his own vessel—shot by the camera mounted on the nose of the RPV now just six miles away—slowly appeared on the TV screen.

Now begins the hard part, he thought.

Jockeying a small lever that was linked to the RPV's guidance computer below decks, the captain gingerly lined up the outline of his boat with the middle of the TV screen. The video image flickered occasionally for the next minute as the captain steered the small airplane toward the fishing-net retrieval barrier erected by the crew.

So far, so good.

Another minute went by and then the RPV reached the crucial "five-mile away" point. Instantly, the RPV's on-board flight system shut down the craft's engine, knocking its flight path slightly off kilter. More juggling of the joystick by the captain brought the RPV back to level.

All of the small aircraft's critically sensitive video systems "locked down" at two miles out, the last step before the retrieval attempt. The TV image quickly faded from the captain's screen as the RPV's video camera clicked off, but by this time, he didn't need the electronic visual aid. Looking out the bridge window, he had no trouble picking up the shape of the green-and-brown RPV as it streaked right toward him.

Ten seconds later, the RPV flew right into the center of the raised net. With a whistle of relief, the captain yelled down to his crew to secure the aircraft and lower the net as quickly as possible.

Within forty-five seconds, they had done so. The whole operation had lasted less than 10 minutes.

* * *

A half hour later, the crew was gathered around the captain's monitor, sharing a pot of coffee.

The captain inserted the RPV's videotape cassette into his playback machine and pushed the appropriate buttons. A color bar appeared on the screen, and the officer quickly adjusted the videotape to the proper hue and tint. Then, after another few moments of knob twisting, he hit the machine's Play button.

The first few seconds of the videotape featured nothing more than footage of the ocean rushing beneath the RPV as it headed for the Cape Cod coastline. Still, this sequence indicated that the RPV's cameras had clicked on at the proper time and that they had done so in sharp focus.

"Looks like it could be a good take," the captain said in a tone slightly more upbeat than his usual somberness. "Image is clear. The color's good. Zoom facility working OK."

"Here comes the coastline now," one of the crewmen said.

At that point, the men put down their coffee cups and drew their chairs up closer to the TV. Two of them began to take notes, while a third operated a stopwatch.

The tape showed the RPV streaking over the coastline at precisely noon, exactly the time dictated by its pre-programmed flight sequence. As soon as it reached the beach, it climbed slightly to clear a long cliff that ran parallel to the shoreline, a place the captain knew was called Nauset Heights. Reaching its prescribed height, the RPV then flew over an abandoned farmhouse and several recently cut hayfields before turning north, toward the small seaport of Nauset itself.

Any doubt that the destruction of the village had been anything but complete was dispelled by the videotape. Few houses in the small town were left intact, and many continued to smolder, now more than two days after the attack. The men watching the TV had seen the pattern before.

"They did their jobs well this time, the bastards," the captain said, his voice thick with contempt.

The RPV went into a wide circle over the village at this point, providing various angles to the ruins of the small Cape Cod seaport.

"Looks like they used mostly rockets and automatic weapons," the captain said, studying the tape with a well-trained eye. "Not so much evidence of napalm or even flamethrowers this time."

"Time at one minute and thirty right now," the man working the stopwatch said. "The wide-angle sweep should commence at any moment."

A few seconds later, the image on the screen flickered slightly, indicating that the RPV's on-board computer had ordered it to break from its circling pattern over the village and climb for a wider view.

Now, as the angle widened, the crewmen were able to see that two paths of destruction led out from the outskirts of the village, one to the north and one to the south.

"No doubt they landed two roaming parties," the captain commented. "Thirty to forty men each, burning and killing as they went. You can see where one unit swept north and the other tried to go south."

"Coming up on the impact site in five seconds, sir," the stopwatch operator said.

Now the captain leaned forward with the rest of the men. The next sequence would be the most important part of the tape.

The image flickered again as the RPV went into a preprogrammed descent and turned slightly northwest of the village.

"There it is, sir!" one of the crewman said excitedly. "God, it looks like a direct hit . . ."

The captain put his hand to his chin and watched the next ten seconds of the poststrike reconnaissance videotape very closely. The blackened, smoking trail of destruction caused by the raiding party heading south came to an abrupt halt at the edge of an enormous crater. Where once a high sand dune stood, now there was nothing but a monstrous chasm. The massive hole—it was more than one hundred yards across and at least fifty feet deep—was still smoking, too, the sand at its bottom and along its rim black and scorched. There was also evidence of many seared bones and skulls.

"It *was* a direct hit . . ." the captain said with a tone of satisfaction. "And it appears to have wiped out that entire raiding party."

He quickly hit the freeze-frame button on the playback machine and then slowly advanced the tape in order to get a better look at the crater.

"Twenty-four miles away and we can *still* hit them that hard," he whispered, almost to himself.

They watched the replay of the crater sequence several more times before the captain finally relaxed. Leaning back in his chair, the captain's face creased in the new lines of an unlikely smile.

"Yes, my friends," he said in a reverent, hushed tone, "They are finally beginning to feel *our* sting."

A short time later, the fishing boat was underway again.

Steering their vessel due east, out into the open Atlantic, they sailed for four hours through increasingly rough seas and in and out of several squalls.

By dusk, they were within ten miles of their destination, and with the coming of night, the sea had settled down to an eerie calm. The captain reduced his speed to one half and allowed the comforting dusk to engulf the fishing boat.

Their home was coming into view now, but in the fading light, the crewmen could just barely see the outline of the warship's massive guns.

Chapter Twenty-four

Yaz woke up to the sounds of a raven crying.

His entire body ached so much, even opening his eyelids was a major discomfort. Then, after he was finally able to blink a few times, he found his vision to be blurry. More blinking cleared it up to the point that he could see his surroundings. But this turned out to be the most painful part of all.

He was inside a tiny room — though "glorified closet" would be a better description. The place was so small, his rusting, squeaky bunkbed just barely fit. All four walls plus the ceiling and the floor were painted in sickly dull gray, the only deviation being the red-paint drawing of a bird just above the room's only door.

A half-filled glass of water was on the floor next to the bunk, as was a piece of crusty bread. Yaz's clothes — the army fatigues he was wearing the night he was captured — were rolled in a ball and wedged between his bunk and the wall. What he was wearing at the moment was a cross between a hospital gown and a very cheesy bathrobe.

His stomach ached worst of all — he was sure he hadn't eaten in at least three days, maybe more. Yet, the piece of stale bread looked anything but inviting. He was sick to his stomach not so much from hunger but from the stench of the cabin itself. It smelled like the dirtiest locker room in the world.

139

Despite being unconscious for most of the past forty-eight hours, it wasn't hard for Yaz to recall just how he had gotten into this predicament. The raiders invaded Nauset Heights less than an hour after Hunter had left to investigate the explosions down in the village. The invaders had come so quickly and in such large numbers—more than forty strong—that Yaz never had a chance to fend them off.

As it was, he considered himself lucky to be alive.

The raiders looked as if they had just walked Dungeons & Dragons horror movie—grizzled, heavily scarred faces, many of them carrying battle-axes that were smeared with dried blood. They had surrounded the farmhouse before he even knew it, and by a series of crude hand gestures, had communicated to him that they would burn down the house if he and Dominique didn't surrender.

At the time, Yaz still wanted to fight, thinking he could hold them off with his M-16 on the chance that Hunter would return just in time to save the day. But Dominique told him no. If they were going to die, she said, she could not bear to see the farmhouse go up at the same time.

So they gave up.

Their captors were immediately struck by Dominique's beauty and this, Yaz told himself over and over, was the real reason he was still alive. From the looks of the men in the raiding party, killing and raping went with the job. Yet, their leader, a man who had only one arm and one ear, instantly recognized that Dominique was much too beautiful to be ravaged then and there. Instead, she was gently bound and gagged and then thrown over the shoulder of the raiding party's strongest member. Yaz, on the other hand, was trussed up with long strands of twine and forced to tramp along like a dog on a leash.

They had descended Nauset Cliff down to the beach and were picked up by a small motorboat that had been commandeered by other raiders. Meanwhile, they could hear the battle back in the village going full blast. In fact, Yaz had not only heard the tremendous explosion on the side of the sand dune, he had felt the shock wave of it as well, even though he had been a good two miles away at the time.

From the motorboat they were transferred to a kind of transparent rubber raft, one that for all the world looked invisible when riding atop the water at night. In a second, Yaz knew that the see-through raft was the reason the raiders had been able to give the illusion that they could materialize right out of the surf.

But the biggest surprise was to come.

When Yaz first saw the submarine he thought he was going to faint. Being a former U.S. Navy submariner himself, he was very familiar with submersibles. But never in his dreams did he think he would ever see a sub as gigantic as the one the raiders brought them to.

His astonishment didn't last long, however. As soon as they were brought down into the sub's control room, Yaz was struck by its total lack of sophistication. Judging from the absence of even the most rudimentary safety and backup systems, he was beginning to wonder how the boat could stay afloat, never mind travel under the water.

At that point, the man who appeared to be in charge of the sub gave Dominique the onceover. Then, with a jerk of his thumb, he ordered his men to take her away, which they did with as much poise as they could muster.

Yaz, in turn, was thrown into a cramped and clammy compartment that held about fifty terrified civilians, all of them women between the ages of eighteen and thirty-six, and many of them from the village of

141

Nauset.

The way things were going, he began to believe that he would be kept inside this crowded room forever. Yet his stay there was surprisingly brief. After only two hours—during which he had traded stories with the women—two guards came for him. He was brought to a man who apparently served as the boat's doctor (though he was as crude and scarred as his comrades), was given a mug of liquid and told to drink. The barrel of the physician's machine gun convinced Yaz that he was indeed thirsty, and drink he did.

He was unconscious ten seconds later.

He reckoned by the growth of his beard that he'd been out for more than two days. Now, with his headache receding, his nose adjusting to the stench, and his stomach starting to grumble, the piece of stale bread was beginning to look pretty good.

He was about to reach for it—just to determine how inedible it really was— when the door of the cabin suddenly flew open and six armed men barged in. Without a word they dragged him from the bed and marched him through a series of passageways that eventually led to the sub's control room.

Along the route, Yaz couldn't help but notice that the lightbulbs illuminating the corridors were getting dimmer by the moment. He was also vaguely aware that the sub was listing to one side. And while the sound of the vessel's power plant operation was roaring unimpeded in the background, the sub itself was moving very, *very* slowly.

They reached the crowded control room to find that the place was in state of pandemonium. Everyone was jabbering at everyone else and speaking so fast in their indecipherable language that all Yaz could make out was an occasional *ya!* and *na!* here and here.

The man he assumed was the captain of the ship was at the center of the confusion. One moment he appeared as if he were in deep discussion with one or two others; the next he was slapping some underling across the face. All the while he was eating a leg of lamb and washing down the huge greasy bites with some kind of sticky red fluid from a tarnished chalicelike cup.

Yaz's guards shoved several of the control-room men out of the way, and with a burst of chatter, made Yaz's presence known to the captain. The man turned and looked Yaz right in the eyes. Yaz simply stared back. The only thing he could say for the man was that his face was less broken, less scarred, and less weathered than the others. His hair was also somewhat shorter, and his beard was fairly combed and trimmed.

He also spoke some English.

"I hear you know submarines," he said to Yaz in a deep, thick accent.

"Who says?" Yaz replied.

"Your woman tells us this," the man stated matter-of-factly. "She says you are a genius in this regard."

Yaz shook his head. There was a slight chance that this man did not smell as bad as the others.

"She is not 'my woman,'" he said, wanting to get the record straight right away. "But she is a very close friend to a very good friend of mine. If any harm comes to her, I will kill the man responsible."

Yaz had unconsciously tensed his shoulders as he said all this, part of him suspecting that he was about to be dispatched by a battle-axe from behind at any second.

But the captain simply waved away his threat. "If she is not your woman, then you shouldn't be so concerned about her," he said, rather nonchalantly.

Yaz was stumped for a counterreply. It was obvious

the captain had other things on his mind.

"Now I ask you . . ." the man said, tearing a gristle-packed piece of meat from the greasy bone, "*Do* you know submarines?"

"I've done some time in them," Yaz replied simply.

"Just riding, or working them?"

Yaz shrugged. "What difference does it make?"

The captain looked around at the gang of smelly, bearded men that had formed a circle around the conversation.

"The difference is your life," he said, his yumping-yippedy tone turning dead serious. "And possibly the life of your friend's woman.

"Now tell me, what do you know about subs?"

Knowing he had little other choice, Yaz prudently took the next few minutes explaining to the captain that he had served as an executive officer aboard the Navy submarine USS *Albany* during World War III.

"Do you know propulsion systems?" the captain asked.

"Some," Yaz answered.

"Then you will help us," the captain replied. He turned to the rabble and tore off a short burst of yips and yaps. They immediately broke into a loud cheer.

Turning back to Yaz, the captain explained that although the sub's powerplants were working at maximum, only a small amount of power was reaching the propeller screws. Plus, the boat's electrical systems were faltering en masse.

"Power-shift differential is all screwed up," Yaz said by way of an instant diagnosis.

The man took another bite of lamb. "Can you tell us how to fix it?" he asked.

Yaz thought quickly and then answered: "Possibly. But first I want to know the whereabouts of my friend's woman and what her condition is."

"What else?" was the captain's reply.

"I want food," Yaz continued, sensing he could extract more from the man. "I want clean clothes and I want freedom for myself, my friend's woman, and all of the civilians you have on board this vessel."

The captain simply shrugged. He was a get-to-the-point type of guy and sensed that Yaz was, too.

"You will be fed," he said, drinking from his chalice. "And given clothes. But you are too late to get freedom for the civilians you spoke of. They are no longer on board. This is a warboat—a *Krig Bat*—and therefore is no place for slaves."

Yaz took due note of the reference to "slaves."

"So where are they?" he asked.

The man took another huge bite of meat. "They were transferred to another boat last night," he said, his words barely understandable with his mouth full. "Only you and your friend's friend remain on board, and we are keeping you both."

"OK," Yaz said. "Then I want to see her."

The captain spit out a piece of fat and ground it into the floor with the toe of his boot. Then he wiped the residue of grease from his mouth with his bare hand.

"You will eat first, get clothes, and then help fix our gears," he said. "And *then,* maybe you will see this woman."

"No," Yaz said firmly, at the same time wondering just how far he could bargain with the man. "I must know her condition first and above all other things . . ."

The captain just shook his head and kind of chuckled in an exasperated way.

"Will you please forget about this female? This 'friend of your friend?' " he said. "She is all right. In fact, she's in the best hands possible."

"Prove it," Yaz said defiantly.

145

The captain let out an enormous, greasy laugh, causing the others around them to laugh, too.

"Prove to me the world is round," he told Yaz in a mocking tone. "And tell me why the sky never catches on fire . . ."

Chapter Twenty-five

Montauk Point Yacht Club

Mike Fitzgerald took another swig of whiskey and re-lit his cigar.

"Some days I wish I was lying on a sunny beach somewhere," he said wistfully, leaning far back in his chair and closing his eyes. "Tub of ice-cold beer in front of me, redheads on either side, rubbing on the tanning oil, keeping the sun out of me face . . ."

"Dream on," Hunter told him grimly. "This ain't like the old days . . ."

They were sitting in the commodore's swanky office on the top floor of the once-luxurious Montauk Point Yacht Club. The multi-million-dollar building, which was built overlooking the scenic Montauk Bay, had been turned into a temporary United American field base. As such, it was crawling with Long Island militiamen as well as regular United American Army troops. A makeshift helipad large enough to handle three choppers plus Hunter's Harrier had been set up in the parking lot, and the entire area had been ringed with defensive weapons and sentries.

The battle at Montauk Point and the subsequent seizure of the raiders' submarine was the reason for all the activity around the yacht club. Once word of the capture of twenty-two enemy sailors had been flashed to Washington—and eventually across the country—the sleepy area around Montauk suddenly became the center of the universe. For it was here that the vicious, marauding invaders had finally been thrown back. Now some people were using Montauk in the same breath as the Battle of Saratoga, Doolittle's raid on Tokyo, the brave stand at Khe Sanh.

But the corraling of the twenty-two POW's had also created the need for interrogation, and that's why Fitz was in town. When it came to grilling prisoners-of-war, the barrel-chested Irishman was the best in the business. In fact, in the past forty-eight hours he had done little else but question the sailors, letting other UA officials deal with the swarm of media types who had camped out by the yacht club's main gate.

Yet with all his experience in the technique of "POW persuasion," Fitz's sessions with the captured seamen had been the strangest by far. As it turned out, language had not been a problem. Fitz had a definite knack for speaking in northern European dialects, and with his knowledge of Norwegian and Swedish, he was able to converse with the prisoners quite easily.

But understanding just what the hell the prisoners were talking about proved to be another matter.

Now it was late afternoon, and he and Hunter were awaiting an open line to Washington so they could give a complete report to General Jones. After that, they would have to start planning for their next step.

Both of them were tired, but The Wingman looked uncharacteristically weary. Fitz knew there was good reason for this, however, for his friend had not stopped to eat, sleep, or even breathe in the past two days. When he wasn't flying long, torturous search patterns off the American East Coast trying to locate other enemy subs, he was arguing, cajoling, and outright bribing people for the jet fuel needed to make the flights. When he couldn't get the fuel, he was helping Fitz with the interrogations, or lending a hand setting up a SAM

148

site or flying close-in chopper patrols along the Long Island beaches.

And in his spare time, he had pored over several dozen books on Viking lore.

Throughout it all, the expression on his face never changed. It was both grim and sad—clear in its yearning for Dominique.

Another few minutes passed, and then the phone on Fitz's desk rang twice. Picking it up, he listened for a moment and nodded to Hunter. "It's him . . ."

Hunter immediately turned on the telephone squawk box on the table beside him and soon all three men were able to talk and hear each other.

"How did the sessions go?" Jones asked through a minor storm of static.

"I've had better," Fitz answered, putting down his cigar and picking up a notebook which featured page upon page of names, numbers, and other various scribblings. "We've got a strange lot on our hands here."

"I'm not surprised," Jones said, the telephone-line connection gradually clearing up.

"If you are ready, General," Fitz continued, "we'll start at the top."

Fitz took the next few minutes explaining to Jones that all of the POW's had basically told the same story.

And what a story it was . . .

As it turned out, Hunter's description of the strange invaders as "modern Vikings" turned out to be quite accurate. Fitz was able to ascertain that just about all of the prisoners were of Scandinavian origin. Moreover, all of them also quite freely admitted they had sailed to North America for the primary purpose of raiding, pillaging, and capturing slaves—especially women between eighteen and thirty-six.

However, when Fitz asked them to identify their overall military commander or a central point where their

149

force was headquartered, the men answered with little more than blank stares. The twenty-two men were all part of one clan. The captain of the submarine—a man who was killed on the beach the night of the battle—was the top man in this clan. And while the prisoners admitted that many clans were involved in the North America raiding campaign, they knew very little about these other groups.

"Clans? That's a new one," Jones said. "Are we to assume then that they *have* no central command?"

"Not one in the typical sense," Hunter spoke up.

Fitz then went on to explain that he had also asked each POW how old he was, where he had grown up, and what he knew about the state of the world in general. Most of them were between the ages of thirty and fifty—old for raiding work. And many were practically ignorant of world events, some of them to the point that they claimed they didn't know anything about World War III.

"For want of a better word, they all seem to be very naive," Fitz went on. "The strange thing is that most of them are very talkative. *Too* talkative. They'll go on forever about a house they built or a bear they killed or an axe handle they carved from scratch and talk to you about it like a little kid.

"Yet they've brutally murdered at least three hundred people so far. And kidnapped at least that many more."

"They're just like the original Vikings," Hunter spoke up again, retrieving information he'd read about Viking lore. "Lack of central authority, definitely clannish, talkative. Their clothes and beards, their simple tactics—damn, right down to sticking that serpent's head on the front of their submarine, these guys fit the description of the authentic Norsemen from a thousand years ago."

"Did any of them say what made all of these clans

150

get together and come here in the first place?" Jones asked.

"Only one guy talked about that," Fitz replied, searching through his notes. "His name was Thurd. Of them all, he was probably the brightest, meaning he could probably tie his shoelaces by himself. He mentioned something about them returning to 'Vinland,' and claiming what was theirs to begin with."

"That's another interesting piece of information, General," Hunter jumped in. " 'Vinland' was what the original Norsemen called the part of North America where they first came ashore—way before Columbus, I might add. It was thought to be up around Newfoundland or Nova Scotia, but maybe as far down as Cape Cod or even farther south than that."

"Well, that would fit in with their pattern so far," Jones replied. "They first showed up in Nova Scotia and have obviously been working their way south ever since."

"And that's one thing we have working in our favor," Hunter told him. "These guys have no finesse. They operate on brute force. They hit a target, rape, pillage, kill, and kidnap, then they retreat to their subs, submerge and surface somewhere farther down the coast.

"What we have to do is be waiting for them at the next likely spot."

There was a break in the conversation as a burst of static came and went.

"Did you get any information about these huge submarines?" Jones asked once the line was clear again.

"Nothing other than they were designed in Oslo by a guy named Svenson and that there are a lot of them," Fitz answered. "And only Thurd, the smart one, knew all that. From what I could understand, the vast majority of these guys were all recruited from the mountains way the hell up in Scandinavia—some of the most isolated parts of the world. You know, dark six months a year. They were trained, probably indoctrinated to a certain degree, and then put on these boats. Apparently they've been raiding parts of Iceland and the British Isles for the past few months, getting their act together before sailing over here.

"However, I did get the impression that different subs have different specialties. One sub might carry just soldiers while another might carry just fuel or weapons."

There was a brief silence as all three men considered the information.

Finally Jones asked a very touchy question: "Did any of them say what they were doing with the people they kidnap?"

Right away, Fitz saw Hunter's face turn incredibly dour.

"No, sir," Fitz replied quickly. "None of them seemed to know anything about the people they kidnapped. They would just turn them over to another boat somewhere out to sea, get supplies in return, and then they'd be done with them. That's why I think they have different boats doing different jobs. The boat captured at Montauk Point was apparently a troop vessel, a *Krig Bat,* Thurd called it. 'War boat' in Norwegian. There weren't any accommodations for the kidnapped aboard."

The static returned now and stayed on the line for nearly a half minute. When Jones came back, it was apparent that he had heard enough for now.

"Get some rest, guys" he said, his voice fading. "We'll talk again in three hours about the next step."

With that, Jones hung up.

Hunter and Fitz each poured themselves another whiskey. Although they drank in silence, Fitz could see that Hunter's anger was building by the second.

"I'm convinced that these guys have a lot of slave

ships roaming around out there," Hunter said bitterly. "And when they're full, they bring all their victims to God-knows-where."

Fitz sadly nodded in agreement. "It's probably something along those lines," he said. "But with no central command point to speak of, it's going to be very difficult to find out exactly what they are up to and what boat is where at any given time. Especially since we've got very little in the way of naval vessels ourselves."

It was true: though the United Americans were strong in ground and air forces, their navy was little more than a few dozen coastal patrol craft and two creaking prewar submarines that would probably sink if they ever ventured out of their dry docks.

Hunter slammed his fist down on the desk. "But there *has* to be some kind of command structure," he said, his voice boiling with anger now. "These grunts wouldn't have to know anything about it. Most of them are as dumb as planks anyway. They're stooges. Thugs. Who else would get aboard those floating shitboxes?"

"Good point," Fitz said, lighting up a new cigar.

But Hunter was smoking now without the benefit of a stogie.

"And we've got hardware they've never even heard of," he fumed. "It's quality versus quantity again, Mike, and this time, I swear it, quality will win out. They can throw as many of their goons onto the beaches as they want, and fuel shortage or no fuel shortage, we'll be able to plaster them."

"If only we could figure out where and when they were coming in a big way . . ." Fitz replied, nodding. "Then we could really put the hurt on them."

An angry silence descended on the room.

"Someone, somewhere, is coordinating all this . . ." Hunter began again, his voice even angrier than ever. "I can *feel* it. Even if these clans don't know what the hell is going on, someone directed all those refineries to be bombed and someone is at least pointing these sub commanders in the right direction, telling them where to be and what to do before every raid."

Fitz was nodding slowly in agreement. "And if that is all true . . ." he said, "then someone is responsible for transporting the people they snatch."

Hunter's face turned as somber as stone. Every time he closed his eyes he saw the image of Dominique, beckoning to him.

"That's right," he said, his words dripping fire. "And that person is going to make a mistake eventually. And I'm going to be right on top of them when they do . . ."

Chapter Twenty-six

Two days later

It was barely thirty minutes after midnight when the Norse raiding party made up of the Finnbogi clan came ashore along a stretch of deserted Delaware seafront ironically named Slaughter Beach.

Unlike the weather during their previous landings, tonight it was raining. The sea was choppy with a high spray, and this made it more difficult than usual for the raiders to land their dozens of large, see-through rubber boats. Once on shore, things didn't get much better. The invaders found the going slow and sluggish due to the high winds, chilly rain, and deep, wet sand.

Nevertheless, they pressed on. There were six hundred and fifty-three of them in all, fully two-thirds of the Finnbogis. Most were armed with AK-47 assault rifles, although a few were carrying old, Czech-made grenade launchers as well as napalm-fueled flamethrowers. Plus, each man was carrying his own intricately carved battle-axe.

Their target for the night was the small city of Milford, located about five miles inland from Slaughter Beach. In terms of likely targets, Milford offered the raiders many of the things they were looking for. First of all, it was the site of a medium-sized oil-processing facility, one which had contained in the past several million gallons of aviation fuel.

Plus, the city, with its population of about five thousand, was lightly defended—so said the clan's advanced scouts, dropped off on the beach two days before. And unlike many of the cities along the American eastern seaboard, Milford had not been abandoned, though the reasons for this were not exactly clear, according to the Norse spies.

Once they had moved off the beach, the clan split into two groups. One party, made up of three hundred raiders and about a dozen rocket launchers, would approach the refinery via Route 36, a seaside two-lane highway. The second group of three hundred fifty would make its way over the sand dunes and through the marshes beyond, putting them in a position to attack the outskirts of the city from the south. Three Norsemen would be left behind to watch the clan's three dozen rubber boats.

A man named Thugg Finnbogi was the commander of the group that would move up Route 36 and attack the oil refinery. A massive individual of rock features and bright red hair and beard, Thugg was hands down the toughest of all the Finnbogis. He had led the clan on the raid at Yarmouth, Nova Scotia, as well as on several towns along Cape Cod, and it was he who had planned the details for this raid on Milford.

Proper dispersement of forces or such rudimentary things as front and rear defense of the unit were of little importance to Thugg, however. Instead of marching down Route 36 in two well-paced columns with scouts on either side watching the flanks, Thugg and his men simply walked down the middle of the rainy, windswept highway en masse, a disorganized mob with little regard for discipline or stealth.

In fact, Thugg considered his biggest concern to be preventing fights among his clan brethren; sharp, violent flareups were a daily, even hourly, occurrence among the Norsemen in general and the Finnbogis in particular.

Thugg's group walked for three miles through the rain and wind before they saw the twinkling lights of the Milford oil refinery off in the distance. Many of the clan members immediately grunted with contentment when they saw their objective. Silhouetted as it was against the glow of Milford itself, they knew the brightly lit refinery would be an easy target for their rocket teams.

They walked another half mile before settling down in a shallow stream basin that was no more than three hundred yards from the perimeter of the refinery. At this point, a number of flasks were broken out, and the clan shared a communal drinking of the hallucinogenic Norse liquor called *myx*. Within two minutes, the warriors were more boisterous than ever, laughing and shouting, their hands gripping tightly the guns and huge battle-axes they would soon bring into war.

Even Thugg was enjoying himself, a state of mind fueled by the mind-altering *myx*. He felt he had something to celebrate: he and his men had met absolutely no opposition so far, and to his untrained military mind, this did not seem unusual.

The second group of Finnbogis, the raiders who would attack and pillage the outskirts of Milford itself, was led by Thugg's cousin, a man named Svord.

Unlike Thugg, Svord was a man of small stature and one of the few raiders who did not sport a beard. Among the Finnbogis, Svord was known as *Stikkende Smerte*—roughly: Sharp Pain—and for good reason. Svord excelled at torture. An expert with both the battle-axe and the knife, he lived for the sheer viciousness of inflicting pain on others. And, unlike Thugg, no one had ever accused Svord of being bright. He was a brutal character in a world of brutal characters.

It was no surprise that Svord was even less sophisticated than Thugg at approaching his target. After a long, damp trek over the dunes and marshes, his clan brothers were seething by the time they saw the first row of houses that marked the outskirts of Milford, Delaware. Despite the late hour, several of these houses had lights on, indicating to Svord that they were full of unsuspecting victims prime for the hatchets and bullets of the marauding Finnbogis.

Svord immediately called his troop to be quiet, slapping several men close by who did not heed his order right away. Then he brought up his four flamethrower teams, and using hand signals, indicated that each team take one of the lighted houses each.

As these men moved into position, Svord called up the *redsel soldats*—the Finnbogis's "fright soldiers"— twenty men who, like him, reveled in dispensing pain. These men always stood at the vanguard of one of Svord's raids, usually being the first—and last—raiders their hapless victims saw. Svord barked a series of short orders to them, most to the effect that they should leave a few victims alive at first, to allow him the pleasure of torturing them himself.

Once these men began the crawl to the row of houses, Svord checked with the family leaders of the rest of the men. No less brutal than the *redsel soldats,* these raiders had simply not yet achieved a high enough status within the clan to spearhead an attack. Within the realm of all Norsemen, that kind of position only came with time and performance in battle.

Several minutes passed while the advanced units worked their way into position. All the while, Svord was nearly panting over the thoughts of the helpless

158

men, women, and children he would soon be gutting with his axe. His only real task—besides spreading panic and fear among the North American *skraelings*—was to bring back at least two dozen women. Only then would the Finnbogis get the supplies that the clan would need to continue this campaign of terror.

At last, two distinctive hoots rose up out of the damp night air. These were the signals Svord was waiting for—his units were in position. One gruff word from Svord and the *myx* flasks were broken out and passed around. Another grunt and the group's buglers began wetting their lips. There was a series of clicks as the clan members checked their ammunition loads one more time. Thumbs were run along axe blades, making sure they were razor-sharp.

Svord took one last swig of *myx* and burped. The time had come for battle.

With one dramatic push, Svord leaped up and stood before the mass of his small army. Axe held high, he let out a shriek that could curdle blood right in the veins. At that moment, the buglers started blaring. A great cry rose up from the rest of the clan. Then Svord thrust his arm forward as the signal for attack.

A split second later, a well-aimed bullet split Svord's skull in two.

Suddenly, the air was filled with bullets and cannon-fire. Tracer shells crisscrossed the darkness, all of them aimed at the mass of Finnbogis who were three steps into their charge of the row of houses. Four heavy mortar rounds landed in their midst in deadly succession. A dozen or so grenades exploded amongst them. Then more mortar rounds, more grenades, more tracers. More death. All of it being delivered with pinpoint accuracy by an unseen force hidden in the brush and trenches around the hopelessly surrounded raiding party.

It was over in less than a minute, the final blow be-

159

ing the riddling of one member of the flamethrower teams who had tried to fight back against his invisible attackers. Caught in an awesome crossfire, the man's tankful of gelatinlike napalm exploded, incinerating him instantly.

When the smoke finally cleared, the only sounds to be heard were the eerie moans of the dying Norsemen and the distant crashing of the waves five miles away. Slowly, methodically, the heavily camouflaged members of the Football City Special Forces Ambush Unit climbed out of their hiding places and approached the field of the dead. Not one of their twenty-four-man unit received so much as a scratch in the violent, brief encounter.

Of the three hundred men in Svord's group, only twelve survived the murderous fusillade. These dozen men, stationed as they were at the rear of the column, had managed to escape while their comrades were being cut to shreds by the intense enemy fire.

Now feeling the same panic they had generated in the hearts of their own past victims, the twelve men threw down their weapons and fled back in the direction of Slaughter Beach.

Only a few of the men in Thugg's column heard what they thought might be the sounds of gunfire coming from the edge of the city, about two miles away.

But not one of these individuals dared bring it to the clan leader's attention. Right now, all they were concerned about was drinking the *myx* and getting on with the attack on the refinery; faraway echoes of what might or might not be gunshots had no bearing on what they were about to do.

Through much pushing and shoving and face-slapping, Thugg finally managed to get his rocket teams in place. The lack of initial fire from the refinery security forces—if, in fact, there were any—made the job of getting the rocketmen into position oddly difficult. These men were used to rushing around, setting up their Milan and Sagger antitank rockets while under enemy fire. Doing it at a peaceful, almost leisurely pace, seemed to go against their nature, and the inevitable arguments and fistfights broke out.

At last, everything was ready. All that remained was for Thugg to check the target through his infrared binoculars and give the opening coordinates to the rocket teams. Usually one, specific structure—be it a fuel tank, a pump house, or a large junction of pipes—would be hit first, ensuring an immediate explosion and a storm of flames which served to panic any defenders.

But now as Thugg glared through the sophisticated spyglasses he saw an incredibly unexpected sight. Not a hundred fifty yards away, just on the outer perimeter of the refinery, there was a line of rocket launchers pointing *at him*. He unwittingly closed his eyes and shook his head, thinking it might be the *myx* that was responsible for what he was seeing. Or perhaps he was somehow getting a back reflection of his own missile launchers.

But after refocusing, he saw the threat in front of him was very real.

"Fire! Now!" he yelled to his rocket teams, but nothing happened. None of the rocket-team crew chiefs had a target yet, waiting as they were for him to sight it for them.

"Fire! *Fire!*" Thugg screamed at his baffled troops, but it was too late. An instant later, he saw the flash of first one, then two, and then a dozen rockets fired at his position.

The carnage that followed was brutal even by Norsemen standards. The three hundred fifty raiders were virtually trapped in the sand basin where they had taken up what they had thought to be only a temporary position. Now, a veritable blizzard of rockets, grenades, and tracer fire rained down on them, instantly blowing some of the Finnbogi to bits while horribly disfiguring others.

Unlike Svord, Thugg had seen disaster in the making. Thus, he had the extra few seconds to realize that their situation was hopeless and, if he stayed, then his entire force would be wiped out.

So with a scream that could be heard over the sounds of explosions and death, he ordered his men to fall back immediately.

The surviving Finnbogis needed no further prodding. Many of them abandoned their rifles (preferring instead to carry only their battle-axes), and scrambled up the far side of the large gulley. Those who were too badly injured to move pleaded with the others to bring them along, but in most cases these men were slain instead. Within thirty seconds of the furious barrage, close to two hundred of Thugg's clan had managed to climb out of the killing zone, leaving behind the remaining wounded to face the rain of missiles and lead alone.

Thugg's party was in wholesale panic by the time it reached Route 36.

Chapter Twenty-seven

The twelve survivors of Svord's unit had been hiding in the dunes at Slaughter Beach for twenty minutes or so when the first elements of Thugg's column straggled in.

Battered, injured, their eyes filled *myx*-fueled panic, the Finnbogis hastily exchanged stories about their mutually terrifying episodes. Never before since the campaign in North America began had the clan suffered such quick, unexpected losses. Nearly four hundred of their men—half the clan itself!—lay dead back at the two sites outside Milford, killed not in the heat of a close-in battle but by surprise and entrapment.

That's what frightened the Finnbogis most. To die in brutal but heroic hand-to-hand combat was not only acceptable to them, it practically assured their souls of a place in Asgard, the gloomy "heaven" of Norse mythology.

But to die in an ambush, before one had a chance to fight back and display his courage, was tantamount to being sentenced to hell.

It took ten minutes for the remainder of Thugg's men to reach the beach, the leader himself being one of the last to stumble in. But no sooner had Thugg arrived when he realized he faced another problem: the small fleet of "invisible" rafts was gone, along with the three men who had been left behind to protect them.

Another wave of panic now swept through the survivors. Not only did they have no means of escape back to the two Finnbogi submarines waiting two miles offshore, they were trapped in a defenseless position—a wide-open beach with only a few sand dunes for cover. Just like on the outskirts of Milford and the gulleys around the oil refinery, the beach offered the enemy a perfect setting for another frightening ambush.

What was worse, the sun was starting to come up.

It was Thugg himself who first saw the jet.

High above him—higher than the small band of circling ravens—was a sliver of dull reflected predawn sunlight moving slowly over their position. Though Thugg knew almost nothing about airplanes—other than the fact that they could fly and some could drop bombs—in his gut he was certain that this aircraft had had something to do with the terrible defeat that the Finnbogis had suffered this night.

The airplane began to circle now, and Thugg let out a wail, shaking his fist at it. This mechanical bird of prey looked as if it were surveying he and his men for its next meal.

Even though Thugg had bullied his cousins into setting up a defensive perimeter on the dunes of Slaughter Beach, it was sloppy and ill-defined. Being a warrior by trade, Thugg could *feel* the enemy approaching, yet it never occurred to him to set up advance positions to prove his instinct right. Instead, he simply sat down in the sand, placed his battle-axe between his legs, and waited.

They were trapped on the beach—pure and simple. No rescue force was coming. The subs were long gone—it was a clan rule that the boats never waited for the raiding parties past sunrise. What was worse, Thugg knew that the enemy probably would not attack them; if they had planned to, the attack would have already commenced and the slowly circling aircraft would have already dropped bombs on them.

No, he was sure that the enemy intended to capture as many of his clan as they could, simply in order to humiliate the Finnbogi name. At this thought he began to openly weep. For a Norse warrior, few things were worse than ending a battle alive and defeated.

The only alternative was for Thugg and his men to die by their own swords. But again this offered little respite. If one were surrounded in battle but had fought bravely, then taking one's own life was acceptable, and a place in Asgard was certain. But to do so only as a means out of an embarrassing and uncourageous position was a cowardly thing to do, one which the gods would definitely find *un*acceptable. These thoughts only caused Thugg to fret more.

A tug on his shoulder brought the clan leader out of his jag.

One of his soldiers, a man named Hogar, had climbed the highest dune and had confirmed Thugg's prediction that the enemy was closing in. Scrambling to the top of the dune himself, Thugg saw two units of uniformed soldiers approaching from the direction of the refinery and another two coming from the south. These troops were backed with tanks and other armored vehicles, and their strength looked to be about five hundred or more.

"Why don't they shoot?" Hogar asked Thugg. "With those guns, they could kill us all without endangering themselves."

"They want to take us alive," Thugg told him glumly. "They want to embarrass us and get information to make it easier to stop the others."

Hogar needed nothing more to be explained to him.

"Gather the cousins in a circle at the water's edge," Thugg ordered him. "We will have a final talk before ending all this."

Two minutes later, the two hundred or so raiders were sitting in the wet sand just feet away from the breaking surf, listening as Thugg explained what was happening.

By this time, the advance elements of the Football City Special Forces Ranger 3rd Brigade had cautiously taken up positions on the far dunes about a half mile north of the trapped Norsemen. Meanwhile, members of the Delaware State Militia arrived at similar positions to the south.

While these lines were being set, a jeep roared up to a dune about a hundred feet beyond the 3rd Brigade's positions and Mike Fitzgerald climbed out. Bullhorn and walkie-talkie in one hand, a notebook filled with Norwegian, Swedish, and Finnish phrases in the other, Fitz spoke briefly with the commander of the Rangers and then crawled up to the top of the dune and stared down at the circle of Finnboggi, twenty-five hundred feet away.

For the next ten minutes, Fitzgerald peppered the damp, early-morning air with broken sentences in the various Scandinavian tongues, telling the raiders that they were surrounded and that they should give up. In return, they would not be harmed and eventually would be put on boats and sent back to northern Europe. Throwing all their remaining weapons into the sea would be the sign that they accepted the offer.

While this was going on, Hunter—who had been circling the scene high above in the Harrier—had landed nearby and worked his way up to Fitz's position.

So far, the operation they'd conceived two days before had worked very well. Deducing that Milford was a likely target for the raiders, Hunter and Fitz had members of the tough Football City Rangers airlifted in and placed along the routes most likely to be used by the highly predictable Norsemen. The resulting ambushes had gone off like clockwork, and now they were attempting to complete the second half of their mission: to capture as many of the raiders as possible for purposes of interrogation. Though not particularly helpful in the overall scheme of things, the first batch of Norse prisoners from the Montauk battle had been so talkative, the United American Command felt that the more raiders captured alive, the better the chances were to determine the motives and movements of the strange enemy.

But as it turned out, dealing with a culture as remote as the Norse was like dealing with someone from another planet—or, more accurately, from another time. This was especially true of the fierce Finnbogi clan.

As humanitarian as it was, the Norsemen on the beach were absolutely petrified at the terms being offered by Fitz via his bullhorn. Giving up without a fight was bad enough. The thought of being disarmed and sent back to their homelands was absolutely horrifying. There was no deeper humiliation for the Norsemen than to be returned home, disarmed and in disgrace.

This is why Thugg and his men virtually tuned out Fitz's messages, although the Irishman repeated them over and over in all languages available to him. For the Finnbogi, only two options were apparent: charge the massed forces on the dunes and certainly be cut down before one of the enemy soldiers were harmed, or throw themselves on their own knives.

Neither was a sufficiently courageous choice.

But as with many times in war, fate intervened.

Hunter's extraordinary sixth sense began buzzing just

167

as Fitz was launching into the fifth Swedish translation of the surrender terms.

He felt *something* was flying toward them, though the vibrations he was receiving from the deepest recesses of his psyche were telling him it was not a typical aircraft.

"Hang on a second," he said to Fitz, just as the man had completed his Swedish translation. "Something's up . . ."

Hunter turned his almost laserlike vision out past the ring of Norsemen, out beyond the waves and gray-blue swells of the sea. Something was out there, and it was flying their way.

Suddenly he saw it. Just a dark, winged speck, skimming barely a foot or two above the waves, a thin line of flame and smoke trailing behind.

"See it?" Hunter said, shaking Fitz and directing his attention toward the incoming craft.

Fitz had to squint for a few moments before picking up the dot against the mass of ocean.

"God, what the hell could that be?" he asked.

Hunter already knew. It was the remotely piloted vehicle he had seen briefly over the village of Nauset right after the raiders' attack.

What happened next would be one of the most terrifying moments in either of the men's lives.

The RPV came straight at them until it reached the shoreline. Then it did a quick bank and headed right over the circle of raiders. Climbing slightly, it went into a tight orbit about two hundred feet above the heads of the bewildered Finnbogi.

Suddenly, another kind of warning went off in Hunter's brain.

"Christ! Fitz, order everyone to take cover!" he yelled almost directly into his friend's ear.

Fitz had been friends with Hunter for years—long

enough to know that in circumstances when Hunter made such sudden requests, it was always wise to follow up on them, no matter how bizarre they might seem at the time.

So recovering quickly from the ringing in his ears, Fitz began screaming through the bullhorn for all of the Football City troops to take cover—and quick! Meanwhile, Hunter had grabbed Fitz's walkie-talkie and was broadcasting the same message to the Delaware militiamen on the dunes to the south.

The next thing they knew, an absolutely horrifying screech pierced the morning air. Hunter dared to look up just as the trio of projectiles were clearing the horizon. They looked white—as in white-hot—and they were trailing three long streaks of deep red smoke.

He quickly saw that as soon as the bone-chilling screech appeared, the RPV had gone into a steep climb. Now the small aircraft had suddenly zoomed out to sea, its small engine sputtering, yet providing enough power to allow the little drone to clear the area.

Within an instant the screeching was so intense, Hunter and the others covered their ears in a vain attempt to block out the frightening sound.

The last thing Hunter saw before Fitz dragged him back down to cover was the small band of ravens scattering away from the beach.

The projectiles landed squarely on the circle of Finnbogi Norsemen just two seconds later.

Hunter had never been in an earthquake before.

But he couldn't imagine any kind of tremor being more violent or frightening than the ground shaking that occurred immediately after the three shells hit the shoreline at Slaughter Beach.

He and Fitz were thrown at least a hundred feet

169

back, both of them slamming into the side of another sand dune only to be covered with a barrage of sand and seawater thrown up by the enormous explosion. Hunter quickly pushed himself up and out of the pile of sand, but for a frightening few moments, he couldn't find Fitz. Digging frantically with both hands, he finally located first a boot, then a pant leg, and finally the belt and holster Fitz always wore. Pulling with all his might on the belt, Hunter was able to yank the squat fireplug frame of Fitzgerald out of the blackened, dirty sand.

Typically, the Irishman still had his cigar in his mouth.

"Mother of God!" Fitzgerald stammered, checking his various body parts to make sure everything was still in place. "Am I really alive?"

By this time, Hunter was up on his knees and brushing the sand from his own eyes. Oddly enough, it appeared as if there were thousands of diamonds on the ground around him. He managed to pick up a handful and saw that they were actually small pieces of glass. The blast on the beach had been so intense and the heat it generated so extreme, that it had actually fused together grains of sand to make millions of diamond-shaped glasslets.

His head still ringing, his mind still disoriented from the shock of the blast, Hunter finally managed to pick himself up and look back toward the beach.

The dune where he and Fitz had been stationed was long gone. From where he was now, he had a clear line of sight to the shoreline.

The Norsemen were gone, too. All that remained was a gigantic, smoking crater at least a hundred feet deep and three times that around that was quickly being filled up by the incoming tide.

"Was it one ours?" Fitz asked, his voice still shaky,

his face encrusted in sand.

But Hunter did not hear the question. Already he was running back through the remaining dunes, past the scores of Football City Rangers who were also just picking themselves up from the blast, back to his Harrier jumpjet.

Fitz had to think a moment as to why Hunter was so intent on getting airborne. But then looking back at the crater, he found his answer circling tightly about a hundred feet above the hole.

It was the RPV, back to survey the damage. Fitz watched intently as the drone orbited the crater three more times, and then did a sharp bank to the east. With a puff of smoke popping from its engine, the drone then accelerated quickly and zoomed back out to sea.

Less than a minute later, Hunter's jumpjet roared overhead in hot pursuit.

Chapter Twenty-eight

Yaz wiped the flood of perspiration from his forehead and leaned back against the bulkhead.

What I would do, he thought, *for just one lousy glass of beer.*

It was more than a hundred degrees inside the power chamber of the Norse sub, and the clammy, oily smell in the air made the heat that much more unbearable. Before Yaz sat a huge, disassembled gear clutch and its hydraulic pump system. Two of the four gaskets that helped seat the clutchworks had worn out, releasing a stream of hydraulic fluid into the sub's power transmission gears. This fluid, in turn, became heated by the motion of the transmission itself, cooked itself into a large sticky mass, and literally gummed up the works.

This is why the sub had not been able to make more than five knots an hour even though its turbines had been running full blast.

It had taken Yaz more than a day just to take the clutch apart. Now he wasn't sure if he had the wherewithal to put it all back together again and make it work. If he did, then he believed that the men on the boat would come to value him even more than now.

But what would happen to him if he didn't? Just one look at the man sitting across the room from him gave him that answer.

The man was a Britisher ironically nicknamed "Smiley." He had no hands, no ears, and no tongue. They were all gone, lopped-off months before by the captain of the boat when Smiley wasn't able to fix one of the vessel's auxiliary turbines within a twenty-four-hour deadline.

Before the mutilation, Smiley had served as the boat's chief engineer, signing on with the crew after the raiders—they being members of the Godthaab clan—attacked his village on the Isle of Wight. After finding out that Smiley had spent ten years aboard Royal Navy subs, the Godthaabs had made him an offer in their typically peculiar fashion: Join us or we'll kill you. Smiley joined.

For a while he'd enjoyed rank and privilege second only to the captain. But when the turbine went down and he couldn't fix it in a day's time, the captain went a-hacking with his knife, reducing Smiley to a partially deaf, handless wretch.

As Yaz eventually learned, the taking of Smiley's tongue had been an afterthought on the part of the captain. While he was in the good graces of the captain and crew, Smiley had learned many things about the Godthaabs—who they were, who supplied them with their boats, and why they were attacking the North American Continent—information only the captain himself was privy to. As soon as he fell out of favor, the captain realized that Smiley knew too much, and that he might one day tell all to someone else. So the tongue came out.

But, oddly enough, just why the captain didn't kill Smiley outright was starting to make some sense to Yaz.

The murals on the walls of the vessel told it all: In the world of these strange foreigners, how one died was extremely important. The paintings depicted raiders dying violently yet courageously. It was clear that, to their eyes, there was no better way to go.

Conversely, it was counterproductive to allow an enemy to die in a manner that might be construed as courageous. This is why moments after the captain had slashed Smiley, the vessel's doctor had the victim in the sick bay stitched up, receiving medication, and on the road to relative recovery.

It was another oddity in the raiders' way of thinking that brought Yaz and Smiley together. Smiley was supposed to be helping Yaz work on the huge clutchworks. But with no hands to hold tools and no tongue to speak with, there was little the man could be expected to do besides sit and watch.

Yet Smiley was an indomitable character. Just because the captain had relieved him of his hands, ears, and tongue, this didn't mean that he couldn't communicate. He still had some hearing left, and this allowed him and Yaz to have many long conversations, via the simple language of Morse code.

They had discovered this mode of communication almost by accident. Yaz had needed Smiley to hold a screwdriver in place while he disconnected the myriad of bolts on the clutch assembly. Using a piece of twine, he had tied the screwdriver to Smiley's right-arm stump and the work went on. But when it came time for Yaz to remove the tool, Smiley made it very clear that he was opposed to the action. That's when he started tapping out messages in Morse Code.

Not being able to communicate directly with a civilized human being for six months, Smiley did a fair amount of gabbing, via frantically rapid tapping. But Yaz didn't mind; with each conversation, Smiley provided him with a wealth of information.

For instance, the Englishman confirmed Yaz's suspicion that the raiders were, in fact, reincarnated Norsemen. The great boats themselves had been built with the help of a Norwegian ship designer named Svenson. This man had owned one of the largest and most profitable shipworks in post-war Europe before someone in league with the Norsemen bought him out for an outrageous amount of gold.

Guilt-ridden and plagued with remorse, Svenson later committed suicide, but not before he had revealed all the secrets to building the huge subs—quickly and economically—to the people acting for the Morse.

The reason why the subs were, on one hand, so efficient, yet, on the other, so unsophisticated was simple: They were built like the famous American liberty ships of World War II. That was, on a kind of assembly-line process, using generic designs, forms, and castings, from the propellers right down to the nuts and bolts. The building process was so elementary that much of the work was done by relatively unskilled labor; anyone who was smart enough to weld Joint A to Joint B could work on the project.

Or as Smiley tapped it, building the huge subs involved "the rational use of a large quantity of unskilled labor building a complex device by way of highly simplified design."

It was not a new idea: the pyramids had been built in exactly the same way.

Nor was there a need for an enormous shipyard in which to build the subs. Because everything was so simplified—no one piece of steel was big enough or heavy enough that two men couldn't carry it easily, for instance—the huge subs could be constructed in rather primitive settings. So even though some were assembled in Svenson's boatworks, many more were built on the beaches of Norway's many shallow fjords.

Smiley claimed that he had seen as many as twenty of the big boats together in one place at one time.

175

However, he had been told that there were as many as sixty or more of the vessels operating in the North Atlantic. Not all of them were used to simply transport raiders. Some hauled coal and supplies for the raiding ships, others simply functioned as transfer vessels for kidnapped victims or captured booty. Still others carried scouting parties and saboteurs; advance troops that could be landed quickly and quietly to recon or prepare a certain target for a later assault.

It was all valuable intelligence, just the sort of stuff that had led the boat's captain to take such drastic action against Smiley in the first place. But despite his nonstop tap rap, there were some things that Smiley was holding back. Once, during a meal break, he had let slip that he had some even more frightening information concerning the raiders' floating army.

Yaz knew immediately from the man's dead-serious demeanor that the information was very hot. Yet Smiley would say no more. That had been thirty-six hours ago. Now, on this early morning, with the clutchworks almost done, Yaz gathered up all his talents of persuasion and gently but firmly pressed the Brit to tell him the secret.

After much cajoling, the mute man agreed.

Tapping quietly and slowly, Smiley told Yaz that he had heard of a squad of four very special subs, ones whose mission had been kept ominously cloaked in mystery.

Called the *Fire Bats*—literally, "four boats" in Norwegian—Smiley said these vessels were worlds apart from the huge, hulking troop and supply boats. Built secretly deep within the bowels of Svenson's shipyard, the *Fire Bats* were smaller, sleeker, and much more sophisticated. As such, they had been built for a purpose other than just carrying raiders to the American East Coast or hauling slaves and booty away.

What that *exact* purpose was, Smiley didn't know. What he *did* know was that the *Fire Bats* were more elaborate inside and out than the big subs because their interiors were filled with equipment salvaged from US and Soviet nuclear submarines that had been damaged or abandoned during World War III.

This equipment, chillingly enough, included systems capable of launching nuclear missiles.

Yaz had no doubts that Smiley was telling him the truth. Only a fool would have spent more than an hour painstakingly tapping out a lie. And his information worked its sobering effect on Yaz quite quickly. Raiding parties of modern barbarians was one thing. Those same barbarians cruising around with nuclear launch capability was quite another.

Despite the heat and the smell and Smiley's incessant tapping, Yaz finally managed to put the sub's transmission gear and pump back together about an hour later.

He sent a message to the captain, who arrived inside the stuffy power chamber several minutes later to watch the tryout of the repair job himself. Taking full note of the officer's long, razor-sharp knife, Yaz took one deep breath and switched on the sub's power-transfer electric generator, the piece of equipment which actually ran the clutch assembly.

To his enormous relief, the clutch moved and the transmission went back to working perfectly right away.

The captain immediately put a bear hug on Yaz that near suffocated him. The officer even tapped Smiley on the head after Yaz mentioned the man had helped greatly in the repair.

The captain then told Yaz that a man with his knowledge of sub workings was valuable to them all. Thus, his talents were needed elsewhere.

With that, he was led away from the cramped, stifling room, leaving Smiley only enough time to tap out a hasty good-bye.

Chapter Twenty-nine

It didn't take Hunter more than a few minutes to get a visual sighting on the RPV.

After launching from the dunes behind Slaughter Beach, he simply followed the thin trail of dirty brown exhaust the small drone had left behind. Moving at a speed of 240 mph, he quickly spotted the craft skimming along the waves heading dead east. Within another twenty seconds he was practically right above it. Then, throttling back to 100 mph, he was able to match its speed.

Taking up a position slightly above and behind the RPV, Hunter knew the easy part was over. Now a bigger mystery remained: Who was controlling the RPV?

The question itself was fraught with implications which, in turn, led to other questions. The RPV was obviously linked with the massive bombardment that had simply obliterated the force of Norsemen trapped on Slaughter Beach. Were the three projectiles which caused the blast actually shot at the Norsemen? Or had they been fired in their support and simply fell short of hitting the American troops on the dunes beyond? Had the same thing happened back at Nauset: when a similar explosion—it, too coming on the heels of a RPV flyover—destroyed a smaller force of raiders?

More important, who had the ability these days to deliver so much firepower? Short of seeing a nuclear device itself being detonated, the massive explosions were by far the most violent Hunter had ever witnessed.

As always, his head was filled with theories, but intuition and experience told Hunter that he'd be wise not to jump to conclusions. War was seldom a clear-cut division of right and wrong.

He *did* know that the RPV was a classic battlefield drone ship, with a TV camera in its nose that was capable of either sending back live pictures of a battle in progress or performing poststrike recon by videotaping the battlefield for viewing once the drone was recaptured.

More importantly, he also knew that the range of small aircraft was not much more than a hundred miles, which meant that its mother ship could be no more than fifty miles off the coast.

Keeping one eye on the RPV, Hunter slowly raised the Harrier up to ten thousand feet and scanned the eastern horizon. All he could see was a single fishing boat making its way in a northerly direction approximately thirty miles from his position.

At that moment his radio crackled to life.

It was Fitz, calling him from the Football City Ranger outpost back in Milford. The Irishman reported that while none of the Norsemen survived the enormous blast, it had caused only minor injuries—blown-out eardrums mostly—to the Football City troops and the Delaware militiamen.

Hunter then briefed Fitz on his intent to track the RPV to its source.

"I've got it in sight and tracking due east," he told the Irishman. "It's got to land somewhere, sometime soon. I'm going to be there when it does."

"Then let me pass on a word of caution," Fitz replied through the occasional bursts of static. "We were lucky here in Delaware that no damage was done by these bastards . . ."

"But?" Hunter asked Fitz warily.

"But other locations along the coast *weren't* so lucky," Fitz said grimly.

Fitzgerald went on to report the disturbing news that other targets along the East Coast had been attacked by the raiders the previous night: the cities of Hampton, Williamsburg, Norfolk, and Portsmouth in Old Virginia; an air base on Cape Hatteras, and the city of Wilmington in North Carolina Free State; Myrtle Beach, Charlestown, and Cape Romain in South Carolina. Nine targets in all. Some were defended by militia and regular UA troops, others were not. Casualties were very high in some remote areas, and in a few places, many hostages were taken. And from all reports, very few of the raiders were killed or captured.

Hunter was so instantly enraged he couldn't speak for a few moments. The sheer audacity of the Norsemen was overwhelming, their brazenness extreme to the point of folly. No matter that they had been handed a defeat at Montauk and one of their subs was captured. No matter that that had failed miserably in the Milford raid. They still appeared intent on raping the American coastline with these hit-and-run battles, all while the entire country was caught up in a state of media-whipped panic and in the midst of a devastating fuel crisis.

And worst of all, for Hunter, the bastards still had Dominique and one of his best friends.

But the news of the increased attacks also told Hunter something about the enemy.

"The scope of their attacks is getting bigger every time," he radioed Fitzgerald. "I think it means that they're gearing up for a major strike, somewhere farther down the coast."

"Could be," Fitz replied. "Though that would still leave the question as to how these guys can all get together and act in unison when they claim there's no central command point."

"Well, that's exactly how the old Vikings used to operate," Hunter told him. "Very little guidance from the top. Back then, the clan elders just used to get their guys pointed in the right direction and then let 'em go."

"It's a fascinating way to fight a war, isn't it?" Fitz came back. "It almost put us heroes at a disadvantage. We can't cut the head off the snake if the snake has no head."

"There's something there," Hunter radioed back, his voice almost raspy with anger. "We've just got to know where to look."

A burst of static interrupted the transmission for a few seconds.

"Keep me updated, Mike," Hunter told Fitz after the line had cleared. "I'll contact you when I know more out here."

Fitz added a word of luck and then signed off.

Coincidentally, at that moment, Hunter saw the RPV take a turn to the north and then settle into a flight path that would take it right in line with the seemingly innocent-looking fishing boat.

Hunter was expecting the vehicle's mother ship to be something a little more elaborate, but already he could see the crew raising its fishing net and positioning it as retrieval barrier.

Ritually tapping his flight suit's breast pocket—the place where he kept a small tattered American flag wrapped around photo of Dominique—he felt a surge of adrenaline roar through him. Instantly, he hit his throttles and put the jumpjet into a screeching climb.

Time to get some answers he thought grimly.

Chapter Thirty

Elizabeth Sandlake rolled over and briefly admired the naked body of the beautiful Spanish woman lying next to her.

The woman's name was Juanita Juarez and she belonged to Elizabeth.

Elizabeth ran her hand up the lovely dark skin of the woman's thighs, over her tight stomach and around her full breasts. Her fingers lightly touched the dark beauty's face and caressed her hair.

What woman would *not* want to sleep with such a beautiful creature? Elizabeth thought.

She's the next best thing . . . Elizabeth found herself thinking.

But in the next moment, she felt all traces of pleasantness wash out of her.

Her head hurt and her stomach was growling. She could feel another brutal hangover coming on. Her own long hair was a jumble of tangles and one touch of her face proved her carefully applied makeup was now smeared and runny.

Looking around in the dim light of the sub's perfume-drenched cabin, she saw that the place was in an outrageous state of disarray. Beside the bed she shared with the sleeping woman were three empty *myx* bottles. A fourth had been spilled sometime during the night and had soaked a large part of the cabin floor. Lying right next to this pool of red liquor was the discarded fighter pilot's flight suit; it too was covered with *myx* stains.

The pilot's helmet and a ceremonial male organ modality were also lying nearby.

The night before had been wild—*too* wild.

The hallucinogenic liquor had flowed more freely than at any other time since she'd been aboard the sleek submarine, known as *Fire Bats Nord,* or Four Boats—North. Her fragile memory told her that no less than seven women had romped in the bed with her and Juanita the night before, taking turns wearing both the pilot's suit and the dildo. At the time, it had been pure unadulterated erotic pleasure. Now, with the onslaught of the morning after, Elizabeth was beginning to regret it all.

This can't go on much longer, she thought as she rolled over and begged her head to stop aching.

Elizabeth was quite insane—but her madness was of a most peculiar nature. True, it was a debilitating, self-destructive psychosis. But she nevertheless willingly gave herself to it. Messianic and nymphomanic, obsessive and schizophrenic, megalomanic and paranoid, Elizabeth had enough loose ends to stock an entire ward of lunatics. But she was not at the mercy of this multilevel complex—she reveled in it.

That was, after all, the best part of the insanity.

She was an educated woman—she held a Ph.D. in the esoteric study of Deep Zone Archeology. But she also had minored in psychology, so she had long ago recognized exactly what was wrong with her and how she had come by the affliction. It was the result her being held in total isolation in deep caves in the Yucatán by the gold-hungry Canal Nazis of the Twisted Cross. It was a simple snap she had felt in her brain that fateful night while locked in the deepest depths of a cavern beneath an ancient Mayan pyramid. After that, her entire life changed.

Now, she wanted nothing less than to rule the world.

Several minutes went by, during which Elizabeth's headache throbbed to new heights of agony.

She turned once again toward the naked Juanita, who was just coming out of her *myx*-induced slumber. A warm caress of the Spanish woman's lovely body eased Elizabeth's pain a bit, a respite she eagerly prayed would continue.

Despite the perpetual red haze of her days and nights, Elizabeth did not consider her attraction to Juanita to be part of her madness. As it was, the Spanish beauty had come to her at precisely the right time in her life, the moment when her brief reign of power at the Canadian fortress was at its peak. It was no exaggeration to say that Elizabeth had been an actual queen there—her subjects being a volatile mix of escaped supercriminals, Amazonian women fighters, and the hired guns of the Guardians. And although the Americans and Canadians had brought the regime to a quick and bitter end, it was not totally unexpected. Ever prepared, Elizabeth, Juanita, and two bodyguards were miles away from the place five minutes after the first shots were fired.

So it was with fondness and memories that she gazed upon the nude form of Juanita. The woman had been involved in the notorious Knights of the Burning Cross fiasco before finding her way to the secret Canadian fortress. Upon arriving, Elizabeth had quickly laid claim to her, especially after hearing that Juanita had been erotically involved with Hawk Hunter prior to her fleeing the American Southwest for the wilds of Al-

185

berta.

This had made a very important connection in Elizabeth's mind; Hunter was a big part of her distorted world, too. After all, it was he who had bravely rescued her from the Canal Nazis. (As a reward she had offered herself to him in many different ways, but, though tempted, he never took her up on any of them.) Then, when she attempted to assassinate the traitorous ex-vice president of the United States as part of her plan to take over America, it had been Hunter who grabbed her gun and saved her from being shot by security forces.

But it was also Hunter who had led the attack on her fortress, thus ending her brief reign as Queen of the Alberta wilderness. However, even amongst her jumbled brain fibers, she knew she had just about dared Hunter to come. After all, what other reason had she for kidnapping his celebrity girlfriend and imprisoning her in the fortress? And why had she arranged to have Hunter's precious F-16 XL stolen as well?

There was something about this Wingman — something that despite her madness she couldn't deny. She knew that he, above others, represented the biggest obstacle in her path to rule America and, eventually, the world. Yet her soul still burned in passionate desire for him. For many nights on end, she and Juanita had lain her bed chamber, deep within the fortress, performing various sex acts on each other while the Spanish beauty regaled her with detailed tales of sex and hypnotism with the famous pilot. These kiss-and-tell sessions had Elizabeth walking around in an orgasmic fog for weeks, intensified as they were by the fact that Hunter's *actual* girlfriend was imprisoned close by in the tower of the castle. Perhaps it was for this reason that Elizabeth never revealed herself directly to this Dominique during her captivity at the fortress.

Later on, after she and Juanita escaped and entered into the long, preplanned negotiating sessions with the Norsemen, she had devised the Sapphic Fighter Pilot "substitute" ritual, to the utter delight of the lovely, sex-starved Norse wenches the raiders kept on board the *Fire Bats.* And even though the distractions were many in the midst of these orgies, Elizabeth still found herself thinking about Hunter during the long, astonishingly carnal nights.

Juanita was fully awake now and Elizabeth was quick to order her to kiss her entire body—slowly, starting at the toes and working her way up in an attempt to drive off the hangover. The Spanish beauty sleepily obliged.

As she felt Juanita's warm tongue pass up one ankle and down the other, Elizabeth's mind felt clear enough for her to consider the day ahead.

It would be a particularly busy twenty-four hours. As soon as she was able, she would be briefed by the captain of the submarine on the results of the many raids carried out by the Norse troopships the night before. Then she had to prepare three coded messages that would be bounced off a satellite and beamed to several points around the globe. One would be sent back to Norway. Another would go to Central America.

The third, and most important, would be beamed to a warship sailing in the middle of the Pacific Ocean, half a world away.

Then she would be briefed by radio by the captains of the other three *Fire Bats,* they being her closest conspirators in her wild, all-encompassing scheme.

Only then would she be prepared for the most important event of the day: her trip to the Great Ship, the *Stor Skute.*

She wriggled with delight as Juanita's tongue finally

187

reached her pubic area and then began a long slow trip to her heaving breasts. Her hangover was now a thing of the past. Her spirits were boosting to manic heights. If all was successful this day, she thought, especially aboard the *Stor Skute,* then perhaps when she returned to the sub, she could convince Juanita to climb back into the fighter pilot's uniform and pick up where they had left off the night before.

Chapter Thirty-one

The retrieval of the RPV had gone remarkably smoothly for the crew of the fishing boat.

They had erected the net barrier, caught and secured the drone, and gotten underway again, all within fifteen minutes' time. And best of all, they had completed their critical covert mission without being spotted.

Or so they thought.

The RPV itself returned in good shape; it had sustained no damage despite being so close to the spot where the massive shells had exploded on Slaughter Beach. Its TV nose camera had worked perfectly, sending back live pictures from the Delaware beach which, in turn, were relayed instantaneously to the ordnancemen on the mothership a farther twenty-five miles from the target. With the RVP's cameras providing the long-distance eye-in-the-sky, coordinates had been instantly calculated and the extremely high-explosive shells deposited exactly on the spot.

Now the fishing-boat captain was straining his vessel's engines to their breaking point. It was especially important for him to reach the mothership as quickly as possible as it would soon be sailing farther south. It was a journey that the fishing boat would have to make also, and the captain had no intention of going it alone.

It was close to 9 AM when the fishing-boat captain spotted the outline of the massive cloud of mist and steam on the horizon.

He let out a breath of relief and then called down to his three-man crew to stow all their phony fishing gear. There was no further need to keep up their disguise as peaceful, innocent trawlers. Now they could return to their real world, that of sea going warriors.

Inside the half-mile-long, manmade cloud sat the mothership. Generated of nothing more than heated seawater, the "smokescreen" wrapped a protective envelope around the vessel anytime a fog bank was not available to do so. While the screen would not fool any enemy on a clear day such as this, it did serve to hide the precise location of the ship within. And preserving the secret of the mothership was the highest priority.

Once the fishing boat was within ten miles of the cloud of vapor, the captain sent out a message in Morse code via the powerful lantern located on his stern. He smiled again when the message was quickly acknowledged.

"Wine and hot bread are waiting for you" the message had said.

For the captain of the fishing boat, there were no better words in the entire world.

Once again he called down to his crew, telling them that they should prepare to tie up to the mothership. The captain was well aware that his men were now going about their tasks with speed and renewed enthusiasm. They, too, were glad to be home.

With one last check of his instruments, the captain slowed his speed to one-third and turned the boat slightly to the north, lining it up with the mothership's strobe light blinking invitingly through the man-made mist of gloom.

Thirty seconds later, the fishing boat entered the artificial fog bank. Ten seconds after that, the captain heard the sound of a jet engine . . .

Hunter couldn't help but stare at his main TV screen in disbelief.

The signals being provided by the AAS-38 pod slung under the jumpjet's left wing were creating an image on the screen that was both amazing and baffling. The FLIR device—as in Forward-Looking Infra-Red—used thermal imaging to find targets at night or in bad weather. Heat thrown off by the target was detected and processed into a remarkably sharp TV picture, similar to infra-red NightScope binoculars.

But the picture that was being bounced back to Hunter at this moment seemed so unbelievable that he thought the FLIR system itself was out of whack.

The target that was registering five thousand feet below amongst the murk of the obviously man-made fog screen was an enormous vessel. Guns of all sizes seemed to poke out of every available space from stem to stern and it carried more than a few missile launchers—both SAMs and ship-to-ship. There were even indications of torpedo tubes both amidships and in the rear. Above it all was jungle of radar and radio antennas that covered the top of the ship's superstructure. Yet strangely, none of them were activated at the moment.

More mysterious was the fact that while the heat image was more or less uniform above and below the decks of the ship—indicating the vessel was crammed with much sophisticated electronic and communications equipment—there was a large evenly spaced "cool" spot running along the entire deck itself. This indicated to Hunter that the deck was made of nothing more high-tech than wooden planks.

But it was the outline of the entire ship that he found unbelievable. He knew what kind of a ship it was right away—its profile was unmistakable. What astonished him was that he—like many others—had believed no ship like this was left on the planet.

He had assumed, wrongly as it turned out, that all the US Navy's massive battleships had been lost long ago.

Suddenly it seemed as if every warning light on Hunter's cockpit panel came on at once.

One moment he was flying undetected high above the artificial fog bank, in the next his Harrier jumpjet was being "painted" by at least three blazing threat-warning radars. Already, as many as a half-dozen smaller SAM acquisition radars were locking in on him, as were twice as many antiaircraft guns.

Everything his instruments were telling him indicated that within three to five seconds, the air around him would be filled with so many missiles and AA shells that even the best of pilots would not survive.

But he was better than the best.

Within a micro-second of the first warning, Hunter had gone on the offensive. In the snap of a switch he had armed his twin Aden cannon pods, putting hundreds of 30mm cannon shells at the ready. In the flick of a button, he likewise activated his pair of wingtip-mounted Matra 155 twin rocket launchers, as well the single Harpoon antiship missile he carried under his right wing.

As predicted, four heartbeats later, the air was filled with hundreds of deadly AA shells and four screaming SA-2 missiles homing in on the strong radar signal of the Harrier.

All of them missed.

Hunter had already yanked back on the jumpjet's vertical thrusters, literally bringing the Harrier to a screeching halt. From this position he watched as all of the high-tech flack passed through the airspace where he would have been if he hadn't slammed on the brakes.

"OK," he whispered, jamming the thruster controls back into the full-forward flight position as the deadly storm of missiles and shells abruptly stopped. "Now it's my turn . . ."

The captain of the fishing boat had to hold his fingers in his ears to block out the roar of the jet engine that had suddenly become so excruciatingly loud.

Looking up through the cloud of mist and steam in no small terror, he searched in vain for the source of the banshee-like engine shriek. But he could see nothing other than the gigantic outline of the battleship and the dirty brown contrails left over from the four automatic, but obviously unsuccessful, SAM launches just seconds before.

Thinking an attack on the mothership was just seconds away, the fishing-boat captain turned his steering wheel hard to the port, bringing him on a course parallel to the huge, slow-moving vessel. At that moment, the scream of the jet engine reached truly deafening proportions. His eyes going fuzzy from the high-decibel roar, the captain nevertheless squinted off into the murk off to his left.

That's when he saw the barest outline of the approaching jet.

It was coming in low and fast, and the first thing the captain noticed was that its wings were so full of weapons and bombs that they appeared to be sagging under the combined weight. Fate had positioned him now directly between the attacking jet and the battleship, but he knew that even as a suicidal shield, his boat would not serve admirably. The weapons being aimed at the battleship were so destructive and powerful they would tear through his little fishing boat as if it were made of cardboard.

There was nothing he could do at this point. Nothing

he could call out to his crew, no prayers that he could say in time. In seconds it would be over for him, and he would die in a less than courageous manner.

But then something strange happened.

The attacking jet did not open fire. Nor did it drop any bombs or launch any missiles. Instead, it roared directly above him, and up and over the main sail of the battleship. Even stranger, none of the battleship's automatic defense systems—from the SAM to the AAA's to the close-in Phalanx Gatlings—opened fire, either.

It was almost as if the pilot of the airplane and the master of the battleship had come to an instantaneous truce. But how? Even a hasty radio conversation could not have delayed the airplane's attack in time.

Somehow the fishing-boat captain knew that it had to be something more . . .

Hunter's psyche was still buzzing after he pulled the Harrier out of its attack dive.

It was a familiar sensation running through him. A wave of intuition had washed over him just seconds before he was to launch the Harpoon missile into the conning tower of the battleship. Some might call it ESP or clairvoyance, but for Hunter it was much more than that. It was the special gift that he had always possessed, the kind of forward-looking psychic radar that, for good or bad, was able to briefly take him several steps ahead in time. It was what made him the best fighter pilot who had ever strapped in. He had always simply called it "the feeling" and the one overriding thing he had learned from it was to never, ever question it.

So it was, as his finger was poised over the Harpoon launch button, just moments before he would have sent the high-explosive-packed missile into the huge battleship's vital organs, something told him not to do it. A psychic voice, crying deep down inside his soul told him that firing on the battleship was not the thing to do, even though it had attacked him.

But with this flash of intuition came more questions, questions that Hunter knew had to be answered.

He brought the Harrier up to twenty-five hundred feet and then banked back down toward the ship. Kicking back his speed to a crawl, he lowered his landing gear and then lined up the nose of his jet with the ship's stern. He was hoping this approach would serve two purposes. First of all, it was the position that would give the majority of the ship's AA gunners an almost unworkable firing angle on him. Second, it was an angle that a jet would least likely take if attacking a ship.

In other words, he was coming up on the ship in the most non belligerent manner he could think of. He just hoped someone understood the gesture.

As it turned out, someone onboard the battleship understood Hunter perfectly.

A man standing on the ship's end rail, wearing a red fluorescent helmet and vest, indicated through a series of hand signals that Hunter should land the jumpjet on the battleship's deserted helicopter pad.

It took a half minute of maneuvering for the Harrier to drift over the end of the ship, its jet engine screaming in the near-hovering mode, its forward speed matched exactly to that of the vessel.

Finally, it came down, right in the middle of the large painted X, without so much as a bump.

The Harrier's engine was quickly cut, the persistent whine of its turbine slowly winding down. Then the canopy opened, and Hunter stepped out.

The man in the fluorescent vest disappeared and another man, he, too, wearing a protective helmet and visor, was waiting as Hunter climbed out of the cockpit, carefully made his way along the fuselage, and finally jumped down to the deck from the wing.

For a few long moments, they just stood there, not moving, each staring at the other through their helmet's protective visors. All the while the noise of the choppy sea and the gradual fadeout of the Harrier's engine filled the air.

Finally, both men took off their helmets at the same time.

To his surprise, Hunter found himself staring into a mask. The man was wearing a tight black cloth that covered his face from the bottom of the nose up and was tied in the back, bandana-style. With its shiny black veneer and the cutouts for the eyes, the mask gave the man an appearance that was a cross between Zorro and the Lone Ranger, with a little of Batman thrown in.

Despite the strange garb, Hunter began to introduce himself.

"I am Major—"

The other man held up his hand. "I know who you are," he said in a thick northern European accent. "Few people in the civilized world don't know Hawk Hunter."

Hunter could only shrug. He was the victim of his own celebrity—but at least he didn't wear a mask.

"And you, sir?"

"I am Wolf," the masked man answered. "The master of this ship."

Chapter Thirty-two

Dominique pulled the strap on her life jacket tight as she stepped down into the large see-through raft.

The sea was choppy, and she nearly lost her balance several times before she finally eased down to the floor of the raft. Looking down through the clear plastic to the dark blue water below created an optical illusion that did little to settle her stomach. The rolling waves made a bad situation worse.

Still, her spirits were high. She was at last leaving the smelly, problem-filled submarine. For some reason, the Norsemen were transferring her to what everyone referred to as the *Stor Skute*—the Great Ship. A second submarine just a hundred feet away was to be her transport to this other, very mysterious vessel, and although this sub looked exactly like the one she was leaving, she couldn't imagine it being anything but an improvement.

Another reason she felt heartened was that Yaz was with her. Although they had been ordered not to talk to each other, he had whispered to her that he, too, was being transferred to the Great Ship because he had shown his expertise in fixing the sub's propulsion problems. He also expressed something that Dominique, too, was feeling: that although they had no idea where they were going or why, at least they were going there together.

Also in the raft were the four Norsemen who would row to the other sub. As it turned out, the ride over to the second boat was a queasy, sloppily executed affair, courtesy of the quartet of brutes. Several times the raft almost capsized, not so much due to the high, irregular waves but because the four Norsemen rowers spent most of the time working against each other. Dominique and Yaz could only hold on tight and roll their eyes as the men argued nonstop over how best to reach the second sub. If there was one myth to be broken in this whole adventure it was that the Norsemen were expert seaman. From all that Dominique and Yaz had witnessed so far, it appeared that just the opposite was much closer to the truth.

Finally they reached the second boat. Climbing up an access ladder and then down into the squat conning tower, Yaz and Dominique noticed that this vessel *was* an improvement over the first simply because the ambient smell inside was that of burnt coal as opposed to human body reek.

Once inside the control room, the captain only briefly turned his attention toward Dominique and Yaz. He went through a series of shrugs and chin scratchings before he held up three fingers and pointed to the clock.

They didn't know just how to take the captain's message. Did it mean that their voyage to the Great Ship would take three hours? Or maybe three days?

Or maybe even three months?

Chapter Thirty-three

The Third Majestic Kingdom of Hawaii

Captain Elvis Q took a long swig of his warm beer and checked his watch.

An impatient man by nature, he hated unreasonable delays of any kind. But now his better half was telling him to calm down, wait it out. The mission had gone on too long and was too important to screw up now.

He was sitting in one of the seediest barrooms he'd ever seen. It was a dark, smelly, poorly stocked, and at this moment, murderously hot. Only the beam of the early-morning sunlight coming through a small crack in a nearby painted-over window gave any indication of the warm, clean air of Honolulu outside. To Elvis, the saloon was a little piece of misery wedged into a large chunk of paradise.

One table away from him sat five men in the midst of a brutal game of poker. There had already been one attempted stabbing and one minor exchange of gunfire between the participants, and the game was barely five hours old. The trouble was, the man Elvis had waited to meet since midnight was one of the players, and at this moment, he was winning big.

Elvis winced as he checked his watch again. Despite his efforts to cool out, he knew that time was running out. The deal he'd come to make several weeks before now had to be done within the next hour. If not, things would simply fall apart and he would be immersed in little disasters, not the least of being that the gang of gunmen who he had hired to guard his F-4X Super Phantom at the nearby airport would go off the clock. He knew that as soon as that happened, his jet would be stripped down to the frame in no time.

But the poker game went on and his boy kept on winning and he could do nothing about that.

Against his better judgment, he signaled the clammy waitress for another tepid beer. All the while he kept counseling himself to stay calm, to be patient and let the world turn for him.

About five minutes later, it did.

Knowing that there was no such thing as pure luck, Elvis had seen it coming from a mile away. His contact had just raked in his fifth big pot in a row when the inevitable accusation of "cheat!" reared its semiugly head.

Two gunshots and the swing of a basebat later, one of the players was out cold and bleeding heavily, and another was contemplating a large hole in his shoulder. Those not wounded played one last hand and then, at last, the game was declared over.

As the injured were unceremoniously dumped out a side door and into a trash-strewn alley, Elvis's contact— and the big winner all around—counted up his money, left it in care of the bartender and then finally meandered over to his table.

His name was Zim. He was a small Oriental man, balding slightly and sporting a range of tattoos plus a pair of gold bottom canine teeth. If a man's importance was figured by the number of bodyguards he employed, then Zim was very important indeed. Elvis had previously counted as many as twelve hired goons swarming around the guy, and that didn't include the jeep full of gorillas he knew was parked outside the barroom.

With the snap of his fingers, Zim had a bottle of no-name liquor thrust into his hand. Another snap and his long, thin cigarette was lit. Finally he sat down directly across from Elvis, and with as much ceremony as he could muster, he withdrew a .45 Colt automatic from his shoulder holster and laid it on the table.

"You want to talk, white boy?" he asked in a sneer.

Elvis stared back at him for several long moments and then reached down into his flight suit's ankle pocket. He came up with an enormous .440 Magnum and placed it on the table next to the now-diminutive-looking Colt.

"I want to talk," he replied.

The display of massive firepower unnerved the already fidgety man, his troop of bodyguards all seemed to take one step forward at once. But he quickly regained his composure and took a long draw from his cigarette.

"So talk . . ." Zim said, a thin, shiny grin returning.

Elvis pulled his chair closer to the table.

"You've got something that I want," he said. "I've been in town for weeks just to tell you I'm here to buy it."

Zim laughed and took a long swig from the liquor bottle.

"Obviously you have never heard of the Oriental art of business negotiation," he told Elvis. "The object desired is never discussed at the first meeting."

Elvis slammed his fist down on the table, the tremor causing the ring of bodyguards to close in even tighter.

"I don't have any more time for your *goo gai pan* bullshit," he said in his thick southern accent. "Tell me the price and let's get on with it!"

Zim smacked his lips and took another drag of his cigarette.

"Typical American," he said. "No patience. No time

to talk. No time to appreciate things . . ."

"As far as I'm concerned," Elvis countered, "we ain't got much to talk about besides what I'm here for."

Zim shook his head slowly, letting a long plume of smoke escape from his nostrils.

"Don't be so sure about that," he told Elvis, his tone turning ominously serious. "I might have something even more valuable to you. But, nevertheless, I can see you are in a hurry, my impatient friend. So go ahead."

Elvis took a deep breath and drew in even closer to the man.

"Let's make it simple," he said. "You have the merchandise, yes or no?"

"Yes," Zim answered.

"And it is for sale?"

"Yes—for the equivalent of one million dollars. Nothing less."

"Gold or silver?"

"Gold. Bars not chips . . ."

Elvis sat back and stared hard at the man. "That sounds too cheap," he said. "What condition is it in?"

"Good condition," Zim replied, sounding like he was offended by the question. "It's all packed in crates, of course. Twenty-three in all, I believe. Every part marked and listed."

Zim took a quick swig of his bottle and an even shorter drag of his cigarette.

"As for the price . . ." he said. "I'm a businessman. I know that sometimes it is best to move merchandise quickly. Besides, I am leaving the islands soon and therefore I must liquidate all my commodities."

Elvis bit his lip; the next question was probably the most important of all.

"Just how did you happen to get it?" he asked the man deliberately.

Zim was caught off guard by the question, a slight

amount of color draining from his face.

"Why should that be of any importance to you?" he stammered.

"'I'll give you half again the price if you tell me how you came by it," Elvis said, staring the man right in the eyes.

What was left of the man's cool facade was now crumbling by the second.

"I cannot tell," Zim said nervously. "I would be a marked man if the wrong people learned that I was selling it to you."

"I'll give you twice the price," Elvis said.

"No," Zim replied defiantly. "You want it, you can have it for the million in gold. But that is all."

That was enough. Elvis knew he couldn't push his luck. Not in this situation. Not in this time or place. The man was getting very jumpy and that was making his goons nervous.

"All right," Elvis told him. "One million in gold bars. We can load it tomorrow morning at 'Lulu Airport and you can get paid then."

"No!" Zim half shouted. "You take delivery within two hours or the deal is off."

Once again, Elvis knew it was not a time to quibble. Still, he had to wonder why someone like Zim—well known in these parts as an ice-water-in-the-veins operator—was so jumpy.

"OK," he told him. "At the airport in two hours . . ."

"Agreed," the man said, his voice returning somewhat to its normally snide timbre.

With that, he stood up, and gathering his bodyguards in tow, quickly marched out of the barroom.

Elvis instinctively checked his watch again. The negotiations had taken hardly any time at all. Not only had the man sold quickly—*too* quickly—he also seemed to be in an awful rush to free himself of the merchandise.

The question was: why?

But first things came first. Elvis had to make a radio call to Maui, the next island over and get a cargo plane waiting there under heavy guard into the air. Then he had to retrieve his jet before it was reduced to the hubcaps.

But he did take a second to finish his beer and contemplate what he had just done. He had the feeling that somehow, somewhere, Hawk Hunter knew that his beloved F-16XL was soon to be in friendly hands once again.

Chapter Thirty-four

Two hours later

The huge C-5 Galaxy circled the former Honolulu International Airport once before coming in for a perfect landing.

Waiting at the end of the otherwise deserted runway, Elvis followed the gigantic plane's progress as it taxied toward him.

If we can get this show on the road within an hour, he thought, *we'll be in LA by midnight.*

It took several minutes for the big cargo plane to reach the prescribed spot and another couple for its pilots to shut down its engines and various flight systems. Already two squads of United American Rangers were disembarking from the rear cargo door, smartly forming a tight defense perimeter around the big airplane. Finally, the front cargo hatch lifted open, giving the big plane the appearance of a huge fish ready to swallow anything in sight.

The first person down the runway was Elvis's partner, the famous Captain "Crunch" O'Malley of the Ace Wrecking Crew.

"Everything still peachy?" he asked Elvis with a sly wink.

"Ask them," Elvis replied, pointing to the small army of Hawaiian gunmen that surrounded the pair of battered tractor trailer trucks parked nearby.

Crunch gave the men a quick lookover and then signaled two UA troopers who were still waiting inside the C-5. The soldiers signaled back and soon were carefully carrying a large steel case down the C-5's ramp.

"One million is all he wanted, eh?" Crunch asked Elvis as the two soldiers laid the cash box at their feet.

"I offered him two if he told us where he got the jet," Elvis replied. "But he wanted no part of it."

"Weird," Crunch said.

Elvis put his fingers to his mouth and let out a long whistle. With that, Zim emerged from the cab of one of the trailer trucks and walked forward, his entourage of goons following behind like baby ducks.

Crunch instinctively pushed the safety off his sidearm. "Let's just hope these guys don't suspect we've got five million more sitting back in the plane," he said.

"Don't worry," Elvis told him. "Mister Zim isn't concerned about money right now. Something else is on his mind."

The businessman walked up and without a word pointed to the cash box. Immediately, two of his bodyguards opened the box and started counting out the gold bars inside.

Two minutes and two grunts later, Zim nodded and slammed the box shut with his foot.

"I'm happy to see that you pay your debts in full and on time," he said to Crunch and Elvis.

"Yeah, big deal," Elvis told him. "Now just get your guys cracking and do your part . . ."

Zim snapped his fingers and was holding a lit cigarette a mere five seconds later.

"There has been one alteration to our deal," he said sinisterly.

Crunch immediately laid his hand on his enormous .357 Magnum sidearm, at the same time nodding to the officer in charge of the UA troopers guarding the airplane.

"What the hell do you mean?" Elvis challenged the man. "You can't go changing the deal now . . ."

Zim flicked away his barely smoked cigarette and then closed his eyes for a moment.

"It is a simple request," he said in a low voice. "I want no more money, or anything of yours that is valuable. All I ask is that you take me and six of my men back to the mainland with you."

The request stunned both Crunch and Elvis.

It was Crunch who started shaking his head first.

"No way, pal," he said. "We ain't no taxi service and that's not part of the deal. Besides, you don't want to go there. There's big trouble back on the mainland. *Very* big trouble on the East Coast. In fact, we wouldn't even be out here screwing around with you at all except our boss told us to."

Zim was becoming very nervous now. Years spent cultivating an image of cool and cunning was lost in a few seconds' time. It was apparent that he wanted nothing better but to get the hell out of Hawaii, and quick.

"I'll cut the price of the airplane," he said suddenly, his gold teeth somehow losing some of the gleam. "You can have it for a half million if you take us."

Crunch had never stopped shaking his head.

"A quarter of a million," Zim said desperately.

Elvis held his hand up at this point. "Hold it," he said. "What the hell is going on? Why do you want to get out of here so damn quick? You just about own Honolulu . . ."

Zim shook his head sadly. "I will have nothing in a very short time," he said. "Nothing will be left . . ."

Crunch and Elvis just looked at each other.

"What the hell are you talking about?" Elvis asked the man.

It took the frightened businessman five minutes to

explain it all, Crunch and Elvis listening with a mixture of astonishment and outright disbelief.

Less than a half hour later, the huge airplane was lifting off from the airport's longest runway, the twenty-three crates containing the disassembled F-16 safely packed inside along with Zim and his six bodyguards.

Elvis's F-4X Phantom took off shortly afterward.

Chapter Thirty-five

The sunlight was fading fast as Elvis flew the powerful F-4X up to twenty-five thousand feet.

Leveling off, he looked to the east and saw the glint of silver that was the huge C-5, heading at full throttle back toward the mainland. He knew that a squadron of F-5's from the Republic of California Air Force would meet the C-5 at about the halfway point and escort them the rest of the way from there. It was the best that could be done under the circumstances.

He, too, would have liked nothing better but to trail the Galaxy back to LA, but he had another mission to perform, one that was as critical as it was last minute.

He shook his head and took a long, deep breath of oxygen.

The last five weeks had been among the strangest of his life. One moment he was training a new crop of United American fighter pilots up in Boston, and the next heading to Hawaii, a satchel of classified papers under his arm and a book of codes in his pocket.

Thus began the mission to recover Hunter's F-16.

Jones's intelligence operatives had been searching for the missing jet ever since the battle up in the Canadian Rockies. A special squad of the Guardians was spotted carting the aircraft away during the early rounds of fighting, escaping amid the natural confusion of warfare. Jones's spies were on the trail of these people forty-eight hours later.

The unlikely group carried the aircraft on a specially

made tractor trailer truck that was adapted to off-road driving. Moving only at night, they made it to Vancouver, Jones's agents just an hour behind.

That's when the airplane and the Guardians simply disappeared.

Jones's men spent the next month combing Vancouver for clues, and their hard work paid off when they questioned a man who built packing boxes down on the city's docks. He had been paid an exorbitant amount of money to construct a total of twenty-three wooden boxes of various sizes and shapes. When the agents saw the crude pencil drawings the man had made by hand, they added up the boxes' total displacement and estimated weight capacity. The total equaled 13,959 pounds, the exact weight of an empty F-16.

Using this tip, the agents then tracked the twenty-three crates to Juneau, where they were bought by a local hoodlum, who once again seemed to have become very wealthy very quickly. Gambling with some heavy rollers one night, this man offered the twenty-three crates as collateral on a big bet. He lost, and the cargo became the property of a Japanese gangster who had slipped an ace into his hand and won the pot with a royal flush.

The Japanese gangster eventually moved on to Honolulu, where he in turn lost the crates to the Hawaiian military officer who was better at cheating at poker than he.

At this point, General Jones called Elvis in and gave him the assignment to go to Hawaii and try to locate the disassembled plane. By the time Elvis made it to Honolulu, the crates had become the possession of a well-known Hawaiian crime boss, who, it was said, planned to sell it in pieces. This gangster was later found floating near the Pearl Harbor monument, the apparent loser in an argument over drugs.

The trail suddenly gone cold, Elvis contacted Jones

and asked what to do. By this time the crisis on the East Coast was getting worse by the day, and experienced pilots like Elvis were soon going to be very much in need. However, Jones told him to stay in Hawaii and try to pick up the scent again.

These orders underscored the importance of the airplane to the country's postwar national heritage. The F-16 was as well known now as Lindbergh's *Spirit of St. Louis* and the *Enola Gay*. But Elvis also knew that Jones's reasons were more personal than that.

The Commander-In-Chief of the United American Armed Forces rightly figured that because the airplane had been stolen from Hunter while he was fighting with the UAAF against the white supremacist armies of the American Southwest, then it was only right that the UAAF do everything in its power to retrieve it. Besides the obvious moral victory in recovering the airplane, the sly Jones knew the gesture would certainly not be lost on a loyal soldier like Hunter.

So Jones had told Elvis to stay in 'Lulu and ask questions and Elvis did just that for two weeks before finding out that the famous airplane had been won in yet another poker game by an individual who turned out to be Zim, the businessman.

Just as quickly, the word on the streets was that the airplane — all twenty-three crates of it — would be sold to the highest bidder.

Elvis immediately radioed Jones, and soon Crunch was driving the big C-5 to Honolulu to deliver whatever money Elvis might need and hopefully carry the airplane back to the mainland.

So now this piece of business was done. The nervous businessman had gotten his one million dollars in gold and his free ride out of the Islands . . .

But not before he had told Elvis and Crunch an incredible story, so incredible that at the beginning they suspected Zim was actually planning an elaborate hoax.

Then they thought he was just plain crazy. Finally he had convinced them not only that he was dead serious but that his tale carried with it such a dire threat to continental America that both Elvis and Crunch knew that they couldn't take any chances. So they agreed to carry him away from Hawaii, knowing that if his story proved true, then he would be just the first of thousands of people who would soon attempt to flee the islands.

Elvis checked his position and fuel load and then turned the F-4X due west, right into the bath of red that was the setting sun. Besides carrying extra-large external fuel tanks, the long-range Phantom was also equipped with several recon cameras. It was only through experience and foresight that Elvis had arranged to have these devices loaded on before he left California for the trip to Hawaii.

Now, as he gazed into the setting sun through his heavily tinted helmet visor, he wondered if the impending disaster that Zim warned about actually lay out beyond the horizon. Or was he just carrying out some enormous joke.

Only time and a lot of miles would tell.

Chapter Thirty-six

Aboard the USS New Jersey

Hunter took another sip from the leather-covered goblet and winced slightly as the bitter lager made its way down his throat.

The barely picked-over remains of the meal in front of him made him long for Dominique's cooking—or even his own. Never had he tasted food so bland, so poorly cooked, or so frigging salty.

Still, he had eaten it—or, more accurately, he had moved the bits of potatoes, cabbage, and practically raw fish back and forth from one side of his plate to the other, while taking only the smallest judicious bites and thus giving the appearance of enjoying the meal.

It was necessary to be polite—of this he was sure. The other men around the table had attacked their chow with unmannered ferociousness, which led Hunter to suspect that this was, in fact, a special occasion, that possibly by his presence a more sumptuous repast had been laid on and the men were taking full advantage of it.

Or maybe they just didn't mind eating slop. But if this was the case, it would still be one of the least unusual things about them.

The first few minutes after landing on the battleship had been riveting and uneasy. After all, the ship had just fired on him, and he had come quite close to launching an antiship missile into its bridge. The fact that the captain— the man everyone simply called Wolf—wore a matinee-idol mask only added to the strangeness of the moment.

Still, Wolf immediately requested that he join him and his officers for his noon meal, and this before Hunter could even fully explain how he had come to discover the battleship by following the RPV.

But by that time, it almost seemed not to matter. Despite the man's disguise, Hunter could almost see a definable psychic aura surrounding the mysterious Wolf. His own strong power of the sixth sense was telling him that this man also possessed intuitive powers. So it was almost as if the ship's captain already knew why Hunter had come.

He was led to the huge dining room that served as the officers' mess. Already there was Wolf's staff of fifteen officers, each one of them wearing a strange, almost comic-book-style navy uniform. After a few goblets full of the bitter ale were dispensed with, the lousy food had been laid on. Through it all Hunter searched in vain for a way to politely question Wolf and his men about what they were doing sailing around in a US Navy battleship, about their connection with the men controlling the RPV, and, most of all, what the hell was the story with Wolf's mask.

But the first few minutes of the meal found the conversation dominated by the other officers. Talking in Norwegian, only bits and pieces of which Hunter could understand, they discussed the weather mostly. When will it change, will it be severe, will it get more placid the farther south they sailed. Through it all, Wolf simply ate and nodded, like a man who was patiently hearing the same story over for the hundredth time.

It was only after the first course of the meal—consisting of watery soup that featured little more than a random carrot floating through it—was finished that Wolf turned to Hunter and spoke directly to him.

"You realize that many of my men consider you somewhat of a saint," Wolf told him in an almost off-hand way. "You saw how they reacted when you first landed."

Hunter had indeed, and this, too, had added to the strange air that surrounded him as soon as he landed on the battleship.

No sooner had he climbed down from the Harrier and met Wolf when a crowd of crewmen had gathered a respectable distance away, dressed in uniforms only slightly less bizarre than their officers. At first these men were simply pointing at him, and a few even waved. But as Hunter was walking toward the officers' mess, the crowd of sailors—now numbering a couple of hundred—did an odd thing. They gave him a round of applause.

This in itself was not all that unusual. Hunter had long ago resigned himself to the fact that he was a celebrity. Without an iota of encouragement on his part, his face had become recognizable across America and Canada before the Big War. As the youngest pilot ever selected to fly the space shuttle, he had made the cover of both *Time* and *Newsweek* in the same week, and his mug had been flooded across TV screens from network news broadcasts to the glut of tabloid TV shows that had been popular at the time.

If anything, his celebrity status had grown in the postwar era, overflowing into the tricky area of legend and myth. He had been at the vanguard of many high-profile missions during the desperate period to rid the American continent of its enemies, and the revived electronic media had dug his picture out of various files and thrown it back up on the screen with each victory.

In the past two years it had gotten to the point where he couldn't go anywhere in North America without being recognized, a definite hazard when the work he was conducting called for him to operate undercover.

Yet these men on the ship who recognized him right away were not Americans or Canadians. They were non-English-speaking Europeans, most of them, and they had hardly been exposed to the drumbeat of the American media.

But as Wolf would explain to him, these men recognized Hunter for a different reason: they had been in action with him before.

"In the Suez," Wolf said simply. "Against Viktor . . ."

The mere mention of the name caused Hunter to involuntarily freeze up. Several years before, Hunter had tracked the maniacal super-terrorist known as Viktor to Suez where the madman was planning on invading the eastern Mediterranean with a huge army. A similarly enormous mercenary force—known as the Modern Knights—had been assembled on ships in England and Spain and charged with thwarting Viktor's plans. However, key to the successful engagement of Viktor's armies was a scheme to launch a series of preemptive air strikes against his legions as they moved up the Suez Canal and thus delay them long enough for the Modern Knights to reach the area.

This holding action was assigned to a band of intrepid British officers who, after hiring several disparate mercenary groups and buying some fighter aircraft, eventually towed a disabled American aircraft carrier to the northern mouth of the Suez Canal, where it served as a platform for the crucial air strikes against the terrorist's army.

Through a series of wild coincidences, Hunter had been "recruited" by the Englishmen for this adventure and wound up being the man in charge of the overall air operations for the mission.

One of the mercenary groups hired by the British was a small fleet of Norwegian frigates—eighteen in all—which provided escort for the big carrier and the tugs that did the actual pushing and pulling. In the series of first clashes against Viktor's armies, the Norwegians had served extremely well, taking heavy casualties in the process. Those who survived linked up with the Modern Knights and played an important role in the subsequent defeat of invaders.

"I knew of this campaign very well," Wolf told Hunter between bites of the tepid, oily fish. "When I set out to man this ship, I wanted good men, men who had been through the Jaws of Hell and had lived to tell about it.

"Many of the Suez survivors had made their way back to Norway and they were greeted as heroes there. I spent months tracking down every one of them I could find. Now, of the fifteen hundred men on board, four hundred of them fought with you against Viktor. Many of them are surprised to find you're still alive."

"I've run into that problem before," Hunter replied.

Eventually, the dishes were cleared away and another round of lager doled out. Instinctively knowing that their part of the meeting was over, the rest of Wolf's officers slowly drifted out of the dining room. Soon, it was just Hunter and the masked man facing each other at opposite ends of the long wooden table.

"Save your breath," Wolf told him just as Hunter was about to open his mouth to ask the first of a hundred questions. "I'll try to explain some of it to you."

"First of all, as you might have guessed, this is the old *New Jersey* . . ."

The USS *New Jersey*. The last Hunter had heard of the ship, it had been rushed out of mothballs for the fifth time and was patrolling the Persian Gulf when the Big War broke out. One of just four battleships the US Navy had refurbished and deployed, Hunter had just assumed that the vessel — like many of America's capital warships — had either been sunk during the hostilities or scuttled after the armistice.

Neither was true, as it turned out. In fact, the ship's most recent history was downright odd, even spooky.

The ship was sailing off the coast of Oman, providing fire support in an effort to keep the Straits of Hormuz open when the ceasefire was declared. As part of the armistice agreement — later found to be bogus — all warring factions were ordered to disarm and destroy their

217

equipment. Witnesses said that when the order went out to US ships in the Persian Gulf to return to the nearest port and comply with the armistice terms, the *New Jersey* simply went into a hundred-eighty-degree turn and sailed away, out into the deeper waters of the Indian Ocean.

When agents of the hated New Order finally found her two months later, she was drifting some two hundred miles off the west coast of Sri Lanka. All of her electronics were up and operating. All of her guns were stocked and loaded. Even the food in the chow hall was warm.

But no one was aboard. The three thousand members of her crew had simply vanished.

Baffled, the New Order agents had the battleship towed to the former US base of Diego Garcia, which was a speck of land in the middle of the Indian Ocean. There the ghostly ship sat, rusting away, its engines unoiled and seized, its on-board systems withering in the brutal heat.

Then the mysterious Captain Wolf came on the scene.

"I heard the ship was capable of being salvaged," he told Hunter. "So I bought it from the Sultanate of Diego Garcia."

It took a full year to refurbish the vessel just to the point where it was capable of going out into deep water.

"Just about everything had to be cleaned, oiled, re-wired, and tested many times before we put to sea," Wolf went on. "The engines proved to be less of a problem than I thought. But things like the propellers and the steering gears all had to be replaced with new parts.

"We finally got her seaworthy and went on a shakedown cruise in the Indian Ocean. We dropped anchor off Sri Lanka, but the people wouldn't let us go ashore because they had heard the ship was haunted. We went on to the tip of Indonesia—which is a very strange place these days—and then back to Diego Garcia.

"Once we thought she was capable, we sailed her around the Cape of Good Hope and on up to England. It was a hell of a voyage, but we were all the better for it.

218

That was about a year ago."

Hunter forced down another few sips of the bad beer.

"But why did you do all this?" he finally asked. "Is there a need for a battleship in Europe's mercenary market?"

Wolf slowly shook his head. "No," he said, his voice again lowering to a somber timbre. "I'm not a mercenary—at least not anymore."

"But how about the time and effort you've put into this vessel?" Hunter pressed. "And the obvious dangers you faced to get to this point? I mean, you are pursuing these Norsemen, are you not?"

"Again, these are questions without easy answers," the masked man answered.

Hunter was stumped. The man was filled with contradictions. He had openly greeted him on the ship like a hero even though he'd sent up a barrage of AA fire just seconds before. He was obviously admired by his crew and he respected them, yet he chose to hide from them by wearing a mask. Hunter had met few people who played everything so close to the vest, almost as if the purpose of his mask was not just to hide his face but also to represent a symbol of his reticence.

"But I *know* you've come all this way in pursuit of these Norsemen," Hunter tried again. "So surely there must be *some* reason for doing what you do."

Wolf stared back at Hunter through his black mask.

"Is there a reason for what *you* do, Major Hunter?" he asked.

Hunter hesitated for a moment. "Of course," he said finally. "Though it's hard to put into words . . ."

Wolf shook his head knowingly. "That's exactly how I feel," was all he said.

Ten minutes later, they were walking on the teak wood deck of the ship.

But no matter how hard he tried, one part of Hunter just couldn't believe that he was walking on the deck of the most famous battleship in history.

Launched in August of 1942 in the midst of World War II, the famous "Big J" — all fifty-eight thousand tons of her — not only saw action in many crucial South Pacific sea battles, she was also on station during the Korean War and the Vietnam conflict, coming out of mothballs both times.

After one tour off Vietnam, the vessel was retired, only to be resurrected again in the early 1980's. Fitted with Tomahawk and Harpoon missiles to complement its already formidible deck weapons, the ship was recommissioned for the fourth time in 1982. It saw action during the chaos in Beirut in the mid-1980's, did some time in the Pacific before being retired again, temporarily as it turned out. She was in her fifth reincarnation when the big war broke out.

Now, as they walked the long, slender deck line, Hunter couldn't imagine the mammoth vessel looking any better than it did at this moment.

At 887 feet long, the *New Jersey* was nearly the length of three football fields. It was 108 feet at its widest point and it boasted a 38-foot draught, meaning more than half the dreadnought's hull lay below the surface. Four giant propellers that Wolf had had painstakingly manufactured by the Omanis, used the 212,000 horsepower produced by the vessel's massive distillate-fueled engines to move the ship at a respectable 20 knots cruising speed.

But of course the real stars of the *New Jersey* were her nine massive sixteen-inch Mark Two naval guns.

With a barrel bore measuring those sixteen inches in diameter and an overall length longer than fifty feet, the gigantic cannons were capable of hurling a high-explosive projectile weighing more than a ton over a distance of twenty-seven miles. Wolf explained that to load and fire one of the guns took a well-trained crew about a minute, during which there was an endless flow of communication between the gun crew, the combat information center, and the bridge. Using as much as eight hundred pounds of gunpowder to fire each shell, just one of these "bullets" could turn concrete bunkers to dust, could release a concussion capable of killing a man a thousand feet away, and could leave a crater fifty feet wide and twenty feet deep.

A barrage of three shells, like the one that had hit Slaughter Beach, could be accurately compared to a small atomic bomb hit.

Firing such guns took a lot of manpower. The Big J had three triple turrets—two forward of the mast and one in back of it. Each triple turret alone weighed seventeen hundred tons and required a crew of seventy-seven to work it, with another thirty-six men stationed below in the gun magazine supporting the gun crew. In fact, manning the guns was such a constant and labor-intensive activity that the third deck passageway that ran beneath turrets two and three was accurately nicknamed "Broadway," for the number of people that used it on any given minute of the day.

After touring the turrets, Wolf led Hunter through a maze of passageways and bulkheads, pointing out literally dozens of cabins and workplaces, all of them in one way or another connected with firing the big guns.

But the sixteen-inch Goliaths weren't the only firepower available on the ship. It also boasted a dozen dual-purpose, semiautomatic five-inch guns which could be used to attack shore targets at ranges up to seven miles, or aircraft flying as high as 4.5 miles overhead, using, like the big guns, a Mark 48 fire control computer. There were also the four Tomahawk cruise missile launchers, as well as four Harpoon antiship missile launchers. Finally, for close-in protection, the ship had four Mk15 Phalanx Gatling guns capable of firing a hundred rounds *a second*. There was also room for four LAMP's helicopters.

The tour eventually led up to the ship's bridge where Hunter saw that the ship was bristling with electronic gear both inside and out. Walking through the all-important Combat Communications Center—the C-Three—he recognized control boards for a SPS-67(V) surface search radar system and a SPS-49 (V) air search radar system as well as a LN-66 navigation radar.

None of these systems were manned, however.

"We can only sail it," Wolf offered as a preemptive explanation. "Navigate by the stars and shoot the big guns where the RPV tells us to. Working this stuff is beyond our capabilities, I'm afraid."

Hunter took a quick scan of the entire C-Three.

Most of the essential systems were locked on automatic, including the ship's AA weapons systems. This told him that, in a strange way, neither Wolf nor his crew had had a hand in a firing at him. It had been the ship's main computer, detecting a possible threat and carrying out its program to fire unless told not to. The trouble was, Wolf's crew didn't know how to countermand the ship's main weapons computer.

Besides the three radar systems and the auto-AA function, the battleship also had an extensive antisubmarine warfare setup that was capable of handling a towed sonar buoy array attachment used to detect enemy submarines. But this, too, was not operating.

"Lots of nice high-tech stuff," Hunter said, admiring the impressive arrays. "It would help you a lot if it was all up and running."

He saw Wolf blink from behind the mask. "We are a ship full of sailors, Major Hunter," he said. "Not technicians. When we refurbished the ship, this equipment was the only stuff on board that didn't need to be overhauled. We've been running it on the simplest modes possible ever since."

Hunter took another quick look around and then said: "Maybe I can help you in a few areas."

For the first time Hunter noticed a brightening in the captain's demeanor.

"You are familiar with these systems, Major Hunter?"

"I could be," Hunter replied wryly. "But we've got to get a few things straight first."

He turned and looked Wolf straight in the eye.

"Our goals seem to be the same," he told him. "I am pursuing these Norsemen, and it's obvious now that you are, too."

Wolf nodded, though somewhat grimly.

"And aside from these electronics, this vessel looks to be in A-1 condition," he continued. "Your crew is well trained and obviously hard-working. And I'm sure that there are enough troubles over in Europe for you to hire this battlewagon out for months at a time. Just seagoing escort duty alone could mean a fortune for you."

Again, Wolf nodded.

"As far as the mask . . ." Hunter said. "Well, I figure that's your business."

"True," Wolf replied.

Hunter took a breath and let it out slowly. "If I teach you how to run all this equipment, and you do so properly," he said, "then you must realize that I am providing you not only with a wealth of information but also with a means to make this ship more efficient, more protected, *more powerful* than it is at this moment.

"But before I do this, you have to level with me. I must insist on your telling me of your true motives."

Hunter fell silent for a moment and tried to figure out whether his words were having any effect on Wolf. But once again, the mask was effective in hiding the man's true emotions.

"In other words," Hunter concluded, "why are you over here, fighting our battles?"

At that moment, Wolf lowered his eyes and shook his head. Then it was his turn to take a deep breath.

"You're a famous man, Major," he said after a pause.

"A smart man, and a respected one. But you know very little about who these raiders are and why they have come here."

Hunter pulled over one of the C-Three chairs and settled down into it.

"Well, Captain . . ." he said, folding his arms behind his head and stretching his legs in indication that he was ready to sit for the long haul, "I guess you'll just have to educate me."

Wolf shrugged and sat down, too.

For the next ten minutes, the mysterious masked man went into depth on the origins of the raiders, confirming some of the information that Hunter had learned from the interrogation of the Norsemen captured off Montauk. Wolf also told Hunter the unusual story behind the construction of the submarines.

But it was the information about the *Fire Bats*—the four ultrasophisticated subs that were capable of launching nuclear missiles—that sent a chill up Hunter's spine.

"Devious forces are at work behind the scenes, Major Hunter," Wolf said. "Ones that won't settle for anything less than total victory."

Hunter could only shake his head in grim agreement.

"From what you say, then I'd have to guess that a central figure *is* behind all this," he told Wolf. "Yet, the raiders we questioned insisted that there is no main plan, that they were acting independently."

"And in their minds, they were correct," Wolf replied. "They are clan members, recruited from some of the most barren sections of Scandinavia. For many of them, the world ends with their second or third cousin. They know no more about military strategy than we do about how to operate all these electronics. All they know is war and raiding. The idea that someone might be behind it all isn't so much beyond their comprehension as it is of no concern to them."

"But someone has to have the guiding hand here,"

Hunter told him. "Someone scoped out and attacked my country's major oil refineries. Someone did the advance spy work for the raids along New England and in Delaware. And someone must be masterminding these Four Boats you spoke about—and their nuclear delivery capabilities."

"You are correct, Major," Wolf said. "In many ways, I believe the raiding submarines are a smokescreen for the *Fire Bats*, just like the campaign to disrupt your country's fuel supplies. The plan, I think, was for the raiders to hold your attention while the people aboard the *Fire Bats* went about the *real* mission, which is to secure several nuclear missiles, and thus increase their chances of holding your country in the grip of . . . well, how shall I say it?"

"Nuclear blackmail?" Hunter filled in for him.

"Exactly," the masked man replied, nodding.

Hunter took a moment to consider all of Wolf's information.

It wouldn't be the first time that enemies of America had attempted to destroy the country's inherent democracy by way of the nuclear menace. The terrorist organization called The Circle had fought two wars and had practically devastated the eastern part of the American continent for a policy based in part on that very threat. So had the Nazi-backed Twisted Cross. But though these enemies had access to nuclear devices, they attempted to carry out their doctrine by somewhat more conventional methods, on the battlefield, armies against armies.

Now it appeared as if the subraiders—or more accurately, the people *behind* them—were trying to overthrow America by much more insidious means. By creating the aura of a brutal, yet in tactical terms, "localized" threat such as the Norse raiders, the masterminds were apparently planning on sneaking in the back door.

But another important question remained.

"Where do they expect to get these nuclear missiles?" Hunter asked Wolf. "I'm sure nuclear *bombs* can be had on the weapons black market. But nuclear *warheads,* with targeting capability and so on, would be a completely different matter."

Again Wolf took a deep breath and let it out slowly.

"Major, more than a year ago, the Red Star clique launched and detonated an air-burst nuclear missile over one of your cities, correct?"

Hunter nodded soberly. It was true, the cultish, anti-*glasnost* Soviet military clique that had ignited World War III in the first place *had* exploded a small nuclear bomb over the city of Syracuse in an attempt to disrupt the ongoing trial of the traitorous ex-vice president of the United States, who had been one of their agents.

"Shortly after that I understand that your forces destroyed the Red Star headquarters in Central Asia," Wolf went on.

Again, Hunter nodded. It was he who actually flew the specially equipped B-1 bomber against the hardened Red Star fortress located at Krasnoyarsk, very close to the Siberian border.

"Well, Major, did you know that just before their headquarters was destroyed, Red Star launched six ICBM's at your country?" Wolf asked.

Hunter was speechless. This was frightening news to him.

"We tracked them from the moment of launch," Wolf continued matter-of-factly. "They were fired from sites near Moscow. Our sensors picked them up the moment they left the pad."

"But none of us here knew anything about this," Hunter said, plainly astonished.

"I'm not surprised," Wolf told him. "You see, these missiles were incorrectly fueled. They did not reach the critical suborbital altitude, and therefore their arming mechanisms didn't respond. They landed well short of their intended targets and obviously did not explode. Thus your country was saved from a very catastrophic event."

226

"To say the least . . ."

"However, while several undoubtedly fell into the ocean," Wolf went on, "several more landed in remote places in eastern North America. The people behind this whole Norse invasion scenario became aware of the tracking of these missiles and from that have apparently located them.

"And it is these missiles—or more accurately their warheads—that they intend to install aboard the *Fire Bats*."

It was the story of his life, Hunter thought. Every time he assumed he had heard it all, something more devastating always popped up.

He felt a sickeningly familiar fire start to build in his gut. Had he been so foolish, sitting proud as wheat up on his hayfarm, to think that the world would suddenly become a civilized place just because he had retired?

"Who is behind all this?" Hunter asked, his voice rising in fury.

Wolf could only shrug. "Just who the overall masterminds are, I don't know," he said. "But I suspect at least one of them may be an American.

"As for the people behind the submarines and the plan to raid your East Coast—that is, those who are providing the smokescreen for the *Fire Bats*—then I'm afraid I know *them* all to well . . ."

Wolf lowered his head further, and for a third time let out a long, low breath.

"You see, it was my brother and my father who sent the submarines against you. And *that* is why I am after them. . . ."

Chapter Thirty-seven

Aboard the Great Ship

Dominique had never looked so beautiful.

She was dressed in a flowing white, low-cut gown made of authentic satin and lace and fastened with clasps and buttons made of solid gold. Her luxurious long blonde hair had been expertly washed, curled, brushed and set, and was now held in place by a delicate strand of diamonds and pearls. Her skin had been gently washed in milk and beer, powdered twice, and then anointed with perfumes made from rosemary and myrrh.

Even her cleavage—substantially revealed in the low-cut gown—had been sprinkled with a fine, glittering dust made from real silver.

She was kneeling on a heart-shaped rug made from lamb's fur, and before her was a goblet made of gold, filled with the thick, mind-altering liquor the Norsemen called *myx*. Kneeling at a discreet distance on either side of her were two lovely female attendants, dressed only slightly less glamourously than she. They, too, had goblets filled with *myx*, though these were made of pewter and not gold.

All around her, the baniquet swelled. There were more than four hundred people in attendance, she would have guessed, with an even split between Norse clan members—dressed up as their crude exteriors would allow—and young women, some of whom were undoubtedly captured as slaves during the recent raids and forced into service.

The banquet hall itself was enormous, taking up more

than half of the promenade deck of the *Stor Skute*. Two long wooden tables ran through its center, both of them pointing to a third, gold-encrusted platform next to where Dominique now was. The wooden tables were crowded with Norsemen, gorging their way through slabs of beef in what was the fifth course of the night. Scattered amongst the men were the scores of semireluctant young women, any one of whom could be flung to the floor or onto the table itself at any moment for the purpose of satiating a Norsemen's whimsical sexual lust.

Through it all, the *myx* flowed freely.

Seated at the gold table, not ten feet away to Dominique's left, was the man they called Verden, which when translated literally from Norwegian meant "world." But in Verden's case, she had come to learn, the name connoted nothing less than "the all-encompassing" or "the everything." It was an appropriate title for the person who, more than anyone else, could claim to be the leader of all the Norse clans.

In appearance, Verden looked the part. Despite the patch over his right eye, his long white hair and beard gave him an undeniable if slightly sinister Santa Claus look. His massive frame—still powerful and muscular despite his sixty-plus years—recalled that of a weight lifter, or perhaps a professional wrestler.

Verden was a strangely quiet and reserved man, Dominique had quickly come to realize, not at all the character she would have imagined would be the top chieftain of the wild and boisterous Norsemen. There was no mistaking that Verden was a man given to long periods of brooding and even depression. Even now, while his minions ate, drank, and molested the evening away, he sat alone at the gold table, his head in his hands, not touching his meal or drink, his only companions being his two enormous, coal-black pet ravens that never seemed to have the urge to simply fly away.

Dominique had been introduced to Verden shortly after

229

she and Yaz were transferred to the Great Ship after a brief three-hour trip in the sub. It was the Norse leader himself who had casually given her a tour of the vessel, explaining that at one time it had been a luxurious Carribbean cruise ship named, appropriately enough, *The Royal Viking Queen.*

Now it served as Verden's floating palace, an unarmed speck of gleaming white surrounded at all times by a protective phalanx of gray Norse destroyers, frigates, and, more often than not, a squad of raiding submarines.

Dominique also found out quickly that Verden was different from the rest of the Norsemen in his candor and outright honesty, though he doled it out in selective measures. Speaking in broken English, the man had explained to her during their tour that, yes, his raiders *were* intent on plundering the East Coast of America. But he insisted in the next breath that they were "entitled" to do so because it had been the Norsemen who discovered the continent in the first place—many years before Columbus. Therefore the land, and its people, were theirs for the ravaging.

Beyond this highly disputable claim, Verden said little more about the motives of his clans. He did mention, however, that although he was the recognized leader of the clans, more often than not, the clan leaders fended for themselves.

"We Norse are like wolves," he told Dominique. "The leader can lead, find food and shelter for the pack. But he is usually not appreciated unless there is big trouble. When one of his brood decides to act independently, all he can do is bark."

Dominique had then asked the Norse leader why she had been transferred to the Great Ship. She would never forget the look that came over him as he held her gently by the shoulders, a slight glistening welling up in his good eye.

In a voice that might have come from a kindly grandfather, he had said to her: "Because you have been selected as my Valkyrie . . ."

And with that, he had left her standing all alone on the deck of the Great Ship.

Dominique knew full well what a Valkyrie was . . .

A crucial component of Norse myth, the Valkyries were maidens of Odin, the godlike character, who, like Zeus in Greek mythology, served as an omnipotent ruler. It was the Valkyries' mission to fly to the battlefield and decide at Odin's bidding who should live and who should die. They also served as conduits of information to Odin, providing him with eyes and ears amongst his domain.

It was also believed, though not generally spelled out in the very few authentic Norse myth texts, that the Valkyries were available to serve Odin's sexual desires. And it was this thought that ran through Dominique's mind now as she watched the banquet reach new heights of drunkenness and debauchery.

As the next course of food—consisting of several dozen roasted pigs—was brought on, it seemed as if more and more of the disinclined young women were being grabbed, stripped, and sexually set upon. Fistfights of varying intensities were also breaking out among Norsemen of opposing clans, the fisticuffs brought on no doubt by the volatile mixture of the psychedelic *myx* and the intoxicating cries of the ravaged young women.

Yet though the storm of drunken wantonness swirled about her, no Norseman dared approach Dominique. Even in their most inebriated state, each man knew that to disturb Verden's Valkyrie in any way would result in the most painful of deaths. Despite the myriad of distractions, Dominique kept a close watch on Verden, thoroughly mystified by what she saw. The man neither ate nor drank and barely did he look up at the raucous scene before him. Rather he spent most of the time with his good eye closed and his head hung down, more like he was a bishop in deep prayer than the presiding member of the banquet-*cum-*

orgy.

Dominique couldn't help but wonder.

What could be worrying him so? she thought.

Deep in the lowest deck of the Great Ship, Yaz could clearly hear the screams, the cries and laughter of the feast.

Even though they were the enemy, and he was their prisoner, Yaz envied the Norsemen who were at that moment eating, drinking, and doing God-knows-what-else six decks above. Just the smell of the beef and ham cooking in the huge galley two levels above him was driving him nuts. All he had to subsist on was a hunk of hard black bread and a dirty gallon jug of incredibly bitter beer.

But at least he was still alive.

He took a long sip of the acrid-tasting lager and contemplated his situation. He was in a tiny cabin barely larger than a closet. A dim bulb provided the only illumination, a lumpy mat served as his bed. Before him was nothing more glamorous than a two-foot-thick, crudely written, badly translated repair manual detailing the unsophisticated guts of each and every one of the *Bats*—as the Norsemen called their submarines. As dictated by Verden himself, Yaz's role in life for the forseeable future was to memorize the book and be ready to advise the Norsemen on what to do when one of their submersible claptraps broke down. To demur would have cost him a finger or an ear, or maybe an even more precious body part at the best, and death at the worst.

So study the guidebook he did.

But now, after poring over the manual for the better part of the last two days, it was slowly dawning on him that like bottles of cheap wine, no two of the raiders' submarines were built alike. Just as Smiley had told him, there were two classes of rudimentary subs: the *Krig Bats* (or war boats) to ferry raiders on their attacks and the *Folk Bats* (people boats) used mostly to transport the human cargo of slaves

232

back to Scandinavia but also as supply and replenishment vessels.

But while the basic design of all these subs was consistent—in almost all cases, Panel A *was* welded to Panel B and so on—the interior layouts were almost always different with each vessel. Some boasted huge galleys, which left little room for sleeping quarters. Others had a surplus area for bunks, yet no kitchen. Some had been built with enough room for so much coal that, if filled to capacity, their buoyancy would have been nil. Others had to refuel almost daily because they carried almost no area for coal storage.

Above all, the electrical wiring and plumbing systems were the most convoluted; some of the boats could barely sustain burning two dozen fifty-watt lightbulbs, while others had power to spare. Many had been built entirely without toilets. Most of the air-circulation systems were a joke, as were the water repurification processes. Just about the only thing the subs had in common was that on-board escape and rescue systems were nonexistent.

Yaz found the reading complicated and frustratingly confusing. Plus, nowhere in the volumes were the mysterious *Fire Bats* even alluded to. Yet it never left his mind that while he was studying the manual, he was also drinking up volumes of valuable intelligence on the enemy. Being able to understand submarine technology had been his life-saving grace so far. And though he hadn't seen her since coming aboard the Great Ship, he liked to think it was what had kept Dominique close by also. It had also given him this chance to learn more about the Norseman's *Bats* than they probably knew themselves.

As an officer of the United American Armed Forces, it was up to him to take as much of an advantage as possible of the mind-numbing yet luckily fortuitous situation.

With this in mind, he set aside the glass of incredibly bitter beer and turned to the next page. Six decks above, it sounded as if the orgy had shifted into high gear.

It was one of the handmaidens who passed the note to Dominique.

Just barely making her way across the chaotic banquet-hall floor, the woman ceremoniously slipped the piece of paper into Dominique's cleavage and then returned to her own rug without a word. Reading the roughly scratched letters, it took Dominique several moments before she realized that the message was from Verden. He had left the banquet about a half hour before, slipping through a side door without so much as a salute from his horde of barbaric soldiers.

Now he was summoning Dominique to his quarters.

No sooner had she reread the note and folded it when two Norsemen, wearing the all-white cloth uniform of Verden's personal security squad, appeared and motioned that she follow them. Like a parting of the waves, these two men cleared a path for her through the sprawling and screaming bodies of the Norsemen and their victims.

She passed unhindered to the opposite end of the hall, not one of the raiders daring to touch her or even look directly into her eyes.

She arrived at Verden's third-deck quarters ten minutes later.

The door was open and the man was sitting on a throne-like wooden chair placed at the far end of the cabin. The room was very dark, six weary candles providing the only light.

In an instant, her two escorts were gone.

"Come in, my beautiful friend," Verden said in his heavily accented, withdrawn, and raspy voice. "It's with pleasure that I greet you. I'm happy that you decided to pay me a visit."

"Your note was an order," she replied, walking to a spot

234

about fifteen feet from the throne. "I had little choice but to obey."

He looked up at her, making an effort to distinguish her features in the dark room with his good eye.

"An order or an invitation," he shrugged, ". . . what's the difference?"

"I am your prisoner," Dominique said. "I must do as you say or suffer the consequences."

He lowered his head to his hand and pulled worriedly on his beard.

"That is true, my lovely," he said in his dreary monotone, grabbing a goblet filled with *myx* and practically draining it in a single swallow. "But you are not like the others. This you must know by now. I have chosen you above them all to be my Valkyrie. This is a position that millions of women would give their lives for . . ."

"And so I must give mine?" she countered.

He poured and gulped another cup of *myx* and then stared hard at her.

"I drink so rarely," he said. "But now that I do, I simply cannot believe your beauty . . ."

"I have had the *myx*," she said, "I know how it distorts reality."

"No," he said, shaking his finger at her. "Your loveliness transcends the *myx*."

"Then it is just another part of your dream," she said, spreading her hands to indicate everything from his throne to the shipload of drunken Vikings. *"This* dream . . ."

Suddenly, Verden's voice became deeper, clearer, and, for lack of a better description, more contemporary.

"Don't be entirely fooled by what you see around you," he told her. "To you, my men and I probably look like actors in an old movie or people drawn in a comic book. But believe me, before the Big War, we weren't all that different from you—you and your 'civilized' American friends."

Another goblet was filled and quickly consumed.

"True, many of my men are from the mountains," Verden

went on. "And from the small villages up near the Arctic where it seems to be dark every hour of every day of every year. Modern civilization was something that intruded in on us only every so often.

"But don't be deluded, my lovely creature, that we are totally ignorant of convention. We know that planes fly and bombs destroy and that men have walked on the moon. We also know that the blood of Eric and Leif and the others runs in our veins, and that it was *they* who first discovered America and not this Italian interloper.

"As I told you before, we are simply returning to recapture our claim."

Once again, he lowered his head and stared into the empty goblet.

"Though, I must admit," he said, his voice returning to its original sad timbre, "that it is the *myx* that makes our blood boil and permits the ghosts of our ancestors to burst through. Then, perhaps, we *do* look like comic book characters."

Several minutes of a stone-cold silence descended on the room. The candles flickered and the ship rolled gently in the Atlantic swell. Verden stayed almost motionless, staring at his empty cup, the aura of despondency almost visible around his hulking frame.

"You belong to another?" he asked her, suddenly looking up.

Dominique slowly nodded her reply.

"And do you think he is still alive?"

"I know he is . . ." she whispered.

"And he will be faithful, even after he knows you're gone?"

"That makes no difference," she said.

He tilted his head up to look at her again. "And why is that?" he asked.

"Because he is looking for me," she replied. "And he will keep looking until he finds me."

Verden reached for his flask and refilled his goblet once

again with *myx*.

"You know him so well, do you?" he asked.

"Yes . . ."

Verden downed the full cup of *myx* in a loud gulp, wiping his mouth with the end of his sleeve. His movements were shaky and almost convulsive now, due to the large quantity of the powerful mind-bending liquor he'd consumed in just the past few minutes.

"But he is not here now," the chieftain slurred. "And you are my Valkyrie. Thus, you shall do what I say . . ."

He drained another cup of *myx,* and coughed hard. Then he poured out another full goblet and handed to Dominique.

"Drink this, my lovely," he commanded. "This and two more . . ."

"And if I refuse?" she asked, trying to stay calm. "Certainly you wouldn't kill your Valkyrie so soon after selecting her."

For the first time, Verden smiled.

"No, my dear," he said, now barely able to prop his head up on one elbow. "But if you do refuse, then I will kill that friend of yours, who right now sits at the bottom of this ship."

Dominique drank the *myx*.

His name was Thorgils, Son of Verden. In the cabin full of clan leaders on the other side of the Great Ship he was the only one without a beard.

Two decks below them, they could hear the orgy reach a new height of ferocity. But frivolities such as eating and *fricking* young slave girls were of little concern to Thorgils and the other dozen men in the room. Before them was a map of the East Coast of America, around which they were discussing the largest Norse assault yet on the American continent.

"The spies tell us that much of the East Florida coast is

still inhabited," Thorgils told them in rapid, tense Norwegian. "The lack of fuel has forced many of the people there to stay put. Plus, the Americans haven't yet started to ship troops and equipment down there by rail, again because of the fuel situation. Therefore the opportunity lies with us."

Thorgils pointed to the multicolored squares of cloth that dotted the map along the eastern Florida coast.

"There are twenty-five targets," he said of the various markers that ran from Jacksonville in the north to Orlando in the south. "You know your clan colors. Those are the targets you should suggest to your men. Each target has three means of access and retreat. When your raiding party goes ashore, they will have a choice of which direction to attack from and how to withdraw. These multiple routes will also confuse the enemy."

The clan leaders murmured in silent approval. It had been this way since the campaign had started. The dozen men—they being the senior commanders representing the twelve major clans that made up the overall Norse raiding force—would come to the Great Ship for a *thing*, the Norse traditional gathering. While their officers and selected warriors reveled in the mandatory prebattle orgy, the clan elders would quietly meet with Thorgils and learn his thoughts for the upcoming assault.

This was not a "strategy session," however—there really wasn't any phrase in the Norse vernacular for such an event. Thorgils drew the map, worked out a timetable, and suggested to the clan leaders where and when to strike. It was up to them to fill in the blanks.

Usually the rest of the clan leaders would simply nod or more likely, grunt their approval of Thorgils's plans. They rarely even spoke. Thorgils was, after all, the oldest son of Verden, and therefore his word was good for them. If he suggested a target and a way to approach it, the clan elders would go along with him more often than not.

The clan heads welcomed this hands-off approach. When it came to making war, the Norse had traditionally taken the less complicated, blunt approach. They knew that there really wasn't any need to go into much detail the night before a battle; strategies, plans, counterplans, and such only cluttered a soldier's head.

Hundreds of years of history had taught them — almost religiously — that in the midst of battle, the highly individualistic Norsemen were best left on their own. This way their minds would be clear, their instincts would be at their sharpest, as would their determination should events turn against them.

So once Thorgils had pointed the way, the dozen clan leaders — each of whom commanded a fleet of five to seven attack subs — would return to their flag boats and pass his recommendations to their subordinates on other boats and they to their crews.

After that, they were all on their own.

"Many of the *Volk Bats* will be available to assist you in the landings," Thorgils told them. "Their captains have secured a number of sturdy landing crafts which will allow you to move your men into the beaches quicker. I think it would be wise to use these vessels if you can."

Thorgils looked around at the twelve men; if there were any questions, now would be the time to ask. But there weren't any. In fact, there was really only one topic left to discuss: the price to be paid to the clans for carrying out the invasion.

"As always, the spoils of choice should be the women," Thorgils told them. "The *Volk Bats* will be waiting after the operation as usual and the exchange rate will remain the same. Supplies will be distributed based on the number of slaves brought back as well as tonnage of booty. However, because this will be the largest, most ambitious operation yet, I hereby declare extra *myx* rations for the clans bringing in numbers over quota."

To this bit of news the clan leaders brightened in an instant. Food, ammunition, and coal made up the staples of the Norsemen's otherwise dreary, violent lives. In many ways, they and their men simply fought and killed and kidnapped just so they could get food and bullets and fuel in order to kill and kidnap again.

But drinking the *myx* changed everything. It was a much-needed relief from an existence that, as dictated by Norse history, was doomed from the start.

And the indisputable fact was that Thorgils and his father controlled the *myx*. Stored in wooden casks and protected like gold in the holds of the Great Ship, the father and son spent much time and effort carefully dispensing it to the various clans in return for the women slaves and booty taken during raids. It was, in fact, the lifeblood of the Court of Verden, the entity around which everything else swirled. Verden and Thorgils could use the strange, highly addictive liquor as an incentive to the most loyal clans, or, by withholding it, as a way of bringing an unruly tribe back in line.

So while many in the clans regarded Verden as a very wise and brave man whom they trusted for the most part, his real power came from the fact that he regulated the flow of the *myx*.

"Once ashore, you men might meet *some* resistance, but not much," Thorgils went on. "We hear that some of the militias in Florida are fairly well trained but others are not. Some regular United American forces are in place several miles back from the coast, but your men shouldn't have any trouble overwhelming them once they move off the beaches and into the cities beyond.

"The attack time should be one hour before dusk on the next day from tomorrow. It will be wise to make sure you are in place in plenty of time."

With that, Thorgils began to fold the map away. This alone indicated the meeting was over. There were no salutes. No wishes of good luck or godspeed. Unlike other cultures, it was not in the Norse tradition to include sentimentality into warfare.

But just as the clan leaders were preparing to go, the

door to the room swung open and a dark figure walked in.

The elders froze as they saw it was a woman wearing a long black gown, her head covered with a hood.

"My Lady," one man said, immediately falling to one knee. Like bowling pins, the rest of the clan leaders did the same. Only Thorgils remained standing, although he did doff his helmet in a slightly more reserved tribute.

The woman threw back her hood and studied the men with her beautiful but cold steel eyes.

It was Elizabeth Sandlake.

"My Lady . . ." the Son of Verden said through strained, whispering lips. "I was just explaining the next attack."

"Is that so?" she asked in a voice dripping with contempt. "Then you won't mind explaining it to me . . ."

Thorgils nearly choked at the sound of her request.

"But My Lady," he stammered. "It was you who . . ."

A stare like a laser beam caused his mouth to suddenly go numb. In the acute anxiety of the moment, he had very nearly given away one of the deepest secrets of the whole Norse campaign.

Now, as the clan leaders watched in anxious amazement, Elizabeth walked to the table in a kind of regal slow motion, and smiled cruelly as Thorgils spread out the map again.

"From the beginning, My Lady?" the son of Verden asked through tight lips.

"From the beginning," she replied, openly mocking him. "Unless you can think of another way of explaining our biggest operation so far . . ."

With the clan leaders more or less frozen at attention, Thorgils took the next forty-five minutes to slowly, precisely, but obviously reluctantly, go over the entire procedure once again.

"Very ambitious" was Elizabeth's reply at the end of the briefing. "And you've made provisions in case there is strong enemy air support?"

Once again Thorgils looked toward her in horror. *Why*

241

would she be asking me that question? he wondered, almost aloud.

"But there will be no strong enemy air support," he replied, his tone leaving no further doubt that he loathed having to reexplain the attack details to Elizabeth. "According to our spy reports, no enemy aircraft of any consequence have been spotted anywhere near the attack points."

"And why is that?" she snapped at him.

Thorgils was becoming just as angry as he was flustered.

"My Lady, the United Americans simply don't have the fuel to move many warplanes to the region," he said, trying his best to keep his composure. "Nor will they be able to move around the few they *do* have on hand to all the various attack points."

"Don't be so sure," Elizabeth fired back at him. "These United Americans have a talent for turning the impossible."

"I doubt that will happen in this case," Thorgils hissed at her, his voice displaying more anger with every syllable. "They might be organized at some points on the ground, but their air capability is frozen. Once the clans get in off the beaches, they will rule the battle. Of this I am certain . . ."

"And of this *I* am certain," Elizabeth shouted at him. "If the United Americans call in even the barest amount of air cover, then the day could be lost for the clans. And that will be your responsibility, Thorgils . . ."

At this point, the Son of Verden completely lost his temper. Something was amiss here—Elizabeth knew more about these plans than he did. What's more, he had discussed every detail with her earlier that day, just an hour after she was secretly whisked aboard the Great Ship.

Now she was trying to trick him, confuse him, *embarrass* him in front of the twelve clan elders. In the constant swirl of intrigue and deception that surrounded the Norse clans and the court of Verden, her attack was a very bad sign for Thorgils.

242

He had no choice but to fight back. With squinting eyes and a red face, he launched into a nonstop verbal strafing of Elizabeth, attacking her intelligence, her rudeness, even her femininity. Elizabeth returned the fire, blow for blow, degrading Thorgils's character, his lack of leadership qualities, and, inevitably, his own sexuality.

The clan elders could not believe what was happening. Although the argument was swaying back and forth between Norwegian and English, there was no doubt as to the viciousness of the invectives that were being hurled in either language. And though the gossip around the clans was that Thorgils and the mysterious American woman had been uneasy allies since the start of the campaign, the elders never dreamed the two rivals would be this open about their dislike for each other.

The climax of the argument came when Thorgils actually raised his hand as if to strike Elizabeth.

But she did not flinch an iota. Instead she just laughed — that frightening, bone-chilling laugh. And suddenly everything stopped. It appeared as if Thorgils, the second most powerful man in the Norse court, had become inert, paralyzed simply by that laugh.

"This can end only with your father, Thorgils," Elizabeth told him, the wicked smile never leaving her lips.

With that, she pulled the hood back up over her head and stormed out of the cabin, leaving the son of Verden frozen in place, his open hand still poised above his head.

Chapter Thirty-eight

Dominique was naked.

She was lying on her back on a bed of pillows placed on the floor of Verden's cabin. Her hair was no longer held in place by the string of diamonds and pearls and her beauti-ful white satin-and-lace gown was nowhere to be seen. Her skin was sticky; it felt like some kind of oil had been spread all over her body, leaving a thin glaze and a highly aromatic smell. She was also very moist around her upper thighs and breasts.

On the pillow next to her were three empty goblets and a half-filled flask of *myx*.

She had just awakened, but for a moment she wondered if she was still dreaming. The cabin, so dark and claustro-phobic when she first arrived, now looked like an enor-mous, brightly lit hall. The candles that had seemed so depleted before were now burning with the intensity of klieg lights. And Verden, standing over her, his hands on his hips, his teeth clenched, looked more like Michaelange-lo's Creator than a rundown, melancholy Father Christ-mas.

Although she was alone on the bed of pillows, she was very aware of the sensation of hands touching her body. Up, over, across, and down, invisible fingers were lightly feeling her, massaging her, gently probing her most private areas. Her nipples were erect like never before, their tips wet with the sensation that some invisible set of lips were lightly sucking on them. She closed her eyes as a familiar feeling began to wash over her. Within a few seconds, her entire body was immersed into a spasm of orgasmic delight.

Through it all, Verden stood over her, shuddering with a similar climax—not moving, not attempting to touch her.

He didn't have to. The *myx* was doing it for him.

The two guards posted outside Verden's cabin felt an immediate shiver when they first spotted the woman in the hood approaching.

"My Lady," they both intoned, going down to one knee and bowing their heads.

"Out of my way," she demanded.

"No . . ." one of the guards said, rising up to his feet quite involuntarily. "The Verden has left strict orders. He cannot be disturbed."

Elizabeth stopped short and simply looked at the man.

"And why is that?" she asked crossly.

The two guards just looked at each other, neither one wanting to speak.

"Answer me!" Elizabeth demanded.

One guard finally had the courage to clear his throat. "He is with his new Valkyrie, My Lady," he said nervously.

"New Valkyrie?" Elizabeth responded with genuine but angry surprise. "He has selected a new Valkyrie without letting me know?"

The guard was terrified. Why would she ask him that question? he wondered.

Elizabeth turned to the second man. "Who is she?"

This man, too, was struck nearly dumb. "A slave," was all he could mumble.

Elizabeth pushed both men out of the way, and with the kick of her boot, burst through the door to Verden's cabin.

The sudden rush of air from the passageway outside extinguished several of the candles—either that or the presence of Elizabeth herself had done the job.

However, the sight of the naked Dominique, writhing around on the bed of pillows, blindly lost in a fog of intoxication, stopped Elizabeth in her tracks. Her eyes immediately darted back and forth along her lovely glistening form.

My God, Elizabeth whispered to herself, *it's her* . . .

Suddenly Elizabeth felt another string snap deep within her brain. In the flash of a nerve, she descended one more step into madness. To her mind, another part of her maniacal plot had just fallen into place. For the woman who she had arranged to have abducted and brought to the Alberta Fortress, only to have her rescued by the great Hawk Hunter, was now stretched out before her, naked and in the thralls of a blinding *myx* stupor.

What goes around comes around. What better confirmation could Elizabeth get from the Cosmos that her quest for world domination was not only predestined, but actually condoned by the spirit world than to have Hawk Hunter's girlfriend back within her grasp?

My dreams do come true, Elizabeth thought as she gave Dominique the once over, feeling her own nipples slowly becoming erect.

Verden was outraged at the intrusion. His face was crimson, and a substantial vein began bulging on his temple. He opened his mouth to say something, but Elizabeth cut him off.

"This is your new Valkyrie?" she asked him, instantly realizing that Verden had no idea who Dominique was, a situation that suited Elizabeth nicely.

Verden was so angry he could not reply. This only encouraged Elizabeth.

"It is good to see My Lord enjoying himself for a change," she told him sarcastically. "The *myx* makes it so much easier, doesn't it? So much better?"

Her eyes dramatically fell to the wet patch around the crotch of Verden's hand-sewn breeches.

"After all," she whispered cruelly, "why bother to touch another human when the *myx* can do it all for you?"

Verden clapped his hands twice, and the two young attending handmaidens appeared from a side door. Working quickly, they covered the now-unconscious Dominique in a silk robe and carried her into an adjoining room.

Once they were gone, Verden turned back toward Elizabeth.

"If you were a man I would have killed you myself," he told her, his voice steaming with rage.

"If *I* were a man," Elizabeth replied, completely unruffled, "I would have killed you first . . ."

Verden shook his head and slumped back into his throne.

He knew there was no point in verbally sparring with the woman. She was a witch—a true, authentic witch—and as such, she drew her powers from a higher plateau than he.

"Why have you come here?" he asked her wearily.

"It concerns the upcoming attacks, my Lord," she said. "They are our most ambitious to date, yet your son is guilty of shodding preparedness."

"In what respect?" Verden demanded.

"He has not made any provisions should the enemy have air support," she told him. "It could prove disastrous for the clans even if they have only a few aircraft on hand."

Verden shook his head. "But I was told that all of the enemy's warplanes were grounded. Frozen in place, due to the fuel situation. After all, it was you who suggested we send our men to destroy their fuel dumps and you who suggested this ambitious attack. Are you now saying that your divine plan won't work?"

"No," she replied forcefully. "What I'm saying is that the United Americans obviously have *some* fuel on hand at their bases. True, they have not been moving their air squadrons around to counter us so far, but this is a strategy based on *saving* fuel, not a complete lack of it."

Verden scratched his hairy chin in thought for a moment. Of all the people aboard the Great Ship, only three—Thorgils, Elizabeth and himself—knew that the real direction behind the seemingly free-wheeling Norse campaign came from those aboard the *Fire Bats*.

Now this woman—this *witch*—was contradicting the very plans she had delivered from the *Fire Bats* in the first place. What did it mean?

Verden wrapped a heavy wool robe around his ample body and then formulated what he thought was a prudent reply.

"What is the worst that can happen?" he asked. "Their few airplanes show up and some of our men are lost. We lost many men on Long Island; many more in Delaware. So what is the difference? We are not seeking to hold ground. We are not an occupying force. Some of our men will be killed, but all of them won't be. Just as long as most of them make it back to their boats with slaves and booty, then the operation will be a success."

"And what happens the next time?" Elizabeth barked back at him. "And the next and the next? The United Americans' warplanes carry weapons that can easily wipe out thousands of men in a matter of minutes. I know. I have seen them in operation. You don't have an endless supply of manpower to draw on. If your casualties are high, then it will affect everything—including the operation of the *Fire Bats*."

Verden cringed at the mention of the mysterious Four Boats. The very words were *verboten*.

"Say no more about that!" he boomed at her. "I don't want to know . . ."

Elizabeth didn't even try to suppress her smile. "And what happens if the battleship intervenes again?" she asked. "What happens if your other son decides to step in?"

Verden's face first drained of color, then quickly became flushed again.

"You are a spiteful and cruel woman," he told Elizabeth. "And I know you are trying to trick me and my son, Thorgils. But I refuse to be a party to your mad games."

Elizabeth laughed right in his face. "You may regret saying that, My Lord . . ."

Verden was too weak to lash out at her. Instead, he slumped into the throne and mumbled, "The only thing that I regret was the day I agreed to cooperate with you."

Elizabeth simply glowered back at him with her dark, hypnotic eyes.

"Believe what you want," she said. "But history will remember that it was *I* who agreed to cooperate with you and not the other way around."

"That is of no matter now," Verden said, reviving slightly. "You have no right to talk of history or speak ill of my family. You have no idea what kinship means to our culture . . ."

At this point, Verden slumped even further into his seat, his right hand just barely supporting his head.

"You have no idea what it means to lose one's son," he said, his voice shaky and low and on the verge of tears.

Despite Verden's obvious distress, Elizabeth pressed on.

"This is not Europe, My Lord," she told the chieftain. "This is not as simple as raiding the Channel Islands or pillaging undefended French coastal villages. We are about to assault a large part of the East Coast of Florida. More than a hundred and fifty miles in all. But Thorgils is treating it all as if we were simply attacking Nova Scotia or Cape Cod. He just doesn't realize the magnitude of the operation or the reaction we may get from the United Americans."

"But what can be done?" Verden asked, his patience finally wearing out. "*You* gave us these orders. We have been planning only to carry out your wishes, and the wishes of those aboard the *Fire Bats*."

Elizabeth just shook her head in defiance. "Any clan leader would have taken into consideration that the enemy would have some kind of air response."

"But how?" Verden asked, once again wearily shaking his head. "We have no warplanes of our own."

Elizabeth's next comment caught on her lips. She stopped herself from speaking, and then she smiled. She had heard the words she'd been waiting for.

"Leave that to me," she said.

Chapter Thirty-nine

Elvis couldn't move any part of his tired body without hearing his joints crack in protest.

He had been flying for what seemed like forever. And because he was flying north and west, it seemed like the large red ball in front of him was in a state of perpetual sunset. The waning light did have its advantages: It made it much easier for him to visually sweep the miles of ocean beneath him, allowing him to shut down all but his critical cockpit controls, thus saving fuel.

But the red glare also gave the surface of the ocean a slightly surreal look. So when he first spotted the group of islands way off in the distance, he thought his eyes were playing tricks on him.

It took his forward-looking surface-tracking radar device to convince him that what he was seeing was not an illusion.

Zim hadn't been lying. Anchored around the group of islands known as the Kures, some fifteen hundred miles northwest of Hawaii, there was a fleet—a *gigantic* fleet made up of warships and armed cargo shies.

Elvis immediately put the F-4X into a steep climb, leveling off at fifty-five thousand feet. Then, as he activated his nose cameras he tried to estimate the number of ships he saw below scattered in and around the small Pacific islands.

He stopped counting at six hundred.

Zim had claimed the fleet was carrying a huge army of mercenaries, Koreans and Chinese mostly, hired by unknown parties to attack America. Zim had heard about this plan only days before and that's why he'd tried so hard to "liquidate his assets" and get the hell off Hawaii. For he knew once this fleet began to sail it would be in Hawaiian waters within three days. His information told him that more than eighty thousand troops were being ferried in the hold of the ships, five times as many as would be needed to take over the Hawaiian Islands.

Elvis was all too aware that mercenary armies of such size, using fleets of such magnitude, were not unheard of in the postwar world. During the fight to liberate the eastern half of America from the hated Circle Army, an East European mercenary fleet of similar size had been stationed off the East Coast, hired by the Circle to join in the fight against the United Americans. It was only after the leader of this mercenary fleet saw that the UA was in firm control of the lands east of the Mississippi that he declined to go through with his contract with the Circle, prudently sailing away without firing a shot. Another famous British mercenary fleet — known as the Modern Knights — had helped defeat the superterrorist Viktor Robotov when he tried to take over the Mediterranean.

And now, here was another huge floating army, hired by someone to attack America. If they did so — and Elvis knew that such gatherings of warships and men rarely did *not* go into action — they'd be able to sweep through the Hawaiian Islands without so much as a sneeze and hit the West Coast head-on. With the crisis on the East Coast at the breaking point, an attack on the west coast would be devastating.

Elvis did two complete sweeps over the islands, taking hundreds of photographs of the enormous fleet. Then, checking his fuel load, he determined that he had just enough to make it back to Oahu.

Suddenly he was struck by a very disturbing notion: Could the attacks on the East Coast and the assembling of this invasion force be somehow connected?

He shivered at the thought, and immediately turned eastward, determined to get back to friendly territory and spread the warning about this new threat.

The surface-to-air missile slammed into his F-4 two seconds later . . .

Chapter Forty

Jacksonville Naval Air Station

Mike Fitzgerald relit his cigar and checked his watch.

"Nineteen hundred hours—he's late," he said to General Dave Jones through a plume of smoke. "Not a good sign . . ."

Jones checked his own watch and slowly shook his head.

"Everything has been so screwed up in the past week, I can't imagine anyone being punctual," he said. "Except him . . ."

As if to prove his statement correct, on the next breeze they heard the distant whine of an approaching jet engine.

"That's him . . ." Jones said simply.

Turning their eyes eastward, they saw a single dim light way out on the horizon. With astonishing speed, the light grew larger and more intense as it came right for them. Within seconds they were able to distinguish the unique silouette of the Harrier jumpjet. A second later the shadow took on a definite shape. Now they could see the navigation lights, the gleam of the cockpit, the red flare of the jet exhaust.

Ten seconds later, the VTOL airplane rocketed over their heads, turned, and quickly slowed to hover. Then it slowly descended for a perfect landing.

Hunter had his cockpit open even before the Harrier's wheels touched the ground. Quickly shutting down all of the plane's systems, he leapt out of the airplane and directly to the tarmac below.

Jones was the first one to greet him. It was an odd reunion for the first few moments—the general had not seen Hunter in almost a year, not since the Wingman went into "retirement." But soon enough they were shaking hands warmly.

"Not the best of circumstances to see an old friend," Jones told him.

Hunter just shrugged. "Duty calls, sir," he said.

Fitz quickly directed them toward the nearby mess hall. It was almost sundown, and the base was dark and strangely quiet—all by design.

"This place *looks* deserted," Hunter said. "Did you get everybody down here in time?"

"See for yourself," Fitz told him as they reached the mess hall.

Hunter had to smile when he opened the door and saw the place was nearly filled to capacity with United American pilots and support personnel.

"Well, *this* looks like a tough crowd," he said with a grin.

"You'd know as well as anyone else," Jones said as he grabbed a pot of coffee and three cups and sat down at an empty table. "They're just itching to get at these Viking bastards. Thanks to your message, they're all hoping this will be the opportunity to do just that."

Fitz poured out three cups of coffee, adding a dash of brandy from his ever-present hip flask to each one.

"Here's to luck," he said, putting his cup up to toast.

"To luck," Hunter and Jones intoned.

"OK, Hawk," Fitz said after taking a long sip of the liquor-spiked java. "Let's have it. How did you get tipped that this big attack was coming?"

Hunter took off his flight helmet and ran his hand through his overgrown head of hair.

"It's so strange, I'm having a hard time believing it myself," he said.

He took the next few minutes telling Fitz and Jones about his encounter and subsequent landing on the USS *New Jersey*.

"Good God, we knew you set down on a ship out there,"

254

Jones exclaimed. "But a battleship? Really?"

"Hard to believe, I know," Hunter told them. "But not only is it floating, it's in A-One condition. Top crew. Top captain. A little weird around the edges, but that's OK. As it turns out, we're all fighting the same war."

Hunter explained that he had been able to get all of the sophisticated sensing equipment aboard the *New Jersey* up and running in a short amount of time. With things such as long-range radar and sonar, plus radio intercept equipment, he and Wolf were able to eavesdrop on the submarine captains as they prepared for the attack on the Florida coast.

"They're so backward, they never thought that anyone would be listening in on them," Hunter explained. "We could have written a book on all the stuff we heard them blabbing about. Times, location, escape routes. The works. That's when I called you guys to get some attack craft down here as quickly and quietly as possible. This way, we can hit them from the air while Wolf and his crew hit them out at sea. It's the perfect trap."

"So it was this Wolf and his ship who wiped out those raiders on Slaughter Beach," Fitz concluded.

"With one, very well-aimed shot," Hunter replied. "From a distance of twenty-seven miles."

"Incredible," Jones said. "I've heard those big battle-wagon guns were accurate, but I'd never actually seen one in action before."

"They use the RPV as their means of targeting," Hunter confirmed. "Then they're able to deliver as many as nine twenty-seven-hundred-pound shells on a dime."

"That's a lot of firepower to be floating around out there," Fitz observed.

Hunter took a healthy swig of his booze-ladened coffee. "To say the least," he replied. "And that's why we're lucky they're on our side, more or less."

"Well, that's my question," Fitz said, casually relighting his cigar. "How come this guy and his ship decided to join the good guys?"

"Refill our cups," Hunter told him, "and give me an extra splash of your secret ingredient. Then fasten your seat belts, gentlemen. I've got a hell of a story to tell you."

Hunter told Jones and Fitzgerald what Wolf had told him.

The masked captain of the battleship was the youngest son of the man who served as the top leader of the Norsemen. Born in a small village in the northernmost part of Norway, Wolf had left home at an early age, traveling extensively throughout the world in the deceptively peaceful years before the Big War.

His father and older brother ran a successful fishing and canning operation and at one time owned as many as a hundred vessels, some of them the size of factory ships. Joint fishing operations with the prewar Russians, Finns, and Germans made the father and son very wealthy—so much so that they were able to wield considerable influence within the Norwegian government. Plus many people in that country knew of them as Norway's version of media celebrities.

"They were moguls," was how Hunter described them. *"Fish* moguls."

Though there was a ton of money floating around, Wolf, the youngest son, never wanted any part of the business. A free spirit, he was happier living day to day, exploring the world. He was also turned off by his father's rather odd spiritual beliefs. For years the old man had boasted that their family was directly descended from the old Vikings—a claim that would have been near impossible to definitely substantiate.

But oddly, as the family's wealth grew, so did this belief, up to the point that each one of the fishing vessels was christened with a Viking-style name, and each captain given a Viking alias, based on the names of the old Norse heroes.

Soon thereafter, the father took on the name Verden and

his oldest son became Thorgils, which was the name of Leif Erikson's son. At that point, the younger son began going by the name of Wolf, simply to preserve his family's original name.

When the Big War hit, there were few places in Europe—alas, few places in the world—that were not affected. However the northernmost part of Norway was one of them. The shockingly brief war passed far to the south, and when it was over, life went on almost undisturbed up in this arcticlike region.

There was a power vacuum in Norway, as well as the rest of Scandinavia, when the war broke out as the democratic governments collapsed. All around the globe, power-brokers, dictators, and opportunists scrambled to redefine national boundaries. Never one to miss which way the wind was blowing, Wolf's father—the Verden—declared within weeks of the armistice that a large section of northern Norway and Sweden was now his *Hvit Kongedomme,* or "White Kingdom."

With the help of Thorgils, he recruited first hundreds, then thousands, of seamen, mostly from his fishing fleet. He fed them, paid them, and then quite thoroughly indoctrinated them, convincing them, as he had convinced himself, that they were modern-day Vikings.

"At some point, about a half year ago, Verden met up with a rather mysterious group of Americans," Hunter told Fitz and Jones. "Criminals of some kind. Eventually an alliance was formed. This group of Americans paid to have the raiders' submarines built, and in no time, the Norsemen began retracing the footsteps of their ancestors.

"Now somewhere in there, they all started drinking this highly addicting kind of booze called *myx.* According to Wolf, this stuff will do everything for you except zip up your pants and light a cigarette when you're done. Sounds weird, but the Norse can't get enough of the stuff. So they trade in their slaves and booty and get paid in food and fuel, but mostly in this *myx.* They've been raiding northern Europe for months, and now they're over here."

"Raping, pillaging, murdering, kidnapping . . ." Fitz said with a mouthful of disgust. "And now addiction. That's quite a tradition to carry on."

"From the bartering side of things, it's the kidnapping that's most important to them," Hunter told his friends somberly. "Their whole campaign turns on how many eligible women they can abduct. These women are then transported back to Europe on their supply subs, where they are bought and sold like sacks of wheat."

Both Fitzgerald and Jones noticed a hard, cold anger come across Hunter as he spoke these words. It was painfully obvious that the fact that Dominique had been kidnapped by the raiders was never far from his mind.

"But what do these American criminals get out of it?" Jones asked, delicately trying to turn the conversation slightly.

Hunter took an extra long swig of his laced coffee and once again ran his hand through his hair.

"That's the scary part," he replied.

He then went on to explain to them what he knew about the *Fire Bats,* the Red Star ICBM warheads, and the plan to hold up the country to nuclear blackmail.

Both men were astonished to hear that Red Star had launched ICBMs at America. But the danger that someone would actually get their hands on those same warheads was even more frightening.

"Then we *are* fighting more than just a large hit-and-run raiding force," Jones said in a grim whisper.

"Much more," Hunter replied soberly.

"Well, somehow we've got to track down these *Fire Bats,*" Fitz said. "That's where the greatest danger lies."

"I agree," Hunter said. "But first we have to deal with the Norsemen themselves."

Jones looked around the crowded mess hall and then back at Hunter.

"Well, we're able to get three squadrons in," he explained. "Anything that was available on the QT *and* halfwise good at ground attack, we brought 'em down."

Fitz pulled out a notebook from his coat pocket.

"To be precise," he said in his thick Irish brogue. "We've got twenty-five A-7 Strikefighters; twenty A-10D Thunderbolts, and a squadron of twelve A-4D Skyhawks. Plus a few F-4s."

"Just what the doctor ordered," Hunter replied.

By bringing in ground attack planes—as opposed to high-speed jet fighters and interceptors—they were arming themselves with the best aircraft to counter the imminent Norse invasion. Although attack planes like the A-7's and A-10's were slower than most high-performance jet fighters, they could carry enormous amounts of ordnance, from big iron bombs to missiles to antipersonnel dispensers. No planes were better suited to stop slow-moving enemy ground troops.

"What kind of stuff will they be carrying?" Hunter asked.

Fitz and Jones finished their coffees at almost the same moment.

"Want to see for yourself?" Fitz suggested.

Ten minutes later, the three men were walking toward one of the base's largest hangars.

Now, with the sun fully set, Hunter was amazed how deserted the large Naval Air Station looked. He could see no lights burning, or hear any engines running. Nor were there any personnel walking about. Even his Harrier jet had been spirited away, towed into a nearby auxiliary hangar shortly after he had landed.

"We just have to assume they have spies everywhere," Jones told him. "Any major activity at this base, or the smaller ones we've set up down the coast, would tip them that we know they're coming soon. So everything, everywhere is under a blackout."

"Plus we've got the Football City Rangers out on perimeter patrol," Fitz added. "If there is anyone out there, they'll take them out, quickly and quietly."

They reached the hangar and slipped inside. The place was illuminated only by dim red-tinted bulbs, ones that cast no shadows.

Hunter instantly took note of the dozen A-10's stored inside the aircraft barn. The squat but powerful Thunderbolts were painted in the light gray-and-blue camouflage scheme more appropriate in the overcast skies of Europe than sun-drenched Florida.

Beyond the line of A-10's there was a row of A-4 Skyhawks, the well-respected, tough little fighter bomber of the Vietnam era. Farther down the line were a half dozen A-7 Strikefighters, another rugged attack aircraft of Navy origin. There were also three F-4 Phantoms sitting in the rear of the hangar.

"We've been able to muster three squadrons in all," Jones told Hunter. "Fifty-four aircraft, total. Most are scattered down the coast. These airplanes here will be responsible for our northern flank up here in the Jacksonville area."

Walking beyond the line of attack planes, Hunter noticed more than a dozen large stacks covered in black canvas tarp.

"Here's a good example of what we'll be dropping on our friends," Fitz said.

He removed the first tarp to reveal a neatly stacked pile of Mk-20 Rockeye cluster bombs.

Hunter felt an involuntary shiver run through him; he knew what a cluster bomb could do. When a cluster bomb—known as a CBU—exploded it sent out dozens of flaming pieces of high-speed shrapnel in every direction.

"The whole idea will be to hit these guys as soon as they come ashore," Jones explained. "Now from what we know about them, the Norsemen tend to stay together in clumps as they move toward their target. Drop one of these in the middle of one of their gangs and you'll shred the whole lot of them."

"And we've rigged up a system in which each airplane, whether its a Bolt, an A-7, or an A-4 can carry twelve CBU's apiece," Fitz added.

They moved to the next stack. Fitz removed its covering to reveal several dozen M116 AZ firebombs.

"Obviously napalm is tailor-made for this operation," Jones explained.

Hunter nodded grimly. The M116 was the granddaddy of all napalm bombs. It was 137 inches long and about 18 inches in diameter. Inside it contained no less than 110 gallons of the deadly gelatin gasoline. On impact, the fiery Jell-O would splash over three hundred feet or more, sticking to and burning anything it touched, from wood to metal to skin.

"We'll put these on the F-4's," Fitz said. "They're the best platform for the job."

Once uncovered, Hunter saw the third stack was made up of a grab-bag of weapons, including everything from AGM-65 Mavericks to Mk-82 general-purpose bombs.

"We'll hit them with this stuff once everything else is gone," Jones explained. "That is, if we need to . . ."

Farther down toward the end of the hangar, a crew of gun mechanics were preparing ammunition belts for the attack planes. The A-7 Strikefighters were fitted with M61 20mm cannon, as were the F-4's and the A-4's. It was the A-10 that carried the biggest gun in town, though. The 'Bolts lugged around the enormous GAU-8/A GE Gatling gun, by far the largest weapon of its type ever installed in an airplane of its type. It was the ammunition for this monster that the gun crews were preparing.

"We're loading them up with HE and incendiary mix shells," Fitz explained, picking up one of the GAU gun shells and handing it to Hunter. The cannon round was more than eleven inches long and weighed a hefty two pounds. Each A-10 would carry 1,350 of these rounds into the battle, each one fitted with an M505A3 impact fuse. The punch supplied by these rounds was more suited to ripping open tanks and armored vehicles. On the human body, they would be simply devastating.

Hunter shook his head soberly.

"It's going to be a wholesale slaughter," Fitz said, almost

to himself. "God, I thought we'd be beyond all this by now."

Jones nodded grimly. "I know these are horrible weapons," he said. "Especially against such an undisciplined opponent. But, let's face it, we can't get sentimental at this point. These guys have to be stopped — *cold.*"

Hunter suddenly flashed on a mental image of Dominique's lovely face and felt a familiar pang of dogged rage thump in his chest.

"My thoughts exactly," he replied quickly.

The three men then left the hangar, and Hunter was shown to his overnight quarters. With the crunch of activity aboard the *New Jersey* — especially the twenty-four hour period that he and Wolf did nothing but listen in on the Norsemen's pre-attack radio broadcasts — he hadn't slept a wink in the past three days. Though that was not unusual for him — he could stay up for many days on end once his adrenaline got pumping — Hunter knew that he had to get sleep eventually so he'd be on top of things once the bullets started flying.

But although the small overnight room located in the base's sick bay featured a comfortable bunk and a large fan to ward off the Florida heat, he couldn't go to sleep.

His head was filled with too many thoughts of the past few days. From the attack on Cape Cod, to the action off Montauk, to the battle on Slaughter Beach, to his contact with the USS *New Jersey.* All of it seemed so compressed in time and space it was almost like a dream.

Then he closed his eyes and once again saw the face of Dominique. With that pleasant antidote to soothe him, he quickly dropped off into a restful slumber.

It would be his last for a long time to come.

Chapter Forty-one

Aboard the Great Ship

Dominique was still groggy when the handmaidens awakened her.

Her throat was parched, her vision slightly blurry, and there was a low ringing in her ears—all side effects, she knew, of ingesting a large quantity of the *myx*. But there was also a pleasantly warm sensation still lingering between her upper thighs as well as around her nipples, and when she closed her eyes, it felt like her whole body was tingling with the last strains of excitement.

Grudgingly, she concluded that a hangover caused by the Norsemen's hallucinogenic liquor was not the worst thing to wake up to.

Although the female attendants could barely speak English, they made it quite plain that they intended on bathing and dressing Dominique very quickly. She was led to the already-filled tub in the room next to her palatial cabin, washed, dried, and anointed with perfumes, all in a matter of five minutes. Dressing in a functional, all-white jumpsuit took only another minute, as did the lacing up of what could only be described as designer combat boots.

Within fifteen minutes of waking, Dominique was standing in the Great Ship's control room, watching as Verden and his son Thorgils completed their morning prayer ritual.

"She is here," Thorgils whispered to his father, as the old man finished his meditation with a low, moaning wail.

The old man creased his wrinkled face and looked

Dominique up and down.

"Do you remember last night" he asked her, his voice deep and solemn beneath the thick Norwegian accent.

She simply nodded, the very thought of the strange, autoerotic episode sending another wave of pleasure throughout her sensory system.

Verden's eyes twinkled slightly, but then he lowered them and became deadly serious. "That was in preparation for the work you must do for me this day."

At that moment, Dominique noticed that a submarine had surfaced and was waiting near the bow of the Great Ship.

The sub wasn't anything like the kind the Norsemen used to carry their troops to battle. It was smaller, sleeker, and painted in shiny black with wild red designs that led up to the frighteningly realistic Migardsom monster head on its bow.

"You must go with Thorgils, and quickly," Verden told her, first pointing to his son and then to the nearby sub. "We are planning the biggest attack of this war and you must be present, or all may be lost . . ."

Dominique slowly shook her head.

"I do not understand," she said in a voice not much more than a whisper.

Verden looked up at her, all moisture gone now from his tired eyes.

"As my Valkyrie, you must observe my men in battle," he told her somberly. "You must see what I cannot. You must hear the sounds that will not reach my ears.

"You must tell me who will live and who will die."

Once again, Dominique shook her head. But before she could speak again, Verden held up his hand.

"I have spoken," he said with deep finality. It was important to him that Dominique leave the ship before Elizabeth realized it, for he was certain the witch would want to claim his beautiful Valkyrie for her own. "Go now with my son," he continued. "He will explain any questions you might have. That boat you see is the fastest one we have, but you must leave immediately so that you will be there when the battle commences."

With that, Verden made a sweep with his hand, and then closed his eyes and began to weep softly. Dominique was then gently nudged by two of Thorgils's personal bodyguards and led to the bow of the Great Ship. Within a few minutes, she was riding one of the accursed see-through life rafts over to the waiting sub, Thorgils and his two grim-faced bodyguards sharing the short, stomach-churning trip with her.

Climbing down inside the conning tower, Dominique quickly realized that this submarine was nothing like the Norse tubs she'd been in before.

"We must go at full speed all day to reach the battle area in time," Thorgils told the commander of the boat once they had reached the control room.

The sub's master quickly consulted a sophisticated TV radar read-out screen attached to the control-room wall. He lingered at it long enough for Dominique to determine that the sub was about two hundred miles off the coast of Florida. The man then checked the control room's clock which read 0700 hours.

"We should be on station with an hour to spare," the captain told Thorgils.

"I pray that we are," Thorgils replied. Then he turned back to Dominique and, taking her by the arm, led her away from the control room.

"Come with me," he told her roughly.

As they walked down the long corridor, Dominique could hear the sub's engines crack to life. Within seconds, she felt the familiar sensation of submerging and moving beneath the surface of the water. But unlike the other Viking subs she'd been on, this one seemed to move through the water like ice on glass. She correctly attributed this to the sub's sleek design, a shape more reminiscent of prewar vessels than the lumbering, monstrous Norse *Krig Bats*.

Everything inside the sub appeared to be high tech, from the steering and navigation equipment to the lighting and

265

vent systems. There was no reek of body odor on this boat. Even the crew members she saw looked high-tech. No scruffy beards or dirty uniforms for these men. Each one was smartly dressed in a neat black uniform, complete with heavy boots and a red beret.

Thorgils led her to the door of a small cabin at the end of the passageway and dismissing his bodyguards with a curt salute, he not too gently pushed her inside.

The room was luxurious compared to the cabins she'd been kept in aboard the larger Norse subs. This room featured a bed not a bed, a small galley, and a locker full of unmarked can goods.

"We have much to do," Thorgils told Dominique once they entered the room. "You must be prepared to carry out the wishes of my father."

Dominique sat on the edge of the bed, now showing none of the pleasing aftereffects of the *myx*. She felt tired, and caught herself trembling slightly. It was the uncertainty of what lay ahead that was causing the tremors. Although her experience aboard the Great Ship had been bizarre, at least she had felt a certain sense of security there. Now she was riding a warship right into what Verden claimed would be the biggest action so far by the Norsemen against the United Americans. And just what her role in the upcoming battle was supposed to be, she didn't have a clue.

Thorgils produced a well-worn notebook from his uniform pocket and opened it to page one.

"These are the instructions for a Valkyrie," he told her gruffly, obviously not relishing the task of explaining it all to her. "You must learn them, *memorize* them, before we reach the battle zone. . . ."

Dominique closed her eyes and tried to will her body to stop shaking. To suddenly let herself cave in to the strange events of the past week would be tantamount to giving up completely. She knew she had to regain some strength, no matter how she did it. Somehow she had to use the situation to her advantage.

She opened her eyes and for the first time noticed that

there was a flask of *myx* hanging from the back of the cabin door. Suddenly her body was revived, her mind flashing with options.

"Go ahead," she told Thorgils, undoing the top few buttons of her tight-fitting jumpsuit. "If the Verden wishes it, then I am suddenly very anxious to learn . . ."

Part Three

Chapter Forty-two

Aboard the USS New Jersey

Wolf stared into the large green eye of the SLNQ-55 surface radar and, for a moment, couldn't believe his eyes.

Just seconds before, the screen had been blank, the only indications bouncing back to the sophisticated radar set being a handful of small weather systems creeping up the North Carolina coast and the occasional flight of seabirds.

But now the long-range radar screen had come alive with blips.

Wolf checked his watch and then made an entry into his ship's log: "Enemy has shown himself at 1630 hours." He shook his head in amazement. Hunter had predicted that the Norsemen would begin surfacing right at this time.

The masked man made a quick check of his present position — fifteen miles off the coast of Fernandina Beach, Florida, and cruising due south — and then punched a brightly red-lit button next to the radar console.

Within seconds, the battleship's insides were ringing with the sound of an ear-piecing klaxon, calling the crew to their battle stations.

Wolf turned his attention back to the radar screen, and as one of his junior officers read from the long list of directions left by Hunter, he fiddled with the SLNQ's various buttons and knobs, finally refining the screen's contrast and focus to peak levels.

"Enter this into the log," he told another officer. "Five groups of subs evident on surface radar at 1645. Position is forty miles south-southwest of our location. Enemy surfacing in packs of three apiece."

The junior officer wrote as fast as he could.

"Three more enemy groups evident now," Wolf continued, never taking his eyes from the screen. "All enemy ships are heading due west. Time is 1646 . . ."

Wolf's gunnery master rumbled into the room, called there by the battle station alert.

"Your orders, sir?" the officer, a Scotsman, asked from beneath a snap salute.

"Prepare all guns," Wolf told him after a moment of thought. "High-impact HE shells, long trajectory powder for the sixteen-inchers. Standard draw for the five-inchers."

The Scotsman snapped another salute and was gone to be replaced by the ship's defensive systems officer.

"Program all surface defensive systems to automatic, with a slave command to manual," Wolf told this man, reading from another set of instructions Hunter had left behind. "Switch on all auxiliary generators for the Phalanx guns and make sure that the magazine is sealed tight."

This officer also quickly saluted and left. Next in line was the ship's intelligence officer, a former Norwegian lieutenant commander named Bjordson, the same man who captained the ship's undercover fishing boat.

Wolf quickly motioned Bjordson to the radar screen.

"There they are," he said, pointing to the staticky white clusters of blips that were now covering the lower left-hand corner of the large screen. "They are coming up in packs."

"Surfacing in full battle formations," Bjordson said, nodding. He had seen the tactic used many times before by the Soviet Navy, yet never on this grand a scale. "They will attack within the hour . . ."

"We should radio the Americans," Wolf said, pushing a button and summoning the control room's communications officer.

"Transmit the last two pages of the log to the American AWAC's," Wolf said quickly as soon as the radio officer arrived. "Top code. Double scramble, reply will be the pass phrase of the hour."

Another button was pushed and the ship's meteorologist appeared.

"What is the exact time of sunset on the Florida coast?" Wolf asked.

The man didn't miss a beat. "Eighteen hundred hours, fourteen minutes, sir."

Bjordson checked his watch. "Assuming that the attack plan is to hit the beaches simultaneously, that will give them about an hour to disembark all their troops," he said.

"That's the time window we have to hit them," Wolf said, nodding grimly. "Once it gets dark, the job will be harder by five times . . ."

"Ten . . ." Bjordson replied.

Wolf turned to the navigation officer who was but five feet to his right.

"How long until we reach our station?" Wolf wanted to know.

"Twenty-three minutes," the officer responded instantly.

Wolf looked back at the SNLQ and pushed a full bank of buttons. The screen suddenly expanded its view, utilizing a grid map that included most of the eastern shore of North Florida. The cluster of enemy subs heading toward that coast was now reduced to a single white dot.

Wolf checked with the officer in charge of reading the SNLQ's directions and then entered a barrage of numbers into the radar's keyboard. Soon enough he had conjured up another white blip, this one blinking every second and indicating the battleship's approximate position twenty-three minutes from then.

"If we hold true, we can cross their sterns just as they are offloading troops," Wolf said, moving his projected course-indicator cursor as if he was crossing the top of a gigantic letter T. "In our sector alone that could be as many as thirty boats . . ."

"Even when they spot us, there'll be little that they can do," Bjordson said. "They can submerge and thereby drown many of their troops or they can stay on top and wait for us to hit them with a barrage."

"A 'turkey shoot' is what the Americans call it," Wolf said somberly. "With us behind them and the American aircraft bombing them on the beaches, it will be a massacre, at least in our sector . . ."

Bjordson just shrugged. Like many of the Norwegian sailors on board, he had no idea whether the Norse fleet included any relatives. There would be no way to know such a thing. Besides, it was useless to worry about it. They were mercenaries. Their job was to kill a particular enemy. This one happened to be, for the most part, Norwegian.

Still, Bjordson could not help but feel a twinge of remorse for his courageous but woefully unsophisticated and highly predictable enemy. As an intelligence man, he knew the Norsemen's mind, and massing for a gigantic attack on Florida made sense. In the past, their brutal, plow-straight-ahead tactics had borne results. So why not try it on a larger scale? Casualty estimates among the Norse soldiers were of no consequence. It made no difference how many of them died—they were soldiers, and therefore to the Norse way of thinking, it was their job to die. It was the results of their deaths that made the difference between victory and defeat.

And Bjordson knew the Norse felt the odds were in their favor. To them it was a simple matter of the numbers: naively relying on their recent smaller attacks on Cape Cod and the mid-Atlantic states, the clan leaders undoubtedly believed that some of their troops would be killed as soon as they reached the shore. But others would not. Some of those units meeting resistance once they moved off the beaches would certainly be battered and destroyed. Yet others would not. Many would invariably sweep past any defenders and advance on the target, and a percentage of these troops would be killed at the target or withdrawing from it. But not all would be. Many would make it back to the beaches to be picked up by the surviving subs, and if past experience was the guide, then that number would be substantial.

Thus, to the clan leaders, the plan virtually ensured that many units would be successful and that tons of loot would be had in return for the operation.

But Bjordson also knew that the anarchic warriors were not taking into account was the possibility that an accumulation of high-technology weapons — as in the United American ground attack squadrons as well as the *New Jersey*'s gigantic guns — were waiting to pounce on them once the attack commenced. It hadn't happened before, so why should it happen now? would be their line of thinking. And if it did, then so what? Wars weren't supposed to be a way of life. They were for dying in.

"Reply code received from American station," the communications officer yelled out. "We now have an open line to the AWAC's aircraft."

"On station in seventeen minutes," the navigation officer told Wolf, anticipating his next question.

"Guns secured" came the radio report from the ship's weaponry officer.

"Defensive systems on automatic lock" came the defensive officer's report. "Will switch to manual on your command."

Wolf finally took his eyes away from the green screen and looked up at Bjordson.

"We'll be in engaging within the half hour," the captain told the intelligence officer. "Better launch the RPV . . ."

Chapter Forty-three

Hunter's entire psyche was vibrating by the time the Harrier lifted off from the Jacksonville Naval Air station.

The adrenaline was pumping through his body like some kind of painkilling drug. His heart was pounding and his brain was locked into its astonishingly computerlike mode.

It was at times like these—the minutes before battle—that Hunter was able to shift his total being into a higher gear.

Movement, thinking, even breathing became simple parts of the whole. The souped-up jumpjet was airborne and streaking eastward, Hunter did not so much steer the airplane as he did merge with it. His thought waves combined with the commands of his on-board computer. The triggers for his gun and weapon-launch systems became mere extensions of his fingers. The unique, variable-thrust engine thumped excitedly in beat with his heart.

He took a long deep gulp of pure oxygen from his mask and closed his eyes just for a moment. The vibrations were now in sync. Heart, mind, soul, and machine were lined up and locked in. He was ready to take on the enemy.

The true revenge for what these Norsemen had done to him—and his peaceful life with Dominique—was about to begin.

He was over the coastline within thirty seconds of take-off.

Already he could see a trio of Norse attack subs, their white hulls turned dull orange in the setting sun, sitting about a mile offshore from Jacksonville Beach disgorging the first wave of troops. A half mile to the south, another trio of subs were doing the same thing, as were another three subs a half mile beyond them.

That the Norse considered this attack as their biggest and most elaborate was apparent right away. Instead of their usual see-through rubber boats, the enemy troops were coming ashore on old-style landing craft—not too far removed from the LCB's and LST's used more than a half century before on the beaches of Normandy. Several other big subs, undoubtably *Volk Bats,* were surfaced about a quarter mile beyond the troopships, and it was they who were providing the landing crafts from their enormous storage hulls.

Hunter brought the Harrier up forty-five hundred feet and throttled back. Even with all his preparation for this moment—both physical and spiritual—he was still amazed at what he saw. The line of Norse subs—war boats and supply vessels—stretched in both directions for as far as the eye could see.

Hunter had seen the estimates of enemy sub strength—there was thought to be about sixty to seventy of the *Krig Bats* troop boats in the Atlantic, and just as many of the supply subs. But nothing could have prepared him for this sight of almost two hundred of the gigantic lumbering submarines, lined up perfectly in groups of two's and three's stretching across the horizon like so many orange keys on a piano.

Each sub was off-loading troops into the landing crafts provided by the nearby *Volk Bats.* Once a landing craft was filled, it would turn right for shore and head at breakneck speed for the white sands of either Atlantic, Neptune or Jacksonville beaches. The scene looked like something out of the original D-Day. Hundreds of white streaks of churned-up foam were left in the path of each landing craft. The difference was the enemy was landing without the benefit of any covering fire.

Hunter's radio was crackling with reports of similar scenes farther down the coast at Vilano Beach, St. Augustine, Summer Haven, even off of Marineland. Within just a few minutes it became very evident that, as anticipated, a good portion of the East Coast of Florida was under attack.

Hunter turned the Harrier due south and went down to twenty-five hundred feet. It felt strange for him to overfly such a large number of the enemy without having to worry about AA guns or SAMs. But the Norsemen had none. Their POW's from Montauk had readily admitted it, and the search of Norse battlefield dead so far had proved them correct.

In fact, with the exception of some antitank type rocket launchers and World War II-style flamethrowers, the Norsemen relied only on their assault rifles and their battleaxes. And their numbers and brute strength.

By quickly estimating the number of subs that stretched before him, Hunter calculated that there were as many as forty thousand enemy soldiers about to hit the beach, and that was just in the northeast sector alone. Against them, the United Americans had nearly seventy aircraft — fifty of them being attack planes, the rest providing recon and communications support — three regiments of Florida militia, and a battalion of Football City Special Forces Rangers. Plus the USS *New Jersey.*

In terms of manpower, the Norse had the UA defenders outnumbered by more than four to one. But it was the technology — the guns, the missiles, and the airplanes — that promised to give the Americans the edge.

Still, someone once said that there is quality in sheer quantity, and this is what ran through Hunter's mind as he screamed over the enemy invasion forces.

And at that moment, the brutal Norsemen seemed like a very formidable foe indeed.

Once he had reached a point just twenty miles north of Daytona Beach, Hunter put the jumpjet into a sharp hundred-and-eighty-degree turn and headed back up north.

The plan was to let the enemy invasion forces reach the tideline and then strike at them—a strategy borne of necessity and experience. For no matter how good the various UA attack pilots were at their jobs, it was always much easier to hit a target that was on terra firma than one that was bobbing up and down in the water.

Now, as Hunter returned to his original position over Jacksonville, he saw that the first wave of Norse landing crafts was just five hundred yards off the beach. With grim anticipation, he reached down and armed all his weapons.

A pair of cluster-bomb-laden A-7 Strikefighters and a fierce-looking A-4 Skyhawk appeared right on time, and after a few seconds of maneuvering, Hunter had joined them in a finger-four formation. A quick glance once again to his south told him that other jet units were also just now arriving over the invasion beaches and that they, too, were jockeying up into their preattack formations.

High above, a Boeing E-3 AWAC's plane orbited the north beach sector, monitoring enemy communications and relaying information back and forth between the attack pilots, the ground forces, the *New Jersey,* and Jones's command staff back at Jacksonville Naval Air Station. Hunter's crash helmet headphones played him a veritable symphony of voices reciting call signs positions, speeds and altitude, all backed up by a low undertone of static.

The voices of war, he thought somberly.

He reached up to his breast pocket and gave it the first of three taps for luck. Inside, a small American flag he had carried for years was wrapped around his most precious possession, a faded, dog-eared, but nevertheless startlingly beautiful photograph of Dominique.

He tapped the pocket a second time.

He had tried—and failed—to avoid thinking about the upcoming hostilities in any other terms but personal. He had learned years ago that the secret of going to war was to become completely objective. Pull the trigger and drop the bombs in the most impersonal state of mind one could rally. This way combat performance was not affected by inner feelings or conceits. All of that kind of mind clutter had to be dealt with before one strapped on the flight helmet.

But Hunter was different, and so were these circumstances.

A familiar fire of anger and rage was growling in his stomach. The Norsemen had attacked his country and taken Dominique from him. He was now in a position to make them pay for both of the equally heinous crimes.

He tapped his pocket a third time — it couldn't get any more personal than that.

On a given signal, his flight split up into two pairs. Hunter was coupled with the A-7 being flown by a Texan named Zak Carson. They would go in first. Lining up to the right of Carson's wing, Hunter rechecked his weapons systems. His wings were nearly drooping with cluster bombs and his Aden gunpods were filled to the max with the heavy-caliber cannon shells. It was a heavy load for the relatively small Harrier, but one push of a button told him that everything was still green.

On another given signal, Hunter and Carson broke off cleanly and banked hard to the left. The maneuver lined them up perfectly with the long stretch of white beach below them.

Their timing couldn't have been better. The first wave of Norse landing crafts were just reaching the wave line, and a few hardy souls had already struggled down the landing ramp and into the shallow, wave-tossed surf.

"Good luck, Hawk," Carson called over to him.

"Ditto," Hunter radioed back.

With that, they both went into a shallow dive, quickly leveling off at no more than a hundred fifty feet.

Hunter took another deep gulp of oxygen and then pulled his gun trigger.

A Norse soldier named Olaf Deiterstrom was the first man of the invasion force to step foot on Jacksonville

280

Beach.

The lead soldier in one of the first Norse landing crafts to be launched, Deiterstrom had been literally tossed ashore when his vessel's door flipped open too soon, causing him to fall out of the boat and into the shallow surf. His clothes soaking wet, his helmet and rifle covered with sand, his blood running rich with *myx,* Deiterstrom nevertheless picked himself up and screaming at the top of his lungs, ran out of the water toward the gray stone wall that served as the beach's breakwater a hundred yards away.

Other landing crafts were hitting the beach at this moment, but Deiterstrom was near-delirious at the thought that among all the members of his clan, the Helgis, he was the first one ashore. It was things like this that pleased his clan chieftain to no end, and no doubt, word would get back to the clan elder about how valiant his servant Deiterstrom had been.

Thus, Deiterstrom knew that even if he were killed at any moment, his place in Valhalla, the heaven of the Norse heroes, was secured.

By the time Deiterstrom reached the beach wall, hundreds of Helgi Norsemen were scrambling off landing crafts and running up from the surf. His reputation as a hero already assured, Deiterstrom decided to pause at the breakwater and wait for the rest of his clan to catch up.

Turning back toward the shoreline, he heard the rising cacophony of sounds that always erupted in the first few minutes of a Norse invasion: the relentless pounding surf; the blood-chilling screams of the Norseman as they ran up from the water; the remarkable tremors running through the sand as thousands of men scrambled for secure footing; the haunting cry of the bugles.

There was also the crackling of gunfire. Many of the Norsemen were firing their rifles, mostly in the air, even though the landing so far had been completely unopposed.

But that was about to change.

Deiterstrom was hastily shaking the sand off his AK-47 assault rifle when he heard a new sound above the racket of hard feet on wet sand, above the rifle shots, above the screaming and the baying of horns. This sound was more frightening than all of these combined. It was a noise that would shake the great Odin himself.

Squinting his eyes to help him see in the fading sunlight, he saw two glints of silver swooping down out of the sky about a mile north of his position. The two objects rapidly became larger and louder, and quickly enough Deiterstrom determined that these were enemy aircraft.

His eyes glued to the fast-approaching jets, it appeared as if their noses were suddenly engulfed in fire. A half second later he saw a long string of small explosions erupt amongst the screaming, running Helgis. Deiterstrom was shocked; the long tongues of flame from the aircraft were ripping into the swarms of charging Norsemen no more than ten feet away from him. Suddenly the air was filled with pieces of bone, guts, blood, and other splattering fluids. Dozens of his clan were literally being blown apart right in front of his eyes.

"This was not supposed to happen!" Deiterstrom cried out as the two jets streaked by.

One mile down the beach, Herman Keasiceau also heard the jets approaching.

Keasiceau was a rarity in the invading army. He wasn't a Norseman at all; he was a full-blood Romanian. Once a captain in the hated Romania Security Forces, Keasiceau was now a middle-aged mercenary, one of the few "outsiders" hired by the Norse for the American adventure. His specialty was antitank rockets, specifically how to load them, fuse them and fire them, complicated procedures well beyond the intelligence level of the majority of Norsemen.

Keasiceau had taken part in both the massacre in Nova Scotia and the attack on the Boston fuel tank farm. During a raid against Charleston, South Carolina, Keasiceau had fired three Milan antitank rockets into a church where hundreds of panic-stricken civilians had taken refuge, instantly turning the all-wood structure into an inferno. He was certain that no one survived.

Now Keasiceau was struggling with several Norsemen to drag their bulky rocket-launching equipment up onto the beach.

Suddenly it seemed as if the dusk sky was exploding with thunder.

Looking to the north, Keasiceau immediately saw the two jets raking the beach with murderous cannon fire. There was no time to think; no time to take cover. In less than a second, the pair of planes flashed by him, leaving a trail of small violent explosions and dozens of squirming, mutilated bodies in their path.

Instantly Keasiceau's body started shaking. The strafing fire had come very close to killing him—as it was, several men were completely cut in half no more than six feet in front of him. All along, the Norse clan leaders had assured their troops that the Americans would have no air support to speak of during this huge operation. Yet now Keasiceau not only could see another pair of jets bearing down on the invasion beach, he also saw that there were many jets crisscrossing high above the beach. In fact, to his terrified brain it appeared as if the entire sky was suddenly filled with enemy airplanes.

At that moment, he realized that the sardine-eaters had fucked up royally. With not a single antiaircraft weapon at their disposal, the Norsemen were like ducks before cannons. Suddenly he wished he was back in his dirty, damp Bucharest apartment.

He stood helpless, frozen to the spot, as the second pair of jets bore down on him. There was no honor in getting killed for him; he didn't believe a whit about the Viking gods and myths and all that dying-brave-will-get-you-to-heaven bullshit. Yet he didn't have time to dive for cover or jump back into the water.

So he grabbed one of the Norsemen and pulled him around as a shield against the approaching wave of cannon fire. They struggled briefly as the startled man realized what Keasiceau was doing. But in another second a string of shells ripped up one side of the startled Norseman's body, their impact being so great that they knocked Keasiceau off his feet and into the shallow water, his hands still gripping the Norseman.

The two jets were gone in a flash, continuing their brutally effective strafing run down the beach. Though he was covered with blood and bits of bone, Keasiceau let out a quick breath, confident that he survived the barrage. With not much effort, the mercenary managed to lift the torn-apart body of the Norseman off him, rolling the corpse into a retreating wave.

"Sucker . . ." Keasiceau murmured as he watched the hapless human shield drift away. All around him were shot up Norsemen, some painfully dying, others instantly dead.

"You're all suckers . . ." Keasiceau thought aloud.

Still laid out on his back, Keasiceau attempted to wash the dead man's blood from his own chest and abdomen. Suddenly he felt a sharp pain in his midsection. Looking down, he was horrified to see a spurt of blood gush from his stomach. *His* blood.

Panic-stricken, he started splashing salt water onto the wound, but this only served to increase his rapidly developing pain tenfold. Reaching down to the area near his belly button, he attempted to stop the flow of blood, but instead he felt a sharp object sticking into his gut just below his ribs.

With one last dying yank, he was able to pull out the object that had fatally torn apart his stomach and lower intestine.

It was the dead Norseman's knife.

Chapter Forty-four

Hunter yanked back on the controls of the Harrier and banked out over the water.

He and Carson had just expended close to their limit of ammunition during the miles-long, nonstop strafing run. Now they were turning back around to fly over the invasion beach once again, this time to drop their cluster bombs.

In the grim task of planning what ordnance to use first, it had been decided that in the initial beach run, cannon fire would inflict the most casualties just when the Norsemen were alighting from their landing craft. Only when they had all landed, and were more or less established on the beach, would the CBU's be dropped to their greatest effectiveness.

Now, as Hunter and Carson completed their long, wide-out loop and once again bore down on the invaders, both pilots could see the destruction that they and the following pair of attack jets had wrought. The beach was literally covered with bodies and the water closest to the shore stained with blood.

Hunter felt like a hammer had hit him in the stomach. Like the majority of professional warriors, he took no pleasure in killing. He had never fired a gun or unleashed a weapon unless it was for good purpose — self-defense or the self-defense of friends and country. And this, he kept telling himself, was no different.

Yet never before had he gone up against such an ill-prepared enemy.

So it was with reluctant quickness that he lined up the

nose of the Harrier with the center of the beach and fingered the jumpjet's weapons-control panel. Up ahead, just a mile away, his extraordinary eyesight spotted a large group of Norsemen that for some reason were clumped together out in the open. Within the span of three quick seconds, Hunter lowered his altitude a hundred twenty-five feet, adjusted his speed to four hundred knots, and put two of his CBU's into predrop mode.

Five seconds and a deep gulp of oxygen later, he pulled the weapons-release lever and felt the corresponding jerk in his wings as two cluster bombs detached from their weapons points and fell toward the beach.

The man in charge of the group of Norsemen gathered in the middle of the beach was named Bven Piki.

A distant cousin to the great Verden himself, Piki was one of the highest-ranking clan members of the surviving Finnbogi clan to go ashore during the invasion. Known for his absolute love of battle and bloodletting, Piki also fancied himself as a divinely inspired battle tactician; a self-infatuation that would prove him fatal, as it turned out.

Piki's landing craft had just made it to shore when the four jet airplanes streaked by, strafing the beach and slaughtering the vanguard of the Norse troops. As the four airplanes banked out over the sea for a second run, a brilliant idea popped into Piki's mind. Urging his men to follow him up to the center of the beach itself, he ordered them to bunch together and stand between one of the pair of black scars that had been left behind by the strafing jets.

Piki's reasoning, altered immeasurably by his consumption of two flasks of *myx* during the trip to shore, was along the lines of lightning never striking the same spot twice. With not enough time to make it to the beach wall or back to the waterline, Piki believed that if he and his men stood where the enemy airplanes had already strafed, they'd be safe.

With no perception of what to do should enemy aircraft

attack them, Piki's men simply followed his orders like sheep. More than one hundred and fifty of them in all, they immediately linked arms and stood together, defiantly growling and yelling as the two enemy planes roared in on them.

The two CBU's exploded fifteen feet directly above the middle of this group, the oddly shaped black bombs arriving so quickly that few of the Finnbogis even saw them fall from the Harrier's wings. It was the CBU's function to blow down, raining a blizzard of fiery, white-hot, high-speed metal on anyone unlucky enough to be caught below. Victims were not so much blown away as they were shredded to pieces.

For Piki's group of hapless Norsemen, death had been instantaneous.

Twenty-five miles to the south of Jacksonville, Mike Fitzgerald was leading a flight of four A-4 Skyhawks over a section of the coastline known as Vilano Banks.

Unlike the smooth white beaches of the Floridian shoreline to the north and south, Vilano Banks was rocky and craggy with coral. It met the Atlantic Ocean with a series of defiant jetties and reefs. The rough terrain had not deterred the Norsemen from landing there, however. Just a few miles inland at a place called Boskins River, there was a string of shopping malls and apartment complexes. Both were favorite targets for the rampaging invaders.

While a modern strategist would have dismissed Vilano Banks as a landing spot in his first breath, plotting instead to land at a more convenient place and approach the target from there, to the Norse way of thinking, it was illogical *not* to land troops on the small rocky beaches and coral reefs. After all, the target was close by. All their troops would have to do was paddle their way safely around the razor-sharp, poisonous coral reef shallows, negotiate the hazardous shoreline territory once they came ashore, scale the medium-sized cliffs, *then* march three and three-quarter miles to the target—all during in the fading light of dusk.

But while the cracked and jutting coastline of Vilano Banks presented a challenge to the Norsemen, it actually provided a grim opportunity for Mike Fitzgerald's flight of Skyhawks. Smooth terrains such as beaches were made for cluster bombs, the wide, unobstructed spaces allowing the thousands of shards of deadly burning metal to disperse in the most effective killing pattern. Conversely, rough, irregular landscapes like Vilano Banks were gruesomely perfect for another, some said, more terrifying weapon.

That weapon was napalm.

Fitzgerald shot ahead of the other three planes in his flight and brought his Skyhawk down to a heart-stopping altitude of fifty feet. Below him, the rocks and shallow pools of Vilano Banks were crawling with Norsemen, each one struggling to get ahead of the other, to make it to the bottom of the dirty green cliffs, to scale the damn things and get on to the target.

Turning the Skyhawk slightly on its left wing, Fitzgerald tried to estimate the number of enemy troops landing at Vilano, but the sheer volume of invaders, plus the waning light, made even an approximate count impossible. For his part, he guessed more than two thousand raiders had already landed, with dozens of additional landing crafts streaming toward the shore along a two-mile stretch.

His quick reconnaissance completed, Fitzgerald pulled up and to the right, quickly rejoining the other three A-4's.

"Safeties off," he called into his helmet microphone.

Three rapid fire acknowledgments burst through his headphones.

"On my lead," Fitzgerald continued. "Going in at a hundred above mean. Pull out to the left. Watch the cliffs . . ."

With enviable precision, the four A-4s broke up into a single line and turned back over Vilano Banks. Fitzgerald went in first, swooping low past the shore's highest peak and unleashing two ghastly-looking all-black napalm cannisters. The bombs hit in a one-two pattern right at the base of the cliff, splattering a blue-orange wash of flaming gasoline jelly over dozens of Norsemen who had just now decided to run for cover.

Fitzgerald's wingman came in next, virtually duplicating his flight leader's pattern and depositing two napalm cannisters about fifty feet from the base of the cliff and covering a natural jetty where men Norsemen had sought cover.

Skyhawks #3 and #4 came in seconds later, dropping their deadly payloads and pulling up quickly to avoid flying into the huge black smoke clouds left over from Fitzgerald and his wingman's bombings.

By the time #4 had cleared the area, Fitzgerald was back again, dropping two more fiery bombs right on a clustering of enemy landing craft. His wingman did the same thing, while the other pair of A-4's concentrated on those Norsemen who were still wading through the reef shallows.

On and on it went, the four Skyhawks methodically incinerating the Norsemen trapped now in the flaming hell of Vilano Banks. When their bombs were expended, the pilots strafed the blazing beaches and the cliffsides. But after a few passes, Fitzgerald knew that further violence would not be necessary. Vilano Banks was now two miles of blazing, smoking holocaust that was generating so much heat, it was actually affecting the air currents over the target. No one anywhere within a half mile of the inferno would live to tell about it.

So with two curt orders, Fitzgerald called his men off and told them to return to base to rearm. Then he dipped his wing and flew over the fires once again, catching an unwanted glimpse of the hundreds of burning bodies below him. "This is not war," he whispered to himself bitterly.

Chapter Forty-five

Aboard the USS New Jersey

Wolf adjusted his binoculars to his masked face, dialed the lenses to their greatest power, and trained them on the southern horizon.

The first thing he saw was smoke, a long, thin column of ashen gray rising above the waterline just where it met the shore. Squinting as best he could, he was able to make out a tongue of flame in the midst of the soot. Then he saw several puffs of red fire appear in quick succession along the horizon. Then he saw more smoke — thick columns of it now, some black, some gray, most dirty white. Then more flames, more explosions.

"All ahead, three-quarter speed," he said calmly into his helmet's microphone. "Battle station roll off now . . ."

For the next minute he heard the crisp, reassuring replies of his officers as they quickly reported that every member of the crew was in the proper battle station and ready.

"What's our exact position?" he asked his navigation officer, who was standing right next to him.

The NO glanced down at a small TV screen on the panel in front of him.

"Six miles off shore, twelve miles north of Jacksonville Beach," he replied. "Speed is up to twenty-two knots . . ."

Wolf checked his watch and did some quick calculations.

"That would give us an ETA in battle area in about sixteen minutes, wouldn't you say?"

The NO did some quick figuring of his own and nodded.

"Not much more than that, sir," he replied.

Wolf handed the binoculars to his executive officer.

"The bridge is all yours," he told the man, readjusting his mask and putting on his battle helmet.

Wolf was out of the bridge like a shot, moving quickly down the passageway and into the Combat Information Center. The room that had been practically closed and shuttered before Hunter's visit to the *New Jersey* was now alive and bustling with technicians, all of them still learning the vast array of weapons and navigation systems in the CIC.

Wolf immediately walked over to the room's largest, most elaborate TV screen.

"The RPV is approaching its first coordinate now, sir," one of the three techs sitting before the screen said.

"Punch it up . . ."

A frenzy of button-pushing ensued, and within ten seconds the big TV was illuminated with a crisp picture being transmitted by the RPV's video camera of the Jacksonville shoreline.

Even in black and white, the absolute horror of what was happening on the beach was evident to everyone in the CIC. The sands of Jacksonville Beach were littered with thousands of dead and dying Norsemen. The foam of the waves was red with their blood. Landing craft were still arriving and invaders were still scrambling up onto the land, but the United American attack jets were bombing and strafing the shoreline at ten-second intervals.

Even from its slow, cruising vantage point some hundred yards off the shore itself, the RPV's telephoto TV lens was able to pick up the graphic effects of each cluster bomb hit and cannon run.

The results looked like an old black-and-white slasher movie.

The scene of the one-sided battle tightened the stomachs of those inside the *New Jersey*'s CIC, including Wolf. It seemed somewhat perverse that their job was to add to the carnage.

Wolf grabbed a microphone and called down to the ship's weapons' officer.

"Is gun turret number one ready?"

"Up and waiting" came the reply.

All the while, Wolf never took his eyes off the TV screen.

"Stand by . . ."

As the RPV slowly made its way down the beach, it found a group of six Norse landing craft that had, for whatever reason, lashed themselves together during the mad dash for the beach and were now just reaching the shore. Invaders were pouring out of the boats in six long lines.

Wolf spotted the enemy boats and pointed them out to the RPV's steering technician.

"There's our first target," Wolf said. "Put the bird into a tight pattern, one and fifty feet up."

The tech did as told, punching Wolf's instructions into the RPV's controlling computer. Within seconds, the TV screen jiggled as the RPV went into a tight orbit above the enemy boats.

"Mark it," Wolf said.

Another technician immediately pushed a series of buttons which automatically sent the targeting information being sent back from the RPV to the weapons officer in turret number one.

"Marked and locked," the technician replied once his computer told him the target info had been fed into the first turret's fire-control system.

"Put the bird up to three hundred feet," Wolf told the flight controller. "And give it a wide-out of two hundred and fifty . . ."

Several seconds went by before the man reported that the RPV was heading for the safer altitude and distance away.

Wolf did one last quick check of his main systems and then said: "Fire when ready."

The radio crackled back immediately. *"Fire!"*

Three seconds later a familiar tremor went through the *New Jersey*. From stem to stern, everything from coffee cups to computer terminals began to shake violently. The sound of three monstrous guns going off at once hit a split second later, a report so loud that even as each man routinely blocked his ears, it still sounded like a shotgun blast being fired a foot away.

The sound of the gun blast gave way to the screech of the twenty-two-hundred-pound shells as they rocketed away from the ship and toward the target. Every man in the CIC who could, kept his eyes on the big TV screen, watching and waiting as the three tons of high explosives raced toward the unsuspecting invaders.

The shells hit 11.5 seconds later.

It was a rare occasion for the men in the CIC, or anyone in the battleship's company for that matter, to see the results of their deadly barrages so immediately. It was normal procedure to have the RPV evacuate the area just as soon as the firing order was given. But in this case, that was not necessary. The RPV had climbed to a safe height out over the water and therefore was less apt to be hit by any flying debris.

Still the explosions resulting from the three 1.1 ton shells hitting simultaneously sent a shock wave through the air that caused the RPV to black out for a few seconds. The back shock reached the battleship several seconds after that.

"Looks like a good hit, sir . . ." the second weapons officer called out.

When the RPV's camera blinked back on, it confirmed the man's estimate with sickening accuracy.

The barrage had landed right on the lashed-together landing craft, instantly obliterating them. The resulting gigantic explosions had simply vaporized the dozens of Norsemen still on the boats while throwing those close by in every direction. The CIC crew watched with open jaws as dozens of bodies — or more accurately *pieces* of bodies — tumbled through the air in slow motion, caught within the deadly, ever-widening fire cloud.

The three rapid explosions also served to throw thousands of gallons of seawater up into the air, where it instantaneously mixed with fire and smoke and just as quickly turned to steam.

The resulting smoky fog temporarily blinded the RPV's camera, causing Wolf to tell the flight controller to direct the RPV out of the prevailing winds and over the target itself.

When the picture cleared several seconds later, the RPV had steadied itself at a point about five hundred feet above where the shells hit.

There was nothing left, of course. No more boats, or bodies or even remnants of bodies. All that was evident was a huge gaping crater which, at that moment, was being filled with rushing seawater. The only indication that a half minute before more than a hundred invaders had stood near the spot was the fact that this seawater was discolored in a shade of TV-video gray that everyone knew in color was actually bloodred.

Wolf took a deep breath and pulled the CIC microphone to his mouth. The RPV's camera was now picking up a trio of Norse subs still offloading troops about a mile of Neptune Beach, with a fourth sub launching landing craft nearby.

"Reload and prepare for next target," the masked man said in a voice just barely above a whisper.

The captain of the *New Jersey*'s fishing boat, Lieutenant Commander Bjordson, had seen the barrage of three massive shells hit the beach, and from his position about a mile and a quarter away, had witnessed and felt their devastating aftermath.

Now he watched as the RPV turned southeast and headed for a quartet of Norse subs about two miles away. Sensing an impending attack on the subs was just seconds away, he knew that even the wake from the violent sixteen-inch barrage could swamp his small vessel. He hit the throttles of the fishing boat and began to put some distance between himself and the three Norse subs.

His role on this fateful day was to act as a backup communications ship between the *New Jersey* and the United American forces on shore and in the air. The high-flying AWAC's planes were just about at peak load coordinating the air strikes along the two-hundred-mile front, and thus there was a need for a close-in support radio ship.

Therefore, ever since the fighting had begun, Bjordson had been plying the waters off the invasion coast, sending information on sub dispersement, enemy troop strengths, and target coordinates to the United American HQ at the Naval Air Station as well as back to the *New Jersey.*

His crew had also taken full advantage of the 20mm all-purpose deck gun mounted on the fishing boat's bow. They had found out very early that the Norse landing crafts carried no weaponry of their own, short of the rifles belonging to the individual troops. So, in between sending out intelligence broadcast, the fishing boat's crew had been firing on any landing craft in their vicinity, sinking several and damaging many others.

While the captain was understandably proud of his crew's accomplishments, the sinkings seemed hardly necessary with the ongoing slaughter up and down the coast. He, like many others fighting the Norse clans on that bloody late afternoon, just wanted to get the whole grisly business over with.

Bjordson yanked back on the throttles after he determined that he was a good two and a half miles away from the doomed Norse subs. Sure enough, ten seconds later, the first three shells from the *New Jersey*'s second battery landed in amongst the Norse *Krig Bats,* blowing one of the war boats right out of the water and cracking the other two like they were dried sticks of wood. The fourth sub, the *Volk Bats* that was carrying the LST's, was instantly swamped, the seawater pouring into its wide-open, vast storage chambers. It went down even quicker than the boats that had been closer to the blast.

The resulting shock wave hit the fishing boat, too, causing it to be tossed about violently in the suddenly swelled waves.

Bjordson had yelled a warning to his men just seconds before—as if they needed any—and all hands held tight as the quick, invisible storm blew over.

"Survived another one," Bjordson said to himself with a breath of relief.

But a moment later he heard an ear-piercing scream from one of his men.

Swinging around in the bridge he saw a huge, dark shape looming up on their portside.

"Christ . . . *no!*" he shouted involuntarily, leaping toward the boat's controls in a desperate attempt to turn away.

But it was too late. The enormous black-and-red *Fire Bat* submarine hit the fishing boat amidships, instantly splitting it in two.

It sunk inside of ten seconds, taking all on board down with it.

Chapter Forty-six

Hunter had just dropped his last pair of cluster bombs from his second reloading when the top of his spine began to tingle.

Deep within him, something was compelling him to change course—to steer the Harrier jumpjet not back to the Naval Air Station for reloading as planned, but out to sea, out beyond the smoke and fire rising from the hapless trio of Norse subs.

Out into the unknown.

Hunter knew better than to doubt this intuition. From the moment long ago when he had recognized his extrasensory perceptive gift, he had always gone with it.

But this particular vibration was different.

As he burst through the funnel of smoke and flames rising from the destroyed subs, *the feeling* was washing over him to the degree he'd never imagined. And although it seemed as if all of his warning-panel lights were blinking at once, he ignored them. What he was feeling could not be picked up on a radar screen or an infrared scope. It could not be detected by a heat-seeking sensor or a microwave beam.

Yet, it was all within and without him. Something way down deep was telling him to get ready . . .

He dipped the Harrier's wing to the east and pulled back on the throttle. Before him lay the depths of the mighty Atlantic and something—or *somebody*—down there was calling to him.

He closed his eyes and gripped the Harrier's control stick

tightly. The vibration from his brain and spine was now running down his arms to his hands to his fingertips and into the jet itself. Suddenly it was as if the airplane knew which way to go. Hunter waited—five seconds, ten seconds, fifteen. Then he took a deep gulp of oxygen and opened his eyes.

Below him was a submarine.

It was apparent right away that this boat was not like the submersible lugs the Norsemen traveled in. This vessel was as sleek and futuristic in design as the Norsemen's troop subs were bulky and cloddish. This submarine was smaller by a third in length and sleeker by a factor of five. It was painted shiny black with bright red highlights and featured an elaborate, bright design that ran right up to the Norse monster head on its bow.

On one hand, the sub's design was reminiscent of the old Soviet Alpha 1-class, with its contoured swept-back conning tower and overall bullet design. Yet Hunter could also see traces of the U.S. Navy's Lafayette class of subs, especially in the deck length and beam. The truth was that this sub could only be a hybrid, designed by taking bits and pieces from other subs and therefore allowing it to be mistaken for any number of submersibles.

But what was unmistakable were the two rows of hatches—four on each side—that were very prominent just aft of the conning tower. These, Hunter knew, were the coverings for missile-launch tubes.

It took less than a nano-second for Hunter to put it all together: he was staring down at one of the *Fire Bats*.

An instant later, the Harrier was shooting straight up in the air. With the gaggle of antennae and radio scopes poking out of the sub's conning tower, it was a good bet that there was air defense-sensing equipment on board capable of detecting him within a close radius.

Now his hands, still linked to the psychic tendons deep within, had rocketed the jumpjet up and away from the mysterious Norse submarine. Up through twenty-five hundred feet, through five thousand. Straight up—not like a bird, not like any other airplane.

Straight up, like a god ascending into the heavens.

He leveled off at ten thousand feet. From this height he could keep an eye on the sub while being relatively sure that they couldn't see him. It was steaming due north, and by evidence of the miles-long, very distinct white seafoam trail left by its wake, Hunter deduced correctly that the boat had just cruised right through the battle area.

He felt an involuntary shudder run through him at the thought of what several nuclear-armed ICBM's could have done during the one-sided battle. Yet the people inside the sleek sub had just borne strange witness to the virtual destruction of the huge Norse raiding army.

And they had done so without firing so much as a single shot.

Hunter's brain switched into overdrive at this realization. Wolf had been right after all. The whole Norse invasion of North America *had* been a smokescreen.

But if this was indeed true—that the Norse invaders' actions had been a cover for yet another, more insidious plot—then it opened up another big question: What were the real intentions of these modern Vikings?

Hunter checked his watch. It was 0710 hours and getting darker by the minute. Yet he found following the sub in the waning sunlight presented no problem. Flying a zig-zag northerly course and trailing the vessel from two miles up and a mile behind, he could still clearly see the long white almost luminescent wake of the *Fire Bats*. Even when it got dark, he knew that his look-down radar would still be able to follow the sub.

And if the damn thing decided to submerge, then he'd fall back on pure intuition to keep it in track.

For there was more than a professional curiosity about this submarine—that had been evident from the moment he spotted it. No, the crackling cauldron within his soul was bubbling for more reasons than just another attack-and-destroy mission. Something aboard the submarine was calling to him—like a siren, it was sending out a psychic message that only his extraordinary internal antenna could receive. But this time the message was not bouncing off his spirit and then going straight to his brain. This time, the vibrations were richocheting off his soul and racing straight to his heart.

And though the storm of psychic messages was complex and overlapping, he knew its presence could mean only one thing: Dominique was on that boat.

Chapter Forty-seven

Aboard the USS New Jersey

For the first time in more than an hour, Wolf was able to lean back and relax for a moment.

The frantic activity that had inundated the CIC for the past hour had now calmed down to a more civilized buzz. Cigarettes were being lit and slowly smoked. Tea and coffee were being passed around. Conversations were being punctuated by relieved breathing and an occasional congratulatory laugh.

And there was reason to celebrate: The *New Jersey* had just gone through its first real sea battle and it had performed flawlessly.

The whole story could be told on the CIC's multitude of TV screens. The surface radar monitor displayed little else besides the lifeless green blips of the dozens of crippled and sinking Norse subs. The below-surface sonar monitor was pinging madly off the dozens of hulks of Norse subs already sunk. The radio-intercept monitor, cued to pick up broadcasts from the Norse subs, was so quiet, it might as well have been turned off altogether. Unlike at the height of the battle, now there *were* no more enemy radio transmissions. There were no SOS's, no calls for help. The remaining Norse subs were dying silently, for most of them, their grand adventure ending in the pale-blue waters off the Florida coast.

But it was the large TV screen that told the biggest story. The RPV was still diligently sweeping back and forth above the Jacksonville coastline, documenting the aftermath of the disasterous invasion attempt. Every sector within the RPV's range looked the same: dozens of wrecked and burning landing craft, hundreds of dead Norse on the beaches and in the nearby surf, burned and sinking subs offshore. The RPV's TV transmission was stark proof that in the zone stretching from Jacksonville flats down to cliffs of Vilano Banks, no invader had made it off the beach.

Wolf finally accepted a cup of tea and spontaneously toasted those sitting around him. From the first shots fired against the Norse troops on the beach to the last barrage sent into the already-burning hulk of a Norse supply sub, the *New Jersey* had wreaked destruction on the hapless enemy that to some might have seemed inconceivable. The total was simply awesome: twenty-three Norse troop subs sunk, another twenty-five left afloat but burning, and six more probably sunk. The total of forty-four, three-gun sixteen-inch barrages fired with pinpoint accuracy at the troops on the beaches had undoubtedly killed literally thousands. This firepower, combined with the unopposed air strikes performed by the United American attack jets, had delivered an astounding defeat that rivaled few events in military history.

Still, after taking a few sips of his tea, Wolf could not shake the feeling that the victory was in certain aspects fairly hollow. As backward and loutish as the Norsemen were, they still had to be stopped. Yet much of the battle had seemed like little more than shooting fish in a barrel. Slaughtering unsophisticated if gallant soldiers did not sit well with a man like Wolf.

So when his executive officer turned and asked him almost nonchalantly: "What next, Skipper?" Wolf felt a chill run through him. Although he knew it wasn't the XO's intention, some part of Wolf's brain interpreted the remark to mean: "Who's our next victim?"

Wolf just stopped himself in time from lashing out at the man. Instead, he clenched his fists and gritted his teeth. He was the captain of the most powerful surface vessel left on the face of the earth, and at times, the job seemed like a nightmare.

"Call in Bjordson," Wolf said quietly. "Tell him to retrieve the RPV and head back. Have the crew go on half stations, except in turret number two. They'll be on alert until midnight when turret three takes over. Prepare the steam screen just in case we have to go undercover."

The XO immediately put down his coffee cup and stood at near attention. He knew by Wolf's tone that the skipper was still operating in the all-business mode.

"Is that all, sir?" he asked crisply.

"One more thing . . ." Wolf told him, nervously adjusting his mask. "Contact the Jacksonville air station. Advise them of our position and tell them we will be standing by for further communications."

The XO saluted smartly and quickly left the CIC. His departure signaled an unofficial end to the respite among those in the war room. Coffee cups were drained, and the chatter immediately died down. Technicians went back to their green screens and weapons officers to their control panels.

But still the XO's question rang in Wolf's ears: What next, Skipper? *What next?*

The answer came an instant later.

It was the air-defense radar technician who saw them first. Two blips, then three, then four, moving rapidly onto his long-range screen, coming in from due east.

"Skipper . . ." the tech called out, watching as three more blips suddenly popped onto the oval screen. "Look at this . . ."

By the time Wolf was staring into the bright green control panel, the number of blips had increased to nine. Within two seconds, four more appeared, and then four after that.

"What's their range and heading?" Wolf asked the man.

A quick check of his instruction manual and another glance at the screen provided the answer to the tech.

"Thirty-eight miles out," he said slowly, "and on their

present course, they'll pass seven miles to our south."

"That's too close," Wolf said under his breath. A second later he hit the ship's attack-warning buzzer.

The klaxon immediately started blaring, and the sounds of men running to their battle stations echoed through the ship again. Suddenly the CIC was bathed in tension once more. Techs rushed back to their screens, weapons officers began readying their guns and missiles systems.

"Could they be the Americans, sir?" the air-defense radar tech asked with a slight gulp.

Wolf shook his head slowly. "Something tells me no," he said grimly. "Those are basic attack formations."

Other sensors were now picking up the mysterious airborne force, warning via a cacophony of buzzers and electronic whistles that the approaching aircraft were not only carrying radar-guided weapons, but that their cockpit radars were locked onto "hot" attack modes.

Three seconds later, the XO was on the radio to Wolf. By that time the number of bogies had increased to twenty-four.

"We have an unknown airborne force bearing thirty-seven miles out and ten miles down," Wolf told the second in command. "Seal everything up, and *fast!*"

The aura of good feeling that had invaded the CIC after the cessation in fighting on the beaches now quickly drained away, to be replaced by an atmosphere of surprise and dread.

"Buck up the air-defense system . . ." Wolf called into another microphone, turning away from the radar screen for a moment. "Program to automatic, with immediate manual override."

When he looked back at the screen, he saw there were now no less than thirty-six blips.

"Is there anyway to ID these guys?" Wolf asked the radar officer, who valiantly reached for the long list of instructions left behind by Hunter.

The second radar man spoke up at this point. "I can tell by the signatures that they are not anything like the UA attack craft," the man said, his voice quavering with concern. "Besides coming in from the ocean, they are moving much too fast for A-7's or A-4's."

From across the room, the main radio officer called: "Jacksonville must have picked them up, too, Skipper. They are sending out an emergency F-O-F signal . . ."

Wolf felt his heart start beating an extra thump a second. The F-O-F signal—for Friend or Foe—was broadcast as a kind of last resort before an accidental—or sneak—attack.

By this time, the incoming force was only thirty-five miles away.

"SAM status," Wolf yelled out.

"All missiles ready, sir . . ."

"AAA guns?"

"Locked and ready, sir . . ."

"Weapons computers?"

"Main is on and ready, sir. Backups on stand-by."

Wolf punched another button. "Activate steam screen . . ."

"We've got a stray indication," the radar officer called out, drawing Wolf's attention back to the massive air-defense radar screen.

The captain followed the man's finger to the tiny, lone blip that had suddenly appeared between the oncoming airborne force and the Florida shoreline.

"Who the hell is that?"

The radar officer dialed the screen to a slightly clearer intensity.

"It seems to be hovering out there," he told Wolf. "It might be a helicopter . . ."

Wolf took a long look at the solitary blip that for all the world looked like an electronic David waiting for the flying army of Goliaths.

"That's no helicopter," he said grimly.

Chapter Forty-eight

On his worst day, Hunter had never imagined the scene that now played out before him.

Hovering at a point 32.6 miles out and 3,623 feet above the sea, Hunter watched with rising trepidation as the swarm of thirty-six black dots moved in and out of the heavy cloud break heading right at him. They were still too far away for normal visual identification—but Hunter did not have to see them to know what was coming.

Deep down inside, he knew this day would come. He just wished it hadn't come so soon.

Like a man about to face death, key segments of the last five years of Hunter's unusual life flashed before his eyes. Five years ago, when the New Order still ruled America and he was the continent's most hunted man, the difference between life and death had frequently been his aircraft, the beloved F-16. In those turbulent days when America had been fractured into dozens of small countries, kingdoms, and free states, and air pirates ruled the skies, Hunter's F-16 had been the hottest bird around—no arguments, no debate. When the civil wars against the Circle erupted, his F-16 held sway over the aerial battlefield, challenging any aircraft the enemy could launch. His subsequent record was a perfect 1.000. In the final battles for independence and in the action against the Panama-based Canal Nazis of the Twisted Cross, his airplane, now converted into the "cranked arrow" design of the ultrasophisticated F-16XL, was in the vanguard of the United American air forces.

Then his airplane was stolen—but not before he had been able to transfer just about one hundred percent of the F-16's avionics and weapons systems out of the fighter and into his present mode of transport, the souped-up AV-8BE Harrier jumpjet.

Even in the slower, less maneuverable if highly versatile AV-8, Hunter had established a kind of one-man rule of the skies over the barely united continent, the main deterrent to the rapidly dwindling number of air pirates being that they never knew where Hunter would be next. To them, he always seemed to be in just the right spot at just the precise time to foil their plans or just to pursue and shoot one or more of them down.

And while the United Americans and the allies boasted a number of hot fighters—notably the squadron of state-of-the-art F-20 Tigersharks employed by the Football City Defense Force—they said that even when Hunter's Harrier had sat idle in his barn back on Cape Cod, a case could be made that it was still the best plane around simply because of the man who owned it.

But myths are myths and legends are lies, and luckily Hunter knew the difference. If he was to accept the mantle of "best fighter pilot who ever lived," then he also could never forget the fact that he was the best because he flew the best.

But this, too, came down to a question of numbers.

It had been the first dictate of the now-destroyed hated New Order regime that the NATO forces destroy all of their military equipment, disarming completely in return for world peace. In the frenzy of technocide that followed, thousands of priceless fighter jets were destroyed, along with the vast majority of all of the US Armed Forces weapons materiel.

As far as he knew, Hunter's F-16 was the only one to escape.

But it was more than that. Not only F-16s had been destroyed per decree of the New Order. Other equally sophisticated, and in some cases, *superior* jet fighters had been demolished. Air Force F-15's. Navy and Marine F/A-18's. Navy F-14's. But Hunter had always believed—or he had tricked himself to believe—that *all* of these hotshit fighters had met the fanatical New Order axe, mainly because he hadn't seen any of them around in the ensuing five years. And with the American continental skies full of antique shitboxes like F-100 Super Sabres and F-101 Voodoos, and maybe an occasional dumptruck like an F-4 Phantom, it had been much easier for him to be labeled "the best."

But now, with his mouth going dry and his heart pounding through his flight suit, Hunter knew all that was about to change.

He recognized the formation right away. It was Navy through and through. Air superiority fighters out front and on the flanks, three rows of fighter/attack craft, a chevron of purely attack planes and missile luggers, and a guard of four air superiority fighters bringing up the rear. Thirty-six planes in all, one deployed air wing of a Navy supercarrier.

Actually, Hunter wasn't one to have nightmares. But in his worst bad dream, he confronted a mass of superlative fighters while he was flying an old biplane, armed with only a water pistol, and there wasn't even any ammo in that.

He felt thrust into the middle of that disturbing vision right now. For just twelve miles from him and a little over a mile above, he could clearly see eighteen F-14 Tomcats, nine F/A-18 Hornets and nine A-6 Intruders. All of them were fully armed. All of them were heading directly for him.

The Harrier was not carrying any air-to-air missiles. Its bomb racks had been packed with cluster bombs, and while Hunter was normally a cautious person to a fault, he had decided not to pack on board his usual compliment of two Sidewinder missiles for the attack on the Florida beaches. It had been a correct decision: the mission simply didn't call for air defense weapons.

308

But now he knew what his psyche had been telling him when it put him in the dream carrying a water pistol with no water.

The jumpjet was armed with an Aden gun pod, featuring two fearsome 30mm cannons. Trouble was, the ammunition he had loaded up on was high-explosive incendiary shells, great for busting tanks and fucking up landing craft, but not so great against other aircraft. Worse still, he was carrying only about a third of a full bag of ammo, the rest having been expended during the air strikes against the Norse.

But the cannons were all he had. And with a total of 114 shells remaining, he thought darkly that it could be a short fight.

But fight he knew he must. Before him was ten times as much sophisticated airpower than he had wanted to believe was still left in the world and they were obviously heading toward predetermined attack targets along the Florida coast. United American targets.

It was up to him to stop them. Or die trying.

As it turned out, he came upon an ally. Two Boeing E-3 AWAC's planes had been dispatched from Washington, DC, to Florida at first report of the impending Norse invasion. They had stayed in the air off the coast for two days, jimmy-rigging their tons of air-detection equipment to scan the oceans below, watching and waiting for the Norse subs to show up. When they did, the flying radio barns with the distinctive rotating radar dish attached to their tops, had served as the battle's main eyes and ears, directing the American defending force to precise locations of enemy landing points and beaming communications back and forth at one decimal shy of the speed of light.

Now, by providence, one of those AWAC's was approaching from the north, flying about a mile above and six miles starboard of the naval air strike force. Hunter had to hesitate a beat and wonder what the AWAC's pilot was doing. The plane was not only unarmed, it was slower

309

than the slowest typical Boeing 707 simply because it spent every airborne moment lugging around a deep dish radar on its back.

Yet, the AWAC's pilot must have been aware of the approaching naval strike force. The gadgets on board an E-3 could detect planes half an ocean away. Why would he approach the enemy force in such an exposed way?

Hunter had no more than a second to devote to this riddle. He had other things to do.

The flight commander of the AWAC's plane was a veteran US Air Force pilot named Logan who had reenlisted during the Circle Wars.

Logan's team of eighteen technicians situated in the body of his E-3 had spotted the formation of naval fighters and attack planes just moments before Hunter did. The thirty-six bogies had appeared out of the sea and onto the E-3 radar screens at a point about sixty-five miles off the coast of Florida. The AWAC's planes, their equipment having been pressed into sea-surface duty, understandably took longer than usual to begin tracking the incoming force.

But when they did, Logan had been quick to sum up the startlingly deteriorating situation.

His first action had been to flash a warning of the approaching aircraft to Jacksonville, Charleston, and Washington simultaneously. Then he talked over their options with his co-pilot, and in a moment of incredible intuition and courage, decided that they would try a fake on the naval strike force.

Praying for the Lord to send him some cool real fast, Logan approached to within five miles of the strike force and then turned on to a course parallel to it. Then, as calm as day, he began his radar dish twirling.

The pilots in the attack force spotted the AWAC's plane immediately, but they, too, were mystified at its actions.

From Logan's point of view, that was the whole idea.

He knew that very few things could break up the attack formation of a carrier strike force once it was heading to target. Enemy interceptors were one, enemy SAM's were another.

But going after pokey AWACs planes would take some discussion among the attackers. Should they ID the plane first before shooting it down? Who would go after the plane, the flanking F-14's or the rear guard? Should they bother at all?

Adding weight to this decision-making process was the fact that, in the naval attack pilots' minds, the AWAC's plane was undoubtedly sending streams of information on their strike formation's range, heading, armament to some control point on shore. If this were true, then not only would the element of surprise be lost to the naval strike force, but possibly interceptors would be vectored toward them.

The naval aircraft pilots had no way of knowing that Logan was not capable of this. There *were* no intercepter aircraft in the area. But by flying alongside the naval jets, even for a few critical moments, Logan was able to convince them that an opposing force was being vectored to the area. In reality, all Logan was buying was time. Time to warn the string of impromptu air bases opened along the Florida coast to suppress the sea invasion. Time to blare air-raid warnings in the few remaining populated areas.

Time to stave off—if only temporarily—what would surely be a devastating attack on American territory.

But unknown to him, Logan's bold plan also provided some important time for the man known—at least until this day—as the best fighter pilot alive.

Chapter Forty-nine

It would be impossible to determine if the F-14 pilot and his backseat radar officer ever saw Hunter coming.

From all indications, they didn't.

One moment the Tomcat was flying on flank formation, closing in to his wingman while the strike leader decided what to do about the sudden appearance of the AWAC's plane. The next moment the powerful carrier-based fighter was plunging into the sea, half its port wing and a third of its port stabilizer sheared off by a surgically precise cannon barrage.

The wingman of the doomed fighter was closest to the action and all he saw was streak of green and red blur by him to the nine o'clock. The next thing he knew, his flight leader was spiraling down into the ocean.

A hasty call back to his radar officer brought a startling report. The enemy plane that had just iced their comrade had not been picked up on the Tomcat's state-of-the-art AWG-9 radar system. Nor had it been indicated on any of the F-14's supplementary infrared detection or radio intercept systems.

"It came out of nowhere" was how the back-seater put it.

As the Tomcat pilot looked back on the downward spiral of smoke and fire that led to the ocean three miles below, he thought a moment and then called the strike leader.

"Flank Four is down," he told the overall commander of the strike force. "Enemy action . . ."

A full two miles ahead of the flank guard, the strike leader was stunned at the news. He had had no indication that anything was amiss. He broadcast the general "under attack" signal to the rest of the strike force, then called over to Flank Wingman again.

"Did you ID enemy type?" he asked.

The flank wingman hesitated briefly before telling the strike leader that no aircraft make was made on the attacker. He stalled another few seconds trying to find the words to tell his leader that the attacker had not been picked up on radar, either.

"Are you saying it was a stealth fighter?" the strike leader shot back somewhat sarcastically upon hearing the "came-from-nowhere" report.

"We're still evaluating" came the wingman's rather obtuse reply.

Now the strike leader had two problems. An enemy aircraft that might or might not be a stealth had penetrated his formation, and an AWAC's plane had used the heavy clouds to his north to play hide-and-seek with him.

However, he was certain that two radio calls would remedy both situations.

With the snap of a mic button he ordered the two outer Tomcats on the right-side flanking flight to go after the AWAC's plane. Then he called back to the left-flank wingman to tell him to break formation and search for the mysterious attacker.

However, the strike leader soon realized he had a third problem: the left-flank wingman did not reply.

Logan was prepared the moment he saw the two F-14's break toward him.

Even old Air Force jocks knew that Tomcats carried heat-seeking AIM-9 Sidewinders for close-in engagements. And the combination of the AIM-9's advanced heat-seeking nose and the tons of hot exhaust pouring out of the E-3's four engines spelled certain disaster for Logan's plane.

But the veteran pilot also knew another thing about the Sidewinder: it was almost a strictly shoot-from-behind weapon.

So now, as the two Tomcats maneuvered for a spot up and behind the Logan's AWAC's, he went into a maneuver of his own. Calling back to his eighteen-man crew to strap down tight and hang on, Logan booted the E-3's throttles up to max and then put the ship into an almost impossible turn.

A few seconds later, the huge E-3 was heading straight for the Tomcats.

The lead 'Cat fired a missile anyway, possibly more out of surprise than anything else. Proving Logan's theory to a frightening limit, the AIM-9L went up and over the E-3, its heat-seeker never locking onto anything hot enough to hit.

The Tomcats had broken away by this time, not in any mood to play chicken with the hulking converted airliner. Pulling into a pair of identical 5-g turns, the Cats once again began jockeying for a rear position on Logan's tail. Once again, the crafty pilot banked his own ship in a nearly impossible turn and wound up—more or less—heading once again for the F-14's.

Two more Sidewinders were fired at him, but again, the heat-seekers fell wanting and they quickly went astray.

But twice fooled was enough for the F-14 pilots. They had already spent too much time and valuable fuel pursuing the big plane, not to mention three wasted Sidewinders.

After a brief radio conversation, the two Cat jocks armed their big nose-mounted six-barrel rotary 20mm M61 Vulcan cannons.

Meanwhile, the strike leader had given up trying to contact his missing left-flank wingman. Leaving control of the strike force in the hands of his second in command, the strike leader jerked his Tomcat into a full inverted climb, looped over, and headed back to the left-flank wingman's last position, his radar officer reminding him that they were about six minutes away from the coastline.

Arriving at the spot within ten seconds, the strike leader could still see indications of two spiral smoke clouds, one "fresher" than the other, leading down into the sea. He put

314

the big Cat into a gut-wrenching dive, pulling up barely three hundred feet above the surface of the water. Two seconds later, he was streaking over the wreckage of the first F-14 to get hit. A few seconds after that, he spotted the wreckage of the left-flank wingman.

There were no signs of survivors.

The first cannon barrage from the lead F-14 tore into Logan's right wing.

Firing from a position almost directly above the AWAC's plane, the Cat pilot had poured it on for about three seconds, an eternity for a fighter pilot to have his finger on the trigger. The resulting fusillade tore up the E-3's inboard engine and sprung numerous leaks in the wing-stored fuel tanks. Yet nothing absolutely critical had been hit.

The second Cat's shooting proved little better. A brief burst, fired way too early, resulted in only a few perforations on the E-3's left wingtip. Now, as the two Cats angrily regrouped for a second run, Logan decided to play out his last card.

Hulking and antique though it was, the E-3 Boeing-707-in-disguise was still an amazing aircraft. It was the first big airplane made to handle like a smaller one. Airline pilots quickly grew to love it for its performance and its survivability. In fact, during its passenger-carrying days, some planes had gone through catastrophic malfunctions and still were able to fly on a single engine safely.

But there was one more secret the Boeing aircraft possessed.

Sensing the Cats were now back in a firing position, Logan once again alerted his now-terrified crew to hang tight.

Then, with the cool of a fighter jock, he ignored the first stream of cannon shells rocketing by his window and put the big airplane into a roll.

The second in command of the carrier Strike Force

315

couldn't believe his eyes.

He'd been watching the curious engagement between the pair of F-14's and the E-3, on one hand silently swearing at the two fighter pilots to hurry up and finish the job, while on the other feeling grudging respect for the E-3 pilot for his evading tactics.

But when the second in command saw the F-14's line up for their second cannon run, he knew the E-3 was as good as dead. So it was with astonishment that he watched the big airplane go into a complete 360-degree roll.

The sight of the E-3 turning completely over looked startling and unreal, so much so, the Strike Force second in command felt a weird chill run through him. It was as if he was seeing it all in a dream. The laws of gravity just didn't support such a maneuver.

But turn over the big plane did, completely confusing the attacking pilots for a fourth time and once again postponing impending doom.

The second in command could barely key his radio mic. He wasn't sure exactly why, but he was compelled to call back to the strike leader and report E-3's nightmarish maneuver.

The strike leader never replied.

Hunter had seen the E-3 roll off in the distance, and even though he had heard the rumors that the old Boeings were capable of such a maneuver, he never believed it until that very moment.

"Dish and all," he had muttered at the time.

Just moments before, Hunter had dispatched his third F-14 in as many minutes, the hat trick plane belonging to the pilot that Hunter was sure served as strike leader for the carrier craft.

Splashing the sophisticated Tomcats hadn't been easy—their radar systems could see as far as forty-five miles away under certain conditions. Yet Hunter had known going in that if any of the shotgun-riding F-14's picked him up on their radar screens, then he would have been involved in a dogfight with a dozen or more of the big, high-tech fighters, and even he would have been hard-pressed to fly away from that.

So the situation had caused him to play it by the seat of his pants.

The key to beating the F-14 was to beat its whiz-bang radar systems. These electronic eyes could not only see forever and in many directions, they could also track more targets than one could count on his fingers and toes.

But they did have blind spots. One of them was straight down.

Seconds after getting a solid visual on the attack force, Hunter had put the jumpjet down on the deck, which in this case was the rolling Atlantic Ocean. Skimming the wavetops, he kept his fingers crossed that the Harrier's radar signature—already fairly small to begin with—would be masked by the natural background clutter created on the surface of the ocean.

He lucked out as he watched the frightening strike force pass right over him up at fifteen thousand feet while he was sucking up sea spray just fifteen feet above the water.

His extraordinary flying skills came into play next.

Turning the AV-8 around on its tail one hundred eighty degrees, he quickly positioned himself directly under the trailing left flank F-14. Then he pushed the Harrier into a near vertical ascent, adjusting a hair-thin flight path as he went along and in effect sneaking up under the F-14's radar umbrella. A pinpoint accurate burst of his cannons destroyed the first Top Gun plane before its crew knew what hit them.

The second F-14 was splashed in an identical maneuver, but the third, the one belonging to the strike leader, proved harder. When he and Hunter caught sight of each other, both were just barely twenty-five feet off the "soft deck" of the ocean. Robbed of his background clutter hiding spot, Hunter had had no choice but to turn into the F-14 and lay on the trigger.

Like the two pilots pursuing the E-3, the strike leader had been momentarily startled by his opponent's bold maneuver. That second's worth of hesitation cost him his life. Before he could get his rear-seater to arm a missile for him to light, Hunter's cannonshells had ripped into the 'Cats' cockpit instantly killing the two-man crew.

But that was all the damage that Hunter could do with his guns. Although he was reasonably sure that he'd eliminated the brains of the Strike Force, he had expended the last of ammunition in doing so. What was worse, his fuel reserves were so low, he figured he had five more minutes of flying left, tops.

By this time the carrier planes were within ten miles of the Florida coast and there was nothing left that he could do to stop them.

As Hunter watched powerlessly, four of the A-6 Intruders—their wings jammed with air-to-ground missiles—broke off from the main body, and picking up two F-14's for protection, veered south. Four of the F/A-18's did likewise, turning off to a course roughly south by southeast.

To Hunter's dismay, the main body of the attack force stayed on a due west course. This could only mean one thing: they were heading for the Jacksonville Naval Air Station.

To make matters worse, Hunter saw that one of the F-14's finally caught up to the pesky E-3 and had fired a Sidewinder into its port wing. The last he saw of the AWAC's, it disappeared into a thick cloudbank, smoking heavily.

With no ammo and only drops of fuel left, Hunter was incapable of preventing the impending disaster. It was almost completely dark now, and the cover of night would give the attackers an extra added shield during their bombing runs. And besides the general broadcast warning he'd transmitted upon first seeing the naval Strike Force, and perhaps a similar warning from the AWAC's plane, there was no way he could know whether his colleagues at Jacksonville knew the attack was coming or not.

In a word, he was helpless.

In the pit of his stomach Hunter felt an anger. A good part of it was channeled toward this new, mysterious, high-tech airborne enemy, but a great deal of it was also turned within himself. He felt that he'd been fooled again by the dark forces of the cosmos, fooled into thinking that all he needed was a jet fighter and his extra large supply of ESP to defend his country and his friends.

Now, as he watched the carrier attack planes perform their prestrike maneuvers flawlessly, Hunter's spirits hit rock bottom. The sub carrying Dominique was long gone by now. And despite his cagey victories against the three F-14's, he still felt like the old gunfighter who had just been thoroughly humiliated by the new kid in town, or more aptly, by the new *gang* in town.

And that gang had enough firepower and radar technology to virtually control the skies over the East Coast of the Continent and attack anywhere just about at will.

He knew from that moment on, things would never be the same in America.

With this devastatingly sober thought in mind—and an empty water gun in hand—Hunter slowly made his way to an inglorious landing on the bloody shore of Jacksonville Beach.

Chapter Fifty

The first wave of A-6 Intruders screamed in on the Jacksonville Air Station at tree-top height, unleashing runway-cratering GP bombs before streaking away into the night.

The F/A-18 Hornets roared in next. Their undersides jammed with Mk-8 Snake-Eye retarded bombs, the first four high-tech strike craft systematically demolished a string of aircraft hangars that bordered the air station's main runway, as well as a line of A-4 attack craft that had minutes before returned from action over the beaches. A second wave of Hornets destroyed the base's main radar station as well as its main fuel depot located nearby.

The Intruders reappeared at this point and, flying at a more reasonable five hundred feet, dropped their secondary loads of GP bombs. The heavy five hundred pound weapons streaked to earth and randomly destroyed buildings and aircraft alike—one string of bombs decimated a group of A-10's that had been in the process of rearming when the enemy air strike came.

The F/A-18s returned and, one by one, strafed the entire base with their awesome Vulcan cannons. All the while, the flight of F-14 Tomcats orbited the target, watching out for any interfering aircraft.

But theirs turned out to be an easy job. All of the United American aircraft were on the ground when the air strike commenced. Lined up and vulnerable to the enemy guns, they were slaughtered like sheep. And even if one or two had been able to get airborne, it would have been an act of needless suicide for the pilots, as aircraft like A-4's and

A-10's were absolutely no match for fighters like the Tomcats and the Hornets.

However, many of the United American pilots wanted to go up at first warning of the impending attack and at least attempt to block some of the enemy aircraft. But General Jones had ordered them into the base's bomb shelter instead. From the second he'd received word—almost simultaneously from the *New Jersey,* Hunter and Logan's E-3 AWAC's plane—of the approaching enemy force and the aircraft it was made up of, Jones knew it would be hopeless to mount a defense. He and his force were outgunned to a maximum degree. At that point, saving the lives of his men was of the utmost importance.

So he had ordered them all into shelters—pilots and technicians alike. And when the last sound of the last departing jet finally disappeared, they emerged from the shelter and walked into a kind of group state of shock. The entire air station was aflame, totally and completely demolished.

In the course of five minutes, more than half of the United Americans attack planes based in Florida had been destroyed.

It took Jones and Fitzgerald nearly thirty minutes to find a workable radio at the base. When they did, all they heard was more bad news. Each of the four UA bases that stretched from Jacksonville down to Orlando had been devastated. Casualties were high, due to the fact that these bases hadn't had as much of an advance warning as Jacksonville had. What was worse, the extent of the destruction and the scope of the attacks led to another chilling conclusion: not just one, but as many as three separate naval strike groups had taken part in the action. This meant that more than one hundred of the high-tech aircraft were in the area. By comparison, there were only one hundred twenty United American aircraft on the entire *continent.*

"It's the end," the normally unflappable Fitzgerald told Jones as they walked stunned through the wreckage of the air station. "The Norsemen *had* been a screen all along.

321

Now we have these airplanes *and* the fact that the *Fire Bats* have nuclear capability to face? It's just too much, even for us."

Jones could only shake his head. He was barely able to speak through his numbed lips.

How could we have been so blind? he wondered bitterly.

Chapter Fifty-one

Kure Island, South Pacific

Elvis finally distentangled himself from his parachute harness and slowly, painfully, lowered himself down the palm tree and onto the jungle floor below.

Depleted beyond words by his hours-long ordeal stuck in the trees, he simply lay on the ground now and wondered if someone could actually die of exhaustion.

An initial survey of his aching body revealed no broken bones—to his great surprise. He was, however, covered from head to toe with cuts and bruises of various sizes and degrees. His left arm was particularly ripped up due to the shattering of his canopy glass when he punched out. Plus, his back was pulsating with deep pain, again the result of the split-second bailout.

But he was alive and breathing and thinking as clearly as he could expect. Now he had to wonder just how long this condition would last.

He had no idea exactly where he was. About a mile away he could still see the burning wreckage of his F-4X Super Phantom, its entire rear quarter gone from the blast of the enemy surface-to-air missile. The sound of waves crashing off in the distance told him the beach was nearby, but this being an island—and a small one to boot—reasoned that a beach was always close by no matter what the location. He had to guess that his stricken plane had traveled at least ten miles before he punched out, and that meant the people who shot the

SAM at him were at least as close.

He couldn't imagine that they would not bother looking for him.

He lay still on the jungle floor for another few minutes, knowing that he had to get up and get hidden, but on the other hand wondering whether it was all worth it. He was after all out in the middle of the Pacific somewhere, on an enemy-occupied island, with absolutely no means of escape. What difference then would it make if he simply decided to stay put and either allow himself to be captured or eaten by bugs?

Putting aside the disturbing thoughts, he forced himself to sit up, and then finally get to a kneeling position. It was hard to determine what hurt the most, his perforated arm or his aching back. Deciding it was a tossup, he took a deep breath and finally got to his feet.

He let the wooziness clear from his head, then, using a nearby stick as a cane, he hobbled out of the thick jungle and onto the edge of a small clearing. It was just past midmorning, he figured, and the tropical sun was beating down on him unmercifully. A searing thirst erupted in his throat, followed quickly by a pang of hunger that felt more like a kick in the gut. He hadn't eaten since leaving Honolulu, and for a brief, frightening moment he wondered if he'd ever eat again.

Rationality returned once again a few seconds later. Despite his desperate situation, he was savvy enough to know that he had to stay military—to the end, if necessary. This meant that if he had the chance, he should try to get some information on this mysterious enemy, reconnoiter their base if possible . . . try to get some answers that, on the slight chance he made it out of this green hell, might be helpful to his country.

With these thoughts in mind, he set out on a path that he believed would take him toward the sounds of the crashing waves.

It took him more than an hour to reach the edge of the cliff. The jungle seemed to fight him every inch of the way, but as he walked in a due east direction, the breaking of the waves had gotten stronger and clearer.

About a half mile away from the cliff, he started to hear other sounds, those of machinery—engines running, wheels turning, tools being used.

Now, as he crawled to the peak of the rocky outledge and looked out onto the beach below, he felt a great rush of air stick in his throat.

Before him was an enormous, sprawling military base and dock facility. He counted at least two dozen ships docked within the island's natural harbor, with another half dozen laying at anchor off the coast. A nonstop stream of smaller craft, supply boats and the like, were shuttling back and forth between the ships and the docks, feverishly carrying men and materiel to the ships.

A small city was sitting at the edge of the docking facility, dozens of plain square wood buildings, each one sporting a bright red-and-yellow flag and a SAM launcher on its roof. A two-runway airstrip lay about a half mile inland from the clutter of buildings, large C-130 cargo planes and Huey helicopters appearing to make up most of its occupants.

Elvis concentrated on the activity along the piers. He could see thousands of soldiers moving about like ants, a frantic buzz of activity that was all the more surprising due to the crushing heat of the midday sun. The soldiers wore a variety of uniforms—some in white, others beige, other in jungle-green camouflage. But the assortment of uniforms itself was a confirmation of something: the soldiers were all mercenaries. Once again, another piece of the puzzle had glumly fit into place.

Despite the extensive buildup along the beach, Elvis knew that the place was just a temporary stop for the hired troops. With the thousands of crates and tarp-covered supply palates overflowing on the docks, it was clear the base was more of a staging facility.

"They're getting ready," Elvis heard himself say.

His attention was caught by a Huey chopper lifting off from the airstrip. Through stinging eyes he followed its flight path as it rose, turned north by northeast, and headed for another island that lay about two miles offshore. It took him only a few more moments to realize that there was yet another facility similar to the one before him on this other island. And out beyond that he could see more islands, and judging from the clouds of brown haze that hung in the tropical heat above them, more bases.

It was at that moment that he wondered if Zim the Honolulu businessman realized how right he had been. An enormous mercenary army and fleet was gathering on these islands. Their ships were covered with guns and soldiers and enough supplies to last for months.

And they all seemed to be pointing eastward.

mum, another piece of the puzzle had slowly fallen into place.

Despite the extensive buildup along the beach, Thyle...

Chapter Fifty-two

Thorgils, Son of Verden, took a deep breath and then opened the cabin door.

Dominique was on the large bed, lying perfectly still, the only indication that she was not asleep being the barely visible stream of tears running from her eyes. Thorgils walked into cabin and quietly shut the door behind him. He had been both dreading this moment and awaiting it with indescribable sexual anticipation for hours.

For before him was one of the most beautiful women he'd ever seen—possibly one of the most beautiful in the entire world. And by his father's orders, Thorgils now had to sexually force himself on her.

Then he would eliminate her.

He was not surprised that his father's belief that this lovely creature would fulfill her duty as a Valkyrie had failed. From the moment she had been captured, everyone who came in contact with her beauty had been blinded by it, the great Verden included. There was nothing in the old Norse myths that stated the Valkyries *had* to be beautiful— it was simply a myth that had grown up around a myth.

But the blind devotion to the Norse way of life, combined no doubt with the daily intake of *myx,* had skewered his father's judgment, and that was the reason he had picked this beauty Dominique to assume the very important position of Valkyrie. The fact that she wanted no part of it once the shooting began didn't surprise Thorgils a bit.

She had been willing at first, though, and it was on this count that Thorgils himself felt the fool. The day before the great battle she had eagerly devoured the mostly ceremonial instructions Thorgils had given her, memorizing them in an incredibly short amount of time, and even at one point reciting them back to him strictly from memory.

Temporarily blinded himself by this display—as well as her beauty and a flask of *myx*—Thorgils had foolishly answered every question she asked about the *Fire Bats* sub. He had even given her a tour of the missile chamber after she had slyly allowed him a glimpse of her exposed breasts while bending down to sensually massage her delicate feet. She had purposely rubbed against him as he told her about the three ICBM warheads sitting atop the missiles inside the tubes—they being recovered from a lake in Nova Scotia, an island off New Hampshire, and a beach on the northern Massachusetts shore respectively.

When she accidentally-on-purpose nuzzled her breasts against him upon returning to her cabin, he spit out everything he knew about the other three Norse nuclear-capable subs: the one that was steaming off the coast of the Yucatan with a landing party ready to search for gold long ago hidden within some ancient Mayan temples, the one that was heading around the tip of South America to take up a position off the Pacific coast of America; and the one that was lying on the ocean floor just fifteen miles off the coast of Maryland, a single ICBM poised to be launched against Washington, DC.

And then on the eve of the great battle, after she had once again recited the responsibilities of a Valkyrie—a mishmash of psychic nonsense that had her determining in no explainable way the number of Norse who would die the next day—she had requested another goblet of *myx* and asked that he join her in drinking it.

Drink they did, until Thorgils felt a fire in his loins of an intensity he had never imagined. Then she slowly undid the back of her gown and let it slip to the floor, revealing the small, short dress that served as her underwear. He made more promises to her at this point—ones he couldn't even remember now—and then she let the undergarment fall.

His *myx*-flooded eyes then beheld a creature of astonishing grace and beauty, a perfectly shaped naked female form that rivaled all great works of art. Lovely pert breasts, an uncanny hourglass shape, upper thighs that led into just the barest hint of light pubic hair, and perfect legs and feet. It was all there, dazzling his intoxicated senses.

What man would not have told her everything?

But then the deflating reality burst in upon him.

Just as it seemed as if she was guiding his hand to touch her naked breast, he felt his body shake with an incredible split second of pleasure—only to feel a damp spot gathering in the crotch of his uniform pants a second later.

At that moment he knew he had been tricked by this woman, and that she was probably a witch.

She had used the *myx* against him, tempting him with her beauty, and he had foolishly fallen for her spell. The result of his folly? Now four people knew exactly what was behind the entire Norse invasion scheme: himself, his father, the woman Elizabeth, and now this treacherous beauty, Dominique.

Even a dolt like Thorgils knew that was one too many.

So it was that when the hour of the great battle came, Thorgils felt like his insides were being pulled in many different directions.

His father's orders were for him to observe the Norse landings and provide a kind of ritualistic eyewitness report on their execution. It was also decreed that Dominique would watch the landings and, through chanting line upon line of mythological Norse mumbo-jumbo, would somehow have an effect on its outcome and the number of Norse who would die.

But no sooner had the *Fire Bats* cruised into the battle area just as the landings began when Dominique told Thorgils in no uncertain terms that she would not partake in the bizarre ritual. Without the ceremonial, yet supposedly essential contribution of the Valkyrie, Thorgils was convinced that not only would many Norsemen die but that the enemy would quickly gain the upper hand and that the entire invasion itself would be a failure.

And that's what happened.

It was a painful moment when Thorgils radioed his father aboard the *Stor Skute* and reported Dominique's refusal and the subsequent slaughter of the Norse clans. The next sound Thorgils heard was a loud clump! followed by a burst of static. Then an underling officer came on the line and told him that his father had taken ill and could no longer speak to him.

Several minutes passed by, and then the woman Elizabeth came on the radio. Her frightening voice intimidating the very radio waves, she told Thorgils of his father's final two orders: first, "deflower the Valkyrie," then, sacrifice her.

And that's exactly what Thorgils intended to do.

Chapter Fifty-three

It was dark by the time Hunter crawled out of the Harrier's cockpit.

He was spent, in mind, body, and spirit. His hands were nearly trembling, his eyes ached, and the pounding in the pit of his stomach felt like it would be with him forever.

Dropping down off the Harrier's wing on to the damp sand of Jacksonville Beach, he felt the grip in his gut tighten up by a factor of ten. There were Norse bodies everywhere. Tangled, twisted and broken, some were missing arms, legs, or heads. Others were contorted into nightmarish positions.

Even worse, the crabs and the seagulls and the insects had already begun their feast.

Despite his exhaustion, Hunter ran. Up through the red-tinged sand, past the fires started by the nonstop bombing of just two hours ago, up and over the sea wall, and onto the deserted street of the one-time resort city. He ran until he was out of breath, and still he kept on running, his flight boots clacking through the deserted streets in such a way as to mimic the sounds of someone chasing him.

Running . . . until his mouth was dry and his eyes were watery. Running . . . with visions of the nightmarish force of carrier-attack craft pounding in his head. Running . . . with the frightening knowledge that the whole world had suddenly changed.

Running . . . with the fear that he could no longer conjure up a clear picture of Dominique's beautiful face in his mind.

Running . . . away from the swashbuckling past and into a very uncertain future.

Running . . .

Chapter Fifty-four

The small white lifeboat was lowered over the side of the *Skor Skute,* its solemn descent lit by the dozens of searchlights piercing the night and underscored by the baleful blowing of ten Norse bugles.

Placed in the center of the wooden boat was the body of the Great Verden. A long silver sword on one side, a symbolic flask of *myx* on the other, the body was wrapped in a white linen sheet that gave it the appearance of a mummy.

Once the boat reached the surface of the water, the bugles temporarily went silent. From the bow of the Great Ship, a solitary Norse soldier fired a flaming arrow into the boat. Then, as the contingent of crew on the converted luxury liner watched along with those on the twenty Norse surface ships and ten *Krig Bats* subs nearby, the flame began to slowly spread along the gunwales of the wooden funeral boat.

The Great Verden was going to his grave.

Elizabeth Sandlake watched the somber ceremony from the bridge of the Great Ship, barely able to contain her glee. Verden had died a coward's death really, she thought. Not by an enemy's sword or bullet but rather by a failure of the heart, the result of hearing about the refusal of his hand-picked Valkyrie to fulfill her duties and the subsequent disaster on the Florida beaches.

He hadn't lived long enough to hear about the devastating air strikes launched against the United Americans.

Now, as Verden's funeral boat drifted away from the Great Ship, the flame on board growing with every second, it was all Elizabeth could do to stop from laughing out loud. Her plans could not have been executed more perfectly if the bumbling Norsemen had been in on them from the beginning. With Verden out of the way, and his son Thorgils in the midst of a *myx*-induced, psychological hangover that would scar him for years, Elizabeth was a queen—again.

This time her kingdom was much larger than the Alberta fortress. Now she ruled over the remaining Norse clans— the surviving leaders having just radioed in their support of her elevation—*and* the men who sailed the nuclear-armed *Fire Bats,* Thorgils included. Plus, she had at her disposal, via a secretly negotiated contract, more than one hundred of the most advanced fighter and attack aircraft left in the world *and* an agreement with the Greater East Asia Divine Warriors' Association who, at the moment, were staging for an enormous invasion of first Hawaii and then the West Coast.

What more would she need to conquer America?

Deep inside the Great Ship, peering through a cracked and stained porthole window, Yaz also watched the traditional Viking funeral ceremony.

Even though he was locked in the small room near the very bottom of the ship, Yaz had been one of the first to hear that Verden had died. He had learned quickly that there were few secrets on the Great Ship; it was simply against the Norse nature to keep anything in confidence. So his guards, excited and talkative as ever, had told him everything: the death of Verden, the defeat of the Norse clans, the massive retaliatory strike by the mysterious naval attack aircraft, the impending doom waiting to befall Dominique.

But as bad as it was, there was one startling fact they'd relayed to Yaz that caused his morale to plunge even further. And that was the treacherous Elizabeth Sandlake—of all people!—now ruled over the Norse.

At first Yaz was stunned. After her narrow escape during

334

the lightning-quick raid against the woman's Alberta fortress, he would have thought that she'd lie low—possibly forever. But the more he thought about it, the more it made a crazy kind of sense.

Who else but her would have the purely maniacal drive, the absolutely ruthless cunning and totally blind fury of ambition to pull the strings behind the whole Norse invasion facade? Who else would be able to cajole, threaten, or bribe all the major players who would have to participate in such a grandiose scheme? Who else was more capable of destroying the delicately reconstructed, still-fragile idea called America?

Now, as the flames completely engulfed the small boat carrying Verden's body, the mournful blaring of the Norse bugles began again. Suddenly another more personally disturbing question popped into Yaz's mind.

What the hell will happen to me? he wondered.

Chapter Fifty-five

Jacksonville Naval Air Station

Mike Fitzgerald wrapped his hands around the broken cup half filled with coffee and tried to draw some warmth from its contents.

Even though the Florida night was a miserably sticky eighty-five degrees, his fingers were cold to the point of being numb.

"Stress," he whispered to himself, trying to explain away his contradictory ailment. "Stress must come with defeat . . ."

He and Jones were sitting in the barely lit bomb shelter, their clothes dirty and in tatters as a result of their efforts to rescue the wounded and retrieve the dead after the massive air strike on the base. The base's only working radio was sitting on the rickety table next to Jones. Until an hour ago, it had been blaring so many messages being sent between the various UA facilities down the coast of Florida that no one would have been surprised if the speaker suddenly began smoking. Now, nothing more than a mild score of static could be heard from the radio. All of the damage-assessment reports had been called in, as had the pleas for help with the dead and dying.

Now the radio was devoid of human voices, allowing those listening to the blur of background interference to contemplate exactly the magnitude of the disaster that had befallen the United Americans. In one day—or more accurately, in one hour—the jewel of the UA Armed Forces their

Air Force—had been reduced by nearly one half. It was a situation akin to Patton losing half his tanks or LeMay half his bombers. Worse even, as the destroyed aircraft and equipment was irreplaceable in the postwar world.

In another corner of the shelter sat the base's telex machine, scrapped and battered from the air raid, yet still in working condition. It, too, had been silent now for hours.

The two men didn't talk. There was nothing left to say. The devastating air attacks all along the Florida coast had left them numb in body, mind, and soul. The uncertainty of what lay ahead for them and for their country was almost unbearable.

Suddenly the telex burst to life, its unexpected clacking startling both of the normally unperturbed men.

Fitzgerald nearly dropped his coffee at the sudden noise. Now he leaned over the machine and read aloud as the words printed one by one onto the faded yellow telex paper.

The message, in two parts, was being transmitted from Jones's office in Washington. Oddly, the preface indicated that the subject matter had nothing to do with the United American's sudden defeat in Florida.

Rather, the first communication was one relayed from the West Coast and sent originally by Captain Crunch O'Malley.

It read simply: "Hunter's airplane secured."

But then the follow-up paragraph briefly detailed the story of Zim, the Hawaiian businessman, and the fact that Elvis had flown westward to investigate the man's claim that a huge mercenary force was gathering in the South Pacific for a strike against the American West Coast.

The message ended with the dire news that Elvis was long overdue in returning from this recon mission.

The telex fell silent for a full minute, and then began clacking again.

The second part of the transmission had to do with a request that Jones had made of his Washington office just hours before the Norse attacks began. It had to do with the somewhat mysterious man, Wolf, the captain of the USS

337

New Jersey. The ever-cautious Jones had asked his intelligence operatives to run a quick check on the man's background, using what little resources they had at present in lawless, totally anarchic western Europe.

The first few sentences of the message confirmed that Wolf was everything Hunter had told them he was: a man who was pursuing his father and older brother in an effort to stop them from spreading death and destruction along the American East Coast.

But the next paragraph held a surprise. Wolf was not the anonymous if eccentric figure he had portrayed himself to be. Rather, he was very well known in some regions of the strife-torn Continent as a kind of postwar Robin Hood, a soldier of fortune who used his skills as a sea-going warrior to help and protect the millions of disenfranchised people eking out an existence in Europe's new Dark Age.

The message concluded with an apt if ironic description: "Wolf is to parts of Europe," Jones's intelligence officer had written, "what Hawk Hunter is to most of America."

Both Fitzgerald and Jones were surprised by the information, but in light of their present situation, it seemed of little consequence to them now. From all accounts, Wolf and his crew had performed extraordinarily well during the recent battle against the Norse. But even a weapon as mighty as a battleship would do little to alter the frightening new balance of power ushered in by the appearance of the mysterious enemy's one hundred high-tech naval aircraft.

The telex fell silent, and once again, so did Fitzgerald and Jones. It was nearly 3 A.M., and all the two men were doing was waiting for morning and wondering what new disasters it would bring.

Suddenly they heard a commotion at the front door of the bomb shelter. Someone was running. Running down the stone steps and down the long, narrow hallway.

A second later, the door to the room swung open and a somewhat disheveled figure bounded in.

It was Hunter.

Chapter Fifty-six

More than a hundred fifty miles to the south, a column of Norsemen lay hidden in a humid and insect-infested swamp marsh, keeping as low to the ground as possible.

They were survivors of the disastrous invasion attempt the night before, and every man was supremely humbled by how lucky he was to be alive. Their sub had been attacked by an A-4 Skyhawk off the coast of Cocoa Beach in the opening minutes of the battle. The jet had dropped two bombs: one had exploded on the sub's stern, damaging its propeller shafts, the other had slammed into the huge forward bulkhead where nearly a battalion of Norse troops was preparing to disembark from the ship and into the landing crafts.

Many soldiers were killed in the attack, including the sub's captain and all of his officer staff. Many more were trapped for a time in the forward part of the vessel. For most of the battle, the sub could not move due to the damage to its propellers. But the smoke and flames belching from its pair of wounds apparently convinced the pilots of the attacking UA jets that further punishment was not necessary.

One man had come to the fore once night had fallen. It was he who not only instructed the rescue crews in freeing those men trapped at the front of the sub but also led the workers who jimmy-rigged a temporary shaft to one of the boat's propellers.

Thus powered again, the sub slowly made its way for thirteen miles until it reached a large sandbar one mile north of Cocoa Beach. Here the sub was beached. When the tide went out, the one hundred seventy-five survivors were able to swim to shore.

Now the majority of these men lay hidden on the edge of the marsh waiting for a squad of scouts to return. The news these men carried with them would determine the fate of them all.

Two hours passed, and the night gradually gave way to the dawn.

Finally, the scouts came scrambling back to the main group—dirty and out of breath, but nevertheless carrying good news. There was a group of abandoned buildings nearby where the Norse survivors could take refuge. The structures were part of a large base of some kind, but the scouts weren't exactly sure of the facility's function. They told wild stories of a wide-open flat space built of concrete in the middle of the swamp and containing enormous towers and at least one huge, strange-looking aircraft.

The rest of the Norse had no time for their tales. They knew they had to get hidden under the roof quickly, before the sun came up. With little fanfare, the one hundred seventy-five men emerged from their hiding places and followed the scouts through the twisting rivulets of the marsh.

By the time the sun broke above the horizon, the one hundred seventy-five Norsemen were standing on the outskirts of the long-ago-abandoned Cape Canaveral.

The unofficial second in command of the group, a high member of the Gothwarb clan named Thunke, stared out at the deserted base and realized that the scouts had not been exaggerating. The place *did* contain many strange, tall buildings as well as mile upon mile of concrete spaces. There were so many buildings, in fact, that the survivors could lie hidden for days, weeks, even months before anyone could find them.

It was the perfect refuge for the Norsemen; all it would take was Thunke's asking for permission from the leader of the group to enter the facility for a closer inspection.

Making his way back through the column of anxious clan members, he reached the small tree where their new leader had taken refuge from the rising, increasingly hot sun. The man was not even a Norseman, but Thunke knew this didn't matter at the moment. The man had fixed the propellers on the sub and had led the rescue of the trapped Norse soldiers. For such bravery, he had attained instant clan leadership.

Now he was giving the orders.

But due to peculiar circumstances, that was not as easy as it sounded. In fact, the only reason that Thunke was suddenly Number Two among the Norsemen was that he was the only one who could speak the new Number One's language.

Now crawling up beside the skinny, beardless, pale-skinned man, Thunke retrieved a tin cup from his belt and a twig from the shading tree. Then, with precise, almost delicate movements, he began tapping on the tin cup.

Immediately getting the full gist of Thunke's message, via the language of Morse code, the partially deaf, mute, and handless Englishman known as Smiley nodded his approval.

planning a descent to pick up and stuff them in the Harrier's hangar.

It was useless. Once Hunter had his mind made up to do something no power on Heaven or earth was sufficient.

Chapter Fifty-seven

Jacksonville Beach

The hot sun rising over the shore at Jacksonville baked the thousands of creatures alternately pecking at the corpses of Norsemen and fighting amongst themselves.

In the midst of the gluttony stood the Harrier jumpjet, its landing gear and lower fuselage covered with caked sand.

Next to the jet was a large sled holding a trio of weapons: one five-hundred-pound general-purpose bomb, one canister of M113 napalm, and a Harpoon antiship missile that contained only a third of the high explosive normally carried in its warhead. Another smaller sled nearby carried a drop tank half filled with aviation fuel and a roll of guide wire and a half dozen pulleys.

Hawk Hunter was working feverishly under the Harrier's wing, splicing the necessary wires and making the necessary connections which would allow him to attach the weapons and the fuel tank to the jumpjet. A red bandana covered his nose and mouth; a pair of industrial safety glasses covered his eyes.

But nothing could block out the incessant squawking and greedy hissing of the multitude of creatures as they continued their disgusting banquet.

If I get airborne within two hours, I might have a chance, Hunter kept telling himself over and over.

Standing up on the beach wall about fifty feet away was Jones and Fitzgerald. They both knew what Hunter was planning to do. But they had also failed in trying to talk him out of it.

It was useless. Once Hunter had his mind made up to do something, no matter how dangerous, it was pretty near impossible to change it.

Besides, Fitzgerald and Jones had little left in the way of spirit reserves. Their whole world had come crashing down on them less than twelve hours before. Trying to convince their friend that he was about to embark on a suicide mission seemed to be just too much for either one of them to contemplate.

Yet, as they watched their comrade hoist the weapons one by one up under the wing of the jumpjet by way of an ingenious series of wires and pulleys, they knew they had to try one more time to save his life.

Blocking out the rising stench on the beach with kerchiefs of their own, the two men tramped through the ghastly red sand and reached the Harrier just as Hunter was attaching the half-filled fuel tank.

"Save your breath, boys," he told them, not even looking at the pair.

"This is crazy, Hawker," Fitz told him nevertheless. "What good does it do anyone if you blow yourself to hell?"

"It's a mission," Hunter replied stoically. "Just another mission . . ."

"It's an *impossible* mission," Jones told him. "Even you won't stand a chance . . ."

"It *still* has to be done—and quick," Hunter said gloomily as he attached the last of the holding wires to the fuel tank. "And I'm the only one within five hundred miles who still has an aircraft in flying condition."

Jones and Fitzgerald could only look at each other and shake their heads.

It all started after Hunter appeared at the destroyed naval air station earlier that morning. He said very little to Jones and Fitzgerald upon entering the bomb shelter. Instead, he drained two cups of coffee and then began a wild

343

search of the still-smoldering base, looking for anything left that he might able to strap under the Harrier's wings.

He located the three disparate weapons in three different damaged buildings, and declining all offers of help from the surviving base personnel, loaded them on a bulky service truck, retrieved the tool sleds, the wire, the pulleys, and the half-filled fuel tank and headed back to his beached airplane.

Now it was almost noontime. He'd been working on the airplane since 7 A.M.

"Suppose I order you not to go?" Jones asked him wearily. "Suppose I ground you, here and now?"

Hunter stopped working for a moment and looked directly at Jones.

"Are you going to force me to disobey a direct order?" he asked his Commander in Chief.

Jones was suddenly speechless. Then he simply shook his head and walked away.

Fitzgerald decided to give it one last try.

Walking up under the shade of the wing, he watched Hunter secure the last guide wire under the fuel tank.

"Hawker, you don't even know what you're looking for," he said, the words not really coming out as he planned them.

"Like *hell* I don't," Hunter shot back. "There's only one way those navy airplanes could have hit us like that. They were launched from an aircraft carrier, a big one.

"Now it's out there, somewhere—and I'm going to find it."

"On a pint of fuel and carrying these three crummy weapons?" Fitzgerald replied somewhat angrily. "You know if it's a big carrier, then it will have SAM's, Phalanx guns, the works, *plus* airplanes that will come out to get you before you even spot the damn thing. You won't stand a chance."

"Maybe not," Hunter replied calmly. "But I still have to try. The alternative is that this country will lose control of its own skies. And you know, when that happens, it will *really* be over."

"But we'll still have those damn subs running around with their nukes," Fitz pleaded. "What about them?"

Hunter turned and looked directly into his friend's eyes. "I'll leave that problem to you, Mike," he said sadly.

With that, Hunter jumped up onto the Harrier's wing, climbed into the cockpit, and began pushing buttons in preparation for starting the airplane's unique engine.

As soon as Fitzgerald heard the low whine of the engine's prestarter, he knew he had only one last opportunity to talk to Hunter, maybe forever.

Running up beside the cockpit, he looked up at his friend and yelled: "What about Dominique?"

Hunter immediately froze, his face turning ashen white. Then he looked down at his friend of many years and said simply: "Good-bye Mike . . ."

The souped-up Harrier lifted off a minute later.

Kicking up a windstorm of sand and debris, the VTOL jet slowly rose above the hardened sand, the screaming of its engine scattering away any remaining sea gulls.

As Jones and Fitzgerald and a small contingent of Football City Rangers watched from the top of the breakwater, the jet hovered briefly over the beach and then rocketed away out to sea in a flash.

It disappeared over the horizon seconds later.

Chapter Fifty-eight

The day passed and night fell and still Mike Fitzgerald was sitting on the edge of the Jacksonville Beach wall, looking out to sea.

The stench that had permeated the air during the day was long gone now. The rising tide had washed many of the dead bodies away, cleansing the sand as it did so. Now the place was absolutely quiet—eerily so. Not so much like a field of battle, Fitzgerald thought, more like a cemetery.

He had been waiting all day for Hunter to return. But now, as the night grew darker, he knew the chances were decreasing that he would ever see his friend again.

Even by the most optimistic calculations, the Harrier's fuel would have run out by midafternoon, four and a half hours ago. And as far as Fitzgerald knew, the jumpjet did not carry any air-sea rescue provisions, such as an inflatable life raft or flare guns.

Still, he spent every second scanning the horizon. And just a few minutes after sunset, he spotted a light way off in the distance, coming right for him.

His hopes alternately rose and sank as he watched the light approach. Although it was moving slow enough to be attached to a hovering aircraft, its color was bright white, almost fluorescent in nature.

He knew the Harrier carried no such light.

Still, the light came straight for him, and within another minute, he heard the distinctive sound of its loud engines. It was at that moment Fitzgerald gave up any hope that it was Hunter. These were not jet engines he heard. Rather, they powered a helicopter.

The light was attached to the snout of a LAMPS ocean-recon helo. As Fitzgerald watched, the aircraft turned over the shoreline and slowly moved up and down the beach, its occupants obviously observing the now-silent battlefield.

After a few moments, the copter went into a hover close by Fitzgerald, and at one point caught him in its searchlight beam.

A minute later, it landed with a roar on the boardwalk next to the breakwater.

Three men alighted from the chopper. All were dressed very strangely. Two of them were wearing a sort of green, yellow, and red costume that would have looked more at home in a comic book. The third was wearing a long black cape over a black uniform and hat.

As the gaudily uniformed men began inspecting something underneath the chopper, the man in the black cape walked over to Fitzgerald.

Fitzgerald knew the people in the chopper were not unfriendly. They would have attempted to shoot him had they been. Now as the lone man walked closer to him in the gathering doom, he saw he was not only wearing a cape but also a black mask over his eyes.

"My name is Wolf," the man called out to Fitzgerald from about fifteen feet away. "Are you with the United Americans?"

Fitzgerald replied that he was.

"My name is Mike Fitzgerald," he said, walking over to the man. "I talked over the radio with your intelligence officer aboard the *New Jersey* just before the battle."

Wolf immediately recognized Fitzgerald's name. "You spoke with Commander Bjordson," he told the Irishman. "He was killed in the closing moments of the battle."

The two men stood and stared at each other for a long moment. Finally Wolf asked: "Are you the only one who survived the air raids?"

Fitzgerald slowly shook his head. "No, there are some others," he said soberly.

Wolf let out a long, troubled sigh. "We saw those airplanes on our radar screen," he said. "We got a warning off to your base . . ."

Fitzgerald nodded. "Yes, I know," he said. "And because of that, and two other warnings, we were able to save many of our men. But all our airplanes are gone, as is all of our fuel. They put us out of action inside of five minutes."

"We tried to locate them after it happened," Wolf told him, his words deep and clear, despite the thick Scandinavian accent. "We sailed out off the coast all day, looking for anything large enough on our radar screens that might be an aircraft carrier. But we found nothing."

"You weren't the only one looking," Fitzgerald replied.

He quickly told him about Hunter's last mission. Wolf was silent for several long moments after hearing the news.

"It's hard to believe that he's gone, too," he said finally, wrapping his cape around him. "We only met a few days ago, and then only for less than a day. Yet I felt like I had known him all my life."

"From what I hear, you and he were very similar," Fitzgerald replied. "You both had the same calling in life, you might say . . ."

Wolf just shrugged and nervously tugged at the corners of his mask. "You've heard of me then?" he asked.

Fitz just nodded.

"The Wingman and I were alike in many ways, yes," he said, embarrassed to admit the secret of his notoriety. "Europe is my home and I love it as much as he did America. We are similar in that we wanted to change things for the good in what is inherently an evil world. That's all. It's really what all men should strive for. Some people just depend on me to do it for them."

Fitzgerald turned and looked out to sea. "Well, we always depended on him . . ." he began sadly. "We always counted on him to come through. And he never failed us. Even when he went up to that farm—'Skyfire' was the name, I think—and finally got back with his woman, we had to drag him out and get him involved in all of this

348

madness."

Fitzgerald had to pause for a moment. Suddenly his words were having a hard time coming out.

"And now, if he is gone," he went on, "then me and my colleagues are the ones to blame, really. We knew he loved his country more than anything else and we used that to such an advantage that he couldn't ever shut it out. He could never escape it. He could never put a barrier between us and himself. It may have finally been the death of him."

At this point, Wolf also looked out on to the empty, darkening sea. Then in a deeply sad tone, he said: "Now you know why I wear a mask . . ."